D1126723

Diana

Diana

R. F. DELDERFIELD

G. P. PUTNAM'S SONS
NEW YORK

For John Steinbeck, who knows SENNACHARIB—*in acknowledgment of all the happy reading hours his work has given me over a quarter-century.*

Part One

Chapter One

TWO miracles occurred that October, the October of my fifteenth birthday. This story begins with those miracles, so I must record them in the order in which they took place; first the miracle of landscape, which was purely personal, secondly the encounter in the larch wood, involving Diana and myself.

I had been living with Uncle Luke and Aunt Thirza for a fortnight or so, and the change of scene, from a second-floor apartment in the Brixton Road to a quayside cottage in a small Devon holiday resort, had done little to cure the wretchedness caused by watching my mother die, or seeing her buried in the hideously crowded cemetery where they laid her.

People were kind. Uncle Luke came up from Devon the day she died and I had no uncertainty about the future, for he assured me of a home the moment he arrived. My mother and I, however, had been very close, for my father, a second cousin of my mother's who shared the same name, had died years before and I barely remembered him. We had shared the genteel squalor of the Brixton boardinghouse and when she wasn't at work and I wasn't at school, we were seldom apart.

On Saturday afternoons, and on fine Sundays, we explored London together. We went to all the usual places—the Tower, Westminster Abbey, Hampton Court. We also went to the Tate Gallery and it was here, only a short time before her death, that she revealed to me the fact that she carried in her mind the remembered scents of West Country gorse and purple heather. This puzzled me at the time, for I knew that she had left Devon as a small child and had never once returned. I knew also that since that time she had lived all her life in cities.

We had been looking at a big landscape by an artist whose name I have forgotten, and the background of the picture was a rich blaze of golden gorse and purple heath, the kind of heath that most people mistake for heather. My mother said, "There John, that's how it is! That's how it looks and that's how it smells!"

The predominant smell at that moment was London fog, seeping through the dome of the gallery, and I made a feeble joke about this but she didn't laugh, just shook her head and said, very quietly, "Ah, but *I* can smell it! It's a kind of frosty freshness. You've got to see it first, though, then when you see it, a picture like that can easily conjure it up."

I forgot this conversation almost at once and I didn't remember it again until that Saturday afternoon, the first Saturday of October, when Uncle Luke, who was paying forfeit of his weekend ramble because he had watched herring gulls all morning instead of delivering furniture, handed me twopence for the bus ride to Heronslea Cross and advised me to explore the country behind Shepherdshey and see if I could identify the holding that we Leighs were said to have farmed for eight generations.

I went off eagerly enough, glad of an opportunity to be alone with my grief and put myself out of reach of Aunt Thirza's well-meant but irritating endeavors to distract me. Uncle Luke had given me directions and I left the bus at the fork, walking down the unsurfaced road to Shepherdshey.

It was a fine, keen afternoon and the road that I later came to know so well was firm underfoot. In summer the Shepherdshey road was thick with dust, so thick that it whirled up when disturbed and settled on the stalks of cow parsley, bending them forward until they were almost horizontal to the road. In winter the track was a slough, without a dry spot anywhere. Only after fine autumn weather was the surface firm as far as the village.

In those days Shepherdshey was a hamlet that had strayed out of an eighteenth-century sporting print. Each side of the single street was lined with humpbacked cob cottages and the only two breaks in the frontages were the general shop on the left and the half-timbered pub on the right. I looked at the pub with interest. It was called The Jolly Rifleman, and I knew it, for it was the place where Grandfather Leigh had drunk himself to death.

Heronslea House, the only sizable home in the area, lay on my left, on slightly rising ground. I couldn't see much of it because it was approached by a winding, beech-lined drive, and further concealed by a clump of tall elms that grew beside the Teasel Brook. At Shepherdshey the brook ran out of its gulley, or "goyle" as they called it in these parts, and the path up to the common followed the stream as far as its sharpest curve, a mile north of the village. On the left of this path were the huge rhododendron clumps of Heronslea House and on the right a broad slope that climbed to Teasel Wood, a vast tangle of fir, spruce, beech, chestnut and dwarf oak.

I was not especially interested in the landscape, not at least until I had left the village behind and climbed the first ridge behind the big house. Then, as I approached the plank bridge that crossed the rushing brook, something stirred under my heart and I began to run without knowing why.

When I reached the first trees of Teasel Wood I stopped and turned around, looking down over the half-moon of timber screening the rear of the big house and beyond it across five miles of pasture to the sea. It was on this spot that the personal miracle occurred. It was here that I first looked upon the area that Diana and I, but no one else on earth, were to know as "Sennacharib."

The sensation was as much physical as spiritual. It was as though something had struck me a sudden blow in the pit of the stomach, a fierce, winding blow that made me reel and reach out to steady myself against the smooth bole of the nearest beech. I saw on the instant the whole sweep of the country, the woods, dove-gray and russet, the white ribbon of road, the smoky, purple woods beyond, the patchwork green of the pasture, the red brown of the plowed land and finally, as a frame to the picture, the pale blue of the Channel on the skyline.

I saw all this but it was the flaming gorse and purple heath that made me cry out, for it lay along each side of the valley like a hoard of guineas flung slantwise across a shallow bowl and at each point where the gold was thinly scattered the purple of the heath showed through, like an imperial mantle spread to catch the money.

It was then that the tag of verse came into my head, the first two lines of "Sennacharib" that I had chanted in the tiled prison house of Brixton Road School:

> The Assyrian came down like a wolf on the fold
> And his cohorts were gleaming with purple and gold . . .

The entire valley—gorse, heath, beechwood, larchwood, elms, brook and all that lay between sea and the moor became mine and because it was mine I named it Sennacharib. Even the white mansion, glimpsed through the wood far below, was included and on entering into possession I experienced a moment of pure joy that has never been mine since. Grief, and a boy's luxury in grief, fell away from me at the memory of my mother's odd remark in the Tate Gallery and I sniffed a long, long, satisfying sniff that brought with it not only a calm acceptance of death but also a consciousness of ancestral heritage, the realization of the presence here, on this very spot, of all the long-dead Leighs who had stood and looked down on Sennacharib in the past. Dead they were and yet they were not, not while I lived; and I was gloriously, exultantly alive.

This was the measure of my discovery on that October afternoon; this was the first of the two October miracles.

I went over into Sennacharib the following Saturday and the Saturday after that. I wanted to know every bridle path, every bush, every fold in the valley between Shepherdshey and the frontier of the London road, where it bordered the common seven miles inland.

It was very quiet down here in the autumn. During those early expeditions I did not meet a soul and when I stood quite still on the edge of Teasel Wood the only sounds that I could hear were the gossip of the larches in Heronslea Wood, or the sudden crackle of bursting gorse pods shooting seeds into the thickets. The oaks and beeches of Teasel Wood never talked unless there was a stiffish breeze, and the air was very still that October, so still that sometimes it seemed to me that everything had stopped growing in Sennacharib and that I was its sole inhabitant.

I came to understand this curious isolation of the area. Geography, and the pace of Edwardian development, had conspired to isolate the area. Our part of the West was a broad triangle, jutting into the Bristol Channel, and the estuary of the Whin and the town of Whinmouth on its left bank had been bypassed when the main railway line drove due west to the county town, fifteen miles inland. Whinmouth had a modest holiday industry and an even smaller fishing and coastal trade, but for the most part Whinmouth folk lived by taking in one another's washing. Such visitors as found their way to the town came down the river road, or via the branch line that ran beside the river. Few of them turned east into the scrub, common and pasture of the Shepherdshey district. This fact delighted me; the fewer people who challenged my right the better I was pleased. But here I ought to speak briefly of my family, the Leighs, although none of them play more than a casual part in my story.

I soon found Foxhayes Farm, where my mother had been born, and shortly afterward I crossed Teasel Wood and introduced myself to my Uncle Mark at his ramshackle riding stable on the edge of my domain. Uncle Mark was the second of my three Devon uncles, Uncle Reuben being the eldest, and Uncle Luke the youngest. Between them, during that first month in the West, I began to make sense out of our family history and learned how, although all were the sons and grandsons of farmers, not one of them had held a scythe or turned a sod since they were small boys.

They were an odd, contrasting trio, with nothing in common but the big, loose-limbed bones and the drifting gait of the Leighs. My mother had spoken to me about this gait when she recognized it in myself. "You can always tell a Leigh by his walk," she said. "A Leigh never puts one foot in front of the other, he drifts like a leaf on a pavement."

As I said, Grandfather Leigh had drunk himself to death, and he accomplished this before he was forty. Up to the moment that his wife died during her fourth childbirth he had been a strict Methodist and was looked upon as being an exceptionally pious man. Like many religious men, however, he challenged the wisdom of his God to interfere with the continuity of a well-ordered life, and when his wife died he was not so much despondent as furiously angry. He marched straight into The Jolly Rifleman on the day after the funeral and ordered rum. Having once tasted it he decided that he liked the flavor and continued to drink it in prodigious quantities until the day came when the landlord refused to serve him.

After that he took to riding his cob farther afield, down into Whinmouth, or over to the Pilot, at Nun's Bay. He was often drunk for days at a stretch but no matter how much liquor he swallowed he never reached the stage where he was unable to sit his saddle and ride off in search of more.

13]

When I got to know the Shepherdshey folk I met people who could talk of his antics during the last two years of his life. They were in the best traditions of the Victorian drunkard and included scenes of the wildest improbability. He must have behaved something like Masefield's hero in "The Everlasting Mercy," smashing up bar parlors and whirling his fists at rash friends who tried to remonstrate with him. One night he stripped himself stark naked and carried a torch up the main drive to Heronslea House. On another he set fire to some of his own ricks and then drove a blue farm wagon at a breakneck pace down the Teasel track and through Shepherdshey as far as the crossroads.

He went to jail several times but the moment he came out he started all over again, and was soon regarded as an intolerable nuisance in the district. Everybody was relieved when they found his cob crushed to death under Nun's Head one morning. His battered body turned up on the estuary cockle sands a week or so later and it was assumed that he had missed the cliff path after leaving the Pilot at closing time.

At the time of his death his eldest son, Reuben, was eight, and the two younger boys, Mark and Luke, were respectively a year and three years younger. My mother was not much more than a baby, and former Methodist friends came forward to give the children homes after the tenancy of the farm had gone to a nominee of the Gilroy Estate, for at that time a cousin of Lord Gilroy was occupying Heronslea House.

Uncle Reuben was adopted by the Methodist minister, who subsequently apprenticed him to Mr. Handford, the founder-proprietor of the little weekly newspaper in Whinmouth. The boy showed an aptitude for printing and was soon a steady journeyman and later the foreman printer in Handford's works behind the newspaper office, in High Street.

Reuben was a solemn, humorless man, a very kind and thoughtful soul, animated by an almost fanatical sense of duty toward his neighbors and employer. In due course he became a town councilor and was much respected, though never very popular in the Whinmouth area. He was a local preacher and a confirmed radical, so that he could deliver an impressive address on salvation or free trade, whichever his audience demanded. I was glad I had been taken in by Uncle Luke and Aunt Thirza. Life with Uncle Reuben would have been more comfortable but very dull.

[14

It wasn't at all dull at Uncle Luke's. Luke had been given a home by a general dealer, who occupied ramshackle premises near the dock. He had never learned a trade but when he grew up he inherited the business, such as it was, and earned his living buying and selling secondhand household goods.

He was not very interested in this means of livelihood and had no business acumen whatever. He was a countryman pure and simple, with eyes and ears for nothing but things that grew in the hedges and fields, or the wild life of the cliffs and the banks of the estuary. His knowledge of birds in particular, and of wild life generally, was prodigious. Everywhere he went he carried a pair of binoculars and everything he saw that interested him he wrote down in fat exercise books that he stuffed into his roll-top desk at the Mart and never referred to once they were full.

He could tell you the smallest details about the habits of unusual birds—what they lived on, when they appeared in Britain, where they nested, how many eggs they laid and anything else about them. He would sit in a hedge for hours with his binoculars glued to his eyes watching lapwings patrol their nests against the descent of hawks. He loved wild flowers, all wild flowers, and could tell you just where to find yellow rattle or round-headed rampion. With colored chalks he could sketch the hue and structure of every insignificant plant that grew in hedge, field or copse.

He was a spare, shambling man, with iron-gray hair and mild, myopic eyes, but despite his gentle nature he could be madly exasperating if one was obliged to work with him. It was often difficult to get through to Uncle Luke, for his brain was hedged around with trefoil, butterbur and bristly oxtongue, or patrolled by protective flights of screaming jays and wailing herring gulls. His wife, Aunt Thirza, treated him like an idiot child. She was a shrewish, bustling, efficient little body, with restless eyes that gleamed from behind gold-rimmed spectacles. She took a fancy to me, however, and almost from the moment I arrived she seemed to expect me to make up for her husband's deficiencies as a provider.

I was expected to work hard but as a reward I was given plenty of pocket money. At sixteen I was virtual master of the house.

Uncle Luke showed a lively interest in my rambles about Sennacharib during the weekends.

"There's a pair of buzzards up there," he said, ignoring the disgusted grunt of his wife. "Buzzards disappeared from these parts when I was a boy and these are the first I've seen in twenty years. Birds are slaves to fashion just like us, and they tire of districts every now and again. I don't know what brought 'em back here but I know what made 'em go. Lord Gilroy's kin had a keeper who was deadly with a rook rifle. He must have shot a dozen and draped 'em on his vermin pole before they up and left. That keeper shot himself in the end, climbing through a hedge into Teasel Wood, and it was about the best thing that ever happened on that estate!"

Uncle Luke never killed anything, not even a fly or a cockroach, and the only thing that could summon him from his endless contemplation of nature was the witnessing, or even a description, of a wanton act of killing. The mere memory of the marksman with the rook rifle, dead more than twenty years, was sufficient to spoil his midday meal.

Uncle Mark, the middle son, was the one reputed to be most like his father. He was over six feet in height and broad as a barrel. His skin was as rough as a last year's apple and his eyes, when they weren't challenging, gleamed with sardonic humor. He was the only member of the family who used the broad Devon bur of his forefathers and his speech was so thick, and so full of archaic idiom, that it was months before I was able to understand more than half the words he uttered.

He had a terrible reputation with women and was reputed to be paying several affiliation orders in the district. Notwithstanding this he always had a roll of filthy bank notes in his breeches pockets and I never did discover how they got there. His livery stable, situated on the far side of Teasel Wood, was a hopeless, ramshackle affair, a motley assembly of clapboard stables and tin sheds, housing a few unclipped ponies, three rawboned hacks, and one well-cared-for gelding that he maintained for his own use.

In his younger days he had been huntsman to the Gilroy pack and was still seen on the fringe of the hunting field, though he never actually attended a meet in case someone should demand his subscription. He was a mean, gruff, picturesque old rascal, and did not go far out of his way to welcome me when I called on him. He was still on nodding terms with Uncle Luke but he and Uncle Reuben detested one another. Uncle Reuben regarded him as a reincarnation of Grandfather during the days of his decline, whereas Uncle Mark dismissed his elder brother as "a bliddy ole humbug, wi' no more go in 'im nor a zick cow!" On the few occasions they met in Whinmouth Bay their greeting was limited to a mutual growl.

It was on the afternoon when I had met and been repelled by Uncle Mark that I first saw the buzzards.

I had hoped to spend the entire afternoon at the stables, but Uncle Mark was in a foul temper over something or other and after looking me up and down with obvious disfavor he simply said:

"Huh! So you'm Miriam's boy, be 'ee? Can you zit a horse?"

When I told him that I had never bestridden a horse in my life he was so disgusted that he swore aloud. I backed away and dodged behind the stables, awaiting a chance to slip back to the woods. He waddled off mumbling to himself and I remember thinking how neatly he fitted my conception of Billy Bones, in *Treasure Island*, and wondering if he too was drinking himself to death on Jamaica rum, like Bones and Grandfather Leigh.

I misjudged Uncle Mark at that time. He was good company once you had learned to take his gruffness for granted, and he never touched rum or any other spirit, confining himself to rough cider which, he declared, "stayed in the legs, didn't maze the ade, an' left a man all his faculties to take full use of such hoppertoonities as come his way!"

By "hopportunities" Uncle Mark simply meant a chance encounter with any obliging women who crossed his path, and his expectations were frequently gratified. At fifty he was a very lusty man and certain types of women were attracted by his heavy masculinity.

I escaped to the tangle of Teasel Wood and across the goyle into the larch and chestnut woods, behind Heronslea House. It was here, on a rail that marked the limit of the park, that I first saw the two buzzards and instantly mistook them for eagles.

They were magnificent birds, the female noticeably larger than the male, with plumage of deep, rich brown and conspicuously lighter patches on the underparts. Their tails were beautifully barred and they sat hunched on the crossbar, their bright yellow feet gripping the decaying bark, their arrogant eyes regarding me with mild disapproval, as though daring me to cross the fence and enter the grounds of the enclosure.

I had a good long look at them before they rose on blunt, mothlike wings and wheeled over the sparsely timbered paddock, uttering a duet of long, mewing cries, a note unlike that of any bird I had ever heard.

Fascinated I watched them soar and drift at about a hundred feet and then, entirely discounting me, they dropped again with wonderful deliberation and perched on the second fence that enclosed the inner plantation.

I don't think I saw the notice board but if I had, the warning would not have deterred me. I climbed the rail and crossed the paddock but the buzzards rose again before I could dodge behind the tree close to them. I ran and leaped over the second paling and through the trees into the wood, but it was impossible to see them here although I could still hear their *Mee-oo! Mee-oo!* from above the feathery heads of the larches.

The wood was new ground for me and I went on down the gentle slope until I broke through to a narrow ride, a glorious, green aisle, as cool and still as a cathedral. It was the kind of wood one reads about and sometimes sees on a calendar cover but rarely discovers, not even in unspoiled country. Rides intersected it and every now and again two rides merged and huge bracken fronds crowded into the slender triangle formed by the junction.

Nearly all the flowers had gone but there were still tall foxglove stems and one or two late campion and lady's slipper. The trees were so closely set that a kind of green mist hung over the wood. There had seemed to be no breeze outside, but in here the faintest breath of wind set the larches tissing and they seemed to me to be whispering the same word over and over again: "Assyria—Assyria—Assyria."

I was standing on a curve of the main ride when I heard a sudden crackle in the undergrowth behind me. Swinging around I came face to face with a keeper, carrying a double-barreled shotgun in the crook of his arm.

I took an instant dislike to the man. He was dressed in rough, patched tweeds, corduroy breeches, gleaming leggings and a drooping, weather-stained trilby, but somehow he did not look like a countryman. His face was too pale and too narrow and his eyes were red and angry, like a ferret's. It was clear too that he was going to be as truculent as most of his kind, for he neighed at me in a strong Cockney accent, as alien as my own.

"Wotcher think *you're* up to, eh?"

Uncle Luke had given me casual advice about trespassing.

"If anyone challenges you offer 'em a farthing damage and walk off without arguing the toss!" he had told me. I had also read about this somewhere and the dignified compromise intrigued me. I happened to have a farthing in my pocket, change from a loaf I had bought for Aunt Thirza earlier in the day, so I plunged my hand into my trouser pocket and produced it as the keeper strode clear of the bracken and faced me in the ride.

"This is for any damage I've done," I said, trying to keep a steady voice, for despite the grand gesture a townsman's fears caused my heart to hammer wildly and I hated the man's red eyes.

With a downsweep of his hand he struck the coin from my hand and thrust his narrow face to within an inch of mine.

"Saucy young bastard! Been after rabbits, you 'ave! Seen the notice, 'aven't you? *Read*, doncher?"

I mumbled that I had not seen a notice and that if I had I would not have entered the wood, but he cut my excuses short and pushed me so vigorously that I staggered back and struck my elbow a sharp blow on a tree. Either the pain, the man's manner, or both enraged me and the spurt of anger gave me a little courage.

"You can't do that to me!" I shouted at him. "I wasn't doing any harm!"

"Shut yer mouth an' open yer jacket!" he roared, shifting his grip on the gun and advancing so close to me that I recoiled from the stench of his bad breath.

"I won't and you can go to hell!" I screamed, my back to the tree and my fists clenched.

Townsman or countryman, he knew his business. In a trice he had dropped his gun and grabbed me above the elbows, whirling me around and throwing me violently against his extended leg so that I fell flat on my back in the bracken. In another second he was on top of me, had lifted me sideways and seized my arm in a half nelson. I cried out with pain and fright but he only jerked the wrist higher and higher, until I almost fainted and began to thresh out with both legs.

"Assaultin' a keeper! We'll see abaht this, cock!" he said, and was in the act of dragging me to my feet when I saw, through a film of tears, a horse and rider walk into view around the broad curve of the ride and heard a girl's voice say:

"Let him go, Croker! Don't be such a damned fool! *Let him go I tell you!*"

He released me at once, jumping back so quickly that I fell forward on my hands and knees. When I regained my feet I saw pony and rider advancing into the main ride and Croker, now harassed

19]

and confused, retreating to the spot where his gun lay in the long grass.

The girl came on slowly, her feet free of the stirrups, her body loose in the saddle that creaked as though very new. Apart from this rhythmic creak, and the almost noiseless impact of the pony's hoofs on the beaten earth of the ride, it was curiously silent in the glade.

There was something stately about her advance, as though she was a young queen riding to acknowledge the obeisance of a respectful multitude, and she sat her pony as though she had never used any other means of progression. This regality, and the utter confusion of the keeper, suddenly communicated itself to me, so that I dropped my glance and pretended to look about for my cap, lost in the struggle.

"You know perfectly well that you're not supposed to do that, Croker!" she said, and her voice, pitched pleasantly low, had a ring of authority. Her presence was so commanding that I began to feel almost sorry for the wretched keeper, now so ill at ease that he had forgotten to retrieve his gun.

He flushed and blurted out:

"He showed fight, Miss Em'rood, proper young d—"

He was going to say "devil" but the girl cut him short, lifting her gloved hand from the pommel of the saddle.

"Bring me your gun—*quickly!* Bring the gun here!"

The man bent, picked up the gun and almost ran across the ride. She took it from him and glanced at the hammers.

"It's cocked, you fool!"

The man began to squirm under her merciless contempt.

"I know it is, Miss Em'rood, but I didn't 'ave it in mind to shoot! Cor Jesus, I wouldn't do that, miss, I was just—"

"You're a liar, Croker! You cocked it to scare him and it might easily have gone off while you were rolling about near it! Then you'd have been charged with murder and strung up and I should have been a witness against you! I would have been, I can tell you! I'd have even turned up to read the notice on the prison gate!"

I suppose this was meant as a joke but Croker did not take it as such. He began stammering more excuses: He was trespassing . . . there's the notice up on top . . . he must have seen it . . . he started the fight . . .

"That's not true," I said, speaking for the first time. "I offered him a farthing damages and said I'd go. Look, there's the farthing on the ground."

While we were talking the pale sun had passed the open part of the ride and I could see the new coin gleaming in one of Croker's heel clips.

The girl glanced at the coin and then at Croker. Severity and the touch of haughtiness left her expression and she smiled. It was a swift, boyish kind of smile and when she spoke again the rasp had vanished from her voice.

"You certainly *will* hang one of these days, Croker! Imagine leaving a clue like that farthing!"

Croker recognized the change in her voice and was pitifully grateful for it. He began to weave more excuses, repeating over and over again that he had strict instructions to eject all trespassers and referring once more to the notice board on the edge of the wood, but again she cut him short with the regal lift of the hand.

"Oh, *stop* it, Croker! Don't *whine* so! I hate people who whine and snivel. And I hate people who hide behind other people's orders. Do you know what you are? You're the sort of person who encourages the Bolshies. People like you would have us all guillotined in no time!"

I am sure that Croker failed to follow her odd line of reasoning and equally sure that it was employed for my benefit rather than his. She returned his gun but he seemed reluctant to go without some assurance on her part that the incident would not be reported.

"After all, I did 'ave me instructions," he mumbled, "and if yer Pa gets to hear about it—"

"You had no instructions to commit assault and battery on my friends!" she told him, and I saw his jaw drop with renewed dismay.

"Gawd, Miss Em'rood, 'ow was I ter know he was a friend o' yours? *Ow* was *I* to know. . . ? He never said nothing!" He turned to me for corroboration. "You didn't, did you?"

"I don't imagine you gave him much of a chance," replied the girl crisply, and then, as though conversation with Croker bored her, she pulled off her riding hat and dismounted.

I had never seen anyone dismount from a horse the way Diana dismounted. She threw her right leg over the pommel and pointed both feet before floating rather than leaping from the horse and then landing with half her weight against her mount's shoulder. It was such an effortless, graceful movement that you wanted to see it performed over and over again. It set you wondering whether it had been acquired after months of practice, or was merely one of a whole repertoire of lithe, graceful movements, like the casual lift of her hand, or the way she moved with the horse when it had walked toward us across the glade. Everything about her had this smooth practiced fluency, even her voice and the movements of her wrist as she gently danced the hat on its elastic chin strap.

To watch her, to be with her, was like listening to a famous actor declaiming well-remembered lines, or hearing a brilliant concert pianist play a familiar passage from one of the classics. There was something exciting and accomplished about everything she did, yet it was the kind of accomplishment that contained no element of surprise or shock, so smoothly and effortlessly was it achieved.

"Hold the pony," she ordered me, "I won't be a moment," and she handed me the reins and crossed to where Croker stood, taking him firmly by the arm and leading him away from me and down the ride in the direction of the house. They walked together as far as the curve and then stopped for a moment out of earshot. I saw her talking to him earnestly, and Croker listening with every mark of attention. Then, with a vigorous nod, he shouldered his gun and marched off between the trees and she came slowly up the ride toward me. It was then that I really saw her for the first time and the second of the October miracles occurred.

She was about my own age and not nearly so tall or mature as I had imagined her to be when she was mounted. Up to that moment, with her hair bundled under the hard little hat, I had judged her to be at least sixteen, but with her lovely hair loose on her shoulders she did not look as old as I and I wondered again at the deference shown to her by such a truculent man as Croker.

From a distance it was the quality of her hair that impressed me, that and the strange transparency of her skin, the paleness of which was so vividly emphasized by her dark chestnut hair. She had a short, straight nose and a small, slightly jutting chin with a single dimple, the largest dimple I had ever seen, a finger's breadth below her mouth. This much I saw as she advanced up the glade, but it was not until she took the reins from me that I noticed her eyes. They were huge and the shadows around them made them seem even larger and more expressive. When she had first approached us, and put a period to the agony of my twisted arm, I had noticed that her eyes were blue, but not until this moment had I realized just how blue they were. They were like the patch of sky between cotton-wool clouds on the calmest April day, or the strip of Channel beyond the first line of sandbanks in Nun's Bay, where the sea floor shelves away from the lip of sandstone and the sudden depth of the water is apparent from the clifftop. They were the blue of Teasel Wood periwinkles, the blue of the irises growing alongside Shepherdshey reservoir; they were Sennacharib blue, a christening gift from the fairy godmother of the woods, moors and cliffs of the lands I claimed.

I looked into their depth for perhaps three seconds while she took the reins from me and swung herself into the saddle with the same effortless hoist as she had left it. I think she must have known that, at this moment, I passed from boyhood to manhood and was hers for life, that everything awaiting me in the future, every ambition that stirred in me, every emotion I was to experience, would be prompted by her dimple, her dark tumbling hair and her eyes. She knew too, as I did, that from then on everything that happened to me that had no bearing on her would be smaller change than the farthing at our feet.

The conquest pleased her, that much was evident by her manner during that first afternoon, but it made no lasting impression on her, so that our relationship was destined to be lopsided from the very beginning.

At the time, however, I did not quarrel with this. Her ascendancy had been established from the moment she lifted her gloved hand to terminate the pain of Croker's half nelson. It was more than that, for she was who she was, the daughter of Eric Gayelorde-Sutton, Squire of Sennacharib and stockbroking overlord of everything in it, a girl in beautifully cut riding clothes, mounted on a sleek, well-mannered pony, a girl who, at the lift of a hand, could make a bully like Croker wriggle with fear and embarrassment.

Against this I had nothing but my secret claim, and that seemed ridiculous in the presence of Diana Gayelorde-Sutton.

2.

The strange thing about that first hour in Diana's company was that I felt no shyness in her presence. We exchanged information about one another as readily as two people who find themselves embarking on a long railway journey in one another's company.

The first thing I wanted explained to me was her name. The keeper had addressed her as "Miss Em'rood" and it seemed an unlikely name, even though I had imagined it to be a surname and not, as it turned out, his interpretation of her Christian name.

"It's *Emerald*," she told me, laughing, "not 'Em'rood'—'Em'rood' is just his way of saying it. He comes from Kent and you ought to understand, for you talk rather like him. Do you come from Kent?"

I said I did but I did not tell her it was unlikely to be the part of Kent from which a gamekeeper had been recruited. Somehow it was terribly important to me to impress her with the fact that Devon was my real home and that my childhood among the terrace houses and tramway clang of the Brixton Road had been incidental. I told her my name and she savored it.

"John Leigh . . . that's a country name . . . *John*, yes, you do *look* a John but it's still not quite right somehow . . ."

Suddenly her eyes sparkled and she dropped the reins, leaning back and putting both hands on her narrow hips.

"I know who you remind me of! It's not John, it's *Jan* . . . *Jan Ridd!*"

The fancy excited her so much that she rocked in the saddle. "Jan Ridd, the big solemn boy in *Lorna Doone!* You're tall and lanky and . . . and serious-looking. Haven't you read *Lorna Doone?*"

Mercifully I had. Only a few days previously I had found a copy in a box of books that had been trundled into the Mart on Uncle Luke's handcart and I had read as far as Jan's escape with Lorna in the snow. I was not sure that I relished her description, "lanky and serious-looking," but on the whole I found the comparison flattering. Jan Ridd was big, strong and fearless and Lorna was dark, winsome and strong-willed, so that at once my mind began to weave a rich pattern of rustic romance in which Keeper Croker was Carver Doone and this girl had been snatched from him after a merciless contest between us. Then my imagination ran against a bulwark of fact, for in this instance the roles of rescuer and rescued had been reversed, running contrary to all accepted courses. It was the girl who had released me from the clutches of Carver, and sent Carver about his business with his tail between his legs.

I returned to the subject of her name, Emerald.

"It's a funny name," I said. "I've never heard it before."

"I don't use it, only Mother insists on using it! It was her idea . . . she named me after Lady Cunard because she's such a terrible snob.

As if a name can do anything for a person—I mean, to make them like anybody else! I always used my second name, Diana. Don't ever call me anything but Diana and don't ever tell anyone about Emerald. You won't, will you?"

"Of course I won't! I like Diana much better. It suits you and I like it. Diana what?"

She laughed again. It was wonderful to watch the play of the dimple and the heavy stir of her hair when she threw back her head. Every moment I spent with her added volume to the tide of worship that rose in me. As we walked along I began to feel lifted on it, just as the earlier miracle in the valley had lifted me, but this time my exhilaration yearned for some form of expression. I wanted to shout and dance and sing. I was no longer John Leigh, odd-job boy at Leigh's Furniture Mart, a clumsy overgrown lout fresh from Brixton Road Council School and wearing a gray serge suit utterly unsuited for a ramble through a larch wood in the company of an angel. I was Jan Ridd, vanquisher of Doones, striding along beside his adored Lorna and conveying her to a place of safety and repose.

"Diana Gayelorde-Sutton," she said, this time with a trace of contempt. "Gayelorde is more snobbery, because Daddy's real name is Sutton and Mother dug up the Gayelorde soon after we took Heronslea. I don't know where she found it, she's very touchy about it when I ask her, but it was all done properly, you know, deed poll and all that!"

I was not at all sure what "deed poll" was but I was beginning to glimpse a formidable picture of her mother, a person for whom it was clear that Diana had no respect whatever. I wanted to know more of her and more of the family, how they came to be here, how rich they were, why it was necessary to name Diana after someone whose name I associated with ocean-going liners and why the family's surname had to be dressed up with the aristocratic-sounding Gayelorde.

She told me a good deal about herself that afternoon and demanded little in return. I told her proudly that my family had once farmed Foxhayes and that I now lived with an uncle in Whinmouth Bay but she showed no real interest in my family or, indeed, how I came to be on the estate. I didn't find out everything about the Gayelorde-Suttons that afternoon but as I walked beside her along the ride she talked very freely and gaily about her life and back-

25]

ground, and I listened to everything she said with respect, awed at being the confidant of such a wonderful creature.

It seemed that the Gayelorde-Suttons, father, mother and daughter, had leased Heronslea from the Gilroy Estate less than a year ago, when Diana's father had made a great deal of money in some kind of business that Diana appeared to understand but was utterly unintelligible to me. It was, she said, something to do with shares, holdings, or mines, either in Africa or South America, she wasn't sure which.

He had been rich before this but was now fabulously wealthy, with another house in London, a horde of retainers and a Rolls-Royce sedan, in addition to the country estate, rustic retainers and two more cars, a Bentley for Mrs. Gayelorde-Sutton and an Austin station wagon for use at Heronslea.

All this was impressive enough but there was more to come. The family went abroad a good deal and when they traveled during the holidays they sometimes took Diana with them. She had been to France several times and to Spain and Italy on two other occasions. When they were in London her father spent most of his time "sitting on boards," which struck me as a strange occupation for a man who owned a Rolls-Royce and two large houses. I was foolish enough to probe her statement and Diana, after shouting with laughter, explained that a board was a group of people in charge of a business, and that her father, aside from his African or South American activities, administered dozens of smaller businesses in the City.

She herself, she said, hardly ever stayed at the London house because she was a boarder at a snob school in Surrey. She would have been at school now but there had been a "lovely, lovely, outbreak of measles," and everyone who didn't show spots had been sent home for "a fortnight's mooch, smack in the middle of term!"

She told me a good deal about her school and I was on more familiar ground here, for I was an avid reader of the *Magnet* and *Gem* and I recognized her school as a girls' equivalent of Greyfriars and St. Jims, where every pupil's father was fabulously rich and famous people arrived in limousines on speech days.

She hated school more than most children, finding all the mistresses "stuffy," and all the lessons "grisly." From her description of the place I knew that I should have liked it. It was certainly a very different kind of school from the one that I had attended in the Brixton Road. All the girls had little rooms of their own and the meals, which she described as so-so, sounded to me like a series of modest banquets.

They even had little parties in the evenings, "to learn how to drink sherry without giggling," and after prep, on winter evenings, one of the mistresses read aloud from *David Copperfield*, or *The Mill on the Floss*. There were plenty of outdoor activities too, hockey, tennis, lacrosse and a game of which I had never heard called "squash," but Diana, although very much an outdoor girl, disliked games as much as lessons. "I kick against anything organized," she told me. "That's why I like riding and that's why I love it down here, with no one but dear old Drip."

"Who's Drip?" I asked her, imagining it to be either the pony she was riding, or a favorite dog.

"Drip is a kind of governess that Mummy got for me," she said, "after Passy-Glassy told Daddy that I wasn't doing any work and must cram during the hols. She's a terrible dreary old thing to look at but she worships me and I can do absolutely anything with her. I should be having conversational French right now but I easily talked her out of it. I said I had a bad headache, and needed fresh air. You'd like Drip, she's a pet really!"

"Then who on earth is Passy-Glassy?" I wanted to know.

"Oh, she's Head at Mount Waring and she's a fearful droop! She's called Passy-Glassy because she's always checking up on accents and one day she threw us into fits by telling us about a girl from the north, who said 'Passs me a glasss' with a strong Lancashire accent. She said it ought to have been 'Parse me a glawse, I want to hev a barthe,' and the whole Middle School went up in smoke at the idea of Miss Endicott-Brookes taking a bath in a glass! She's as fat as a barrel, you see."

It was a silly story I suppose, but it made me laugh, partly because Diana was clever at imitating accents but more, I think, from relief that she was so gloriously free of snobbery, and this made an association between us possible.

I don't think I had ever met anyone quite so free of class prejudice. I knew that I possessed a strong Cockney accent, for already the Devonians in Whinmouth Bay had made me conscious of it, but Diana minded it as little as my trespass of her father's property and from the first moment we were alone she always treated me as a social equal.

At the time I mistook this for a natural broad-mindedness on her part; it was only later that I discovered that it was a deliberate act on her part, part of her ceaseless counteroffensive against her mother.

While we had been talking we had followed the ride that led to the eastern edge of the wood and suddenly we emerged from the trees and looked down over the valley. I forgot Diana for a few moments as I studied the view, for I had never seen it from this angle, and the impact of all that color was so powerful that it made me run ahead of her until I came to the extreme edge of the escarpment. Then I looked back and saw her framed against the green backcloth of the larches and I knew that she was the jewel of Sennacharib and as rightly mine as any part of it.

I made a vow then that somehow, at some time, no matter how many difficulties interposed, or how long the conquest took me to achieve, I would marry Diana Gayelorde-Sutton and we would live together in that big white house, the roof of which I could just glimpse from where I stood.

3.

She kicked her pony alongside and looked down at me curiously but even at that stage of our friendship it wasn't necessary to explain to her how I felt about Sennacharib.

She said, "You love it, don't you, Jan? You feel about it just as I do! You *do*, don't you?"

I don't think I was surprised that she had guessed my secret so quickly. Somehow it had never really been a secret from her.

"It's Sennacharib," I told her, and recited the opening lines of the poem.

She didn't laugh, or look blank, or quarrel with them in any way but sat perfectly still on her pony, looking over my shoulder and down the golden hillside to where the Teasel crept between folds to Shepherdshey, then up the further slope into the blue-black vastness of Teasel Wood.

It was one of those magic moments that comes perhaps twice in a lifetime, the moment before a single word, or a sigh of wind, breaks a crystal of pure happiness. We stood together for perhaps a minute and then the buzzards came drifting over the wood, mewing their soft, plaintive call. The moment passed as we saw them dip across the elm clump in search of fresh wind currents.

"How would you like to come home for tea?" she said, when the birds had disappeared. "There's no one there but Drip and me, and Drip won't mind, she's always saying I spend too much time alone."

I tried not to show elation, mumbling something about muddy boots and the Whinmouth bus, but she ignored excuses and kicked the left-hand stirrup iron.

"Jump up behind," she said. "Nellie can easily take two of us."

"I've never been on a horse," I protested, for the second time that afternoon.

"This isn't a horse," she said, "so do as I say, and hold me around the middle!"

It was as much an order as any she had given Croker. I put my foot in the free stirrup and climbed on the pony's broad back, clasping my hands around her narrow waist and letting my legs swing free.

"Tighter!" she commanded. "Or we'll part company on the bends. Giddup, Nellie! Stir your stumps!" and we were off at a brisk trot, heading back into the wood and down the broad path toward the house.

It wasn't a very comfortable ride but what it lacked in comfort it made up for in exhilaration. Soon I was clinging to her as a drowning man clings to a breakwater and even the fragrance of her hair could not obliterate the fear of being hurled from my seat and flung against the trunks of the close-set firs that replaced the larches farther down the slope. At the same spanking pace we left the wood and entered the level paddock leading to the kitchen garden and stables. Then a madness entered her and she urged Nellie forward, shouting and kicking furiously with her heels.

The pony did not seem to mind its double load and broke from rolling canter into a stretched gallop, streaking across the grass and clattering onto the cobbles of the yard at top speed.

I did not know then that a horse needs no urging when its head is turned for home, but neither did I know that it always stops outside its own stable door. It did so now with an abruptness that sent me flying over Diana's shoulders and onto the cobbles under its feet. The impact drove all the breath from my body and stripped the skin from my knees and knuckles.

Diana did not even leave the saddle. When I struggled to my feet she was helpless with laughter.

"You should have braced!" she gasped. "Braced back, directly we passed through the arch. I say, you haven't really hurt yourself, have you?"

I had but I wasn't going to admit it to a girl. My knees and knuckles were smarting horribly but I thrust my hands in my pockets as Diana slid down and a bowed old groom clumped out of the house and led Nellie into a lighted stable.

"I'm all right," I said. "It was fun, but I did tell you I'd never been on a horse before!"

A middle-aged woman, with graying hair scraped back into a tight bun and a permanently worried expression creasing her bespectacled face, appeared on the stone platform that projected from the rear of the house.

"What's happened? Who's that? I was worried about you," she called to Diana. "It's long after teatime!"

"Oh you're always worried about something, Drip," Diana called back. "I've brought someone to tea and we're both ravenous! We'll have it in the kitchen."

"You can't entertain guests in the kitchen," Drip said. "You know very well that your mother would be furious."

"She won't know unless you tell her, so don't fuss, Drip. Just call through and tell Cook we'll have crumpets. Do you like crumpets?" she said, turning to me, and when I said I did she took me by the hand and ran up the steps to the kitchen door where Drip was waiting to usher us into the house.

We went along a dim passage and into the large, cheerful room in which there was a great deal of heavy oak furniture and a large fire burning in an open grate. There was a wonderful smell in here, a smell made up of baking bread, lamp oil and smoldering wood. Diana peeled off her string gloves.

"Good Lord, you're bleeding like a stuck pig!" she suddenly exclaimed, staring at the blood on her glove. "Take him down Hangman's Drop and let him wash off, Drip. Let me see!" and she seized both my hands and stared at the gravel rash. "That's nothing at all," she went on. "Put some powdered alum on them. I know there's some in there, I used it this morning."

Drip cluck-clucked almost continuously but she did everything Diana ordered her to do, taking me down three steep steps into a washhouse where there was a big, lead sink and enamel bowl. The room was at least three feet below the level of the kitchen and Diana, who had a nickname for everyone and everything, always referred to it as Hangman's Drop.

Drip, whose real name was Miss Emily Rodgers, superintended the washing and cleaning of my cuts and bandaged a long graze on my knee. She was a simple, sympathetic little body and I didn't envy her chaperonage of a high-spirited fourteen-year-old like Diana.

"She hasn't even introduced us," grumbled Miss Rodgers, when Diana's voice came to us from the kitchen, where she was now beguiling the fat, freckled cook. "Are you one of the boys she met at the Conservative gymkhana in the summer?"

"No," I admitted, "I got lost in the woods higher up. I live in Whinmouth Bay and my name's Leigh, Jan Leigh."

"Well, Jan," she said lightly, "don't let her lead you into any mischief. She'll try, mark my words. I'm not firm enough with her, I know, but she's got such a way with her, and she always does exactly what she chooses to do the moment her mamma's back is turned. There now, that doesn't hurt any more, does it? Come and have tea and then I'll get someone to take you home."

We found Diana lifting the cover from a silver muffin dish stacked high with dripping crumpets. I was ravenously hungry and so, it seemed, was she, for between us we ate a dozen, finishing off with huge slices of rich plum cake.

I don't remember enjoying a meal more than I did that evening. It wasn't simply the food, which was plentiful and beautifully prepared, or the presence of Diana, bubbling on the edge of laughter as she maintained a running fire of teasing aimed at poor Drip and the cook. I think my delight stemmed from a sense of pride arising from where I was and from the coziness of the warm kitchen overlooking the stable yard, where the autumn dusk was creeping in from the woods and isolating the yellow glow of the stable lamps. There was a kind of timeless comfort and security in here, a sense of being wanted that soothed the ache of my mother's death and stilled the upheaval that had followed it, and when Drip, in response to Diana's urgent pleas, brought in her musical boxes, a final drop of delight was added to my cup and I remember thinking how wonderful it would be to live like this always, here, with Diana, in the very heart of Sennacharib.

Drip, or Miss Rodgers as I always preferred to think of her, was a collector of musical boxes, some of them very old and intricately constructed. Her favorite was one made of mother-of-pearl and crowned by a willowy woman in a high-waisted frock and a Quality Street bonnet. It played "Allan Water" and the pure, tinkling notes brought a lump to my throat.

I was surprised and pleased to discover that Diana was affected by the tune, for when I looked at her halfway through the second playing I noticed that her huge eyes were brimming with tears and that she did not seem in any way ashamed of them but let them brim over and roll slowly down her cheeks. I had already noticed how beautiful she looked when she was angry but there in the lamp-light, sitting quite still as the music box tinkled out "Allan Water," she looked like a girl out of one of the eighteenth-century portraits I had seen in the Tate Gallery. Her presence filled the room and the whole universe became a place of enchantment.

"I think Mr. Leigh had better get ready to go now," said Miss Rodgers when the tune tinkled to a close. "His people will be getting worried about him and he's missed the last bus from the cross-roads."

I was so surprised and flattered at being referred to as Mr. Leigh that I did not hear Diana tell the cook to order the car. It was not until Diana grabbed me by the hand, pulled me into the passage and through a white door into the hall that I realized it was now half-past six and that Aunt Thirza would have been nagging Uncle Luke about my absence since the half-past-five bus had arrived in Chapel Square.

I had a fleeting glimpse at the front part of the house, a large oval hall studded with dark oil paintings and spread with Persian rugs. There were several closed doors leading out of it and I had time to notice the lovely proportions of the staircase that swept in a wide scimitar curve to a three-sided gallery, a gallery lit by a huge crystal chandelier.

"We've got electric in this part of the house. We put in a plant to make our own," Diana told me, "but the current isn't strong enough to supply the back regions yet and Daddy says it'll need another dynamo. I don't care if we never have it, I like the lamp-light in the kitchen. Where shall I tell Redman to go?"

Redman was the chauffeur who was waiting, capped and booted, just inside the porch. He said "Good evening, sir" when I came up with Diana but he shot me a shrewd sidelong glance nevertheless.

I told Diana I had better be put off at the bus center in the square, but that it was not necessary to have a car to convey me home, for I could easily walk.

"Don't be so feeble," she snorted, "it's four miles and dark as a bag! Drop him at the bus center, Redman."

"Yes, Miss Emerald," he said and managed to convey the impression that he by no means relished the assignment but would perform it as a personal favor to her.

She followed me out on the half-moon of the graveled approach and the chauffeur opened the rear door and held it while I climbed in. The car was Mrs. Gayelorde-Sutton's Bentley, and far larger and more luxurious than any car I had traveled in up to that time.

Redman walked around and got into the driver's seat, but before he could let in the clutch Diana opened my door again.

"Oh, there's one thing I'd forgotten," she said, a little breathlessly. "You can go anywhere in Sennacharib when I'm back at school, and I'll see that Croker and the others are told about it. Good-by, Jan. See you again sometime—next hols perhaps."

"Yes," I said, "and thank you for everything . . . it's been wonderful . . . I . . ."

The chauffeur moved off then, just at the moment when a huge dog, either a Great Dane or a St. Bernard, ran barking from the house and thrust his great muzzle into Diana's hand. Greeting the dog she seemed to forget about me and as the car sped down the drive I twisted around and looked back at the house, only to see that the front door was now closed and that a single spotlight shone out over the portico, picking out the tall Doric columns that graced the front of Heronslea.

I was the tiniest bit put out by the speed with which she had withdrawn, but soon I forgot this in rich contemplation of all the wonderful things that had happened since Croker had jumped at me out of the wood. I found this contemplation so rewarding that I forgot I was traveling in a chauffeur-driven Bentley, owned by the wife of the overlord of Sennacharib, and only awoke from my daydream when the car stopped and Redman's voice rasped from the speaking tube. "This is it, I think!"

He didn't say "sir" and he didn't jump out to open my door.

Chapter Two

THE first week in November brought a series of violent southwesterly gales. One after the other they beat upon the coast, drenching the town with fine, sticky spray, knocking holes in the promenade and reducing to debris such of the beach huts as had not been dismantled and carted away for the winter.

I had never seen seas like this and I enjoyed the spectacle very much. I liked to stagger along the esplanade, with the wind in my back, and scramble over the landslip rocks to Nun's Bay Head, where a little coast guard hut had been built on the highest promontory.

From here you could see the coastline from the estuary in the west to Nun's Bay in the east, an entire seascape of heaving brown mantled in misty rain. The roar of the breakers provided a continuous undertone to the shriek of the wind, as it made its first landfall after a three-thousand-mile haul across the Atlantic.

When the tide was out and the sandbanks were exposed it was sometimes possible to see the stark remnants of the *Bonadventure*, the wreck that had given a name to this part of the coast. Uncle Luke told me that the great ship had gone aground there in the early nineteenth century and that almost everyone aboard it, including a company of nuns on their way to the West Indies, had been drowned. Most of those that the sea returned were buried in Whinmouth but two were interred on the little island, now known as Nun's Island, that stood about a mile out to sea. When the clouds lifted I could see the mouse-shaped rock with its thin covering of trees and scrub and farther east the abandoned lighthouse, put there by Winstanley years before his more famous lighthouse was built off Plymouth.

I did not go out to Sennacharib until late in the month and when I did I discovered that the gales had played havoc with my valley.

Two of the giant elms on the edge of the Heronslea rhododendron plantation were down, and one of the avenue beeches had fallen across the drive and was being cleared by estate timbermen. The Teasel Brook, which Diana and I had last seen as an insignificant stream some two yards wide, was now a brown torrent carrying a flotsam of twigs and leaves out of Teasel Wood. At Shepherdshey Bridge the water was almost up to the arch and the village street was ankle deep in frayed thatch, broken tiles and sodden twigs from the Heronslea timber.

I went on up the Teasel for a mile and found that the October colors had faded. The gorse guineas had turned to a dull copper and the purple sheen of the heath was rust red. It was still an exciting spectacle but its full glory had gone. There was loneliness in place of the mellow welcome of a month before.

I entered the estate boundary, partly to test the strength of the license Diana had promised me, but also in the vague hope of seeing her or getting some news of her. I met no one, not even Croker, who I suppose was busy clearing the rides behind the house, where the gales had done considerable damage among the larches and firs.

In the following month, as Christmas approached, my uncle's business took me to Shepherdshey Village several times in one week and I came to know some of the folk who lived there.

They were a picturesque community, almost untouched by the twentieth century and in some ways as archaic as the tumble-down buildings they occupied.

There was Half-a-Crown Sam, the village cretin, so bowed and hunched that when seen from a distance he looked almost round. Sam was a professional idiot, with a smooth shining skin and great tufts of yellow hair peaked up like the hair of a circus clown. His eyes were the lightest blue but could narrow to the merest slits when someone invited him to demonstrate the trick that earned him his name—a choice between a half crown and a halfpenny. He invariably chose the halfpenny, muttering that it was less trouble to carry away. Shepherdshey people told me that he had been amassing money by this means for close on thirty years, so perhaps he wasn't really an idiot at all.

There was Ada Macey, the shrill-voiced proprietress of The Jolly Rifleman. Ada said she could remember my Grandfather Leigh taking his first noggin of rum the day after he buried his wife. She had a high color and hard eyes and her reputation had penetrated as far as Whinmouth Bay, where she was said to have two husbands, the landlord, Jack Macey, and his man-of-all-work, Harry Venn. Jack, so the story went, had been reported missing early in the war, and Ada had married Harry soon after Armistice Day. She was not in the least put out when Jack turned up in 1919, and since then all three had continued to live lively but by no means quarrelsome lives in the ancient hostelry, west of the Teasel bridge.

It was difficult to imagine Ada as a source of solace to one man, much less two. She was sharp-featured, short-tempered, and not averse to boxing the ears of any male customer who crossed her. I delivered some furniture there on one occasion and happened to scratch the paint off the banisters on my way upstairs. Her protests followed me down the street as far as the crossroads and some of her expressions were such as the Whinmouth fishermen used when trippers walked over their nets spread to dry on the quay.

Across the street from Ada's pub was the village general shop, maintained by a swart, foxy little man called Pat Bristow. Pat was a bachelor and his bosom friend was the sexton, Nathaniel Baker, who seemed to spend all his time seated on Pat's counter.

Nat was a huge, slow-speaking man and the main occupation of these two consisted of issuing a running commentary on every customer who passed the window.

They were ruthless character slayers and in any less tolerant community would have soon been summoned to answer a slander writ. Pat would lay the accusations and wait for Nat's thoughtful corroboration. Having secured it he would then cast about for new charges in respect of the next person to pass the window. Both male and female sinners were referred to as " 'er."

"There 'er goes, ol' Nell Josling, looking as though butter wouldn't melt in 'er mouth!" Pat would say, jerking his pipe stem at an elderly woman on her way to the bus stop. "Wouldn't think to look at 'er she owed me four-pun-ten, would 'ee? Owes everyone over Whinmouth, so I hear. Ought to county court 'er, I ought, but I'm zoft. That's my trouble, zoft as a feather bade I be!"

Nat would ponder the customer's shortcomings for a few moments before adding: "They zay 'er insured old Trev Josling bevore 'er passed on. Dree-hundred-pun I 'eard it was. Tidy sum for a man in 'is condition, dornee think, Pat? And him a-bade two year or more, bevore us got round to burying 'un!"

Then Ada Macey would appear in the porch opposite to shake a mat and Pat would abandon the Joslings in order to comment on Ada's experiment in polygamy.

"Going on long bevore 1914 it was! I used to stand here an' zee 'em bob upstairs the minute old Jack Macey went out to his allotment. Time it to the split second they would. First you'd zee Jack, spade in hand, then Harry carrying out the empties, then Ada taking off her apron on the way upstairs. Always in a hurry *she* was, but Harry, he took his time like. He'd watch Jack out o' zight around the church bevore he went up, then draw isself a pint on the way up, never mind 'er shouting for him from the best room! Makes 'ee laugh, dorn it, blamin' it on the war?"

Then Nat would add his corroborative evidence regarding Ada's character in earlier life: "Never no different she wasn't! Smut Stover was the first there when she was fifteen. Zore 'em once I did, in the corner o' the churchyard when I was a choirboy. Fine place to start eh, top of a grave, but it's true. Smut gimme a penny to forget what I zee!"

Smut Stover, the man they referred to, was still about the village. He was a notable poacher, always at odds with the keepers on the Heronslea estate and on Lord Gilroy's coverts farther east. He was a cheerful ruffian and a crony of my Uncle Mark, who was said to have nameless business with him. Perhaps this accounted for Uncle Mark's roll of notes, for Smut was half a gypsy and was regarded as a thief as well as a poacher.

There were respectable folk of the community, of course, but I had no occasion to meet them at that time, for they never patronized Uncle Luke's Mart. They consisted of several farming families scattered around the area and one or two retired folk living in remote houses on the east side of the brook.

The farmers were as backward as everyone else in Shepherdshey. One never saw a tractor at work in the fields, only big, lumbering carts, painted sky blue and drawn by huge, patient shire horses. The vicar, Mr. Shelton, was as out of date as his parishioners.

He looked like a character in a *Punch* cartoon, trotting to and from the vicarage in shirt sleeves, a black bib and rusty clerical hat. He spent most of his time with his bees and usually had to be fetched from his hives on the edge of Teasel Wood when he was wanted to visit the sick, or perform a ceremony. He was said to be deep in the pocket of the Gayelorde-Suttons and dined with them whenever they were in residence. Another regular visitor to Heronslea was Colonel Best, V.C., a Zulu War veteran, who had taken part in the defense of Rorke's Drift and received an assagai wound that left him with a withered arm. The village as a whole, however, thought very little of the new occupants of Heronslea, dismissing them as foreigners, or "foggy-do-men." Everyone whose father had not been born in Shepherdshey was a foggy-do-man and the Gayelorde-Suttons, particularly Mrs. Gayelorde-Sutton, were objects of derision, welcome enough for the gifts they distributed at Christmas and at various fetes held in their grounds but far short of what the villagers called "real gentry," like the Gilroys.

The steady milking of the Gayelorde-Suttons was the principal hobby of the villagers. Mrs. Gayelorde-Sutton was invited to become president of every social group and a fairy godmother to every activity sponsored in the area. Her delight in these forms of patronage ensured a steady flow of funds, jumble, produce and free labor, and in return for these bounties the villagers were ready to eat as much feudal pie as she set before them, mumbling their thanks, tugging their forelocks and laughing heartily at the provider the moment she drove away in her Bentley or Rolls-Royce.

During that first winter I wondered how much Diana knew of this rustic charade or whether she cared two straws what the village folks thought of her parents, but soon I had an opportunity of assessing Mrs. Gayelorde-Sutton myself and guessing at the reasons for Diana's hostility toward her mother.

One afternoon, about a week before Christmas, I was left in charge of the Mart while Uncle Luke attended a sale. Business was slack, so I settled myself in the office corner, where I could watch the door and give the remainder of my attention to *Silas Marner*. The Mart was a treasure house of old books. There were trunks and tin chests full of them and I was never at a loss for reading matter.

I heard heels clicking on the slate slab outside the main door and looked up to see Diana standing there. She was standing sideways to me, talking to someone out of my line of vision.

I slammed the book shut and jumped up to greet her, but at that moment she shrugged and moved away as a well-dressed woman came through the doorway. I guessed at once that this was her mother, the celebrated Mrs. Gayelorde-Sutton, so I swallowed my welcome and remained quiet in order to get a good look at her.

She was a great deal younger than I had imagined, not more than thirty-three or thirty-four, and so stylishly dressed that anybody in a town like Whinmouth Bay would be sure to turn around and stare at her when she passed by. Skirts were at their very shortest just then and this made her look almost girlish, for her tailor-made costume finished well above her knees. She had very shapely legs and smart shoes, with heels that looked almost as long as her feet.

She was not particularly good-looking and possessed few of Diana's striking features but the general impression she gave was one of sensational smartness, like a model on the cover of an expensive periodical, the kind of magazine you see people reading in first-class railway carriages. She had dark, close-cropped hair and greenish, slightly prominent eyes. She was medium height, with a neat figure somewhat too thin. The only thing about her that reminded me of Diana was her chin, well rounded but very firm, too firm for a woman as willowy and elegant as she.

I studied her and was a little disturbed by what I found. There was something arrogantly aggressive about the way she sauntered around our pathetic display of goods, as though she were doing us a favor by just being there and was afraid of touching things as she tip-tapped among kitchen chairs, tables, mangles, washstands and battered commodes.

Then I heard her voice and realized instantly why the people in Shepherdshey made unpleasant jokes about her. It wasn't a woman's voice at all but a voice that belonged to an extravagant puppet. Its accent was so strained and strangled that it made you feel ashamed to listen and it struck me at once that her voice was in key to her personality, a whole jigsaw of effort and contrivance in striking contrast to her daughter's effortless way of moving, talking and smiling.

When Diana moved and smiled everyone about her relaxed. The person at whom she smiled wanted to acknowledge the rhythm and orderliness of the universe, for contact with her made you feel tolerant and generous *inside*. When her eyes sparkled you knew that it was good to be alive and that everything was going to turn out all right in the end.

Mrs. Gayelorde-Sutton's presence had an exactly opposite effect. It made you feel tense and apprehensive, as though you were walking over rough ground in the dark and not sure what you would bump into, or how much you would be hurt in the process. It armed all your defenses against indignities and humiliations and even when she wasn't addressing you the sound of her voice talking to somebody else made you feel edgy and small.

I've thought a good deal about Mrs. Gayelorde-Sutton's accent in the last twenty years. I've even gone to considerable pains to get it down on paper, but to do so with any accuracy is almost impossible, for it was the kind of accent that didn't use any rules regarding the articulation of vowels or the emphasis of syllables. It was meant, of course, to be a high-hat accent, the kind the best people have used since accents became stock-in-trade in this country, but hers overreached itself so ludicrously that it plunged down into farce and was lost in a whirl of despair, laughter or downright incredulity, according to how important she was to you.

I knew that she was important to me because I was already hopelessly in love with her daughter, and the first dry crackle of her voice made me shy away in alarm and want to hide myself behind Uncle Luke's junk.

I was still standing there, book in hand, when she swung round and tip-tapped into the Mart, her prominent eyes roving here and there for someone to hector. That was the very worst thing about her; you were always absolutely certain she *would* hector, it was so clear from the way she walked and held herself. Diana trailed along behind, almost submerged, I noticed, under this tide of arrogance.

Then Mrs. Gayelorde-Sutton spied me, rooted to the spot in our pigsty of an office.

"Boy!" she pronounced. "Come over heah, boy!"

I edged forward like a pupil of Dotheboys Hall anticipating a sound thrashing.

"How mache is *thet!*" she said, flicking her hand from the wrist and indicating a marble-topped washstand marked ten shillings in Uncle Luke's chalked scrawl.

I made a bad mistake straightaway. Licking my lips, and trying hard not to look at Diana who was now standing immediately behind her mother, I said that the article was marked and could be sold for ten shillings, plus delivery charges.

She screwed up her mouth, already very small, into a pink ball about the size of a florin.

"Ai ken see it's marked, boy! Ai've got eyes in mai head! Is there no adult on the premises?"

I quavered that I was in charge during the temporary absence of Mr. Leigh, but that I had his authority to sell anything that was priced.

She thought about this for a moment and then Diana suddenly spoke up. She did not look at me, and gave no sign at all of recognizing me as the boy to whom she had once extended the freedom of Heronslea and entertained in the kitchen less than three months ago.

"You'd better tell him we're buying a lot of things for the cottages," she said, quietly. "Then he'll probably let you have everything a lot cheaper."

I welcomed the compromise. Up to that moment I had been wondering what on earth a person like Mrs. Gayelorde-Sutton could want with our stock. I had seen some of the furniture inside her home, and the very least of it would have been unlikely to find its way on to Uncle Luke's handbarrow. I realized now that she was furnishing some of the Heronslea estate cottages and that made her presence clear. I managed to master my awe and embarrassment in the prospects of doing a profitable piece of business in Uncle Luke's absence and enjoying the handing over of money when he came in, cold and tired after six hours at the auction.

"We could certainly come to some arrangement like that," I said briskly.

She laughed at that and her laughter was like a gleam of sunshine, but sunshine on a February afternoon, without a particle of warmth in it. It was a laugh that made you wince and stammer, and what made it so much worse for me was Diana's silent presence.

I was rescued by Uncle Luke's entry. He came in trundling his handbarrow and even the presence of three chamber pots, roped to the barrow rails by loops of cord, did nothing to reduce the relief his entry afforded me.

"This is Mrs. Gayelorde-Sutton, from Heronslea," I muttered. "She wants some pieces for her cottages, Uncle Luke!"

She whipped around on me like a striking cobra.

"How do you know who I am?" she snapped, and it seemed to me that Diana disembodied herself into the windowless part of the store. I had realized my mistake as soon as it was uttered, however, and this time I was ready for her.

"Everybody knows you in Whinmouth, ma'am!" I said, and it was almost pathetic to see her bridle at such a hoary way of compliment-ing a customer.

"We hev been renovating on a considerable skeale," she told Uncle Luke, who was not particularly impressed by her. "Mai husband and I hev rebuilt all the cottages on the spinney side of the avenue and we shall be buying somewhat extensively, providing, of course, that we don't quarrel over praices!"

Uncle Luke, who treated every customer alike, assured her that this was unlikely and switched on a naked electric light in the angle of the store made by the office partition. As she followed him across the Mart I saw Diana jerk her head toward the main door and I gladly took the hint, slipping outside and across the road to the edge of the quay, where she joined me.

"Didn't she know about me?" I asked, breathlessly, for the en-counter had shaken me badly.

"Good Lord, of course not," said Diana. "I don't tell her anything important."

The words warmed me through, thawing me out and uncoiling the knots in my inside.

"I've been up to Sennacharib several times since," I said, "but I've never even seen Croker. You've had a lot of damage up there, haven't you?"

"Don't let's waste precious time on small talk," said Diana, shortly. "She'll be out in a minute and she wouldn't even trade here if she saw me talking to you! Have you seen our buzzards again?"

I told her no and she smiled a secret kind of smile.

"I have," she said. "I saw them yesterday. I've got a thing about those buzzards, Jan. They only show up when we meet, so I knew I'd see you today. I saw them from my bedroom window but you won't ever see them unless I'm there."

It made all buzzards lovelier than birds of paradise and I accepted her prophecy on the spot.

"Will you be at Boxing Day meet?" she wanted to know. "We're having it at Heronslea . . . it was always at Teasel Wood, but Mummy's decided to give a lawn meet and the Master has fallen in with it because there'll be plenty of everything—you know, stirrup cup and all that!"

"Muffins?" I said. My knowledge of hunting ritual was lamentable but this query made her laugh so much that I had time to feast my eyes on her and notice that she wore a rakishly tilted Cossack cap and that her soft brown curls cascaded from beneath it and lay thickly upon her shoulders. She looked more grown up than when I had last seen her, but perhaps this was because of her London clothes and elegant Russian boots, which were tight-fitting and as high-heeled as her mother's.

"You don't eat muffins on horseback, Jan," she said, but the touch of mockery was compensated by her easy use of the name she had given me. "You've grown even taller and broader, yet you aren't sixteen. When *are* you sixteen?"

"Next October," I said, trembling a little, "October the 6th."

"I'll remember," she said and then, looking across at the ramshackle shed: "What exactly do you do in a dump like this?"

"I help my uncle, we buy furniture at sales and sell it again at a small profit."

"Is that all?"

"Well, yes, I suppose so. We deal in secondhand books, of course, and sometimes sell bits of china and other antiques."

"It's not much of a job, is it? Why don't you get a real job?"

Up to that moment I had been rather proud of the position of right-hand man to the proprietor of the Quay Furniture Mart. It had seemed to me a much more important job than those occupied by most of the Whinmouth Bay boys who had passed school-leaving age. Most of them were grocer's errand boys, or newspaper and milk deliverers. Her obvious contempt, however, wrought an instant change in my heart. Suddenly the job of wheeling used-up furniture about on a barrow seemed mean and degrading and I knew that I would have to seek an occupation that found more favor in her sight. The prospect elated rather than depressed me. I said, rather recklessly:

"Oh, this is only temporary. I've got my eye on something much more exiting!"

"What?" she demanded.

"You'll find out when the time comes," I promised, and my stomach contracted as I reflected that the prospect of finding an exciting job in Whinmouth Bay was remote indeed.

She didn't press the point but simply looked me up and down, a half-smile playing hide-and-seek around the corners of her wide mouth. Finally she nodded, as though she had made up her mind about something.

"You're sweet, Jan. I like you because you're different!"

[44

I could have fallen at her feet on the quayside. I could have told her that I was worth ten of Jan Ridd when it came to adoring and protecting the girl I loved, but I had no words at my command, and even if I acquired them I was aware that I had nothing to buttress a declaration, not even a job that she considered superior to that of a glorified errand boy in the seedy old store of an unfashionable seaside town. I realized that my declaration must wait and all I said, in a desperate endeavor to prolong this delicious conversation, was "How do you mean, different?"

"Oh, just different," she said, and then: "Most boys of your age are show-offs!"

She turned and walked back into the store and I followed her at a safe distance. Uncle Luke called to me from the shadows and asked me to help him move a washstand into the center floor space and after that I was fully occupied, dragging furniture to one side and calling out the prices to Uncle Luke, while Mrs. Gayelorde-Sutton probed and peered and squeaked among the dusty stock. She finally settled for a small vanload and Uncle Luke reduced the total price by more than 20 per cent. I decided that for one so fabulously rich she was careful with halfpennies.

She bought one thing for herself, a pretty porcelain vase that she singled out in order to demonstrate her knowledge of china. From time to time Uncle Luke bought pictures and ornaments at the sales, but he could never afford to compete with the dealers for articles of any value, and this vase was Victorian and of little account.

"I'll take the little Rockingham vawse," she said, when they had agreed on a figure for the furniture, and when Uncle Luke, who was a lamentably honest dealer, explained that the vase was not Rockingham but of a much later date, her mouth again contracted into a pink ball and she called upon Diana for corroboration.

"Aim'rald," she said, pronouncing the name with a sighlike emphasis on the first syllable and then almost ignoring the "rald," "wouldn't you say that this was Rockingham? Laike the figures in the small kebinet in the morning room?"

Diana drifted over but nothing could induce Uncle Luke to sell an article under false pretenses. He said, very firmly, "It's not Rockingham, ma'am. If it was it certainly wouldn't be priced at fifteen shillings!"

"It's slightly chipped," said Diana, woodenly, "and inside it's full of hair cracks."

45]

"I'll hev it anyway," said Mrs. Gayelorde-Sutton, and put fifteen shillings on the table. "Rep it carefully and put it in the car, boy."

Diana shrugged and moved away again, while I wrapped the vase in tissue paper, placed it in a cardboard box and carried it out to the Rolls which was parked some distance down the quay.

I hoped that Diana would follow me out but she didn't. When I opened the door I found the rear compartment was full of dogs. They were handsome, amiable dogs, not disposed to resent a stranger. One was the huge beast that I had seen Diana fondle when I was driving away from Heronslea, and I saw now that it was a Great Dane. Half obscured by its vast bulk was a sleepy, golden Labrador, with a spiked red collar, and behind the Labrador a silky cocker spaniel who sat up and whimpered. I put the box in the glove compartment and petted the dogs, noticing that they all had their names and addresses engraved on their collars. The Great Dane was Beau, the Labrador was Sheila, and the spaniel was Flop. I wondered which of them was Diana's and whether it was she who had named them. Then Diana and her mother came out and I heard Uncle Luke promise to deliver the furniture by carrier's van and Diana and her mother got into the car, both without another glance in my direction.

As they drove off I hoped that Uncle Luke would close the store and go in to tea, because I yearned to slip away to my bedroom, light the gas fire and savor everything Diana had said during our brief conversation. I had plenty to think about—the fact that she considered me important enough to keep my visit a secret and not attempt to pass it off as a chance encounter with a village boy bribed by muffins and plum cake to keep his mouth shut about a bullying keeper. There was also her frank use of the name Jan and the admission that she considered me sweet, though I was not sure that I liked the adjective. Then there was the more flattering statement that she found me different. In fact the whole atmosphere of our second meeting had been distinctly encouraging, so much so that I made up my mind to go to any lengths in order to deliver the goods to Heronslea. I also decided to attend the Boxing Day meet despite Uncle Luke's strong disapproval of fox hunting. I went to bed happier than I had been since the evening of the second October miracle.

As it happened, the furniture was not delivered until after Christmas.

Ned Gilchrist, the carrier who undertook our deliveries, was booked all that week and although I begged him to accommodate us, and told him that the good will of people like the Gayelorde-Suttons was important to us, he was unable to fix a delivery date earlier than Old Year's Eve, so I had to wait until Boxing morning before I could hope to see Diana again, and then I knew that I would have no chance of talking to her alone, for a local meet, especially a lawn meet on a bank holiday, was certain to attract half the population of Whinmouth Bay.

It was just as I thought. The exodus from the town after breakfast on Boxing morning required the attention of the entire local police force, a sergeant and two constables, and apart from the buses and a few private cars conveying people to the Shepherdshey crossroads, the road was thronged with cyclists, pony carts and groups of pedestrians in their Sunday best.

I resented this invasion into Sennacharib and set off rather sullenly on Uncle Luke's ancient cycle. On the way I passed half a dozen horsemen and three or four pigtailed girls riding plump ponies. I reflected bitterly that these people would have the privilege of spending an entire day in Diana's company, whereas my own contact with her would be limited to a respectful gaze from the edge of the lawn and perhaps a wave of recognition if I was lucky enough to be noticed in such a crowd.

I was unduly pessimistic. In the first place, I soon forgot the stir and chatter around me in the glory of Sennacharib, now looking its winter best in strong December sunshine. The beeches that lined the approach to the house were splashed to their summits in red gold and every rusty leaf glittered with tiny beads of moisture, so that the trees looked like a long row of golden candlesticks sprinkled with silver dust. The sky between them was a cloudless blue and the air was so clear and frosty that it made your eyes and nostrils smart. The turf of the outer paddock was rimed and springy underfoot, and behind the house, which stood against the long slope of rhododendrons and Scotch firs like a squat wedding cake, was the high, feathery crest of the larch wood, the dearest spot in Sennacharib, for it was here I had met Diana.

The graveled forecourt, immediately in front of the portico, presented an animated scene by eleven o'clock. About a hundred people were sitting their horses there and sipping stirrup cup from glasses carried round on silver trays by members of the staff wearing spotless aprons and long Edwardian streamers. I recognized the fat cook dispensing pasties from the terrace, and at the first stroke of eleven the huntsman released the pack from a station wagon and they poured onto the gravel, trotting with noses down and tails up around and about the horses until they were chivvied into a dejected group by the cries of the hunt servants and the pistol cracks of their long whips.

The Master himself, bull-necked Doctor Kingslake, stood on the terrace chatting to a tall, squarish man with a head that looked far too big for his thin neck. Somebody close by said that this man was Mr. Gayelorde-Sutton, so I paid the group on the terrace special attention. Presently a groom led two horses around from the stable yard and I watched him hand the reins of the smaller horse to a younger man and then move over to assist Diana's father to mount.

Gayelorde-Sutton climbed up very awkwardly and when he was there he sat slightly forward, with his legs stuck out at wide, ungainly angles. When the groom moved away he wobbled slightly, then steadied himself by gathering reins and crop into a tangled ball. Then I forgot him, for Diana came out through the tall French window and it seemed to me that the chatter all around us subsided as she drifted across the terrace, took the reins of the smaller horse and floated up into the saddle, settling herself like a bird on a nest and making some last-minute adjustments to the girths.

She looked as enchanting as ever in a dark blue habit, fawn jodhpurs and a blue hunting hat crammed down over her curls. I was still gazing at her when somebody nudged me and I turned to find that it was Nat, the sexton of Shepherdshey, whom I had last seen sitting on the counter of the Shepherdshey shop.

Nat was commenting on the uncertainty of Mr. Gayelorde-Sutton's seat and doing so in the tone of tolerant contempt that all the Shepherdshey folk reserved for foggy-do-men and foreigners.

"Look at 'un," he muttered, "zittin' there like he was hatching out a pan o' live coals. Gordamme, the bliddy vool'll break 'is bliddy neck if they 'as any kind of a run! They won't though, never do Boxing Day, not with 'alf the bliddy county standing around and sp'iling the scent wi' they ol' charrybangs and whatnots! Be a laugh though, wouldn't 'er? Praper job if the pervider of all this 'ere toddy valled flat on 'is face afore they so much as got goin'!"

I deduced from Nat's speculation that Mr. Gayelorde-Sutton was a beginner, and now that he was mounted I edged closer to get a better look at him.

He was far less impressive than Mrs. Gayelorde-Sutton and on horseback he looked almost pitiful, for you felt that you wanted to stand around and catch him when, as must soon happen, he fell down on one side or the other.

His head was so round, and his body so square that the contrast was almost grotesque, and while I could see some slight physical resemblance between Diana and her mother I could see nothing at all to connect this nervous, awkward man with the girl who sat beside him, looking as if she had grown out of the glossy creature she was riding.

Then the Master mounted and called gruffly to the hounds, who shook off their dejected look and trotted up to him adoringly as he addressed them by a string of John Peelish names. When they had gathered, and he had tossed back his final flagon of stirrup cup, the crowd surged in and the huntsman blew a long, tuneless blast on his horn.

The thought of not being seen by Diana made me bold enough to push through the ranks of followers and cross the drive to where she was sitting her horse. The riders were beginning to close up behind the Master and she touched her mount with her heels and passed within a few feet of me, frowning slightly, as though irritated by the impeding presence of so many pedestrians.

"Hullo!" I faltered, touching her foot rather desperately, and she turned in the saddle and glanced down at me. Her frown disappeared and she smiled rather absently.

"Hullo, Jan! Glad you could get here. Are you going to follow on foot?"

"Are we allowed?"

"Of course. We'll be drawing Big Cover behind the house to begin with, and after that we'll probably move over to Teasel Wood. I should go there first and get away from this awful mob."

The horn sounded again and the followers fell back, forming up behind the last of the horsemen and moving around the western clump of rhododendrons toward the paddock over which I had galloped on Nellie. I grabbed my bicycle and pedaled madly down the drive and along to the village, where I left my bike in the yard of The Rifleman and continued on foot along the path beside the brook as far as the long sloping hill that crowned Teasel Wood.

Nobody followed me, they were all pounding after the field in the broad rides behind the house. I could look down on it here and, although field and followers were invisible under the close-set trees, I could hear the horn and presently a chorus of faint halloos.

I waited up there until after one o'clock, and my patience was rewarded. Just as I was thinking of surrendering to the pangs of hunger (I had been so excited that I had been unable to eat more than a spoonful or two of porridge for breakfast) there was a wild outcry from the far side of the brook and I saw the huntsman and one or two other riders burst through the gorse, jump the brook and pound up the slope directly toward me, led by about a dozen hounds in full cry.

Then I saw the fox, a brown, unhurried streak, daintily picking its way among the half-exposed roots of the gorse and heading, no doubt, for the shelter of Teasel Wood on the crest of the slope. He was invisible to his pursuers but I had him in view for several minutes and saw him turn right-handed to approach the trees at an oblique angle.

I marveled at his coolness and the deliberation he showed in threading his way through the obstacles that lay in his path. For a moment or two I forgot Diana and the hunt in a prayer that he would find sanctuary before hounds overtook him.

He made it with three hundred yards in hand and even tricked them into thinking he had headed directly up the slope, for they kept on until they had overrun his scent and reached the edge of the wood where I was standing. There they paused and ran aimlessly to and fro while the huntsman pounded up, his horse snorting with the effort of breasting the slope and glad enough to check while his rider glanced left and right, screwing up his nut-brown face in an effort to guess the likeliest line.

His sharp eye caught sight of me where I was standing against a tall pine.

"Did you see our fox, sonny?"

"Yes, sir," I said, "he ran along under the hedge and went in there!" and I pointed in the opposite direction to that taken by the fugitive, indicating a stony track that wound along the edge of the wood toward the common proper.

He did not thank me, for which I was grateful, but simply shouted, "Left-handed, Charlie!" to a farmer on a huge gray, who had breasted the slope behind him. Then he bellowed some jargon to the hounds and cracked his whip, driving them around the left-hand curve of the wood and riding out of my line of vision.

Seeing him from below, a stream of riders who had negotiated the brook now bore off at a sharp angle, spurring to overtake him on the gentler slope of the hill.

I was so frightened by the effects of my lie that I did not dare to watch any longer but retreated into the wood and took up a position in some hazel bushes beside the broad cart track that cuts Teasel Wood into two equal halves.

Dismally I wondered what Diana would think of such unsporting behavior and I was almost sick with shame and fear when I heard them pounding back along the cart track, slowly at first, then more resolutely as a stray hound picked up fresh scent outside the wood and drew them on at a brisker pace.

I stayed hidden in my cover when the huntsman, cursing like a madman, thundered by, followed by the farmer on the gray and after him three or four more riders, including the Master, who was so tall that he had to lie flat on his horse's mane to avoid low-hanging branches.

There was a fallen fir a few yards up the path and the huntsman jumped it, but all the others thought twice of setting their horses at the jagged cluster of broken branches and picked their way around near the small crater dug by the roots.

At last, after a dozen or so had gone by, along came Diana crouched low in the saddle and calling softly and persistently to her mount.

She was moving in long, easy strides and made straight for the fallen tree, adjusting her bunched reins as she went and shouting "Up, Glory, *hup!*" as the horse rose and cleared the highest branch by a good six inches. They made a perfect landing on the far side of the obstacle and I remained hidden in the hazel bush until the last of the field had cantered by, still shamed but for all that secretly pleased with myself, for my stratagem had at least enabled me to see Diana in action and Diana riding a fence that had scared all but the professional in the field.

The hunt went whooping away over the arable land in the direction of the sea and I stayed in the wood long enough to watch the stragglers toil across the gorse hill in twos and threes, their horses finding the plowland heavy going after the beaten rides of the estate thickets.

Last of all came Mr. Gayelorde-Sutton, his hat swinging on its guard, his reins, crop and string gloves tangled into a skein and held against his stomach by his wrists, while his fingers groped and groped for the lifeline of his mount's breastplate. He was only moving at a shambling trot, and as his forlorn figure crossed the skyline I could not help wondering whether active participation in the hunt had been his idea or his wife's. In spite of his money and cars, in spite of his undisputed sovereignty of Sennacharib, I felt sorry for him. I was always to feel sorry for him, for then and later he always had the air of an ungainly, unpopular child, bullied by a vain parent into entering a contest that could bring him nothing but bruises and humiliation.

Halfway along the brook path I came face to face with Drip and she recognized me at once.

"I thought you'd be riding, Jan!" she said and the warmth her greeting showed told me that she was predisposed in my favor and might prove a valuable ally. I pulled off my cap and admitted that I was not yet a good enough horseman to hunt but hoped to join the Pony Club and become proficient in the near future.

"That's a very sensible outlook, Jan," she said. "Emerald thinks everybody has got as much confidence as she has, and because she's a girl all the boys she knows try to outdo her and get into trouble of one sort and another. Are you walking back to Whinmouth or did you come over by car?"

I said I had cycled and wished I could think of some way to rid her of the impression that I was a member of the same social set as the rest of Diana's contemporaries. I hated the thought of her finding out who I really was, where I lived, what I did for a living, and how impossible Mrs. Gayelorde-Sutton would consider me as a squire for her daughter, but I lacked the courage to make the necessary confession and see dismay creep into Drip's lined face. Then she gave me something else to think about.

"I'm on my way to Miss Westcott's, at Hawthorn Cottage by the crossroads," she said. "She's collected a parcel for me from the midday bus. I went into Whinmouth for it on Christmas Eve but it wasn't ready. It's Emerald's Christmas present and I think it's going to be a big surprise for her!" Drip smiled. "She's a very difficult girl to buy for, you see, because she's got everything a child could possibly need or want. If I tell you what it is you won't repeat it to her and spoil it, will you?"

"Of course not!" I promised, and added that it was unlikely I should see Diana again before she went back to school for the Lent term.

"Then I'll show you when we get to Hawthorn Cottage," said Drip. "I think I'd like to know what someone her own age feels about it."

We turned into the village street and walked up the gentle rise to the crossroads. On the way Drip talked ceaselessly about Diana and, although she told me little that I did not already know, she made it clear that she was as much Diana's slave as I was, and a far more unselfish one to boot, for her livelihood depended on Diana's progress and good behavior, and from what I had seen of the relationship of governess and pupil it was obvious that Diana dictated her own terms to this gentle, friendly soul.

I also gathered that Drip was terrified of Mrs. Gayelorde-Sutton.

"Her mamma is very keen to bring her on," she explained plaintively, "but Mrs. Gayelorde-Sutton is away such a lot and nobody else has any kind of authority over her. I'm sure I haven't and I know that her father hasn't. She can coax him into promising anything, even when it runs contrary to her mamma's wishes, and that sometimes makes trouble for all of us! It's not that she's naughty, mind you, she's the most lovable gel in the world when she wants to be, but she's not afraid of anything or anyone, except perhaps her mamma, and when she's down here she likes to run wild, you know, the way she did when she put you up on that pony and raced across the paddock into the yard. She needs somebody much stricter than me, I'm afraid, but I think I'd break my heart if I couldn't watch her finish growing up, now that I've had her so long. You see, Jan, I'm a kind of auntie about six times removed, and I was her nanny before I was made governess."

Drip had been talking half to herself as we went along but now, as we reached the gate of Hawthorn Cottage, she suddenly recollected herself and smiled.

"There now, I am a goose. As if you'd be interested in all this chatter! Just wait there and I'll pop in and see if the present has come, I won't be a moment." She tripped up the path and disappeared into the cottage without knocking.

In less than a minute she was out again, carrying a large oblong carton that appeared to be heavier than she could comfortably manage. She set it down on a stone garden ornament and whipped off the lid in a flurry of pride and excitement.

"There!" she said. "What do you think of *that*?"

I gazed at the contents in wonder. The box was full of exquisitely bound books that fitted into a neat, backless bookshelf, the kind of shelf made to stand on a large bedside table. The edges of the pages and the lettering of the authors' names and titles were picked out in gold and the bindings were of tooled Moroccan leather, with a silken bookmark hanging from each spine. I went down on my knees and examined the titles, a fanfare of all the titles I had already gathered into my own private box at the Mart, *Robinson Crusoe, Treasure Island, Kidnapped, Tom Brown's Schooldays, Huckleberry Finn, Silas Marner, The Mill on the Floss, Pilgrim's Progress, Water Babies, Westward Ho!, Don Quixote,* and half a dozen more; but these were more than just books, each was a work of art, exciting to look at and thrilling to handle.

"It's an absolutely wonderful present, Miss Rodgers!" I exclaimed and saw that my unconcealed delight brought her intense pleasure, for she flushed and bit her lip, as though about to burst into tears.

"I . . . I'm so very glad you think so, Jan . . . I thought and thought and then, about a week or so ago, Diana happened to make a joke about how she used to plague me into reading one more chapter before I turned out the light. I picked all her favorites, you see, and strictly between ourselves, they're *my* favorites too. I thought she'd have them for always and maybe remember me when she dipped into them, perhaps when she has children of her own and begins reading aloud to them."

"*Lorna Doone* isn't there," I said suddenly. "She likes *Lorna Doone,* doesn't she?"

"The case only held seventeen," said Drip, so apologetically that I instantly regretted my comment, "besides, I . . . I just *had* to draw the line somewhere. They were rather expensive."

I wondered how much the Gayelorde-Suttons paid her and how many weeks' salary had been paid over the counter for this wonderful demonstration of affection. The thought, together with Drip's eager expression, formed a lump in my throat, so that I could only blurt out once more that it was a marvelous Christmas present and that Diana would be certain to value it above all her more spectacular possessions.

Drip was so delighted with this halting speech that she gave me an impulsive hug and said that I was a nice boy and must come to tea again during the holidays and hear another of her musical boxes, one that played "Lass of Richmond Hill." Then, as she was replacing the lid of the box, she had an inspiration.

"Why don't you buy her *Lorna Doone?*" she suggested. "You're quite right, *Lorna* was always a great favorite with her, but of course, you must know that, mustn't you? After all, you're Jan, aren't you?"

"It was Diana who christened me Jan," I told her. "My proper name is John. I like Jan much better, though," I hastened to add.

"Well, if you haven't already got her a present it might be a good idea, don't you think? I know they've got a copy in Beatty's because I saw one. It won't be exactly like these, of course, because these had to be specially ordered from Agnews', in London, but it's a very nice edition, in dark blue, for seven-and-six."

I said it was a very good idea and thanked her for showing me the books. Then I said good-by and began to push my bike up the long hill. As always, whenever I had seen Diana, I had plenty to think about on the way home.

3.

Uncle Luke paid me ten shillings a week and I was expected to save half this sum for my clothes. There was nothing in my money box because Christmas had emptied it and New Year's Day fell before another payday. I couldn't ask Uncle Luke for an advance, for my money was always doled out by Aunt Thirza and I knew that she would ask me why I needed it so urgently. I hadn't told either of them about Diana, sensing that they would raise a whole string of objections to my associating with a family like the Gayelorde-Suttons. Drip's idea was a nuisance in some ways, because the raising of seven-and-sixpence occupied my thoughts all next day, and I wanted to devote my attention to the much more important problem of finding a job that Diana would consider a worthier occupation for a Jan Ridd than that of carting kitchen furniture and chamber pots around town on a handbarrow.

I had already given long and careful thought to this problem but as yet had not produced a solution, not even a temporary one. I even went so far as to borrow one of Uncle Luke's nature notebooks and jot down a list of my possible qualifications. They were not impressive. I discovered that I was an inch and a half above average height, nearly a stone above average weight, could swim two lengths of the Brixton Baths breaststroke and one length backstroke, had written a composition on "A Day at Hampton Court" that had been included in the school magazine during my final term at school, and had since shown a mild aptitude for getting bargains in the slow bidding that opened the local auction sales.

There was, so far as I could see, nothing here to indicate that I would one day develop into the kind of man whom Diana Gayelorde-Sutton would admire and respect. Physically she seemed to find me pleasing but I was aware that men who earned their living by physical accomplishments—lifeguards, gymnasts, athletes, and even policemen and professional boxers—seldom became the masters of large country estates, with a string of hunters and several expensive cars.

I finally decided to put the problem on one side until I had settled the more immediate one of finding seven-and-sixpence for the blue *Lorna Doone* and until I had had an opportunity of questioning Diana as to the type of occupation she would consider fitting for a future husband. It was necessary, I felt, to explore the ground very carefully before making a decision that might lead me into another blind alley.

I set these thoughts down now across an interval of more than twenty years and it may seem an exaggeration on my part to claim that, at the age of fifteen and two months, I was already planning my life along lines that led directly toward marriage and the overlordship of Sennacharib, with Diana as vice-regent, but I know that it was so. I realize now that the normal pursuits and dreams of a boy played but a small part in my development after the October miracles; I was now the victim of a twin obsession, the ownership of a country estate, and the sharing of that estate with Diana Gayelorde-Sutton. Everything I dreamed, and everything that I pursued, had to do with one or other of these ambitions. I was not as yet physically in love, for Diana was too remote and far too elevated in my imagination to encourage me to ponder the act of touching her hand, or breathing one word to her of my devotion, but I know now that her mere presence uplifted me and inspired me in a way that all the heroes of romantic fiction had been uplifted and inspired by their sweethearts and wives.

Perhaps my insatiable appetite for books had something to do with it, or perhaps my spirit, badly bruised by the recent death of my mother, responded to the spontaneous friendliness she had shown a gawky boy who had settled among strangers. It may have been either or both of these things that drew me to her, or it may have been the fact that she represented, in a single attractive human being, all the good things of life, and all the comforts and security that spring from wealth and the manifestations of wealth.

I solved the present problem by an act of sheer desperation.

On the following day, when the last post had gone and I had abandoned hope of being able to take her a surprise parcel, I remembered that there were one or two articles of furniture in the Mart that had been put on one side to await the collection by the Council refuse van. They had been brought away from the last sale, where the auctioneer had included them in a final lot as too battered and broken to be itemized, and Uncle Luke loaded them onto his barrow in one of his absent-minded moods. When he saw their condition he flung them aside as items unlikely to coax coppers from the lowliest customer.

I went out and took a good look at them. There was a three-legged chair, a cabin trunk with its lid hanging on a single hinge, and a badly frayed wickerwork plant stand. All the pieces were there and I set to work on them by candlelight, for there was no electric point in the repair shop. We often restored furniture, so I had all the right tools and a gluepot.

In less than two hours I had completely repaired the chair, rehinged the lid of the trunk and replaited the frayed patches in the plant stand.

I estimated that we could now ask fifteen shillings for the three items and I carried them up to Aunt Thirza in the flat we occupied behind the Mart and told her that I had spent the evening working on them.

Aunt Thirza was a parsimonious soul and I knew that I could count on her commendation. She did not disappoint me. When I told her I was going to ask Uncle Luke to price the items at five shillings apiece she at once opened her purse and extracted three half crowns. "This'n to encourage 'ee in the belief that someone'll buy everything, providing 'er's furbished up to look praper," she told me.

I slipped out at nine o'clock the next morning and ran along to Beatty's, in Chapel Street, to buy *Lorna Doone*, telling them to leave it unwrapped because I wanted to write in it and wrap it myself.

I should have liked to buy a card to go with it, but the purchase of the book consumed my entire capital. During the lunch interval I took the gift to my room and sucked a penholder throughout the greater part of the dinner hour while composing the inscription.

Finally, I wrote: *To Diana, a New Year gift, from Jan, with all my Love.* I hesitated a long time before I added the final words but finally decided that they could pass as a formality and could not be taken to mean anything forward on the part of the donor.

I now had to wait three days until the carrier called for the goods that Mrs. Gayelorde-Sutton had bought before Christmas, for I had made up my mind to give Diana the present rather than risk a maternal interrogation that might follow the arrival of an unexpected parcel.

On the last day of the year the van arrived about eleven o'clock in the morning and Aunt Thirza packed me some sandwiches to take for lunch, as I was expected to stay and help with the unloading. My one fear was that Diana might not be sufficiently interested to come over to the cottages when we arrived or, worse still, that her mother would superintend the whole operation and keep us in view all the time.

I was lucky again, for not only was Diana awaiting us at the entrance to the drive but at once hopped on the tailboard and gave the driver his directions. She was dressed for work too, in blue jeans, a green sweater and a scarlet beret. She told me that her mother and father had returned to London the previous day and that Drip was expecting me to tea when the job had been completed.

"It won't take us all the afternoon," I protested, though secretly overjoyed at the invitation. "We shall be finished about three and the van will be going back."

"Oh, I've fixed all that," she said, airily. "I telephoned your uncle and said we wanted some help clearing out one of the cottages and that you were to stay and sort out anything he might want to buy."

"Good Lord!" I said, aghast at her nerve. "Whatever did he say to that?"

"He said it would be all right and you could come home on the bus at six. Why should he object? You're not scared of him, are you?"

"No," I said, "not of him, but I'm scared of your mother."

"Well, most people are," she said tolerantly, "but she's well over two hundred miles away, thank heavens! Praise Him from Whom all blessings flow for Boards!"

The van branched off the main drive and lurched along a narrow track that led through rhododendrons to the cottages, built on the Teasel side of the big paddock. Somehow it was much easier to be myself with Diana when she was dressed in hand-me-downs, a dirty sweater and the beret. On all three of the previous occasions that we had met, her expensive-looking clothes had intimidated me, but today she looked just like one of the fishermen's daughters who played and flirted on the quay outside the Mart. I asked her about her Christmas gifts (being careful to drop no hint about my present) and she said that she had been given a silver toilet set by her mother and that the horse I had seen her riding on Boxing Day was a combined Christmas and birthday present from her father. She made no mention of Drip's wonderful gift.

This led us on to discuss the Boxing Day hunt and she told me that they had run the fox to ground at Nun's Bay, where it had entered a cliff earth too deep to be opened with the crowbars. They had hung around there most of the afternoon, and apart from the initial gallop that I had witnessed it had been a blank day.

I had half a mind to tell her then that it was I who had saved the fox by misdirecting the huntsman but I checked myself, fearing that such a confession would endanger our relationship and spoil what promised to be a wonderful day. I had made up my mind that I would tell her but in my own time, when our friendship had thrown out stronger roots.

We got through the unloading in double-quick time and the van left soon after two o'clock.

"Now," I said, finishing my sandwiches, "where's all this other stuff I'm supposed to look at?"

She laughed and shook her curls. "Why, Jan, you great booby, there isn't any! I made that up. I guessed you'd have to go back and I wanted you to stay, but it's perfectly all right, you can say none of it was worth buying."

I wasted no time pondering her ethics. I was far too flattered by the discovery that she wanted my company enough to invent lies to get it. The sky was overcast and rain was threatening, so I imagined that we should now return to the house. Instead, however, she suggested that we go up through the larch wood and across the common to another wood that I had not yet explored but had seen from a distance on the day of my encounter with the keeper.

"It's the most exciting place in Sennacharib," she said, "because it's got the Folly in it."

"What's the Folly?" I asked and she told me that it was a kind of tower, built by one of the mad Gilroys nearly a hundred years ago, and was not ruinous and abandoned but quite habitable and just like a corner tower of a French château on the Loire.

It sounded well worth exploring so we set off at once, Diana having called to a woodsman and told him to tell Drip that she had had lunch with the furniture men and would be back at dusk for tea. I was on the point of giving her my present then but I decided it would be better to wait until we got to the Folly. The book was carefully packed in my knapsack, along with Aunt Thirza's thermos flask and sandwich tin.

We climbed the main ride of the larch wood and crossed the fenced paddock to Foxhayes Common. The Folly was in a large, straggling copse that occupied the highest piece of land on the estate, apart from Overhang Head, above Nun's Bay on the coast. This wood was not a plantation but a wild and lonely jumble of dwarf oaks, chestnuts and silver birches, and as we drew near it I could see the top of a leaded conical tower peeping from the seaward edge of the timber. I thought it very odd that I hadn't noticed such an incongruity before. It was, as Diana had described, just like a corner of a castle in an illustrated fairy-tale book, the kind of tower where giants and ogres lived and old women spun magic charms. It was exciting enough, but the excitement it generated was tinged with fear and I was at a loss to understand why anyone had chosen to build a tower in such a lonely spot, or what possible purpose it could have served when first erected.

Diana said she had wondered the same things and had sought information from the oldest estate worker, a man whose father had been a keeper at Heronslea when the house was still occupied by the Gilroys.

"The man who had it built was a bit of a loony," she told me. "He used to come out here and sit by himself for days on end, or so old Venner told me. At one time it had little cannons on the top floor and Lord Gilroy's cousin, or whoever it was who built it, used to play his violin up there. Poachers wouldn't go near the place, Venner said, because they all thought it was haunted after he died. There was even a story that people heard a violin playing there long after he was dead and gone, but I don't believe in ghosts, do you?"

I said I didn't, but the Folly, when we came to it, was the kind of place that encouraged you to believe in them wholeheartedly, particularly on a gray December day, with a cold wind blowing from the northeast and the surrounding common looking pinched and defeated, as though it awaited a spring that would never come.

There was an overgrown path leading to the doorless porch and a flight of church-tower steps to the upper rooms, of which there were two. The triangular steps were hewn out of solid stone and were still in good condition, so we climbed up, passed through the middle chamber and reached the top room without any difficulty.

It was lighter and more cheerful up here, for we were now above the level of the nearest trees and could look down over the whole stretch of country between the tower and the sea.

Sennacharib was laid out like a map, with the blur of Teasel Wood to the east, the blue spirals of smoke marking Shepherdshey in the center, and the vast green clump of the Heronslea grounds to the west. Beyond the road you could see the red and gray huddle of Whinmouth and the estuary, and if the day had been clear the far side of the Whin would have been visible, as would have been Nun's Island in the bay to the north.

Up here the sense of gloom that the first sight of the Folly had provoked was exorcised by the magnitude of the prospect and Diana, noticing my exhilaration, said, "You like it, don't you, Jan?"

"Yes," I said, "it's a marvelous place! Does anyone come here now, anybody but you?"

"No," she said, "not even the keepers. I know that because they were surprised to hear it was still safe to climb and you can see by the briers at the entrance that nobody ever uses the path. I'll tell you what, Jan, it can be *our* place. I won't ever bring anyone here but you and if we ever want to meet, and it isn't possible to make proper arrangements, we can have the Folly as a *thought code*—you know, a prearranged rendezvous that doesn't need any message—we'll just *know* we can always meet here! Later on I'll sneak some chairs and a table, and perhaps a bit of carpet and some tinned stuff and an oil stove for cocoa. It'll be like the cave in *Tom Sawyer* or that place on the cliffs where Stalky and Co. used to hide."

I was overwhelmed by a plan that plainly indicated that I was progressing at a prodigious rate, but the mention of Stalky and Co. suddenly reminded me of the gift and I took it out, my throat dry and my hands shaking a little.

"It's for you, my New Year present," I said, blushing. "I met Drip at the hunt and she said she'd forgotten to include this in that wonderful set she gave you."

The presentation took Diana completely by surprise. She stared at me with parted lips for a moment and then she swallowed twice, very deliberately, and began to tear at the wrappings. I watched, enjoying every second of her suspense, and when she saw what it was, and had cooed her delight over the inscription, I was ready to burst with pride and satisfaction.

"*Why, Jan!*" she cried, holding it close against her chest. "This is the nicest present anyone ever gave me . . . no, no, I *mean* it . . . because—well—you haven't got much money and this is like . . . like Daddy giving me a thousand pounds, if you see what I mean!"

I don't know how much Mr. Gayelorde-Sutton was earning in 1927 but the book represented three quarters of my weekly income. If he was drawing fifty thousand a year from his investments, as he did into the middle part of the thirties, then her extravagant comparison probably wasn't far short of the mark.

It was easy to see that she had been reared against a background of dividends and shares values. The first thought that came into her head was the cost of the book and what the outlay had imposed upon the investor, but a more generous reaction followed as soon as she had reread the inscription and flicked through the pages.

"It's the *thought* that's exciting, Jan! You're like old Drip that way. The presents I got from Mummy and Daddy don't really mean anything, you see? They forget until I come home just before Christmas and then they suddenly remember that something is expected of them and rush out and splosh money on the first thing that comes into their heads. It was that way with the pony and the dressing set."

I didn't feel that I could take undue credit for the gift. Although an accomplished liar herself, Diana always made you feel that way, you shied away from pretense and wanted to tell her the whole truth, whatever the consequences.

"As a matter of fact it was an afterthought on my part," I admitted.

"I got the idea from Drip, when she showed me the marvelous present she had for you."

"I don't care, I still think it was wonderfully sweet of you, Jan . . . there, that's *how* sweet!" and she placed the book on the broad window ledge, took my face in her hands, and kissed me on the mouth.

Sensations are difficult to recall over a gulf of twenty years. You always promise yourself that you will remember the best of them but you seldom do, not really, not in the active sense. There have been half a dozen moments in my life of which I could have said I was ecstatically happy, and each of those moments was a spontaneous gift from Diana. This, I believe, was the first of them, not only because it was the first time that I had been kissed by a girl and because that girl was Diana, but because her impulsive affection somehow transformed me from a boy to a man, marking that transition as nothing else could have done.

Adolescence, at least for the male, is a slow, tedious business and not so exclusively physical as is generally believed. I think that its progress involves so many workaday things, things like wages, the lack of privacy in tiny households, the attitude one is obliged to maintain toward parents and employers and even the attitude of bus conductors and civil servants. I had been doing a man's work ever since I came to the West and I had always been treated like a man by Aunt Thirza and Uncle Luke's customers, but I had never considered myself anything more than an overgrown boy until Diana's lips touched mine and I caught the fleeting scent of her hair and my senses registered the pressure of her fingers on my cheeks.

I don't recall whether I returned her kiss but I do know that I must have communicated something of my emotional turmoil to her, for her hands instantly left my face and she had to combat a flurry of embarrassment, rare for her but powerful enough to make her turn back to the window and change the subject.

"Do you ever go to dances in Whinmouth, Jan?"

Her abrupt change of manner shocked me. Somehow it depreciated the value of the kiss.

"No," I said, with a touch of sulkiness, "I can't dance."

"Of course you can," she said impatiently, "anybody can nowadays, there's simply nothing to it but walking around to a rhythm! We have a dance every Saturday at school but it's a bore dancing with girls. I have to be a gentleman because most of the girls are smaller."

63]

Talk of her school always interested me, possibly because it was so unlike any school I had attended or visited. From the odd scraps of information she imparted I had conjured up a picture of a kind of social university, where the emphasis was on deportment rather than on dates, sums and irregular verbs.

"What are you going to do when you leave that place?" I asked her, not because I was anxious to know, but because I wanted her to do the talking, leaving my faculties free to imprint the memory of the kiss upon my mind.

"Oh *that's* all mapped out," she said, scornfully. "It's all rather dull and I'm not at all sure I mean to go through with it! I shan't leave till I'm seventeen and then Mummy's determined to send me to Switzerland to be finished. She plans to keep me there about a year, rubbing up on languages and then I'm to go *en famille* to Paris before coming back to be presented."

I had a vague notion what "being presented" and "finished" meant but not the slightest inkling of the meaning of "*en famille*." I never minded displaying ignorance of this kind to Diana, so I asked for more detailed information.

She said that nearly all girls who were finished in Switzerland remained on the Continent for another year or so, living with a French family in order to become fluent in at least one other language. I said that this would probably be fun, but she shook her head and pointed out that her mother would be certain to select a family where boarders were heavily chaperoned and never allowed to leave the house alone. She went on to say that the sister of one of her friends was already domiciled in such a household and had written home to say that it was worse than being in prison.

I asked her to explain to me exactly what being presented entailed.

"Well, it's a kind of here-I-am ritual," she said, laughing. "It happens when a girl is about eighteen and she is prepared for it, the way you get prepared for confirmation. When it happens you have what is called 'a season.' A season means you stay in London and go to parties and naturally you have a big party of your own. The idea of the parties isn't for fun but an opportunity to meet suitable boys."

"Boys to go about with?"

Diana threw back her head. "Oh Jan," she protested, "you're so sweet—*no*, boys who'll propose to you!"

I at once turned my face against seasons and muttered darkly that

I had always supposed that this sort of thing was terribly old-fashioned nowadays and that even wealthy people married for love, the way they always did in books.

"Oh that's so," she said lightly, "but the man you happen to fall in love with doesn't have to be poor, does he? Some of them who come to the debs' parties are, of course, as poor as church mice if you did but know it, and all those are on the lookout for a girl with money, but money wouldn't influence me one way or the other, so long as the man I accepted *was* somebody!"

"You mean a . . . a knight, or something?" I asked, guardedly.

"Goodness no!" said Diana, laughing again. "Titles don't mean a thing nowadays. You can buy them if you want to—in a roundabout way, that is. Mummy's been after one for Daddy for years now, but it takes time and it's got to be done tactfully. She'll pull it off, though, mark my words! No, what I mean by *being* somebody is somebody who had done something out of the ordinary, somebody like, well, like Scott of the Antarctic, or Evans of the Broke, somebody I could look up to and who didn't give a hoot whether Daddy was well off or not, but wanted *me* as a person. The point is, people like that usually haven't got money, not real money, that is."

Then and later I was fascinated by Diana's phrase—"real money." Our views of money were poles apart. Any money was real money to me but it wasn't to her; "real" implied something over the five-figure mark, the kind of money I associated with film stars, and people like her father.

Her declaration gave me hope, however, for at least I was getting the kind of information I needed. I made up my mind to get more.

"What would you like to do when you leave school, apart from what your mother has mapped out for you? I mean, if it was left to you, would you go around the world or something?"

"Not me," said Diana, promptly, "you can have globe-trotting for all I care! Travel isn't anything like as exciting as it's cracked up to be. There's nowhere like this, for instance, at least not where I've been so far. France is flat and bare, and Switzerland is sickeningly picture-postcardy. Italy's all right in some ways but it's ever so smelly and I'm glad Mummy and Daddy are going to Africa on their own in the summer, because then I shall have you and Sennacharib all to myself for seven glorious weeks!"

Suddenly she stopped talking and looked at me speculatively for a long moment, sucking her finger and "freezing" her enormous dimple. "Do you know, Jan," she went on at length, "I think that's what I like about you—apart from your nice wide shoulders and your long eyelashes, I mean—you *feel* about this place as if it was something alive, like an animal. That's exactly how I feel but I don't think I'd have known that if I hadn't met you that day in the wood. What would I do if I wasn't packed off to Switzerland to be finished, and then hauled home for all that presentation flimflam? *I know* what I'd do"—she stood clear of the window ledge and interlocked her long fingers—"I'd run a riding school, hunt all the winter and swim all the summer. I'd teach *you* to ride, so that we could go long hacks together and in the evenings I'd give parties—not the kind of parties that Mother gives, where dreary people stand around nibbling those soppy little sausages on sticks but *real* parties, where we all danced on the terrace and had midnight swims and talked and talked, you know, about interesting things, like books and plays and being in love."

The mention of books was the one chord I recognized in this rhapsody and I pounced on it, recalling my pitiful little success with the essay on "A Day at Hampton Court."

"Would you . . . you *marry* a writer, Diana? A famous one, of course!" I added, seeing a puzzled expression cross her face.

She put her head on one side so that her dark curls swung freely in what I thought an enchanting manner.

"A writer? Ye-es! I think I would, providing he wrote the right sort of books, of course. I wouldn't care to be the wife of a writer like Edgar Wallace, for instance, but it might have been fun to have been, say, Mrs. Kingsley, or Mrs. Robert Louis Stevenson! A writer would never be dull, would he? He'd always be surrounded by other interesting people, you know, painters and sculptors and famous people of one sort or another. Yes . . ." she finally made up her mind. "I *would* like to marry an author, Jan!"

There was so much that I wanted to say to her but I needed time and leisure to think it out. I had a conviction now that our relationship was entering a new phase and that it might be fatal to make rash promises I had no power to keep. A vague plan was already forming in my mind but it needed time.

"Can we meet on Saturday, Diana?" I asked her. "I might have something important to tell you."

She pouted. "Oh dear," she said, "I won't be here on Saturday. I should have gone back with Mother and Daddy but I wriggled out of it because I knew you were coming. I tell you what, why not write to me about it? I'll give you my school address too, at least I'll give you a day girl's address to write to, because old Passy-Glassy has a nose a yard long and if she recognizes letters in male handwriting she redirects them to parents! Here"—she whipped a tiny diary and a stub of pencil from the pocket of her jeans and scribbled an address on it—"write to me as much as you like and then I'll be one up on Sheila Bryanstone. She's always showing off about the sloppy letters she gets from the boys she meets in the hols."

I took the address and as I did so I saw through the open casement that dusk was creeping across to the edge of the wood and lights were showing down in Shepherdshey hollow.

"We'd better be going, Diana," I told her. "It'll be dark before we get back."

She looked out of the casement and then picked up her book, opening it at the flyleaf and rereading the inscription. "All my love . . ." she repeated and then, shutting it abruptly: "Do you mean that, Jan, really mean it?"

"Why yes," I said, grateful for the fading light, for I knew that I was blushing, "yes, of course I meant it."

The half-smile that was so peculiarly Diana's flickered at the corners of her mouth.

"You mean you haven't got a girl already?"

"No," I said, using the Whinmouth term for an adolescent courtship, "I'm not 'going' with anyone, if that's what you mean."

"That's funny," she said, half to herself, "I always imagined that a boy as big as you and going to work . . ."

She trailed off, as though turning something over in her mind, and then quickly looked at me, with serious eyes.

"You won't see me again until next hols. Wouldn't you like to kiss me, Jan?"

If she had said that before we entered the Folly, before I gave her the book and she had responded with the impulsive kiss given in acknowledgment, I should have been far too shy and gawky to have responded, but I had grown very appreciably during the last half hour, and when she stepped closer and tilted her face I felt no embarrassment, only a great surge of warmth and ecstasy, that lifted me higher than this—the highest point in Sennacharib. I kissed her very softly on the mouth and I think she must have known then that it was the first time I had ever kissed a girl. Then, as gently as I kissed her, she took me by the hand and led me down the staircase and into the wood. As we came out on the path to the paddock there was a flutter of wings in the oak on the very edge of the copse as our buzzards rose and wheeled above the larches below.

Neither of us remarked on them but Diana's fingers tightened on mine before she released my hand to climb the rail and jump down into the field.

Chapter Three

EARLY the next morning I put on my best suit and went around to the building behind the High Street office of what my Aunt Thirza described as "The Gospel According to Saint Reuben"—that is, the headquarters of Uncle Reuben's *Whinmouth & District Observer*.

I had been there before, of course, but my visits had been impersonal. Then the machines that were engaged in grinding out handbills and posters, and the lumbering great flatbed on which the *Observer* was printed each Friday had been no more than a source of clatter. Now I looked at them with respect, for I knew that they underpinned the bridge I so desperately needed to approach even the most tentative claim to Diana, or Sennacharib.

It was the usual small-town printing office, employing half a dozen men and boys, all wearing indescribably filthy aprons. The machines appeared to me to be but a slight improvement on the apparatus of William Caxton, seen in the famous picture depicting the patronage of Edward IV. Each machine was surrounded by bulkheads of type cases at which men stood, plucking at type and slamming their gleanings into what to me looked like metal pencil boxes. Over all hung a rancid smell of machine oil and printer's ink, together with an air of quiet absorption.

Uncle Reuben greeted me with the professional heartiness of a habitual public speaker.

"Well, young feller-me-lad, and what can we do for you today?"

I had learned to ignore his forced breeziness and look-smart-about-it manner, for I knew that he possessed qualities of kindness and patience. I spoke up without fear or embarrassment.

"I want to be a reporter, Uncle," I told him, adding a conciliatory "I'm quite prepared to start at the bottom."

He stared hard at me for a moment or two and then laughed. A laugh was a luxury in which he rarely indulged.

"God bless my soul!" he exclaimed, laying down his "pencil box" and thrusting both hands into his apron pocket. "Whatever gave you that idea, John? Was it Uncle Luke or Aunt Thirza? Have they decided you're not cut out for a junk merchant?"

"No," I told him, "I think they like me working for them, but there's no future in it."

Suddenly he looked pleased and studied me for a long minute; then he said:

"I daresay you're right at that! It isn't a real trade, like printing. What you really mean, I imagine, is that you want to learn to be a compositor?"

"No," I said pompously, for one glance had assured me that Diana would regard printing as only slightly less degrading than junk dealing, "it's writing I want to do, writing for the paper. You see, I think I'm going to be a writer someday and words and phrases are the tools of my trade."

This impressed him more than it should have done. How was he to know that the statement had been lifted from a book on writing for the radio, borrowed from the local library?

"Come with me," he said briefly, and led the way between type cases into a poky little office behind the flatbed.

It was lit by a single, begrimed skylight and its sole items of furniture consisted of a roll-top desk, a cane-bottomed chair and a vast array of paper, all kinds of paper, from galley proofs and posters to dog-eared ledgers and offcuts. The hardboard walls were plastered with old posters and trade calendars and there was one impressively bold notice that said: FOLLOW YOUR COPY, EVEN IF IT GOES OUT THE WINDOW. The desk likewise was a litter of proofs—"pulls" I later learned to call them—and in here the smell of ink and oil was subordinate to that of my uncle's vile tobacco. He swept papers from the chair and sat down, groping for his pipe.

"A reporter," he began, "has to be observant. Are you observant? Take a quick look around this office and then close your eyes. Ready? Now then, what's in this pigsty?"

I reeled off a list of nearly two dozen items that had remained in my memory and he was obviously struck by my powers of observation.

"That's very promising," he conceded, "but supposing I sent you to report a funeral, what would you find out?"

"Who was there and who read the burial service."

"Good! And a wedding?"

This was more ponderable so I took my time.

"What the bride had on and what all the people had given them for presents," I suggested.

His eyes smiled. "That's not a bad guess," he admitted, "except that we don't print the presents unless they pay threepence a line for them! Well, you seem to have the right instincts but can you write shorthand?"

I told him that I was willing to learn, adding that I had taught myself to type on Uncle Luke's ramshackle Oliver. When he rose I saw that I had pleased him.

"I don't know why this never occurred to me when your mother died," he said, absently. "It was very remiss of me, for you shouldn't have wasted time in that wretched furniture shed. That's no kind of job at all for a bright boy like you! I shall have to see Mr. Priddis, of course, but I think I can talk him into it."

This was disappointing. I had forgotten for a moment that Uncle Reuben did not own the paper and printing office.

"But everybody says you run the paper, Uncle Reuben," I protested.

"Everybody says wrong," he replied gravely. "I only do as much as I do because Mr. Priddis hasn't been very well lately. Now run along and don't say anything to anyone until you hear from me."

I gave him my promise and went out the back way into the yard. Twenty-four hours later I was junior reporter on the *Whinmouth & District Observer*. Not content with riding two horses, I had cheerfully committed myself to riding three.

In 1927 the *Observer* had a circulation of about three thousand. This doesn't sound much but it was impressive for all that, as the local population did not exceed twelve thousand and we reckoned to sell an *Observer* to four out of every five houses in Whinmouth Bay.

It was owned and nominally edited by Nick Priddis, a man in his mid-sixties and a chronic sufferer from asthma. People were not much mistaken in supposing Uncle Reuben to be the real editor, for

Priddis' ill-health had prevented him from active participation for some years and he spent most of his time in his cottage up the coast.

Uncle Reuben did most of the original writing and I stress the word "original" because at that time less than a third of our copy was written by any member of the staff. About half of it was shamelessly snipped from the columns of the *County Press,* a much larger and more important journal, published biweekly in Whinford, the county town. Much of the remainder was sent in by local contributors who viewed the act of publication as adequate reward for their efforts.

The economics of the paper baffled the uninitiated. Advertisement space was sold at two shillings an inch, and even less if the advertiser was a regular. The *Observer* sold at one penny but local news agents were charged eightpence a dozen, ninepence if we had to deliver. The ready money that did flow into the office came in via small ads, at threepence a line. Lists of wreaths in funeral reports and lists of wedding gifts in wedding reports were the main sources, and petty cash was also supplied by the lucrative set pieces—births, deaths and marriage announcements and the "return thanks" panel that invariably followed a funeral. For the rest, the paper existed on quarterly payments for larger advertisements and on the steadier proceeds of its printing office.

The *Observer* had a curiously old-fashioned format. Its front page was devoted exclusively to standard advertisements, built around a huge, blurred block depicting the Whinmouth esplanade as it had looked in the eighteen-seventies. This picture set the tone of the publication. One only had to glance at the bathing machines, the little girls in pantaloons and the lowering clouds in the background, to know that the inside pages would be solid wedges of close print, diffiult to concentrate upon and impossible to skim. It gave the paper a dull, self-righteous aspect. It said, in effect: *You may look in vain for sensation in here. Whatever is written down happened just so, whether you like it or not!*

Uncle Reuben was perfectly capable of going out and about town to collect information for the inside columns, but the printing office was the only one for miles around and his presence was needed there as supervisor. He therefore welcomed the idea of having a boy to send here and there for raw material that he could shape into news at his desk under the dirty skylight.

Usually he only had to snip the reports from *The Whinford Times,* rewrite the introductions, change the headings and send the copy down to the keyboard operator to be used in our paper. This meant that most of the paper had to be printed in a single day and a night, and it was becoming clear to Uncle Reuben and his employer that the business would not stand the overtime rates entailed by this makeshift process. The mainstay of the firm was the printing office and my uncle was needed in there to set type and operate the keyboard for the Monotype.

I had a brief interview with Mr. Priddis, the owner, on the day I started work and, although I was to see little of him during the years I worked on the paper, he impressed me as a man with original views on journalism. I never afterwards forgot his handling of my initiation.

He looked like a Victorian actor, tall, spare, and all knees, knuckles and black eyebrows. He had a strong, resonant voice and punctuated his lecture with deft applications of a nasal spray, the use of which might have brought him physical relief but seemed to irritate him to a point of frenzy.

"So you're Reub's boy? What's your name? Well, I don't imagine we shall see much of one another—curse this bloody contrivance—I've got a cottage up at Hartland and have to spend most of my time there. The air's less oppressive, or so they tell me. Reub says you've got a nose for news. What do you say, hey? Drat this pestilential invention, don't know why I use the damn thing—listen, sonny, since you've volunteered for the treadmill your uncle will expect you to put your back into it. *People!* That's your job from now on, people around here—nowhere else, just around here—what they do, what they think, what they eat, what they wear, how they get on with their wives, how they don't—devil take this blasted thing—nothing outside matters, see? Governments fall, war breaks out in South America, records are smashed—earthquakes, plagues, revolutions—none of it matters as much as who runs the woolly stall at the Missionary Sale of Work. There's a coronation in Westminster Abbey—not your business! You've got your eye on the choice of a Carnival Queen right here, d'you follow? Curse this bloody squirt—that's all, boy, that's all!"

It was, too, for Uncle Reuben had entered in with some proofs and jerked his head toward the door, indicating that the explosive interview was over. I made a bewildered exit and a few minutes later I was on my way to get an account of the Whinmouth Club's away match, from the strongly partisan source of the man who won it by kicking a last-minute goal.

Mine was no slow, painful apprenticeship wherein I was led, step by step, from the petty sessional court to a coroner's inquest, from the interschool athletics contest in Harbor Meadow, to the autumn production of the Whinmouth Thespians. I was picked up and flung headlong into the torrent of local politics and social activities, hearing something fresh almost every hour and marveling at the complexity of what I witnessed and learned.

To the impersonal spectator, Whinmouth Bay was a deceptively tranquil community—"dead-and-alive," visitors called it—but to an inquiring boy, engaged in recording its day-by-day history, it seethed like a hot spring. I was so frantically busy during those first weeks, and so tired after my scurryings about the district and my two-hour stint at shorthand after supper, that I barely had time to think of Diana or Sennacharib. At first I was nervous of making mistakes and sometimes I was homesick for the humdrum peace of Uncle Luke's Mart, but on the whole I enjoyed my new importance and a front-row seat at every event that took place in the triangle between the estuary of the Whin and the eastern edge of Teasel Common, the boundaries that marked the extremities of our territory.

I was the impersonal witness at family tragedy and family celebration. I attended concerts, council meetings, lectures, sports meetings, dances and every kind of social function. I got to know every face in town and I saw the inside of every kind of dwelling, from the three-roomed cottages on the quay to the detached houses that stood in their own two-acre plots in the area west of the Shepherdshey road. I was absorbed in the business of becoming if not a writer, then at least a professionally observant chronicler of British provincial life and, as I say, I had almost forgotten how and why this transformation in my life had taken place until the morning that I received Diana's letter.

I went up to my room with wildly beating heart, turning the blue envelope over in my hands and noting the elegant flourishes on the J in John and the L in Leigh, for Diana's handwriting was new to me and as exotic as everything else about her.

It was a chatty, affectionate, schoolgirlish letter and succeeded in putting the *Whinmouth & District Observer* right out of my mind for the next forty-eight hours.

My Jan [*it began*]—

As you don't seem disposed to write to me, as you promised, I'm breaking all the rules (social as well as Passy-Glassy's) by writing to you first.

School is as dreary as ever and I'm counting the days until we break up for Easter. Before that, however, we've got Lent exams and I'm sure to flop at practically everything, for I've slacked all term and it's partly your fault, because I've been waiting and waiting to hear from you about our lovely Sennacharib and whether you've been to the Folly again and if you think of me as much as I do of you! (This is awful, I'm absolutely throwing myself at you!)

Seriously though, I have been awfully disappointed by your silence, and have made an absolute nuisance of myself with Marion. (She's the day girl whose address I gave you to write to.) I must have asked her about fifty times whether there was a letter for me and now the hateful thing says no before I can ask! I had another and special reason for writing. Is it possible for you to come to London on Saturday? This may sound absolutely mad to you but there is a good chance of us being able to meet, in fact you could take me out somewhere if you wanted to and it would be a terrific adventure and a marvelous score over the school rules! I'm not going into details in this letter, *a* because you mightn't be able to make it, and *b* for the more likely reason that you've cooled off and are going about with someone in Whinmouth Bay, in which case tear this up and forget all about it and me. If you *can* come to town, however, write and say so at once and I'll write again by return and give you all the instructions for what our Lorna would have called "a tryst."

All my love dear Jan,
DIANA

There was a single cross, artfully contrived out of the final flourish of her signature, and when I saw it, after rereading the letter for the third time, my hands shook with excitement.

I would have liked to have written a long letter in reply, telling her all about my new job and making it sound much more glamorous and exciting than it really was, but I had a busy day ahead of me and conditions were not conducive to composing my first love letter. Ordinarily I should have waited until I did have a chance to write, but the prospect of actually seeing her was more urgent than the desire to pour out my feelings on paper, and if she was to have time to write back and explain how and where I could meet her it was essential that I reply by return.

I worked out a plan to get to and from London. There was a semifinal Cup excursion from Whinford and I knew that I could borrow Uncle Luke's bicycle and ride it to Whinford Junction on Friday, in time to catch the train at 10 P.M. I could leave the bike in the station yard against my early morning return on Sunday, and the prospect of such an exhausting journey involving the loss of two nights' sleep made the occasion additionally romantic. I wrote a hasty letter explaining my plan and said that I would follow any instructions she sent. Wednesday and Thursday passed in an gony of anticipation. Then, on Friday, her second letter arrived. It said briefly that I was to meet her outside Swan & Edgar's, in Piccadilly Circus, at three o'clock on Saturday afternoon and that I need not reply as she would be passing the rendezvous at that time in any case. The letter contained no endearments. It was blunt, very much to the point and, as I was to discover with the years, entirely characteristic of Diana when she had business to conduct.

I told Uncle Reuben that I wanted to take advantage of the cheap excursion and would like his permission to skip the tedious folding routine of publication day.

He was a good deal surprised at my request, so much so that I did not dare to pretend to a sudden interest in professional football but told him a lie that troubled my conscience. I said that my object in wanting to visit London was to put flowers on the grave of my parents.

He was very touched by this and instantly granted me leave, doubling the burden of my conscience by giving me ten shillings to buy flowers from himself, Uncle Luke and Aunt Thirza. I had no option but to take his money and it burned in my hand. I told myself that I would have to go to the cemetery now whether I had the time or not.

At the last minute I adjusted my plan and went to the junction at Whinford by train, taking Uncle Luke's bike in the luggage van and catching the main-line train in good time. I was far too excited to sleep and sat hunched under the feeble compartment light reading *Lorna Doone*. The romance had become a kind of litany for the worship of Diana.

It was drizzling when I arrived at Waterloo and still wanted an hour or so to daybreak.

I left the station and walked along York Road and over Westminster Bridge toward the Houses of Parliament. It was a dank and dismal morning, and the Thames looked still and sinister in the glow of the Embankment lights. An early tram whined past as Big Ben struck five, telling me that I still had ten hours to fill before meeting Diana. The dreariness of the scene deflated me and I thought how strange it was that, although I was a Cockney born and bred, I should feel so lonely and desolate in the heart of my home town, so much so that I was already beginning to feel homesick for the rusty bracken of Teasel Slope and the dark smudge of Folly Wood against the skyline of Foxhayes Common. The tug of homesickness set me thinking deeply. Why was it, I wondered, that such a remote and rustic corner of England exercised such undisputed sovereignty over my heart, and that after a few short months of the least impressionable period of childhood? Was it the drag of an ancestral memory, or had it nothing to do with long-dead Leighs but everything with a fourteen-year-old schoolgirl, whom I had met but half a dozen times?

When the first gray streaks of dawn began to show over the river I stirred myself and decided that what I needed to cheer myself up was a wash, a brush-up and a hot meal.

I found all three in the Covent Garden area and after some bacon and eggs, and three cups of drayman's tea, I shed my pensive mood and was not even depressed by the prospect of traveling all the way to Brixton to visit the double grave. Somehow it seemed to me that this dismal obligation would be an act of finality, a final breaking of ties that held me to my drab London boyhood. I told myself that my mother, who could conjure up the smell of Devon gorse and heath after a separation of forty years, would surely have approved my new allegiance to Sennacharib and understood my almost physical repugnance for the huddle of slate, asphalt and yellow brick of which some Cockneys are so proud.

I spent Uncle Reuben's ten shillings and seven-and-six of my own on a large armful of daffodils and narcissi and caught a southbound bus to the cemetery. By midday I was back in the Strand and after a modest lunch in a snack bar I walked up Whitehall to spend an hour in my favorite museum, gazing once more on the bloodstained shirt Charles I had worn at his execution and the pathetic skeleton of Napoleon's horse, Marengo. I wondered whether Diana would share my enthusiasm for museums, or whether she would demand more sophisticated entertainment. When the clock said two-twenty-five I decided that it was time to find out.

I walked up to Piccadilly Circus, arriving far too early. The usual group of anxious-eyed pedestrians were drifting up and down the block, each endeavoring to give an impression that the appointment they had anticipated was of small importance, yet each betraying the same kind of nervous apprehension that I experienced. If ever we met in London again, I decided, it would have to be at a more original rendezvous.

I had no idea from which direction she would come, or what means of transport she would use, so that when, on the stroke of three, a taxi pulled up beside me I did not glance at it until the door slammed and a voice on the brink of laughter said, "Don't scowl so, Jan! People will think we're married and I'm an hour or so late!"

She looked more grown up than ever. I had been half-expecting a girl in a school uniform and one of those dreadful floppy hats, but here she was in the smart little suit that she had worn at the Mart —"mufti" she called it, and added that it was only permissible when you were taken out by one's parents. She had an outdoor coat over her arm and a little yellow straw hat, close-fitting and trimmed with tiny wings, like the hat worn by Gretchens in traditional Dutch pictures. I felt painfully shy in my ready-made suit of gray serge and a soft collar held in place by a narrow tiepin, but from the first moment she seemed to sense my awkwardness and set to work to overcome it, taking my arm and in full charge of the expedition.

"First, somewhere to sit and gossip," she said. "How about Lyons, in Coventry Street? I've got until eight o'clock and it'll take us forty minutes to get back to school. There's a train at seven-thirty-five and you can travel with me as far as the suburban station."

I was impressed by her efficiency and air of dispatch. It was as though she had been planning every moment of our meeting, anticipating each contingency before it revealed itself.

Fresh from Devon, I was bewildered by the swirl of traffic, but she guided me across to Eros and then over the wide stretch of Coventry Street as though I were one of her big, obedient dogs.

Even in that press of buses and taxis, however, I was conscious of the firm pressure on my forearm and the rhythmic bob of her brown curls that now seemed suspended from the rim of her little yellow hat. Delight in her company swelled inside me and with it came a kind of delicious dependence on her judgment and gently exercised authority.

When we reached the Corner House I made a big effort to assume my responsibilities as a squire. I piloted her to a corner table, far enough away from the orchestra to enable us to converse without raising our voices. It was the post-lunch lull and they were not busy. The waitress brought us tea and cakes almost at once and the orchestra tuned up and began to play excerpts from *The Merry Widow*.

"Jan, you're looking wonderful!" she said, with enthusiasm. "I'm so thrilled you could make it, because I went to so much trouble and it would have been absolutely awful if you hadn't been there after all. Just think, I might have run the risk of being expelled, all for nothing!"

"Expelled? Good Lord!" I exclaimed. "You don't mean . . ."

"Why, naturally!" She laughed and squeezed my hand. "If I was caught here with a boy Passy-Glassy would have a seizure! When she finally came around she'd phone Mummy and I'd be out on my ear in twenty-four hours. This is positively the worst thing you can do short of bringing a man into your cubicle and I don't think that's ever been done, at least not in my time, though May Didcott is supposed to have done it the week before she stowed away for Switzerland."

I would have liked to have heard more of May Didcott, but first I wanted to learn how Diana had arranged our meeting in the first place.

"Oh, it was all very simple really," she said, gaily. "You see, we get one day each term out with our parents and everyone usually takes half-term, which was nearly a month ago. Mummy and Daddy were away in Nice at half-term, so I had a day due to me and they came for me after breakfast this morning. I've just left them at home."

"But you couldn't have," I protested, remembering my five-hour train journey from the West.

"Silly! I mean home up here, in Palmerston Crescent. It's only me who thinks of Heronslea as real home. I don't think they'd go there much if it wasn't for me, or if it wasn't the thing to do—you know—to have a place in the country and play at being a squire weekends."

"But if you're supposed to be with them, and they think you're supposed to be back at school, how on earth can you stay out until eight?" I asked.

"Oh, that's where the brains come in," she replied, lifting the teapot that the waitress had set before her and beginning to pour. "I know that you take sugar, but I forget whether you have milk in first."

"It doesn't matter," I said, impatiently, "tell me what you did."

"Well, I simply told Mummy that I had to be back by three for an important hockey match but I didn't tell her until it was too late to get hold of the chauffeur, so then I had to go by taxi and the taxi brought me here instead of taking me back to school. I was lucky in one respect though. Mummy would have told the driver where to take me and he might have followed his instructions in spite of the big tip that I had ready, but just as he arrived the phone rang and Mummy answered it, so *I* gave him his instructions instead and just kissed Mummy good-by at the door! Now then, that's enough about me, tell me everything about your new job. I'm terribly proud of you, Jan, perhaps because I had a sort of feeling you were just bragging up at the Folly and that when I came home at Easter you'd still be mucking about that awful furniture store. Do you go to fires and wrecks and attend murder trials?"

"I would if there were any," I said, guardedly, "but so far there haven't been. I did go out after the fire engine once but it was only a chimney fire in a semidetached on the Shepherdshey road. I like it, though, and it's going to be exciting when things start happening in the summer. Uncle Reuben says that the spring is always the quietest time because it's only the visitors who get themselves into trouble and give us the more sensational stories—you know, boating tragedies and beach rescues."

She made me describe everything I did and even asked me to write something in shorthand on the paper napkin. I wrote: *You look very beautiful today!* and she teased me into translating. Then, when I could think of nothing more to tell her, she said:

"You don't know how lucky you are, Jan, to be more or less grown up and earning your own living. Look at me, marking time and likely to be, for years yet!"

It was characteristic of Diana, then and later, to subscribe to the popular fiction that money and a cushioned background were obstacles that stood in the way of full enjoyment of life. She would always pretend that the circumstances surrounding her stifled self-expression and encouraged a general flabbiness of outlook. I don't think that she really believed this, even then, but she found it useful as a banner of rebellion against externally applied discipline. It was also a challenge to her mother, the kind of challenge that she was making now, by sitting in Lyons Corner House instead of returning to school.

I remember that all the charm she exercised over me did not prevent me from debating this claim and that we had an amicable argument about it on the spot. I must have sounded very pompous when I pointed out the obvious advantages of a good education and of the opportunity to travel while still at school, and of all the glittering by-products of wealth, such as ponies and a legal claim to every square yard of Sennacharib.

"Well, all I can say is I'm jolly glad *you* haven't got it anyway, Jan," she said, when I had run out of the advantages of being Emerald Diana Gayelorde-Sutton, of Heronslea, Devon, and Palmerston Crescent, W.9., "because what I admire about you is the fact that you stand on your own feet! That's what makes you different from all the other stuffed dummies Mummy introduces into the house. They're all at public schools, of course, and they take the kind of background that I have for granted, but there isn't one of them who could learn to be a reporter as you have, and on top of that I don't think any of them would take this much trouble just to see me, so there!"

I could have sat there all the afternoon and evening hearing her talk like that, but the restaurant was filling up now and if we wanted to make the best use of our few hours together it was time to move.

"Have you anywhere special you'd like to go?" I asked. "I suppose you've been to the Tower and Madame Tussaud's, and all that. If it had been better weather we could have gone on the Serpentine for a row. I used to go there with my mother sometimes."

"I thought we might go to the pictures," she suggested. "There's a double feature at Marble Arch, a film about Nurse Cavell and a new comedy called *Just Imagine*. How would you like that?"

I said I should like it very much and called the waitress, who had been hovering around our table rather impatiently. It was nearly half past four and all we had ordered was tea, cakes and a second jug of hot water.

I paid the bill and we caught a bus to Marble Arch. A Pathé Gazette feature was showing when we went in and we had time to settle ourselves before the comedy started. I didn't often get the opportunity to go to the cinema because we didn't have one in Whinmouth Bay, so I was determined to enjoy myself, apart from the nearness of Diana. She asked me to help her off with her coat and when it was folded across the empty seat in front she let her shoulder touch mine and presently she took hold of my hand in the most natural way possible. I wouldn't have changed places with a prince of the Indies.

The comedy was an original one to a cinema-goer fed on Harold Lloyd and Buster Keaton. The hero was transplanted into the world of the future, where laughs depended upon his reactions to the new habits of society. I remember how I laughed when, having visions of a large, satisfying meal, he was given a small vitamin pill and exclaimed, "Give me the good old days!" I remember, too, how Diana laughed, and how secretly shocked I was, when a couple put money in a slot and a baby slid down a chute, giving the hero an opportunity to make the same remark, this time in tones of the strongest disapproval.

The Nurse Cavell film impressed us both tremendously and stoked up a tremendous hate for the suave German generals.

Looking back it seems strange that a cinema audience could wax so indignant over the execution of a single British nurse, but in those days Belsen and Lidice were nearly twenty years away and not even Germans used phrases like "total war" or "liquidation."

When we emerged into the foyer we were still in a patriotic fever and I was touched to notice that Diana had been weeping in the darkness and did not appear to be in any way ashamed of the fact.

"I think she was wonderful, just wonderful!" she said, dabbing her eyes. "Daddy showed me the place in Brussels where they shot her but it didn't seem very important then. Gosh! *I'd* like to do something like that, you know, stand up to all those bullies because you believe in something!"

"I'd jolly well come and rescue you long before you got shot!" I told her, identifying myself with Jan Ridd once again, and she squeezed my arm and said that she knew very well I would but that it was high time we caught the bus for Victoria, for we dared not risk missing the train.

It was at that moment that Yves de Royden stepped up and whipped off his cap with a courtly flourish. I looked at him with interest because I thought he was very oddly dressed. He looked very well-to-do but somehow frumpish as well, in his pepper-and-mustard tweed suit and a kind of cravat, instead of a conventional collar and tie. His trousers were unfashionably tight at the ankle, for it was the era of wide Oxford trousers, and I noticed that he carried an ebony-handled cane which he tucked smartly under his arm as he bowed.

"Why, Yves," exclaimed Diana, delightedly, "what a place to run into you! Whatever are you doing over here? Buying more horses?"

The young Frenchman looked at me as I stood slightly behind Diana. I was feeling, and doubtless looking, miserably embarrassed but Diana at once introduced us. "This is a journalist friend of mine, Yves, a Mr. Leigh, from Devon. Jan, this is Yves de Royden. You must have heard of his father, Hervé de Royden. He won the Ascot Gold Cup with Dantonist a year or so ago, and he's quite famous, isn't he, Yves?"

The French boy smiled and extended his hand, his fingers barely touching mine. He was about seventeen, tall and thin, with narrow hips and shoulders, like those of a girl. After the apology for a handshake he turned his attention to Diana and asked three rapid questions in perfect but slightly pedantic English.

"You have been to the films? You like the picture? You are on holiday from school?"

The faint impression of effeminacy was charmed away by his excessively good manners and adult bearing, but notwithstanding this I hated him, then and there, for he seemed to me to be typical of the kind of rival I should have to face in the future. I recognized that he was so much more a part of her world than I could ever be and my nervousness made me rather rude. I said, gruffly:

"We've got to catch that train, Diana!"

He turned his charm on me, repaying good for evil and making me feel more inferior than ever.

"You have a train to catch? But I will take you there! I have a car outside. It would be a great pleasure."

"Oh, you're an absolute darling, Yves!" exclaimed Diana. "Just wait till you see his car, Jan, he wrote me about it. Why, this is wonderful luck, we might have missed that train getting a taxi. Come on, Jan, and you'd better step on it, Yves, it's Victoria!"

She hustled us out of the foyer and he led the way to a side street off Cumberland Place, where a low-slung and exotic-looking cream sports car was parked. It was a Lagonda, the kind of car I had only seen in magazine advertisements. There were no rear seats, so Diana squeezed in between us and we zoomed off down Park Lane, passing every vehicle that showed ahead.

He drove superlatively well, maintaining a consistently high speed but taking no chances. Speech was impossible owing to the rush of air and roar of the engine, but I heard Diana shout "Lovely! Lovely!" as we skimmed past the sentry boxes outside Buckingham Palace. In a very few minutes we were at Victoria and Diana was telling me to buy two tickets for a place called Sanderstead, one single ticket and one return.

When I rejoined them in the yard they were still talking beside the car, but as I approached, Yves drew himself up to attention and extended his hand to its fullest extent, the way all Frenchmen shake hands. Then he gave a little bob toward Diana and to my intense astonishment took her gloved hand and raised it lightly to his lips.

"Until Ascot then," he said, and Diana replied:

"If I can manage it. It's in termtime, you know, but I'll talk Daddy around. Good-by, Yves, dear, and thanks so much for the lift. I adore the car, it's an absolute scorcher!"

He nodded once more to me, wriggled into the car and roared off into the traffic. To my great relief Diana seemed to dismiss him at once. "Come on," she said, seizing my hand, "we'll get a carriage to ourselves if we look spoony enough!"

We went to the far end of the waiting train and although one middle-aged man did ignore Diana's look of savage disapproval as he stepped over our feet, he got out at the third station from the terminus and we made the remainder of the journey alone.

The advent of Yves de Royden and his splendid car had blunted the fine edge of my pleasure and she was quick to notice the fact.

"Why, Jan," she said, smiling and propelling herself toward me, "I do believe you're jealous! You needn't be, silly. I wouldn't *dream* of falling for a foreigner. Yves is a nice foreigner, of course, and fabulously rich but I never think of him as a real man, not like you. Why, if he had to take part in a fight he'd probably kick and scratch! They all do, you know, like Brigadier Gerard in the box fight."

She knew exactly how to banish my gloomy thoughts and by the time we had passed another station I had almost forgotten Yves and his outlandish courtliness.

"I've had a wonderful day, Diana," I told her. "It's one of the best days I remember, like that one back in October, when we met for the first time."

"It's funny, Jan," she mused, tilting her head, throwing out her legs and turning in her toes, "but I can't imagine we've only known each other about six months. It seems as if you've always been part of

Heronslea and the Devon half of me, if you see what I mean. Sometimes I feel I'm two quite separate people, the London Emerald and the Devon Diana. I like Diana best, of course, and when I'm with you I grow right away from the other person, so that she seems a stranger. At first I thought it depended on where I was in the flesh but now it doesn't somehow, it's got to do with you, the way you look and talk and even walk. Just now, for instance, in the car I mean, the fact of you being there kept Emerald at a safe distance. Does this sound crazy to you? I'm sure it must because you're so . . . so very much *one* person all the time!"

Before I could think of an answer her practical streak reasserted itself, summoned by the hoarse shout of the station porter calling the name of a station.

"It's the next stop," she warned, "but don't get out until the moment the train is moving and then go right across the bridge and wait for the next up train. It's just possible that there might be someone from school on the platform. Now there's one thing we've got to settle. How much have you spent, I mean altogether, including your fare?"

"Good Lord," I protested, "that's nothing to do with you!"

"Oh yes it is," she said briskly. "I asked you up here and you can't afford to splosh money around. There was the fare and the café and the pictures and then these railway tickets. Would two-pounds-ten cover it, or is it more?"

In view of the fact that the return ticket to Devon had only been ten-and-sixpence, two-pounds-ten was getting on for double the amount I had spent but I was horrified at the thought of her financing the excursion, or paying one penny toward the costs of our entertainment.

"I wouldn't dream of taking your money," I said, flushing. "It's . . . it's been wonderful meeting you like this and the man always pays, you know that, Diana."

She looked at me gravely for a moment. "All right, Jan," she said. "I knew you'd make a fuss, so I'll have to make it up to you some other way. We shall be in in less than a minute, so you'd better kiss me, that is if you want to."

In the early stages of our long courtship it was always Diana who took the initiative, not only about when we should meet and how we should occupy our time but when we should embrace or even hold hands. She was so much more adult than I was, and we both knew it, but that occasion was the first that I was more than a passive partner in the act of kissing.

I put my arms around her and kissed her in what I hoped was a fair imitation of the couples on the films and her response was frightening. As our lips touched she tightened her grip on my neck and shoulders, pressing her cheek to mine and murmuring, "Jan, Jan, you belong to me! You're my Jan, aren't you? You *are*, aren't you?" Then I forgot to be frightened and began to drown in a sea of sweetness, so engulfing that I did not even hear the porter shout "Sanderstead" or sense that the train was drawing to a halt.

She pushed me away, jumped up, and pulled her coat from the rack. I noticed then that her eyes were wet and that they had the same look of intensity that I had seen in them when she had gathered up her reins and ridden straight at the fallen tree on Boxing Day.

"Good-by, Jan," she whispered. "I'll write! I promise—good-by, darling Jan, *my* Jan!"

Then she was gone and I heard her footsteps pattering along the platform. The train jerked and I remembered just in time that I too had to alight.

I flung myself out of the carriage and came down on one knee, jarring it painfully, but I was up again at once and waited in the shadows between the station lights until the train was out of sight. Then I crossed the bridge to the up platform, feeling nothing of the smart of my knee but walking in a blissful state of suspension between the greasy planks of the steps and the sky. In this ecstatic trance I somehow found my way back to Waterloo.

I slept most of the way home and when the train ran into Whinford, about half-past four, the night had cleared and the sky was bright with stars.

My road home to Whinmouth Bay ran alongside the river and it was here, in the silence broken only by the steady crank of Uncle Luke's ancient machine, that I emerged from the trance and was able to set about marshaling my thoughts and enjoying the sense of achievement they brought to me.

A little over thirty hours ago, I reflected, I had traveled over this same route toward an uncertain destiny, for despite my new-found confidence in myself, and in Diana's encouraging behavior in the Folly on Old Year's Day, there had remained deep down in me a

[86

nag of doubt that she would ever grow to regard me seriously. I had difficulty in ridding myself of the thought that my devotion was simply a scalp to hang on the belt of a spoiled child. Now I no longer had any doubts. Not only was I cheered in retrospect by the encounter with the French boy and by the lightness with which she had dismissed him, but as positive proof of her love I had the image of her tear-stained face when we parted and her whispered claim on me as we had kissed one another and she scurried out of the compartment.

I repeated her words over and over again to myself and each repetition brought more comfort and reassurance. I no longer pondered the outcome of her presentation parties, or feared her mother's opposition to our preposterous courtship. Whatever the future held in store for us, wherever she was sent, however long we were separated, I knew now that Diana and I belonged to each other for all time and that nothing else was of the smallest importance.

By the time I rode into Whinmouth Bay the sky was paling over Nun's Head and the shadows on Whinmouth Flats, on the western side of the estuary, were deeper in contrast. I no longer felt tired and jaded, for the fifteen-mile ride had seemed like five. Instead of going home to bed I propped the cycle outside the Mart and walked along the old jetty at the Point.

This was my favorite part of Whinmouth and I had a secret perch here, under the barnacled timbers near the lock gates. It was still barely light and being Sunday morning there was no one astir. I climbed down the piles and sat looking out over the wide estuary, waiting for sunrise to succeed the false dawn.

It was quiet and pleasant down here. Out on the bar gulls were wheeling over the shallows, wailing greedy protests at one another. The soft tide lapped the timbers of the jetty and across the river one or two early lights were showing under the hills. I always used to think of this scene as the Mississippi and it did indeed correspond in many ways to Mark Twain's vivid descriptions of the big river, for if you took a slantwise view it was heavily timbered on each side and it never occurred to you that open sea lay on the immediate left.

I sat here a long time, my legs swinging from the crosspile, thinking and thinking about love. I thought about it in relation to all the people I knew, Uncle Luke and his querulous Thirza in their poky little bedroom over the Mart, Uncle Reuben in the loneliness of a bed-sitting room behind the High Street, the landlady of The Rifleman and her two husbands over at Shepherdshey and, from thence, to the graceful, porticoed Heronslea, home of Diana and her ill-assorted parents.

I wondered about the relationship of Mr. and Mrs. Gayelorde-Sutton, he with the big, wobbling head and square, clumsy body, she so elegant, groomed and stilted, and it puzzled me that these two people could have created a vital and adorable creature like Diana. People always said that if you want to see what you are getting when you lead a bride to the altar you should look closely at her mother, but how could this apply in my case? What link could exist between the eager, sparkling girl I had left on a suburban platform and the silly, prancing woman who mangled her vowels and performed such monstrous antics in order to impress dour old countrymen like Big Nat, the Shepherdshey sexton? Why had a financial wizard like Mr. Gayelorde-Sutton chosen such a creature for a mate? How could he suffer her to act such a charade, day in and day out, when his friends and business acquaintances must surely snigger behind their hands every time she opened her mouth? Was she like that when they were alone together?

Did she continue to twist every "i" into a strangled "aiee" when they went to bed together? Would she be more inclined to regard me as a social equal if I did the same thing, or if I learned to ape the courtliness of a boy like Yves de Royden and kiss her hand when I was introduced to her? Or was all this flummery due to money and nothing else? Did the mere possession of property and a big bank balance regulate her attitude toward everyone she met?

I was unable to answer any one of these questions but they were idle and irrelevant in my present uplifted mood. What anyone else thought about pledges exchanged between Diana and myself was unimportant. What mattered, *all* that mattered from now on, was that we belonged to each other, as surely as Héloïse belonged to Abélard, Romeo to Juliet, Jan to Lorna.

When the shadows had lifted from the western bank I got up, stiffly. My bruised knee was paining me but I paid no attention to it. I scrambled up the timbers of the jetty and regained a quay now crowded with screaming herring gulls and lesser black-backed gulls, quarreling among the lobster pots over gobbets of gutted fish.

I let myself into the apartment above the Mart and crept along to my room. No one was about so I did not wait to make tea but turned in and slept the clock around.

Chapter Four

DIANA'S Easter holidays commenced on April 1st but she did not come down to Devon for the first week. She wrote to me from London a day or so after breakup to say that she would meet me at the Folly "very early in the morning" on the day after her return. I set the alarm for five A.M. and it was still dark when I cycled up the chalk road to Foxhayes Common and entered the Heronslea estate from the rear. I left the bicycle on the track leading to Heronslea Woods and climbed the spiral staircase of the Folly just as the sun was breasting Teasel Wood and every bird in Sennacharib was awake to greet it.

I had never seen Sennacharib in springtime and its beauty, viewed from the open casement of the Folly, made my heart ache. Every bracken frond of the common was laced with dew and beyond it, across the green downslope of the larch wood, I could just make out the white smudge of Heronslea House. Where the sun touched the southern slopes the primroses were growing in great, trailing clusters along the edge of the plantation, so thickly as to form a yellow hedge.

Our two buzzards were astir, drifting lazily over their favorite hunting ground of the paddock. Every now and again one of them would pretend to swoop, dropping a hundred feet or so, but never pushing home an attack. I remembered then that Uncle Luke had said buzzards were cowardly birds, always waiting for easy prey and never attacking anything that might fight back, but this morning it seemed to me that they were enjoying the wind currents and their mastery of flight rather than searching out a meal.

I was still watching them when I saw something twinkle on the fringe of the larches and after a moment or two Diana rode into the paddock. She was mounted on her big piebald, Sioux, and was leading a saddled pony.

I could see her more than a mile off, moving toward the Folly at a slow trot, and the sun made the stirrup irons flash like naked swords. I watched her with quiet pride, sitting her splendid Sioux as nonchalantly as her celestial namesake, and when I waved from the window she urged the horses into a slow canter that sent the pheasants karking from the bracken and a pair of pigeons whirring out of the oaks beside the Folly.

When I was sure that she had seen me I ran down the staircase and out into the clearing. The sparkle of the morning glowed in her cheeks as she threw a leg over the pommel and slid to the ground with one of her breathless, good-to-be-alive laughs.

"Isn't this wonderful, Jan? I thought it was the kind of morning you should learn to ride! Slip Nellie's irons down and let's see how you look. How did you get here so early? I made sure I'd be first. Come on, get up, for Sioux is raring to go!"

I obeyed without much enthusiasm, remembering the last occasion that she had bullied me into climbing up on Nellie, the dun pony she was leading.

I did not fear a fall so much as I dreaded to look ridiculous in her eyes, but Nellie seemed quiet enough on the leading rein and when I was awkwardly astride, Diana proceeded to give me my first lesson in horsemanship. I would have preferred a quiet walk along the primrose banks and the chance of starting a hare or fox from the dew-beaded gorse, but Diana was adamant. Once embarked upon the subject of horses she pursued it to the exclusion of all else.

"Hands down—elbows in—*no*, don't turn your toes out! Press in and up, with the strain on the balls of your feet. That's the way you learn to grip with your knees and you won't even stay on old Nellie until you learn to do that. Don't sit *forward*, Jan, not unless you want her to gallop! Loop your reins—look—like this, you're holding them bunched, just like Daddy."

"I feel like Daddy!" I told her, but she stuck to the lesson with the single-mindedness of a professional.

"Relax, Jan—don't *hunch*—you aren't going to fall off so long as you listen to me. Relax, and let all your muscles except your thighs go slack. *That's* better! Now, I can't have you on the leading rein at your age, so tie it up and let's go!"

We jogged out of the wood and across the common to the moor. She rode alongside and kept looking doubtfully at my feet, occasionally tapping them with her crop. After a mile or so I began to feel more confident and presently she shouted something to Nellie, who rolled into a slow, easy canter, pushing ahead of the collected Sioux and widening the gap between us.

I was astonished then to discover how easy it is to sit a cantering pony. I did not know that Nellie was all of twenty years old and that countless children had learned to ride on her broad back. Then Diana flashed past me and blocked the narrow path, forcing Nellie to drop back into an uneven trot, and I had all my work cut out to maintain balance, especially after one foot had slipped from the stirrup and I pitched forward, clutching frantically at Nellie's mane and rolling first to one side and then the other.

"Well, I've seen a lot worse," said Diana, smiling, when at last she wheeled and grabbed Nellie's drooping reins. "You've got long legs and you'll be all right when your muscles build but you'll have to practice for hours and hours until you can hardly limp around."

"If we're going to ride every morning," I protested, "I'll have to get the proper togs. These trousers ruck up and I've rubbed all the skin off the inside of my knee."

"I'll have a square foot of skin off your bottom before I've finished with you!" she promised. "When you come out tomorrow bring corduroys. They'll do to begin with but never mind about riding now, let's walk back to where your bike is, I've got to explain the scheme I've worked out for the rest of the holidays. Now listen carefully and do everything I say, then we can be together all the time until I go back."

The plan had the hallmark of Diana's shrewdness and reckless gaiety but she explained it in the matter-of-fact tone she invariably used when advancing a harebrained scheme aimed at getting her own way.

"You see, Mummy would squash it flat if she thought we had even a mild crush on one another," she said, frankly, "so I had to think out a foolproof wheeze to explain your presence in Sennacharib for the rest of the hols."

"You can't mean to keep on buying loads of Uncle Luke's furniture," I protested.

"Good Lord, no," she said, impatiently. "You work for a newspaper now, don't you? Well, this has to do with a newspaper, and Mummy'll fall for it hook, line and sinker, because she's an absolute glutton for publicity, even publicity in a little local rag like yours."

It was the first time Diana had spoken slightingly of *The Whinmouth & District Observer*, and I should have challenged her had I been less enthralled with the prospect of spending days in her company. She was right in claiming her plan to be foolproof, however, for it was based on Mrs. Gayelorde-Sutton's snobbery. Providing my employers proved co-operative I didn't see how it could fail.

The idea was that my paper should set about collecting information for a series of weekly articles on Heronslea House and the history of the estate as a whole. I was to be introduced into the house as the gleaner of these facts and then either Uncle Reuben, or someone else, was to collate the information I had gathered into a series of features. The scheme was to be sparked off by a telephone call from me to Mrs. Gayelorde-Sutton, after which I was to sell the idea to Uncle Reuben as having originated from her.

It worked surprisingly well. Uncle Reuben liked local features, though I had a hard job to prevent him from undertaking the fact-finding tour himself. When I pleaded that I needed experience, however, he gave way, and so it was that I donned my best suit and dutifully presented myself at the front door of Heronslea House, equipped with a notebook, three well-sharpened pencils and such confidence as Diana had been able to instill into me during that morning's riding lesson on the common.

I had expected Diana to fly to the door the moment I arrived but when a traditionally disdainful butler led me into the circular hall and across it to a sunny room overlooking the small terrace, she was nowhere to be seen. I was shown a chair and told to wait until it pleased Mrs. Gayelorde-Sutton to attend to me. I don't know whether Masters, the butler, had been informed of the reason for my presence, but I gathered from his manner that I was not the type of guest he was accustomed to admit to his mistress's writing room.

It was an interesting room, especially if you knew Mrs. Gayelorde-Sutton. The walls and bureau photographs screamed her pretensions toward life membership in the Upper Ten. There were several oval oil portraits of bewigged gentlemen and brocaded ladies, a signed photograph of a recently deposed king, more photographs of groups of fashionably dressed people, including herself and husband taken on a racecourse somewhere, and a cabinet crammed with china, part of her Rockingham and Bow collection.

The furniture was mostly French. There was a large writing table, with slender legs and a mass of gilded ornamentation, a lovely rosewood escritoire, decorated with a pastoral motif on its bow front and a set of ribbon-backed chairs, with seats that matched the yellow curtains of the room. Although in many ways a ludicrously counterfeit squireen, it was clear that Mrs. Gayelorde-Sutton possessed genuine taste. There was absolutely nothing wrong with her ideas of furnishing a large country house. Life with Uncle Luke, and attendance at scores of auction sales, had taught me a smattering of these matters and I sensed that everything in the room was what the dealers would call "right," just as she herself always looked "right," until the moment she opened her screwbag mouth and spoiled a good impression by strangled vowels and overstressed consonants.

Suddenly she swept in and subjected me to a long, disapprovingly intense scrutiny.

"The reportah from the peepah? But you're only a boy! I expected someone oldah, *mech* oldah!"

Luckily I had anticipated this and made haste to explain that I was a mere fact assembler and that the proprietor of the paper would write the actual articles.

I must have been learning fast about Mrs. Gayelorde-Sutton, for I scored a direct hit by a deferential tailpiece to the effect that this assignment was considered the most important one our paper had ever undertaken and therefore demanded the maximum preparation.

"Oh, I see, I see!" she murmured and then, after a moment's reflection: "Ai'm far too busy to spend mai taime explaining everything to a boy, but there's something in what you say. We don't want to rush the business, do we? Ai think perhaps the best idea is to get mai daughter to show you around; then you ken read me what you've written, before submitting it to your editah."

She opened the door and called, "*Air*-m'ald . . . *Air*-m'ald . . . !" There was the same painful sigh in her pronunciation of the name as I had noticed on the occasion when she visited the Mart. "Come in here, Air-merald, Ai want you to meet someone!"

The strong element of farce in the situation made me want to giggle but I forced myself to maintain a mute, respectful expression while Diana was summoned and solemnly introduced to me. Her play-acting was far better than mine. She even managed to look petulant when her mother instructed her to escort me around the house and grounds and tell me what she knew of its history.

"How long is all this likely to take, Mother?" she demanded, implying that she regarded the entire business as a terrible bore.

"As long as Ai think fit, deah!" said Mrs. Gayelorde-Sutton tartly, and I noticed the deep-rooted antipathy that existed between them, even allowing for the fact that Diana was only playing a part and that her mother was addressing her in front of a stranger.

"All right, all right, I only asked," grumbled Diana, "but I don't want to spend the entire holidays cooped up in the house!"

It seemed to me that Diana was overdoing her show of reluctance but I later concluded that she was merely strengthening the knot that was to hold us together for the next three weeks. Her apparent truculence irritated her mother and made her determined to exert her parental authority. She gave Diana a little lecture on the importance of her escort duties and stressed that everything she said was liable to appear in print. Diana played her like a fish, pretending to warm to her duties as soon as Mrs. Gayelorde-Sutton pointed out that the tour was to include a careful inspection of the entire estate and that this would mean rambles about the grounds.

"Does he ride?" she inquired demurely and winked over her mother's shoulder.

"Oh yes, ma'am," I told her, "I learned over at the Tally-Ho Stables, a year or so ago."

"There then," said Mrs. Gayelorde-Sutton, with a certain amount of relief, "you can ride over the estate but Ai shall want the interiah covered first, you understand? All the chinah and pictures and particularly the Dutch and Italian gardens and McCarthy's hothouse displays. When we've sorted it out," she added, turning to me again, "your employer will hev to send a kemerah up heah, so now I'll leave you to my daughter and you can show me what you've done when it's time to go. Start in the library, Air-m'ald, and ask Mrs. Beddowes when she's ready to let you go upstairs."

"Yes, Mother," said Diana, dutifully. "Come this way, will you, Mr. . . . Mr. . . . ?"

"Leigh," I said, promptly, and followed her out into the hall, closing the door behind me.

Thus began the charade that lasted the greater part of the Easter holidays, and from everyone's viewpoint it proved a remarkable success. The articles were compiled to Mrs. Gayelorde-Sutton's satisfaction, the *Observer* filled its center page without the aid of scissors and pastepot, and Diana and I had license to associate whenever we wished. Although it all began as an elaborate joke it soon developed into something more for me. To anyone at all receptive to beauty and good craftsmanship, an inspection of Heronslea House and estate was a rewarding way of spending an April day. Diana was at first incredulous, then mildly amused by my enthusiasm.

"You're taking it all so seriously, Jan," she complained, when I begged her to allow me more time in the library. "Nobody ever *reads* the books in here, they went with the house and they simply aren't readable, none of them."

"They smell exciting anyway," I said, and Diana laughed and gave me an affectionate little hug.

"Oh, you're a funny boy, Jan!" she exclaimed. "Funny but nice! You know"—she stood back and regarded me as though making up her mind about a purchase at a counter—"I really think you *are* going to be someone after all. I'll tell you what. For the house tour I'll hand you over to Drip. She's got quite a pash on you and I'll get all my chores done before we start outside and combine this nonsense with some real work on the horses. I've got heaps of letters to write and an awful French holiday task and by the time I've done you'll be through in here."

Without waiting for my agreement she pulled me up the broad staircase, composed of stairs so shallow that one had little sensation of climbing, and along one of the curved corridors to a little suite beyond the schoolroom. This was Drip's quarters and as we went in she said:

"Drip's in our secret, of course, so you might have to grapple with her conscience! She won't give us away, however, so you don't have to put on an act with her."

It was soon clear that poor Miss Rodgers was having a great deal of trouble with her conscience, and because I was genuinely fond of her I was unable to share Diana's detachment. It did not take me long to discover that Drip was very well aware that my world re-volved around Diana, and also that I was no more than a glorified errand boy with whom her charge was consorting in brazen defiance of her mother.

Miss Rodgers (I find it difficult to write of her as "Drip") was torn between her adoration for Diana, her genuine kindheartedness, her liking for me personally, and her obvious duty to her employers, but Diana was correct in her assumption that our secret was safe, for Drip's awareness of responsibilities as governess was outweighed by more personal considerations. After a good deal of preliminary tongue clicking and half-hearted protests she consented to take over Diana's duties as guide.

"I don't like all this hole-in-the-corner business, Jan," she admitted, as soon as Diana had left us alone. "After all, I am supposed to be responsible for her whenever her mother isn't here, and although I don't see why you and she shouldn't be friends, I don't like being a party to a shameless deceit."

"It isn't really a deceit, Miss Rodgers," I pleaded, "because we really are going to print the articles. Besides, I like the job and I think Diana's mother will like what we do, so in the end everyone'll be happy, won't they?"

"Yes," said Drip, doubtfully, "but I think you'd better tell me a little more about yourself, just in case anyone finds out later on. I mean . . . well . . . Diana's mother *is* rather fussy whom she asso-ciates with in the holidays, and I can't help feeling that she might be furious if she found out that Diana had tricked her like this, if you see what I mean."

I saw what she meant far more clearly than the amiable little governess imagined. Diana's mother would be less inclined to ex-plode over being so outrageously hoodwinked than over the dis-covery that her expensively educated daughter was gaily associating with a boy who had recently graduated from a secondhand furni-ture store to the post of junior reporter on an insignificant country newspaper, and a boy, moreover, who had left a council school at the age of fourteen and used a reedy, Cockney accent that placed him on a footing with the village boy who cleaned the silver.

My tour of the house in the wake of Drip served to emphasize the existence of the vast social gulf between us. Before I had in-spected half of the sixty-odd rooms of the mansion it was plain that the Gayelorde-Suttons were far wealthier than I had supposed. I followed Drip from room to room with mounting dismay. It was like being taken on a conducted tour around Blenheim Palace, or Compton Wynyates. Drip let me browse in the library and jot down notes about some of the pictures on the staircase. There was a Cotman landscape and several small Fragonards. Down in the vast drawing room was a group of Isabey miniatures and two portraits by Raeburn. I knew very little about pictures and was content to make notes on the insurance figures quoted by Miss Rodgers, but my association with antique dealers had taught me something of the value of the French furniture in the ground-floor apartments.

The furniture alone would have merited a four-day sale and attracted every reputable dealer in London. There were samples of almost every well-known English craftsman of the eighteenth century, as well as a number of exquisite French pieces, of the kind I had already noted in the writing room.

There were Aubusson screens, Chinese carpets, Burgundian tapestries and Sheraton sideboards, loaded with Georgian silver. There was Mrs. Gayelorde-Sutton's personal collection of china ranging from early Chelsea and Plymouth, to exotic groups and centerpieces of Rockingham, Worcester, and Bow. There was a small armory containing chased Spanish morions, exquisitely wrought Italian armor, and a dozen cases of handsome dueling pistols, collected, I was told, by Mr. Gayelorde-Sutton during his various Continental trips. There was a little conservatory, full of oddities left by the Gilroys and containing, among other interesting exhibits, the charred stump of a stake at which the last witch of the district was said to have suffered. Dotted here and there among all these splendors were scores of framed photographs, each of them featuring the Gayelorde-Suttons during their swift rise to power during the opening years of the decade.

It was an early photograph of Mr. Gayelorde-Sutton wearing knickerbockers and deerstalker hat and taken alongside an early model of an open touring car that prompted me to ask Miss Rodgers if the family had always been rich, or whether, as was freely rumored in Shepherdshey, they had acquired their vast wealth during the 1914-18 war.

I saw by the instinctive tightening of the governess's lips that the question challenged her honesty.

"Well er . . ." she temporized, "Diana's father has always been very clever, of course, and he was doing quite well *before* the war, importing something or other from South America, but money makes money, doesn't it? It was really *during* the war that he came to be really well known, not in the newspaper sense, you understand, not like Rudolph Valentino or that man Lind something or other, who flew the Atlantic last summer, but among the city people who seem to make money without doing anything in particular."

"But what does he really *do?*" I asked, for it seemed important to me that I should know this once and for all.

Drip wrinkled her pudgy little nose and looked very uncomfortable.

"I . . . I don't really know," she admitted. "I don't think anyone here really knows, except that it's something to do with . . . with high finance, and . . . and *selling* something to the government. Perhaps it's something like he was doing before the war—that was nitrates, I believe, Chilean nitrates. I do remember that because I saw some illustrated charts hanging in his office when I had to call there the day war broke out."

That was as much information as I got at that time about the source of the Gayelorde-Suttons' wealth, but before Diana came to claim me and continue our tour of the gardens, Miss Rodgers asked me into her little sitting room adjoining the nursery and talked to me seriously over a cup of tea and some of her favorite muffins. I could see that she was still very worried over our association and at length she forced herself, much as she hated to pry, to explore the future of a friendship between Diana and myself.

"I . . . I know you're very young, Jan," she began, her pendulous cheeks flushing, "but I've got a dreadful conviction that you're . . . well . . . beginning to feel the same way about Diana as I do, and I can't see how you'll be able to stop getting *hurt* later on. You see, I've known Diana from the minute she was born and she's always been this way—thoughtless and terribly impulsive, always rushing into things that she thinks of as . . . well . . . as *adventures,* I suppose. I don't mean that she's silly enough to imagine she's in love, or anything of that nature, and I suppose I shouldn't even say that to a boy of your age anyway, because I'm sure you won't let your mind dwell on that kind of thing for years yet, but I do think a young person can be hurt as much by a broken friendship as grown-up people are hurt by love affairs, and I don't like a nice boy like you being picked up and . . . and well . . . *led* to believe things and then dropped and laughed at, do you know?"

[98

Despite her obvious good intentions I found myself resenting her estimate of Diana. I suppose I failed to make sufficient allowance for the fact that Miss Rodgers had been reared in a Victorian atmosphere and accepted rigid class distinctions without in the least resenting them. It seemed to me at that time that she was being stuffy and old-fashioned, as well as slightly disloyal to someone who had never hinted at the social barrier between us, except as a fence to be crossed and recrossed in defiance of her mother's edicts.

I fell back on a rather surly justification of myself as a not altogether impossible squire for the daughter of wealthy and distinguished parents. Drip's halting references to impending disaster had touched my pride in a way that Diana's frank acceptance of parental opposition had never touched it, and I said, without looking at her:

"I'm not going to stay a small-town reporter, Miss Rodgers. I'm going to get on a bigger paper and be famous, so that in the end we won't have to pretend any more and then Diana and I can be married without any fuss!"

Poor Miss Rodgers was so startled by the mention of the word "marriage" that she dropped her pince-nez spectacles on the carpet.

"Jan, you . . . you mustn't *think* about things like that," she protested, her plump hands fluttering as she groped for her glasses. "You must see that just saying them puts me in a dreadful position. I don't know what to say, I simply don't know *what* to say!"

She trailed off miserably and I was sorry then that I had confided in her. At the same time, I felt the necessity of convincing her that it was quite possible for a boy of fifteen and a half to be hopelessly in love, and that I would not accept her disqualification on grounds of age quite apart from those of class and education.

"People grow up quicker than they did when you were young," I declared, quoting from a newspaper feature I had read a day or so before, and feeling a hot flush creep into my cheeks. "I'm nearly sixteen now and all the boys about my age in Whinmouth have a girl they like better than any other girl. I've never met anyone who could compare with Diana, not just to look at, I mean, but as a person, as someone who's wonderful to *be* with. All the girls in the town seem so . . . so feeble compared with her, and she seems to like me, otherwise why should she go to all this trouble so that we can be together?"

Miss Rodgers seemed to consider and for a moment the concern left her expression. When she spoke again she sounded wonderfully gentle and understanding, so much so that instantly I changed my mind about her and was glad that I had forced the matter out in the open.

"You haven't got a mother or father, have you, Jan?" she asked and when I told her they were both dead she folded her hands on her lap and smiled, her faded blue eyes radiating so much kindness and comfort that I swallowed quickly and had to look away.

She went on: "I'm afraid I'm a romantic, Jan, just like you, and what you've just said makes it clear to me that I was quite wrong to pooh-pooh the idea of being in love at your age. You *are* in love, the right kind of love, and I don't suppose anything I can say will stop you being, not for a year or so at all events. All I want to say now is that you must realize Diana isn't in love in the same way, perhaps because she hasn't grown up as fast as you, or perhaps because she's had so much of everything. That means that she hasn't developed in the way that you've had to develop, partly, I think, because you lost your mother and father at a time when you most needed them but more so because you've been pushed out in the world to earn your own living. All the other young people Diana knows have still got two or three years more of schooling ahead of them and this friendship with you is a kind of game to Diana. Although I'm sure she likes you very much, most of the fun to her is just having you around and scoring over her mother; that is, doing something that she knows very well is strictly forbidden."

She paused a moment and then added, "I don't suppose this makes much sense to you now, but I think you'll see the wisdom of it later on. I'm going to have a little talk with Miss Diana and it's going to be tonight!"

She got up and smoothed her dress, looking so resolute that my heart sank at the prospect of our association being severed there and then.

"If you say anything like that to her I won't be able to see her, Miss Rodgers," I pleaded. "You needn't be frightened I'll do anything you wouldn't like. I'll just go on being friends, the way we are."

I thought, fleetingly, of our secret meeting in London, and of the despairing kiss that Diana had given me as the train drew into the station. I wondered what Drip would say and do if she knew the whole truth of our association to date, and whether such knowledge would cause her to regard the matter less sympathetically from my point of view.

"All the same, I'm going to talk to Diana," said Drip, "but don't think for a moment I'll say anything at all to her mother, or that I'll make it any more difficult than it already is for you to see one another. To begin with, that would only make Diana more determined than ever, and the truth is I'm thinking of you more than her because you're the one who is going to be hurt most and I won't have that, ever, do you understand? I won't *have* that!"

I left Heronslea that day without seeing Diana again and my thoughts were so wretched and confused that I made no attempt to sort out the notes I had made, but retired to my room after supper on the pretense of doing this and sat for a long time watching the moon rise over the estuary beyond the empty quay.

Whichever way I looked at the situation, I could see no hope in the immediate future and I slowly came to hate Drip for what seemed to be a monstrously unjust interference in our lives.

I set the alarm for five o'clock again and cycled up to Foxhayes to watch the dawn, but although I hung about the Folly for almost two hours Diana did not appear and I freewheeled back to town in black despondency.

Diana's failure to keep the tryst seemed to me clear evidence that all was now known to her mother, and quite apart from the misery of losing her I began to feel very apprehensive of my reception at the office.

I did Drip a grave injustice. There was no showdown. Uncle Reuben was just as interested in the articles as ever, and was obviously expecting me to bus over to Heronslea for the next day's note taking. He even complimented me on the material I had already gathered and said that if I wished to knock it into a draft article, without first submitting it to him in detail, I was welcome to try as soon as I returned.

His attitude was puzzling but not nearly so puzzling as Diana's. She greeted me the moment I entered the drive, and talked gaily of a book that she had unearthed dealing with the history of the house and estate under the Gilroy who had built the Folly.

We inspected the Dutch garden as she chattered on about this and that until I had almost persuaded myself that Drip's nerve must have failed her at the last moment and that she had never, in fact, had her talk with Diana. Then, as we passed the box hedges and entered the Italian garden, I thought I detected a nervous brittleness about Diana's chatter, as though she were only talking in the hope of preventing me from voicing the subject uppermost in my mind. This conviction grew until at last I was unable to keep silent any longer and blurted out: "Well, did Drip say anything to you last night, Diana? Anything about us?"

She stopped in the middle of a sentence and looked at me sharply, her head on one side, her thumb pulling her lower lip.

"What does it matter what Drip said? Who cares about Drip's opinion one way or the other? I told you she wouldn't give us away and that's all that counts, isn't it?"

"No," I said, glumly, "it isn't, and what's more you must know that it isn't!"

She looked at me then with an expression I had never seen in her face. It was hard and challenging, as though at any moment her eyes would blaze with anger. When she spoke her voice was equally harsh and strange.

"Why should you say a thing like that? Just exactly what did Drip say to you about me? What made you afraid of coming here?"

"I'm not afraid, Diana," I protested, "it's just that . . ."

"You *are* afraid, Jan! All the sparkle's gone out of you. Yesterday it was fun and today you're as jumpy as a cat. You'd better tell me everything Drip said and be done with it."

I told her, withholding nothing, and she heard me in silence, keeping her gaze on me in a way that made me feel wretched and ashamed.

"Is that all?" she said, when I had finished.

"All I can remember," I said, sulkily.

She stayed quite still for a moment, reflecting.

"You know what she was getting at," she said at length. "I mean, what she was *really* driving at when you peel away all the cotton wool that she wrapped it in and all that gaff about me encouraging you just to spite Mother, and so on?"

"She didn't seem to me to beat about the bush very much," I growled.

Diana threw back her head and laughed. It was not her pleasant abandoned laugh, the one I loved to hear, but an expression of unspeakable contempt, contempt for Drip, for me, for Heronslea House and everything in it.

"People like Drip always go all around the mulberry bush to soften the blow," she said. "They think they're doing it out of consideration for people but they aren't, you know, it's just lack of guts on their part. Drip's a dear old thing in many ways but she hasn't the spunk of a rabbit. She ought to have said exactly what she meant while she was about it."

"What did she mean, Di?"

"Simply that nothing could ever make you into the sort of person that I should care to be seen with—outside Sennacharib, of course. Just that you weren't 'our class' and never could be, and that everything about you was wrong, clothes, accent, outlook, everything! Well, do you believe that? Because it's what you think that really matters, Jan. Do you believe it, deep down, inside you?"

Did I? I think I did on the rare occasions when I could escape from the web of romantic dreams I had been spinning since the day Diana had ridden out of the larch wood and rescued me from the keeper. I had changed my job because of her. I had obeyed her every command, as a dog runs to a whistle. I had lied to myself, to Uncle Reuben, to Aunt Thirza, to her mother and even to Drip, simply in order to continue dreaming, but if I was once seriously challenged could I continue to fool myself? Would I ever convince myself that Diana and I could ever really belong together, or would I wake up and face the fact that no efforts on my part would ever establish a relationship between us that was capable of outgrowing the friendship of two adolescents, a pair of kids who had absolutely nothing in common but a love of the woods, fields and hedgerows?

I was searching for words to convey this to her when suddenly she took pity on me and her expression softened. She took hold of my wrist and ran her fingers up the sleeve until they were pressing my forearm. Her touch was like a salve, soothing the raw wound of my pride and injecting vigor into my dreams. Confidence and self-esteem seemed to radiate from her finger tips and flow through into me, the glow warming every nerve in my body.

"What you need is a tonic, Jan, a real, live tonic! Meet me at Whinmouth Station after lunch and we'll go out after it, but don't ask me about it now, just be there. We're going on a little trip somewhere."

"How far?" I asked, astonished at both proposal and change of mood.

"Oh, not so far," she replied, gaily, "ten or twelve miles. We'll be back before dark and by that time you'll have things straighter, a whole lot straighter, I promise you."

That was all she would say at that time and we devoted the rest of the morning to an inspection of McCarthy's spectacular hothouses and banks of blooms. I made various notes, but my mind was not on my work, it was probing and probing into the mystery behind Diana's knowing smile and her brisk, businesslike manner.

I left Heronslea shortly before lunch and gobbled a meal in time to be at our little railway terminus by two o'clock. About ten past Diana came into the booking hall and without glancing in my direction went straight to the window and bought tickets. I heard the clerk say, "Two returns, Castle Ferry, two-and-four, miss," as he gave change.

"Why on earth are we going to Castle Ferry?" I wanted to know, as we passed the barrier.

"You'll find out as soon as we get there!" was all she would tell me. "Now don't keep pestering me with questions and let me enjoy my surprise. I know what I'm doing, I *always* know what I'm doing, Jan!"

I knew her well enough by then to keep my curiosity to myself and find other topics to talk about. Fortunately an obvious one was at hand, for Castle Ferry was a fishing village a dozen miles along the coast and to get to it by rail one had to travel inland to the county junction and then, by branch line, southeast through the pine and bracken country beyond Teasel Wood and the boundaries of Sennacharib.

I had been there once before and knew it for a picturesque little place, just beginning to enjoy popularity as an artist's colony. It was too picture-postcardy for my taste, the kind of seaside one sees in scores of amateur water colors, all pebbles, white cottages and heeled-over boats draped around with nets and lobster pots. It had, I suppose, plenty of conventional charm but lacked the solitude of Sennacharib, or even the strident vitality of the rural slum that is often the hard core of towns like Whinmouth.

We had our heads out of the window all the way and vied with one another in spotting landmarks, but before we reached the junction the fact that we were alone in a railway compartment reminded me of the short railway journey we had made together in London, and I began to hope that Diana would say something to stage a repetition of the moment of parting. She was not, however, in a romantic mood, for when I let my arm rest on her shoulder and lightly brushed her hair with my lips, she ignored the gesture and said, rather pointedly, "Look, Jan! You can just see the top of the Folly above the wood."

We left the train at a point a mile or so from the coast and walked down the steep lane between high, flowering hedgerows to the foot of the village, where a shallow stream emptied itself into the bay that divided Castle Ferry into two unequal halves.

The castle, a rounded ruin, was on the far side and under it was an old tavern, The Sloop Inn. There was no bridge and people who wanted to cross from one part of the village to the other used a rowing boat that was hauled along a taut cable by hand. There was no regular service. Ferry customers crossed the shingle to where the boat touched shore, and if the ferry was on the far side the ferryman, who spent almost all his time in the pub, was summoned by a hail.

Easter was gone, the summer season had not yet begun, and there was hardly anyone about. The boat was moored on the far side, so we put our hands to our mouths and shouted in chorus. Nothing happened for a few moments, then the ferryman emerged from the Sloop, a fat, shambling man in a fisherman's jersey and a battered yachting cap. He waved his arm, very irritably I thought, and began to haul the boat toward us.

"Take a good long look at this Johnny, Jan," said Diana as the ferry neared us, "because he's the reason we're here."

The ferryman was worth noting. He was the most picturesque old ruffian I had ever seen, a cross between a W. W. Jacob's illustration and a buccaneer run to seed. He was aged, I should say, between sixty and seventy, and his face was a flabby ham, framed in tumbling iron-gray locks that were almost as long as a girl's. His complexion was light mahogany but not pleasing, for grime filled the crevasses of his huge ears. His eyes were as soft and blue as Diana's, but the cunning squint in them changed to a surly contempt when he saw that his passengers were only a couple of youngsters and therefore unlikely to pay more than the requisite halfpenny. Seen at close range his bulk, and particularly his belly, was immense; when he seated himself in the bows preparatory to hauling on the cable, the stern was out of the water until we had stepped in and sat down. He smelled very strongly of beer and when he opened his mouth to jam a clay pipe between his discolored teeth I saw that his tongue was horribly furred. One way and another, he struck me as being an extremely unsavory old man, the kind of pseudo-fisherman who hangs about quays cadging from visitors, who usually tell one another: "Here is a real old salt, the kind that are getting rare these days." We had our own contingent of longshoremen at Whinmouth, but none of them were quite so repellent or professional-looking as this one. His hands were as big and rough as everything else about him, and the tar from the cable had ingrained itself as high as the wrist. He looked to me as though he had never washed since he was a boy and apart from the reek of beer it was an unpleasant experience to travel with him, for he also exuded an odor of stale sweat.

He said nothing to us during the five-minute crossing and only grunted when I handed him sixpence, twelve times the fare. We got out and took the path up the knoll to the castle and I saw him stumble into the pub the moment he had moored the boat.

"Well?" said Diana, throwing herself down on a level stretch of grass beside the tower. "What do you think of Dan'l?"

"I think he's a complete phony," I said, "and a pretty smelly one at that!"

"Not a character? Not a tarry chip of Old England?"

"No," I said, "not on your life! Chaps like him are ten-a-penny in Whinmouth, but most of them wash once in a while and all of them say thank you when they get a tip."

She curled her legs under her and leaned back on her hands, the familiar smile playing hide-and-seek round the corners of her mouth, while her eyes regarded me with affectionate mockery.

"Look, what is all this?" I demanded. "What's he got to do with us being here?"

"He's the tonic I told you about," said Diana, "he's your private pick-me-up."

I was always ready to stand a great deal of chaff from Diana but that day I was too nervous about the immediate future to put up with her teasing indefinitely. I said, shortly, "For goodness' sake say what's in your mind and let's begin at the beginning!"

"All right," she said, softly, inserting a grass stem into her mouth with the casual grace she displayed when she slipped from the back of one of her ponies. "Dan'l is Mummy's father and my grandfather!"

I jumped as if I had found myself sitting on a wasps' nest, utter incredulity depriving me of speech for nearly a minute. At last I found my tongue.

"That . . . that ferryman! . . . *Your grandfather!*"

"Uh-huh!" she said, enjoying every moment of my outraged astonishment. "His name is Daniel Best and Mummy is his youngest daughter. She doesn't know that I know, of course; in fact, nobody knows that I know except you, but it's true, all right, and if you look really hard you can see it, at least I can, because I've seen Mummy without make-up."

"I don't understand," I said, weakly, "I just don't understand how the chap and your mother . . ."

I trailed off, for it was impossible to contemplate the relationship, much less put it into words. I thought back to the first glimpse I had ever had of Mrs. Gayelorde-Sutton, tip-tapping on her high heels into Uncle Luke's store, splendidly arrogant in her elegant clothes and addressing me as though I was something left behind by the tide. I remembered how she had screwed her small, red mouth into a tight ball of distaste and called in strangled vowels to Diana, "*Air*-m'alde! *Air*-m'alde! Come heah, Air-m'alde, Ai want you!"

I compared her mincing charade with the sour, uncompromising heaviness of the ferryman Dan'l, searching my memory for some characteristic, or suggestion of a characteristic, that might link them as father and daughter, but my mind shied away from the possibility, not only on account of its staggering improbability but because, deep in my heart, I was feeling the first stirrings of pity for Mrs. Gayelorde-Sutton and wanting to absolve her from a relationship with a sullen drunkard who smelled vilely of sweat and stale liquor.

"How did you find out? Why are you so sure?" I asked, holding on to a tendril of hope that this was just one of Diana's elaborate jokes.

"I'd always wondered about Mummy's people," she said. "I think I began to suspect something years and years ago, when I first realized how terribly phony *she* was and why she tried so terribly hard to convince even me that she came out of the top drawer. Then I got a clue from a book of check stubs she left lying around and did some detective work among her papers before coming over here to make sure. It wasn't all that difficult, it only needed common sense and luck. She pays him to stay away, you see, and as long as he gets regular beer money and his cottage rent paid, he never gives any trouble. He isn't anything like as truculent as he looks, just rather pitiful, I always think."

"Do you mean you actually rooted about among your mother's things for clues?" I demanded.

"Certainly, and don't expect me to apologize for it," she said sharply. "I've a right to know who my own grandfather is, haven't I?"

I conceded her this but remained doubtful of the ethics of her action.

"Does he know . . . about you?"

"Well, he knows I exist, but he certainly doesn't recognize me. That was obvious, wasn't it?"

I thought for a moment and then began to ponder her tortuous motive in bringing me here, introducing me, so to speak, to the family skeleton. I remembered the word she had used—"tonic." What exactly did that mean? How was knowing about Dan'l a tonic to me? Then, quite suddenly, I saw her object and she realized that I had understood.

"Well, Jan, do you catch on? Does it make sense now—why I brought you here, I mean?"

I said, "I imagine it was to prove to me that your family wasn't really any better class than mine, Diana."

"I should say you had the edge on us if anything," said Diana, laughing. "I've seen all your uncles and none of them measure up to our Dan'l, do they?"

Suddenly she whisked out of her bantering mood and her eyes became serious. "Don't you *see*, Jan, it isn't what you are, it's what you become that matters! If Mother had just broken away from a family like that and struck out on her own, I think I should have admired her, but as it is, what possible right can she have to choose my companions and lay down rules and regulations for me? She doesn't just laugh at Dan'l, or give him enough money to lie low. She doesn't even send him out of the country—she's too scared to do that and wants him fairly handy where she can keep an eye on him. It's almost as though he was a criminal, and in a way he's worse than a criminal to her, certainly worse than a criminal with a public school background. It makes me absolutely sick when people like her and Drip look down on somebody like you, someone who earns his own living, and tries to keep himself decent on a few shillings a week! I brought you to see Dan'l in the hope that it would help you to see straight, the way I've seen since I was old enough to sit up and take notice. If a person like you wants to change enough, he can always do it. Thousands of people have had worse starts and become all sorts of things without being ashamed of what they were born, as Mummy is. I suppose I've got a thing about this snob business because I've been hedged in with it all my life, and when Drip came up with her pi-jaw last night I wanted to hit her. Then I was angry with you, for letting her persuade you to eat humble pie and pull a forelock at squire's house. Don't *ever* eat humble pie, Jan, and don't ever pull forelocks! If you do I'll hate you, and I don't want to hate you because you being in love with me is the nicest thing that's ever happened to me!"

Her logic wasn't very original but I still think hers was a remarkable outlook for a fifteen-year-old girl who had been brought up to regard almost everyone about her as a social inferior. I know that at the time I admired her for it tremendously, and that my heart, already hers, swelled with pride because she had faith in me and was prepared to go to such lengths to prove it. I loved her honesty and courage. I loved her high spirits and irrepressible sense of fun. I loved her grasp of realism and utter lack of pretension and I was beginning to respond to her physically in a way that was new to me, despite our occasional kisses and childish protestations. This would doubtless have happened before, but until her latest declaration my awareness of her eager, elfin prettiness had been held in check by her unattainability. I had been ready to serve her, to perform any and every feat she demanded of me. I had been eager to worship but, if necessary, to do my worshiping from a respectful distance. Now, within a few months of my sixteenth birthday, I wanted to possess as well as worship, I wanted to begin training as the man who would ultimately soar to the ecstatic position of mastery over her, and as I watched the afternoon sun light up her hair and breeze stir the uneven fringe that seemed always to be reaching for the arch of her left eyebrow, I made up my mind that I would commence that training without confiding in her and then lay my accomplishments, one by one, at her feet as the forfeits of rapture.

We sat there a long time watching the empty bay, talking of other things, apart from beery old Dan'l and what kind of childhood her mother must have had in the crowded cottage that he continued to occupy behind the boat sheds. Then we climbed down from the castle and ordered a Devonshire tea in a tiny gift-shop-cum-café under the red cliff, afterwards recrossing the ferry piloted by her grandfather, who became embarrassingly servile when presented with Diana's half crown at the point of disembarkation.

We had to share the compartment back to Whinmouth, which distressed me, for I had made up my mind to kiss her without awaiting her usual invitation. As it happened, with three other people in the carriage, I was obliged to remain content with letting my hand rest on hers as we sat close together on the dusty cushions. I saw her to the bus stop shortly before dusk and then, with singing heart, went home to sort my Heronslea notes and file my latest memories.

Chapter Five

DIANA returned to school the last week in April. By the first week of May I had made my plans and put the two of them into operation.

I had learned a good deal in the holidays. It was plain that Diana was not prepared to share her life with a man whose achievements were limited to chronicling small-town events, and while my present job was good enough to be regarded as a training ground for wider fields, I realized that I must look ahead for something more spectacular and certainly more rewarding. In the meantime I decided to employ the interval by overhauling my social equipment, leaving my career in abeyance until I was experienced enough to apply for a post in Fleet Street.

It was still nearly three years before the great industrial slump of the early thirties and the word "unemployment" did not, as yet, loom very large in Whinmouth. I went so far as to discuss my future with Uncle Reuben and although he shook his head when I told him, with the brashness of youth, that I was determined to see the world and start by getting myself a job on a national newspaper, he commended my ambition and promised that when the time came he would do everything in his power to help me.

"You'll find that every middle-aged reporter in Fleet Street dreams of running a little provincial weekly like ours, John," he warned me. "Taken all round, there's a lot to be said for being a big fish in a small pond. Up there they earn good money, of course, but it's a rackety life and most of them end up by drinking too much or go to the bad in one way or another. However, I'm not so old as to realize that you won't want to spend the whole of your life in a place like this, and I think you're bright and willing enough to merit something more than a job on a small paper you aren't ever likely to own. Let's shelve the whole business until you're eighteen; then we'll get Mr. Priddis to give us some introductions and try our luck in somewhere a bit bigger than Whinmouth Bay. In the meantime we'll give you a raise to thirty shillings a week."

I thanked him and was ready to leave it at that but privately made up my mind to do something about improving my position before another two years had elapsed. In the meantime, as I say, I reached out in other directions. I learned how to ride properly and began to acquire a working knowledge of French.

The riding lessons were easily arranged. I went over to Uncle Mark's stables, determined to improve my acquaintance with the old rascal. Having studied his battered signboard, which proclaimed lessons were given and liveries received, I demanded to be taught to ride and offered a fee of five shillings per lesson. Uncle Mark was pleased, I think, by my forthrightness, and by my sly admission that I was presenting myself in defiance to staid Brother Reuben's advice.

"You'll get nothing but dirty stories from that scoundrel," he had warned me, when I told him of my intention. "He'll take all your money and give you nothing better than a filthy taste in your mouth!"

I didn't repeat this comment to Mark but I told him that Uncle Reuben had dismissed horsemanship as a giddy pursuit for the idle rich, and that was enough to put Mark on his mettle.

"Damme, I'll teach 'ee for nowt if you've a mind to learn praper!" he growled, and when I told him I had already had a few lessons on one of the Gayelorde-Sutton ponies he looked me up and down much as Diana had done after persuading me to ride Nellie at the Folly.

"Do you think I'll ever make a really good rider?" I asked him.

"I dunno!" he grunted. "Us'll zee when us gets 'ee up!"

He brought out an old cob called Justice and taught me to mount and dismount, and having expressed grudging satisfaction that I "zeemed to get the 'ang of it better'n most o' the young bleeders," he saddled his own horse and took me over the common, thumping out the rhythm of the trot on my left thigh until it was sore to touch.

After that we made remarkably good headway. I slipped out to Uncle Mark's three or four times a week, and by midsummer we had exchanged Justice for a lively mare called Polly, whom I took over some of the smaller jumps in Mark's grid, behind the stables.

I worked very hard, for I was absolutely determined to surprise Diana when she came home for the long holiday, and Uncle Mark became almost amiable as he watched my progress. The day we galloped round Teasel Wood and finished a neck-and-neck race by clearing a fallen spruce in the ride approaching his premises, he rolled from his sweating mount and waddled over to wring my hand in both of his.

"Giddon, us'll 'ave 'ee 'untin' in no time!" he exclaimed. "Damned if you ab'n got a natural zeat, me boy, aye, an' bliddy gude 'ands too, or my name ain't Leigh! I'll tell 'ee what, you come yer an' zaddle up Polly any time you've a mind to, and you tell that bliddy preacher of yours down in the town that Mark's done more to making a man of 'ee than ever 'im an' 'is penny backscratcher 'as!"

Uncle Mark disapproved of my association with the *Observer*, which he always referred to as a penny backscratcher, an implied criticism of the lavish praise it doled out to its regular advertisers in reports of their various social and political functions. I said very little about my riding to Uncle Reuben, however; indeed, I kept it a close secret from everyone, for I was now itching to demonstrate my prowess to the only pair of eyes that mattered.

In the meantime I was making steady if less spectacular progress with elocution and French, under the tutelage of Miss Beddowes, the daughter of a former king's messenger, who lived in one of the big, detached houses on Foxhayes Hill. Miss Beddowes taught elocution free of charge at the local evening Institute. She was a prim, rather leathery little spinster with a passion for dispensing education among the deserving poor. She ran the local Book Club that did duty for a county library in Whinmouth, and we became friends after I was able to help her in an appeal for unwanted books to stock the club shelves. It was through me that she was given a case of classics from Uncle Luke's store and she was so grateful that she invited me to tea in her big, old-fashioned house on the hill.

She was an energetic little woman whose undoubted talents as a teacher had been wasted while caring for invalid parents. Now that both were dead, and she was comfortably provided for, she was trying to make up for lost time by throwing herself heart and soul into all kinds of social work. Apart from running the Book Club and teaching at the Institute, she was a leader of the Girl Guides and the only female member of the Urban District Council. She was not, at first acquaintance, a very likable person, being entirely without a sense of humor and very much inclined to take herself too seriously, but I grew very fond of her later on and exploited her shamefully when she suggested that I should try to shed a Cockney accent that was beginning to crossbreed with West Country brogue.

From these lessons it was an easy step to elementary French, and I was gratified to discover that I had a mild flair for languages. Perhaps the work seemed easy because I was young and eager, or perhaps the real spur was the prospect of astonishing Diana in yet another field of accomplishment. At all events, Miss Beddowes was pleased with my progress and spared no pains to bring me to a point where my own interest in the subject supplied the main impetus.

I was totally ignorant of French when I came to her but this, I gathered, was an advantage.

"You've nothing to unlearn," she said crisply, when I apologized for my utter ignorance of the subject, adding:

"It's quite dreadful when one reflects that of all the thousands of children who are taught French at school not one—not *one*, mind you—can make himself or herself understood when they set foot at Calais. The trouble is, of course, that the method of teaching is ridiculous, quite ridiculous! A child is bored with unintelligible grammar before its ear is attuned to the language. Now you have a dozen of my oral lessons and listen to my set of records on the phonograph, and I'll have you speaking French as well and better than you can speak English before the next Christmas!"

She did not quite justify this boast but she went an appreciable way toward doing so. She spoke perfect French herself, having lived in France during the greater part of her youth, and all that summer, when I had completed any *Observer* assignments, I cycled up to the big, red brick house on Tuesdays and Fridays and sat in Miss Beddowes' study, listening to her carefully articulated conversational French and the excellent supplementary lessons on the horned phonograph. I can see her now, across the years of slumps, booms and wars, sitting bolt upright in a high-backed chair and making a series of careful mouths as she struggled to perfect my accent, both in French and my mother tongue. Sharp at nine o'clock the elderly maid would enter with cocoa and biscuits, and there was a fifteen-minute break while we talked town politics over refreshments. Then on would go the phonograph and lesson until the chiming clock on her mantelpiece struck ten, when she would rise, dust her plain dress with her hands, and say, "Well, John Leigh, that's all for tonight! Remember, you must *think* in French, beginning as soon as you wake, pull back the curtains, and say, 'Does it rain? Is the sun shining? Is my breakfast ready? Did I dream something pleasant?'"

These questions became for me a litany of the French tongue and throughout that summer I was always dreaming something pleasant, although the majority of my dreams came by day as I walked and cycled about Whinmouth Bay, filling my notebooks with lists of mourners, the names of stall holders, and ratepayers' complaints about the smell of decaying fish on the jetties.

Most of the daydreams were inspired by Diana's letters, a spate of which flowed steadily through the letter box all that summer. Their tone differed somewhat from the letters I had received during the previous term. It was at once more serious and more affectionate, sometimes almost frighteningly so, for I think that Diana's stage of adolescence coincided with an upsurge of competitive romance among her friends at school. It was, as she confided later, the Thing to maintain a passionate correspondence with a boy friend, and as time went on, her letters became more liberally sprinkled with dears, dearests and darlings, each of which lifted me to a slightly higher plane of ecstatic contemplation.

There were photographs too, all kinds of photographs, snaps of Diana sitting on a log and displaying plenty of shapely leg, snaps of Diana in a hitched-up gym costume, snaps of Diana in a one-piece bathing costume, looking archly aware of her swiftly maturing figure, and each letter and photograph was read and studied a dozen times before being placed in a special box that I had acquired to receive them, a box shaped like a small treasure chest, with a lock and clasp wrought in the likeness of a heart pierced by an arrow.

It is easy to look back on the joy these letters brought me, and dismiss the romantic impulse as the emotional outlet of a half-grown youth, but what letters reach us in later life that compare with those exchanged by adolescents believing themselves to be deeply in love? I don't know whether the delight of receiving them was more or less than a grown man might feel on getting a letter from his fiancée, but I do know that I looked for the postman as impatiently as a shipwrecked sailor watches for a smudge of smoke on the horizon, and when Bill Clipper, the postman, hesitated outside the Mart before pushing one of Diana's blue and gilt envelopes through the letter box, I had to stifle a shout of triumph and then force myself to walk slowly downstairs, retrieve the letter and scamper off to my room to enjoy it in solitude.

One day, toward the end of June, she wrote saying that she had spent a day at Ascot and that Yves, the French boy we had met at the cinema, had been there with his father, the famous race horse owner. I was sick with jealousy all that week and some pictures that appeared in one of the smarter periodicals, showing a group composed of Yves, Diana, and their respective parents at the races, depressed me still further. Yves looked the complete man about town, with an expression of polite boredom on his thin, aristocratic face, but Diana, who was wearing a cloche hat and a flowered frock, looked utterly unattainable and almost as grown up as her mother, who was flirting a parasol and in the act, it appeared, of aiming a salvo of tortured vowels at the bland-looking Count de Royden. That was one picture of Diana that did not go into the chest. It was torn to fragments and dropped over the edge of the wharf.

A week later much better news arrived. Her parents, she informed me, had now departed for Capetown, and would be absent from England until the end of September. This meant that she would be virtually unchaperoned throughout the whole of her summer holidays. I began marking off the days to July 27th, the last day of term.

During the final week's vigil I busied myself with certain preparations. I bought a wicker chaise-longue, a light, aged armchair, a pair of rugs, an occasional table, and a wall bookshelf, and transported them, piece by piece, up to the Folly.

It was no easy task, for I dared not hire a carrier, not even as far as the point where the path led onto the common, and the transfer of the chaise-longue through acres of brambles from the Foxhayes road to Folly Wood occupied me the whole of one Saturday afternoon. The couch was too long for the spiral staircase, so the evening was spent in hauling it up to the top room of the tower by means of an improvised pulley.

The armchair was easier to carry since I was able to upend it on my head, but its passage from the ground to the tower casement proved hazardous, for it slipped its cradle halfway up and crashed down, almost pulling me after it.

By Sunday of the last weekend before Diana was due, however, I had furnished the tower room to my satisfaction, even adding an oil stove in case we should want to cook and a couple of framed reproductions, one of Botticelli's "Venus Rising from the Sea," and one of Fragonard's "The Swing," both stolen from Uncle Luke's store.

I should have liked to have lit a fire in the broken grate but I was afraid that the chimney would catch fire and someone would see the smoke. The crumbling old room looked cozy enough when I had finished, with a westering sun shafting through the unglazed windows and patterning the plaster walls, and I surveyed it all with quiet pride, reflecting that here was yet another surprise for Diana and one calculated to bring her special delight, for it was she who had suggested furnishing the Folly but had forgotten about it in the turmoil of the Easter holidays.

Once or twice during my comings and goings I caught a glimpse of one or other of Mr. Gayelorde-Sutton's keepers in the paddock behind the larch wood, but never once did I see the buzzards who lived there. It was strange how faithfully they fulfilled Diana's early prophecy concerning their appearance. They never showed up unless we were together.

On the morning of the day she was due to arrive I thought up another surprise, arranging with Uncle Mark's hired man to have the old cob, Justice, brought into the stables for the night and left to await my collection. Diana had written to say that she would arrive late at night and that I was to meet her as usual at the Folly, about seven A.M. the following morning. By six-thirty I was over at Uncle Mark's, had saddled Justice and ridden him over to the meeting place, tethering him under the trees and mounting the stairs in order to watch Diana ride from the wood on Sioux. I knew that Nellie, the pony, was out to grass and that she was very difficult to catch, so I banked on Diana leaving her free until she could bridle Nellie herself. Any horse or pony would come for Diana; she only had to lean on a gate and coo, holding the bridle behind her back.

A few minutes after seven I saw stirrups flash on the edge of the wood and Diana came cantering out of the trees and across the paddock, taking a section of broken rail at a bound and calling softly to the big horse as it loped across the heather to Folly Wood.

She was bareheaded and the sun gleamed in her hair, turning it momentarily from dark chestnut to ash blond. When she was within fifty yards of the tower, Sioux scented Justice and whickered, and from my high vantage point I could detect Diana's surprise as she turned in the saddle and saw the cob tethered to the oak. Then I could wait no longer and pelted down the staircase, risking my neck in a frenzy of joy attributable not only to the pleasure of our reunion but to being abroad in Sennacharib on a warm summer's morning and living in the same world as Emerald Diana Gayelorde-Sutton.

I had some doubts that the endearments in her letters were conventional expressions and that, after the exchange of so many extravagantly romantic phrases, we should both feel shy at the actual moment of meeting. I think I was slightly apprehensive about this despite my excitement, but I need not have been, for the moment I emerged from the tower Diana dropped Sioux's bridle and ran to meet me, her face alight with the same joyful expression as I had noted when we kept our first tryst in Piccadilly.

She was as free of inhibitions as a child at a Christmas treat, throwing her arms around me and kissing me half a dozen times, squeezing my shoulders and laughing as she kissed.

"Jan, Jan, this is wonderful, wonderful!" she exclaimed, when she had paused for breath. "There was I, cursing everybody for not catching Nellie and spoiling our first morning's ride, and you've thought to bring your own horse after all."

"I've got lots of surprises," I told her, "come and see the first of them," and I pulled her up the staircase and proudly displayed the tower room, watching her prance from item to item with more delight than I had dared to hope when toiling through the brambles with that unmanageable chaise-longue.

"It's wonderful!" she announced. "We can come here whenever we like, especially when it rains. You've got pictures, books and a stove . . . we can make tea and fry sausages . . . oh, it's lovely, Jan, and I love you for it!"

Then she kissed me again, more expertly this time, and the world stood still while I let my hand run along the back of her head. The scent of Sennacharib was in her hair and its freshness and sparkle in her eyes. I thought I had never seen anything so enchanting as the sweep of her long eyelashes, or the bloom on her cheeks.

"I'm so terribly in love with you, Diana," I told her breathlessly and she put her lips to my ear and whispered, "Me, too, Jan! Darling, darling Jan! Me too!"

It was strange how swiftly and cruelly the magic of that morning was shattered and how the second of my surprises, the one that I had judged would please her most, was the cause of our first quarrel, a quarrel that, notwithstanding its triviality, was to leave a small scar in my heart that never wholly disappeared.

We returned to the wood and cantered knee to knee over the common as far as the Teasel bridge. As we went along, Diana glanced at me approvingly and I knew that she was noting my vastly improved seat and general management of a horse. Then my vanity urged me to make a false move, how false and ill-advised I could never have guessed, for it was to strike at three things that were fundamental in Diana's nature—her almost hysterical demand for independence, her pride in what she considered the most important of her achievements, and her love of horses.

At the corner of Teasel Wood, where the timber track skirted the northern boundary and ended by cutting across a corner of the covert and out to Uncle Mark's stables, I suggested we should change horses and race the last half mile. I was quite confident of being able to hold Sioux and secretly mortified by Diana's frank expression of doubt on the subject.

"She's very fresh, Jan," she said doubtfully, "and I honestly don't think you'd better."

I had told her nothing of my lessons under Uncle Mark or the fact that I was regularly riding Polly, a mare of sixteen hands and often as much of a handful as the piebald Sioux. I wanted her to discover these things for herself and that was the real reason why I had brought the old cob to the first meeting, for I had planned to appear on Polly the following day.

"Oh come on, let me show you how much I've improved," I argued. "After all, you made me learn to ride, and if you're afraid of your own handiwork . . . !"

"Oh I admire you for wanting to, Jan," she said earnestly, "but I don't want her to run away with you and spoil your confidence and she will, you know, she's got a funny temperament with beginners and after all you *are* still a beginner."

This made me more determined than ever. I slid from Justice and threw her the reins.

"You climb down and I'll show you how much of a beginner I am!" I boasted. "I'll give you a head start and be at Uncle Mark's gate by the time you and that old screw have come into the straight."

"All right, Jan," she said quietly, "but take it easy. Don't touch her with your heels and keep her on a tight rein every inch of the way."

She dismounted and swung up on Justice. I got one foot in the stirrup and then shouted, "Away you go!"

The cob moved off in a collected canter and Sioux, savage at seeing her mistress disappear, bounded after her, so quickly that it was several yards before I could settle myself in the saddle and sort out the double bridle. When I did, and had Sioux well in hand, Diana was about thirty yards ahead, flying down the path and throwing up a screen of dust and chippings in her wake.

Sioux was certainly a flier. I gave her her head and she tore over the ground, overtaking and jostling Justice before we reached the wide curve. I was drunk with pride and as Diana swerved to give Sioux more room I shouted, "Take the brakes off!" and swept past her without consciously noting her unsmiling expression as she crouched to avoid low-hanging foliage on the inside of the path.

I think I managed the horse well enough and rode straight at the fallen spruce that marked the end of the gallop. I cleared it, or nearly so, for there was the slightest jar as I forced Sioux to slacken her pace. We slowed down reluctantly and as we pounded up to Uncle Mark's gate there he was, leaning on folded arms, his big red face a study of delighted astonishment as he saw me bring the big mare to a standstill and leap from the saddle.

"Gor damme!" he exclaimed. "What you got there, Jan? 'Er's a praper job."

At that moment Diana came in view and I could see that she was driving the cob as fast and faster than he could go. When she came to the spruce tree she crashed through it rather than over it and Justice, landing badly, pecked and dug in his forefeet, throwing Diana over his head and into the blackberry bushes alongside the path.

Then I knew terror and ran toward her, shouting, as she rose unsteadily to her feet and picked up her crop. I reached her at a run as she was dusting dried leaves from her jacket, but she did not look at me when I stopped just short of her.

"Good Lord, Diana!" I gasped. "Are you hurt? You came a fearful cropper! I ought to have warned you about the jump but I forgot."

"Yes," she said almost inaudibly, "you ought."

She looked straight at me then and I saw a very different person from the eager, sparkling-eyed girl who had thrown her arms around me less than an hour before. Her eyes were now smoldering with rage and her wide mouth, the mouth that had covered my face with kisses so recently, was clamped into a crooked line, as though it was holding back a howl of vexation and injured pride.

She looked at me like that for a few seconds and I squirmed under the glance, for it had in it not only rage and hurt pride, but the kind of contempt she had used to humble Keeper Croker. Then she brushed past me to the gate and snatched Sioux's bridle from Mark's hand.

On the edge of tears I ran after her and caught her by the arm just as she was passing in front of Sioux preparatory to mounting.

"Diana!" I quavered. "I'm terribly sorry about the jump. I thought I'd—"

I was going to blurt out my excuses, to confess on the spot to the part Uncle Mark had played in my tuition and how much I had wanted to surprise her, but she gave me no opportunity to submit this abject apology. Suddenly she pointed to the small fleck of blood on Sioux's shin. It was nothing much, just a scratch caused by one of the twigs of the spruce.

"You big show-off!" she screamed. "You cruel, stupid, clumsy lout! I never want to set eyes on you again, *never*, do you understand!"

Then, as though to make her meaning doubly clear, she stood back and swung her open palm at my face, landing a box on the ear that sent me staggering. Before I had recovered my balance she was in the saddle, had jerked Sioux's head around and was thundering down the ride toward the common. She cleared the spruce with a foot to spare and I gaped after her, my hand still clamped to my crimson cheek.

Uncle Mark spoke from the gate on which he had continued to lean throughout the entire incident.

"Ah," he murmured, "there's sperrit there. More real sperrit'n I ever zeed in a maid!"

I said nothing. Turning my back on him I went around behind the stables for my bicycle.

Diana was not the only one to show spirit that morning. For nearly a year now I had been completely under her spell and ready, if necessary, to lie down and die for her, but that did not mean I was ready to concede superiority to a fifteen-year-old schoolgirl, even such a girl as Emerald Diana Gayelorde-Sutton. This was my first experience of feminine unpredictability and I had no philosophy to match it. I had been lifted to the heights and cast to the depths in a period of less than an hour, and as I thought back over her behavior it seemed to me to display grossly bad manners and a lunatic's illogicality.

For a time my loyalty to Diana sought excuses for her. I told myself that she had been shaken and scared by the fall, that she had been upset by the graze Sioux had received at the jump, that she had lost the race after a good head start and was mortified by a defeat at the hands of a beginner. None of these reasons, however, justified the humiliation she had imposed on me in the presence of a witness, and my resentment was increased by the memory that my stock with Uncle Mark, a veteran admirer of pretty girls, had been reduced to nil at the very moment when it should have soared, for I had planned to introduce him to Diana with a great show of nonchalance. I pedaled myself into a fury during the ride home, arriving hot, bad-tempered and ready to quarrel with anyone.

As it happened the means for working myself into a tornado of self-pity were to hand at the office, for when I reached there someone was complaining to Uncle Reuben that I had done some careless reporting on a funeral the previous week and inserted the family mourners in the wrong order of precedence, thereby sparking off a family row. This kind of thing was often happening—the Whinmouthians set great store upon precedence in lists of mourners, and we usually had a good laugh about it the moment the indignant customer was halfway down the High Street. Today, however, it seemed to me that the entire world was conspiring to make what had promised to be a wonderful day into a hell of trivial irritation, and instead of apologizing I argued and then told Uncle Reuben, in the hearing of the complainant, that I was fed up with the pettiness of Whinmouth Bay and everybody in it. This was heresy to Reuben and he lost his temper, not only with me but with an unlucky printer's devil who had just upset a frame of type and wasted two hours' setting time. I was glad to escape from the strained atmosphere of the *Observer* and brood on my miseries in private during a walk over to the sports pavilion to get the latest scores of the tennis tournament.

Here, on the well-kept courts adjoining the squat pier, I found fresh fuel for my resentment against humanity. Whinmouth Sports Club organized a very popular open tennis tournament and first-class amateurs came from all parts of the West to take part in it. They were the kind of young people who spent the entire summer traveling from tournament to tournament in sports cars, and today they were a bitter reminder of Diana's class, the pampered children of the rich, who were never expected to earn money but were experts at spending it. I hated the sleek good looks of the girls and the studied heartiness of the men. I envied them their gay blazers and cars, their easy confidence and haughty bearing toward the ball boys and oafs like myself who were obliged to treat them with respect. They drifted about between sets calling one another "old bean" and "old thing." The men drank small whiskies and soda and flirted with the girls, while discussing games in incomprehensible slang.

Somehow the day passed with an interschool sports meeting, a couple of weddings, and a fruitless quest in search of details regarding a street accident. When I came off duty about eight o'clock I was slightly cheered to see that the sky was overcast and hear a rumble of thunder over the bay. That meant the stuffiness of the day would dissolve in one of our heavy local thunderstorms and all the visitors, particularly the tennis amateurs, might get wet! By nine o'clock the storm had burst and rain was slashing across the estuary, while thunder crashed and lightning flickered in a way that exactly suited my mood. I went to bed early, resolved to think out the phrases of a long farewell letter to Diana composed in terms of dignified sorrow. This, I thought, would be more calculated to wound her than would an explosive renunciation of my homage. Before I had made up my mind how to open the letter I was sound asleep.

Something awakened me with a start and I saw that it was almost one A.M. The downpour had ceased and the thunder was rumbling away on the other side of the river but steady rain was coming down and the guide light on the edge of the wharf, opposite my window, was the only relief in the inky blackness of the bay. I lay still listening for a moment and then the sound that must have awakened me came again, a loose rattle on the windowpane, as of sand or fine gravel flung from below.

I was out of bed in a second and had my head out of the window, peering down on the wharf. For a moment I could see nothing, then I detected the vague outline of a solitary figure standing on the edge of the narrow pavement and looking up.

"Jan!" it called, piteously. "Jan, it's me! Diana! Come down and let me in, Jan, I'm soaked!"

It was some seconds before I was able to persuade myself that I was not dreaming. Then, without stopping to put on the old mackintosh that I used for a dressing gown, I grabbed a flashlight and slipped downstairs and along the passage to the front door.

Aunt Thirza was a fanatical bolter and barrer. There was never anything worth stealing inside the house, and Uncle Luke cheerfully relied on a sixpenny padlock to keep thieves out of his store, but his wife went through an elaborate ritual of locking up each night and I knew that I could never open the front door without disturbing the household. I put my mouth to the letter box and directed Diana to go down the passageway to the kitchen door and opened the door leading to the yard. Diana came in dripping and I was still too astonished to utter a word of greeting.

Luckily for her, Aunt Thirza had another idiosyncrasy. She kept the kitchen stove going winter and summer. I turned on the light and stoked the fire, as Diana kicked off her sopping shoes and crouched close to it, extending her hands to the blaze and looking at me with one of her sly, sidelong grins.

"Well," she said, "aren't you going to gloat?"

"What on earth's happened?" I wanted to know. "What made you come down here at this time of night and in all this rain?"

She settled herself in Aunt Thirza's favorite wooden chair. "Conscience, I suppose," she said. "I was going to leave a letter if I hadn't been able to wake you. Look, I've got it ready, but there's no point in your reading it now. This is a much cozier way of confessing, Jan."

"It won't be very cozy if my aunt wakes up," I said. "If she finds me entertaining a girl at one in the morning, there'll be a fearful to-do."

"Where do they sleep, at the front?"

"Yes, in the room immediately over the store."

"I guessed they would, that's why I took the risk of throwing shingle. The awful thing was I wasn't absolutely certain of your bedroom. I was going to slip the letter through the door and bolt if anyone else popped their head out of the window!"

"How the blazes did you get down here at this time of night?"

"I borrowed the head gardener's cycle, it's always propped up against his cottage. I didn't mind that bit, it was fun riding through that deluge, and the lightning over the woods looked ever so pretty. I oughtn't to have liked it really, because coming here and getting so wet was a sort of penance, and you aren't supposed to enjoy penances, are you?"

There was nothing penitential about her. She was as gay and sparkling as the day we had first met and I had a strong conviction that, however abject her mood had been when she started out, the excitement of riding three miles through a thunderstorm, in the middle of the night, had offered more than adequate compensation for the discomfort suffered.

"Let me read the letter you were going to leave," I demanded.

She hesitated and the fleeting smile at the corners of her mouth worked wonders on my bruised spirit.

"Nnno," she said at length, "it's far too abject! I'd sooner tell you what's in it and keep what's left of my pride."

She ripped the sodden envelope in two halves and stuffed it into the coals. Then she turned toward me, put her arms around my neck and laid her wet cheek alongside mine.

"I'm terribly sorry I was so beastly, Jan darling, as sorry as it's possible to be! There, say I'm forgiven!" and she kissed me twice, once on the mouth and once on the forehead.

Her lips were the only warm part of her. When I put my arms on her shoulders I realized that she was soaked through and shivering. Then I suddenly realized I was in pajamas and quickly released her, stepping away so nervously that she threw back her head and laughed aloud.

"Why, Jan, you're blushing! I believe you're still a bit scared of me but I really can't blame you, can I, you surely haven't ever entertained a girl in your pajamas before! If you'd like to slip something on, I won't stop you and maybe you could find something dry for me. I don't want to catch cold and spoil the first week of the holidays."

It was in my mind to say that the holidays were already spoiled for us but then I realized that this was no longer true and that whatever had happened up at Uncle Mark's that morning was more than atoned for by her presence here and her affectionate apology. Then I had another shock, for she returned to the fire, pulled her sweater over her head and swiftly unzipped and stepped out of her short gray skirt. She shed her clothes as easily and naturally as if she were undressing in the privacy of her bedroom. With a start I pulled myself together and told her I would try to find some things she could wear, but I warned her to be as quiet as possible, for Uncle Luke was a light sleeper and would certainly rouse Aunt Thirza if he heard movements about the house.

I crept back to my room and foraged for a pair of corduroy slacks that I had outgrown and a roll-necked pullover that I used when I went swimming before breakfast. I also put on my mackintosh and slippers and on the way downstairs I pulled the chain of the toilet, hoping thus to account for any movement that had already been overheard.

When I re-entered the kitchen she was sitting before the fire wearing only a silk heliotrope slip. Her sweater, skirt, stockings, shoes and beribboned panties were spread on my aunt's clotheshorse.

She enjoyed my obvious embarrassment and smiled when I offered her the slacks and pullover.

"In a minute, Jan, let me get warm first. You wouldn't happen to have a comb handy, I suppose? My hair's in a dreadful state, look at it!"

Her hair was certainly very wet and clung to her cheeks but it looked as pretty as ever, slightly darker than usual but retaining all its luster and vitality. I found her a comb in Aunt Thirza's workbox but when I offered it she said, "You comb it, Jan, I'd like that!"

"You ought to have something hot to drink," I said, looking her over with a tenderness that almost choked me. "I could make some cocoa, provided we got rid of all the evidence afterwards. Would you like cocoa?"

"Yes," she said, "but while it's brewing do my hair."

I put the kettle on the hob and got out the cups, milk, sugar and cocoa can. Then I took the comb and stood behind her chair, letting the damp tresses run lovingly through my fingers. I think it was by far the pleasantest task I was ever engaged upon.

"Now tell me why you came," I said.

"Now I'll tell you why I got in such a tizzy," she replied, leaning back and lifting her long legs onto the fender. "It wasn't really because of the jump, or the graze you gave Sioux, and it wasn't because you beat me and made nonsense of what I said about your being a beginner. All those things had a little to do with it, I suppose, and I was a bit rattled by the fall, but when I had time to think about it I knew what it was that had really upset me. It was your going to someone else to learn and taking away the only real advantage I had over you. Does that sound stupid to a man?"

It did really, for any one of the reasons she had dismissed would have made more sense to me at the time. It was hard to understand why she should have resented Uncle Mark's tuition, or what perverse line of reasoning made her regard her familiarity with horses as a hold over someone whose experiences in that field were so limited.

"You see, Jan," she went on, "the main thing I admire about you is the fact that you stand on your own feet and earn your own living, and the only accomplishment I had to compete with that was my riding, and being able to patronize you when we were together. I had a feeling that it was my handling of horses that impressed you more than anything else, and apart from that it was nice to be able to teach you something that you weren't likely to learn from anyone else. It was a kind of present but better than money, if you like."

The kettle began to steam but I was reluctant to stop combing. I let it simmer for a moment and said:

"Riding is only one of the things I like about you, Diana, and it isn't the most important by a long chalk. I like the way you accept me and take awful risks to be with me and I don't see how anyone in my position could keep from being terribly proud that someone as rich and lovely as you bothers to want me around. That was why I spent so much time at Uncle Mark's, learning to ride properly, and that was why I've been going up to Miss Beddowes' twice a week to learn French and how to speak properly. I don't want you to have to apologize for me wherever we go, and I've never forgotten what you told me over at Castle Ferry, about a person being anything they wanted to be, providing they wanted it hard enough."

"What's this about your learning French?" she demanded. "You never said anything about it this morning."

"It was to be another surprise, like furnishing the Folly and the riding," I said ruefully.

"Tell me about it."

I told her and she listened with the closest attention. When I had finished she reached up and took my hand in both of hers, pressing it down to her small breasts and holding it there. There was absolutely nothing provocative about the gesture. Like all Diana's gestures it was simple, natural and spontaneous. I could feel her heart hammering through the damp slip and the exquisite contact made the stuffy little room swim before me.

"That's the loveliest thing anyone's ever done for me, Jan, and it makes me love you more than ever! I did notice too, about the way you spoke, I mean. I'm not a snob about anything, especially accents, but it is the kind of thing I meant when we talked at Castle Ferry last hols. If speaking without an accent gives you more confidence, then it's right, and I think you were brave and clever to think of it. Say something in French, Jan!"

I said, "To learn French correctly one must think in the language. One must wake up in the morning, go to the window and say, 'Will the sun shine today? Am I hungry? Do I want my breakfast?'"

She squealed with delight, so loudly that I had to shush her.

"Jan, that's marvelous!" she exclaimed. "You've got a better accent than old Flossie, our Mam'selle. Say something else!"

I was so elated by her praise that I forgot all about Aunt Thirza and sang a verse or two I had learned from the phonograph, the opening lines of the inevitable *"Au Claire de Lune."* She looked at me with shining eyes.

"Well, who would have thought it! And you did it for me! Would you do *anything* for me, Jan? Would you?"

There was a kind of teasing ecstasy in the question, as though the contemplation of her power was intoxicating and she wanted to proclaim it.

"I'll make you a nice cup of cocoa and then you'd better put on my things, bundle up your wet clothes and get on home before someone finds us and sends a cable for your people," I told her. I said it casually but I felt very far from casual. The delight of being alone with her in the middle of the night was only slightly held in check by the fear of bringing Aunt Thirza down and having to go into a wealth of humiliating explanatory detail.

We sipped our drink and talked on. She seemed quite unconscious of her state of undress and I don't think that the fact that she was sitting in front of me, clad only in a semitransparent underslip, had any other effect upon me than that of increasing my wonder at her loveliness. Zest for life, and uninhibited enjoyment of the occasion seemed to me to be radiating from her smooth white shoulders and pink toes, and I thought I must have been mad to have felt so bitter and resentful about her a few hours before. Now it was enough to live in the same world; anything additional was a bonus.

About two-thirty we washed up the cups and then crept back into the kitchen to see if her clothes were dry. The stockings and panties were so she slipped them on, laughing when I turned away and saying, gaily, "Poor Jan, I'm always embarrassing you! I wonder if the real Jan blushed the first time he saw Lorna dressing."

"The only thing you and Lorna Doone have in common is the

habit of getting swains into awkward situations," I said, partly in jest but also to mask my shyness.

"And love for our particular Jan!" she said, and suddenly caught up my hand again and pressed it to her cheek, like a child demonstrating affection toward its parent. Then, as suddenly, she let my hand drop and stood away.

"Now, how do I look? Good enough for the road?"

She looked as lithe and supple and feminine as when she was dressed in her own expensive clothes. Even my ill-fitting slacks and grubby jersey could not deprive her of natural grace. We crept across the yard and retrieved the gardener's bicycle from the passageway. I walked with her as far as the end of the quay. The rain had ceased and the cobbled paving stones gleamed under the yellow glow of the guard light.

"Am I quite forgiven, Jan?" she said, as we went along.

"Nothing you could do would ever make me stop loving you," I told her, soberly. "If I never saw you again it wouldn't make any difference to how I've always thought about you!"

She stopped and looked at me across the bicycle. The lamplight shone in her hair, as she put her head on one side and said, "Dear Jan, I think you honestly believe that."

"I do believe it," I said.

"Kiss me good night, then."

We kissed lightly across the machine and then she swung herself onto the saddle with the same easy grace as she displayed mounting a horse. I watched her pedal away toward the High Street, remaining still under the light and listening to the rattle of the mudguard long after she had disappeared. Then, on feet that seemed not to touch the ground, I went home and upstairs to bed.

Chapter Six

I HAVE described this quarrel at length because it marked the very beginning of a subtle change in our relationship.

Up to that time the initiative had always been Diana's. She was the democratic little ladyship, I the adoring swain. Never, during our various meetings, had she gone out of her way to emphasize the social gulf between us, but whenever I reflected upon our friendship I did so with a kind of reverence, as though I were acting in a play in which she was the star and I an insignificant, walking-on character.

After our first quarrel and the midnight scene in our kitchen, the relationship between us altered. I lost none of my admiration for her but my pleasure in her company was no longer qualified by awe. I don't think she was conscious of this change, or of the more important fact that all future adventures and expeditions we shared taught me something new and vital about her.

I have a few special memories of the weeks that followed. My work enabled us to meet almost every day and Diana would occasionally appear at some of the local functions I attended on behalf of the paper.

I would see her waving at me from behind the ropes at an athletic meeting and would hasten over between events to ply her with ice cream and a free program. She would drift into a Methodist Sale of Work, or even the annual general meeting of the National British Women's Total Abstinence Union, taking a seat at the back and waiting for me to finish my work before plying me with questions about the activity I was reporting. She even appeared in the specta-

tor's gallery of the petty sessional court and sat through several tedious hearings, listening with the closest attention to the charges,
evidence and decisions.

I was sufficiently vain to imagine that she attended these local
events in order to see me as much as possible, but I had to admit, as
time went on, that this was not the case. Small-town life was totally
unfamiliar to her and she was the kind of girl who welcomed the
unfamiliar and applied to it an eager, questioning mind. After the
first court session, for instance, she plagued me to explain everything
I knew of the rules of evidence and the difference between indict-
able offenses and offenses that could be disposed of summarily. She
also wanted to learn something of local politics and this led us to the
council chamber, where she was fascinated by the apparent acrimony that existed between our local diehards and the group of business people styling themselves progressives.

Whinmouth Bay was expanding very quickly in those days and in
the vanguard of its advance was a former jobbing builder, now a
hotelier, called Singleton. Already a comparative newcomer like myself could notice changes about the town, evidence of Singleton's
reiterated boast to put Whinmouth on the map.

Through the early part of the twenties his had been a lone voice;
but now, as the first postwar decade drew to a close, he won over a
group of adherents, small businessmen who felt that they stood to
gain by equipping the town to cater for a bigger influx of holiday
makers.

Thus, almost imperceptibly, Whinmouth began to lose its Peg-
gotty qualities. The promenade was extended, neat flower beds and
parking areas began to replace the sand hills, a council estate was
built where the Foxhayes road entered the town, and a rough-hewn
swimming bath took shape in a rocky natural basin east of the jetty.

I witnessed these changes without either resenting or welcoming
them. Uncle Reuben was a progressive and lent the *Observer's*
weight to the business interests. Looking at Whinmouth Bay now,
and remembering what it once was, I have the strongest sympathies
with the old-fashioned councilors, men who fought a rear-guard action to keep the rates low and retain what was left of the town's
salty charm. I remember that Diana was more farsighted than I and
argued strongly against the Singleton group at the time, pointing out
that no amount of money or enterprise could convert our isolated
community into a serious competitor with the big, established resorts

and that we might as well nurse the benefits of that isolation as long as we could.

In this way we managed to see a good deal of one another but there is a curious blank in dating my memories from the first day and night of that summer holiday. I can recall a number of incidents but I can never assemble them in chronological order. Reckoning back, I know that when we met that first morning on the common I was fifteen and a half and Diana had just passed her fifteenth birthday, but from then until prior to her departure for Switzerland, a period of nearly two years, the development of a boy and girl friendship into that of young man and woman is confused and episodic. I am only sure that each highlight in our friendship taught me something new about her, filling a blank space in the picture of Diana that I carried about with me every waking hour. It was like coloring a printed outline in a child's painting book, and the portrait was never wholly completed.

There was the day she asked me to row her over to Nun's Island, the inviting conical rock that broke the surface of Nun's Bay and lay about a mile from the mainland of Sennacharib's coastal border.

I had asked Uncle Reuben to tell me about this islet and about the wreck that had given it its local name. He, in his grave way, had referred me to the files of the *County Press*, where I read all I could learn of the tragedy in which the vessel foundered during the southwesterly gale and all hands save one had been lost.

The grim story intrigued Diana and as we rowed along the coast from Whinmouth and struck out across the bay toward the island, she made me recount every detail. Was it a paddle steamer, like the one Grace Darling went after? How many nuns were drowned? How many crew? Did they find all the bodies? Was there any salvage? Who was the survivor, and what explanation did he give of the calamity?

I told her all I knew, and she was particularly interested in the recovery of the bodies, all but two of the crew having been found during the next few days and buried in a common grave at Whinmouth Churchyard. I had to promise to take her to see this grave and then she wanted to know if the two missing bodies were ever found. I had been saving this as a dramatic climax and told her that they had come to light years later, a pair of clean skeletons, found by Crusoe Jack, the lobsterman who once lived on the islet as a recluse and remained there until comparatively recent times. These two sailors were Negroes, firemen or greasers who had been trapped below when the vessel wedged itself on the rocks, and their skeletons were found after a particularly heavy gale had smashed the remaining timbers of the wreck and uncovered a deep drift of sand between the ridges.

"What happened to them then?" she demanded, her eyes shining with interest.

"Crusoe Jack buried them up near the trees," I told her, nodding to the tiny copse of pine and dwarf oak that crowned the highest part of the island.

"You mean they were actually buried in unconsecrated ground?"

"Well yes, I suppose so. Uncle Reuben told me that Crusoe Jack— he was as crazy as a coot—didn't say anything about finding them for months and then nobody bothered to have them dug up again and examined. I read the adjourned inquest report in the *County Press* and after Jack had described how and where he found them, the coroner said he saw no point in exhuming them and carting them over to the mainland churchyard; it had all happened so long ago."

"Well, I think that's terrible!" exclaimed Diana, to my great surprise. "I think we ought to *do* something about it."

"What on earth can we do?" I protested.

She thought for a moment, biting her lip, and then, as our skiff grounded on the tiny beach about a hundred yards west of the wreck, she jumped into the shallows and ran ashore shouting, "Come and show me the graves, Jan!"

We went up a gully and climbed the knoll to the trees. Apart from a magnificent view there wasn't much to see. The island was about two hundred yards long by a hundred yards wide, and the slopes below the knoll, which boasted some twenty trees, were covered with couch grass and a low, fungus type of scrub. On the southern slope, facing the open sea, was the ruin I recognized as Crusoe Jack's shanty, now nothing but a roofless structure of pine boughs and driftwood, with a stone chimney and a pebbled floor. We poked about for a spell and eventually found the graves or rather grave, for there was a single mound with a cross fashioned from driftwood, now leaning at an angle of forty-five degrees. She stood and stared down at it for so long that my own interest began to wane; I was more eager to inspect what remained of the actual wreck.

"He didn't even carve the names," she said at last. "Good Lord,

Jan, they bury dogs with more dignity and I'll tell you the heart of the matter, it's because they were only black men!"

This aspect of the resumed inquest had not occurred to me and I readily agreed that the lack of ceremony was probably due to the fact that the two men had belonged to some other religion—that, and the lapse of years between the sensation of the wreck and their discovery as a pile of bones. Suddenly she caught me by the arm and I recognized the expression that always heralded some extraordinary and involved plan.

"Can you get off tomorrow evening and bring the boat along as far as the landslip below Nun's Head, Jan? I could meet you there and we could do it. . . . I'll have all the things we shall need and I can ride over on Sioux. I'll hobble her in the meadow, behind the Pilot Inn, and pick her up on the way back."

"Well yes," I told her, quite bewildered, "I could row along and pick you up easily enough but—"

"Don't ask any more questions now, Jan," she said imperatively. "I'm not sure whether I can manage it without help, but I'd like to try and I'd like to do this on my own—all on my own, do you understand?"

She would not explain any further and seemed then to dismiss the fate of the two Negro firemen, dragging me down the gully to the humps that were all that remained of the wreck and pointing out the barnacle-covered frame that had once been the paddle wheel of the vessel. She seemed preoccupied during the pull back to Whinmouth and when we said good-by and she rode off on the gardener's ill-used bicycle, she seemed hardly to be aware of me until I called after her and reminded her of our appointment the following day.

"That's right," she said, "about five o'clock! I'll be here on the beach."

She was, too, a lonely little figure, squatting on a lobster pot, with the great red wall of Nun's Head rising behind her like a backcloth in a pantomime. As I pulled around the rocks and hailed her she jumped up, flourishing what looked like a cross, of the kind Peter the Hermit held in my illustrated volume of *The Crusades*.

"What on earth have you got there?" I asked, noting that she was in a high state of excitement, so much so that she could not wait for me to beach the skiff but dashed into the water and flung herself down in the stern, nearly upsetting us.

"We're going to have a proper burial service," she said. "It's high time it was read, and you're going to officiate! I'd like to do it myself, of course, but as I'm a woman it wouldn't be right; it would seem too much like a joke and this isn't a joke, it's terribly in earnest."

I gaped at her for a moment and then looked more closely at the cross. It was neatly jointed, freshly varnished, and finished off with plain black lettering that read: *Two Unknown Seamen. R.I.P.*

She watched me nervously as I examined it and then, when I looked at her, she began to blush, looking so adorably pretty and confused that my throat went dry and I wanted to fall on my knees before her, kiss her hands and tell her what a lovely, exciting girl she was and how proud I was to act as her partner in such an enterprise.

"Then you . . . you don't think it's silly, do you, Jan?"

"No," I said, truthfully, "I think you're very wonderful to think of it, Diana."

She was pleased with that and we rowed out to the islet in silence, a silence we enjoyed. When we had beached the boat and thrown out the anchor she took my hand and led me along the high-water mark to gather anemones, and then, as the sun touched the rim of the bay and sent a flood of red-hot brass across the water, we climbed the knoll and replaced Crusoe Jack's rotting pole with our cross. I remembered then that I knew barely a word of the burial service and mentioned as much, almost in a whisper. The hush, the solemnity of the act, and Diana's nervous excitement had combined to extinguish the last sparks of frolic from the occasion.

"I've thought of that," she said and from a satchel worn as a shoulder bag she produced a handsomely bound Book of Common Prayer, with the silk marker inserted in Service for the Burial of the Dead.

She placed the anemones at the foot of the cross and then took her place at the foot of the grave, first covering her head with a white scarf and tying the ends under her chin.

"Go on, Jan," she prompted, very gently, "don't be afraid." And when I still hesitated, fumbling with the prayer book: "You needn't think God doesn't approve, I'm sure He does. I'm quite sure He put the whole thing into my head!"

I was grateful for this assurance and at once began to read, clumsily at first but with mounting confidence. I remember shuddering a little when I came to the passage about worms destroying the body, but I cheerfully raised my voice on the cadences of the Ninetieth Psalm. When I had worked through to the piece preceding the final prayer, Diana spoke the responses and our voices rose together in that quiet, lonely place, with only a curious herring gull as an audience. When at length I closed the book and coughed with returning embarrassment, I noticed that her eyes were brimming with tears but I was too near shedding them myself to remark upon the fact. She said, after an awkward pause, "Thank you, Jan dear, you read it quite beautifully," and she took my hand, squeezing it as we walked through the soft sand to the boat.

I lay awake a long time that night pondering what we had done. It seemed to me that the incident had revealed an entirely different Diana from the girl whose exploits included thwarting her mother, tearing about on horses and poking fun at the conventions piled up around her.

It seemed that I had stumbled across a Diana in whom a religious training was something more than a convention, someone who took her recent confirmation seriously, who had an adult sympathy for the friendless and underprivileged, and I wondered if this helped to explain her championship of me when I was in the grip of Keeper Croker's half nelson, or her deep humility after the quarrel we had at the stable. I fell asleep at last, luxuriating in the memory of Diana standing with downcast head, her back to the sea, her white scarf fluttering in the evening breeze, and somehow, in trough of sleep, this endearing memory transformed itself into a picture of Diana standing in her bridal veil before the altar at Oare Church. She was undoubtedly Lorna but I was not conscious of standing beside her as a devoted Jan.

2.

Not all my recollections of Diana's exploits at this period in our lives were as solemn or serene as the latter-day burial service. One particularly is in direct contrast, an uproarious occasion about which I can never think without a chuckle.

This was the intrusion of Alice, the prize sow, into the Conservative Fete held in the grounds of Heronslea, and it revealed to me yet another aspect of Diana, the reckless practical joker, forerunner of the Bright Young Thing who intrigued British newspaper readers a year or so later.

It must have been during the early summer of 1931, when the

country was approaching the financial crisis that unseated Mac-Donald's short-lived government. The Whinmouth constituency was predominantly Conservative and had never returned anyone but a Conservative Member. Our Member at this time was Major Fayne, a terse, soldierly man and, as might be expected, high in favor at Heronslea House where he was a frequent visitor.

Mrs. Gayelorde-Sutton was a very active Conservative. She was president of the Constituency's Women's Association, and organizer of a seasonal succession of Conservative functions, one of which was the annual May Fayre, an ambitious project organized for the dual purpose of raising funds and propagating the gospel according to Stanley Baldwin and Mabel Gayelorde-Sutton.

I attended all these functions as a matter of course and had already acquired the journalist's blasé indifference to politics, regarding them more as a source of copy than the means of advertising a social system under a party banner. It was shortly before the advent of aggressive fascism and fascism's chief exponent at that time, the lamented Benito Mussolini, was regarded as a huge joke by Conservatives, Liberals, and Socialists alike.

As the date for the May Fayre approached, marquees and side-shows sprouted on the broad lawns of Heronslea House, and Diana, together with some of the more socially elevated young locals, were enlisted as usherettes, all the girls being attired in the Quaker uniform of high bodice, gray ankle-length skirt and starched headdress.

Diana did not take kindly to this form of regimentation and the fuss, the uniform, and the inroads these events made into her freedom had already colored her political outlook.

"It's absolutely daft!" she complained to me, the evening before the Fayre, when I had slipped over to Heronslea on the pretext of getting advance data. "Quakers and Puritans weren't Conservatives, were they? They lopped poor old Charles' head off, didn't they? And a good job too, if he was anything like Major Fayne and all the old hens who cackle around him up here. Talk, talk, talk, all about what's happening to their filthy money! As if that was the only thing that mattered to the country! You aren't a Conservative, are you, Jan? I shall loathe you if you say you are!"

I said I supposed that I was a Liberal, like my Uncle Reuben, but she declared that she was going to vote Red when she was twenty-one and that what was needed anyway in Parliament were lots more women who would not be so beastly careful of their dignity. By this I inferred that Diana inclined to the Left because her mother was so staunchly Right.

"If they must put us in fancy dress," she went on, "we ought to look like orange girls, at the time of Nell Gwyn, you know—something off the shoulder, to get the men to buy more programs and draw tickets and suchlike!" She looked despairingly at the array of tents and stalls that had transformed the broad sweep between the terrace and the Shepherdshey road into a genteel fairground. "Well," she added, "I'm praying for rain. That'll put the kibosh on everything!"

"It rained last year," I told her, "but they all crowded into the marquee to hear the Member's address. You couldn't breathe in there and Uncle Reuben said they didn't give him elbow room to write notes."

At the thought of a damp and dripping fiasco she cheered a little. "Come and say hello to Alice," she invited, and when I inquired into the identity of Alice, she told me that Alice was the Heronslea prize sow who, together with a lusty litter, was being offered by Mrs. Gayelorde-Sutton for the fete skittle prize.

Alice was the kind of prize that only Mrs. Gayelorde-Sutton would offer. She was undoubtedly the largest pig in the West. Penned in a temporary sty under the avenue beeches, she lumbered to and fro like a malevolent dinosaur, herding her squealing litter out of range of Diana's bamboo cane and grunting maledictions on those who had transferred her from a comfortable paddock sty to a few square yards of unfamiliar enclosure.

"I love pigs," said Diana, dreamily, "they're so gloriously antisocial. She's very unhappy in there. Do you think we could let her out and give her a bit of a root around under the trees?"

"No jolly fear," I told her. "You leave her where she is! She looks a killer to me and if she got loose there would be hell to pay and I'd be sure to get mixed up in it somehow."

"Well," said Diana, "I'll tell you what, the minute old Pumpjaw"—this was Diana's pet name for the Honorable and Gallant Gentleman representing Whinmouth—"pauses for breath, and all the other old pumpkins on the platform start billing and cooing, you nip out to the old coach house. I'll meet you there with some choice refreshments and wine. The only thing good about this show-off is the grub, it's going to be scrumptious!"

I promised to keep the appointment and went about my business.

The following morning a glance at the sky told me that Diana's prayers were about to be answered. By midday the rain had begun to fall, lightly at first but very heavily by midafternoon, the time fixed for the Member's address. Provision had been made for this contingency and everyone crowded into the vast marquee. By the time Major Fayne had got under way the heat inside the tent was suffocating, the sour smell of wet canvas and crushed grass combining with that emanating from the clothes of three hundred damp constituents, packed on benches each side of a narrow gangway.

I was wedged under the platform and not unhappily situated, for there was an exit flap within a few yards of me and a current of air kept the people on the platform awake throughout the long-winded address. The people farther back, however, began to get restive as Major Fayne swam through a sea of Socialist disasters toward the global trouble spot in Manchuria, and thence to the value of the pound. He was about to inveigh against Snowden's monetary policy when there was a ripple of laughter at the back of the tent, followed by a volley of startled exclamations and then two individual screams, as loud and piercing as those of a radio heroine.

Major Fayne stopped speaking but remained standing, his overworked jaws agape, his slightly poppy eyes fixed on the scene of mounting confusion at the extreme end of the long marquee. Then Mrs. Gayelorde-Sutton jumped up and shouted something and after that there was a sudden scramble on the part of the platform party to climb down and head for the exit.

As they all tried to do this in unison, and because the trestle platform was high and there was only a single pair of steps, the result was a confused struggle just above my head. A row of potted hydrangeas broke away from their fastenings and fell onto the press table, scattering mold over myself and the *County Press* reporter and adding to the general tumult. Mrs. Gayelorde-Sutton rushed past me as I was picking myself up and I saw that her face was white with rage.

I hurried after her toward the flap but the platform contingent had now reached level ground and was trying to charge the exit in a body.

Major Fayne fell headlong over the taut guy rope and somebody, with more loyalty than sense, stooped to pick him up, so that others fell and I was turned back into the rapidly emptying body of the marquee and the heart of a scene of wildest confusion. It was like an illustration from an improbable book of Irish country life. Alice's litter was advancing rapidly up the narrow aisle between the close-packed seats; a yard or so behind, grunting and snorting like a mad elephant, came Alice herself. Behind Alice dodged two of the Heronslea estate workers, armed with goads, both screaming directions at one another and obviously out of touch with a deteriorating situation.

The constituents, mad with fear, were scrambling out of the marquee in every direction, the majority diving under the side curtains, others battling their way to the open flap behind Alice's cautious pursuers. As I watched, aghast at the shambles, the marquee emptied like a tube and Alice followed her squealing litter out through the platform exit.

I was too shocked to see the funny side of the incident and after gathering up my notebook I went into the open and pushed through the chattering, gesticulating Mayfayrers to the coach house. Inside, weeping with laughter, was Diana, and I knew at once that she had been responsible for the appearance of Alice at the meeting.

It was some minutes before she could speak.

"Oh Lord! Oh Heaven! Did you see it? Were you there? Did you see the laughter turn to terror the minute Alice showed up in pursuit of the babies?"

I had to laugh too, but the reflection of what might have resulted from such a reckless practical joke sobered me almost at once.

"It was a crazy thing to do, Diana," I protested. "Supposing she'd savaged someone? Supposing there had been a real panic and people had got trampled?" Then my journalistic curiosity prompted me. "How on earth did you manage it, anyway, and how do you know you won't get found out? Your mother would half kill you for this, it'll make her a laughingstock all over the county!"

"If I tell will you swear to keep mum—for ever and ever?"

"Yes, of course."

"Even though you're a reporter?"

"You don't imagine I'd sneak on you, do you?"

She stopped laughing then and looked at me with her teasing, half-mocking expression, eyes half-closed, head inclined to one side.

"Dear Jan," she murmured, "it's very flattering to have a newshawk like you put love before duty." Then, seeing my face cloud, as it usually did when she made fun of me, she put both hands on my shoulder, kissed me on the cheek and told me how she had waited until everyone except the Heronslea staff was inside the tent and then let her horse Sioux out of the paddock to graze among the stalls.

"I knew anyone who was around would try to catch Sioux before she bumped into anything, and you know how difficult she is to halter if I'm not about. Well, it worked just as I knew it would. They all went after Sioux, who cantered around behind the house, and when they were out of the way I drove Alice's litter toward some meal I had scattered outside the marquee. When they were nicely clustered there I let Alice out, knowing that she'd make straight for them and that some of them would trot into the tent. I didn't bargain for such a complete uproar, though! The people at the back were ever so glad to see the piglets, because they were so bored, but they all lost their heads when Alice appeared. Don't worry, Jan," she added, seeing that I still looked harassed, "I let her loose for a bit last night and the estate hands think the pen was insecure. I won't get into trouble over it."

"*They* might!" I grumbled, remembering Mrs. Gayelorde-Sutton's savage expression during the scramble for the exit.

"Oh no," she said calmly, opening a basket and offering me savory pies and sandwiches, "I thought of that! I warned Mummy last night that Johnson, the pigman, thought that Alice ought to go back to her sty on the day but she pooh-poohed the idea and told me to tell Johnson to leave Alice where she was. She always knows all the answers, you see, and this might help her to learn to listen to someone else for a change! Here, have some pâté, it's good, and open this bottle of hock I pinched for us. I brought a corkscrew."

I took the bottle and drew the cork, my misgivings less than half resolved by her assurances.

"All the same, I bet there'll be repercussions," I said gloomily, and, as always where Diana's family was concerned, my pessimism was justified. Mrs. Gayelorde-Sutton's counteroffensive opened the following Saturday, and I narrowly missed becoming its first victim.

Uncle Reuben always stayed in the office on Saturday morning, mainly for the purpose of hearing complaints. We could always rely on a steady stream of irate readers each Saturday, people whose names had been omitted or misspelled in a sale-of-work notice, or the principal mourners I have already mentioned, whose claims to precedence had been jumped by mere in-laws in a funeral report.

Uncle Reuben never lost his temper with these idiots and nearly all of them were soothed by his bland explanations. I was engaged in plotting next week's tide table when the door flew open and in stormed Mrs. Gayelorde-Sutton, with her big-headed husband in silent tow and everything about them promising a brisk engagement. She flourished a copy of our paper under my nose but I wasn't unduly worried by that, because we had carried a straight report of the incident and there was nothing in it that had not appeared in the *County Press* on the previous day. Uncle Reuben offered her a chair but she refused it, demanding to know the identity of the reporter who claimed to have witnessed the appearance of Alice into the marquee. When Uncle Reuben gravely indicated me she whipped a small newspaper cutting from her handbag and pushed this under my nose.

"Then Ai suppose Ai have yew to thank for this!" she shrilled.

Before I could protest, Uncle Reuben relieved her of the cutting and glanced at it briefly. It was a piece written by the columnist of a London Socialist weekly, in which the writer had made use of the advantages to be derived from the preoccupation of ex-Premier Baldwin with pig breeding. It was a heavy little gibe, beginning:

> We are interested to hear that Stanley Baldwin's interest in pigs has spread to his backbenchers and that one of them, the Honourable and Gallant Member for a West Country Constituency, is now more Catholic than the Pope, inasmuch as he actually invites pigs to his public meetings. . . .

There was a crude cartoon clipped to the extract, the drawing portraying the Whinmouth Member and a hawk-visaged supporter (who might or might not have been a caricature of Mrs. Gayelorde-Sutton herself) standing on a platform and addressing a row of attentive pigs. It was entitled "Pigs in Clover."

I was wondering how Mrs. Gayelorde-Sutton came to connect our little paper with the report and cartoon but her next declaration solved the mystery.

"There were only two pressmen acktually present in the marquee," she wailed, "and one of them was *thet* boy! Now Ai've been assured by the *County Press*—a respectable Conservative organ, I might add—thet they had no contact with the London papers as a whole, or this scurrilous publication in particulah!"

"And what makes you think it originated from us?" asked Uncle Reuben, innocently.

For a moment Mrs. Gayelorde-Sutton seemed disconcerted, then she rallied and did her best to intimidate him with her hard blue eyes.

"You *must* hev!" she said. "How else would they have heard of it?"

Uncle Reuben regarded her sadly. I have never admired him so much as I did on that occasion, for somehow he made a reality of the vaunted majesty of the British press, standing, as it were, four-square as the champion of free speech from Paine and Cobden onwards.

"Mrs. Gayelorde-Sutton," he said, consciously inserting a heavy sigh into his voice, "this incident actually occurred and was faithfully and fairly reported in two West Country papers. Copies of those papers have since been mailed all over the world and their contents, I don't doubt, have since been read and digested by journalists of every political creed and shade of opinion. There is nothing, so far as I am aware, to prevent any such journalist using this factual base as the skeleton of a partisan gibe at you and your party. We can hardly be held responsible for the use made of our straight reporting in any corner of the globe!"

It was a dignified rebuke, magnificently delivered, for somehow it conjured up the picture of the arrival of a bundle of *Whinmouth & District Observers* on the busy quays of Hong Kong or the railway sidings of Chicago, where hordes of white, black and yellow journalists were queueing to seize and comment upon the intrusion of a fat sow into a marquee full of Whinmouth Conservatives. It absolved us from all consequences of their several interpretations, at the same time elevating us to Olympian isolation, alongside the shades of W. T. Stead and the late Lord Northcliffe. Its effect upon Mrs. Gayelorde-Sutton, however, was less salutory than upon her hitherto silent husband, who rose, a little stiffly, and laid a restraining hand upon his wife's glove, addressing her in a thin, nasal voice that I now heard for the first time.

"Come, come, my dear," he said, quietly but not meekly, "you've had your say and you've got your answer! Go back to the car while I have a private word with the editor."

To my intense surprise she obeyed him. Without a word of protest she swung round on her stiletto heels and clacked out of the office, leaving behind her a pleasing aroma of perfume to join hopeless battle with the reek of dust, printer's ink, moldering newspapers and Uncle Reuben's semilethal tobacco.

"Well, sir?" demanded Uncle Reuben, his tone hardening now that he found himself addressing a member of his own sex. "I trust you are satisfied with my explanation? Not that I am under any obligation at all to offer you one, even supposing it was I myself who had telephoned Fleet Street. This is fair comment, you understand? Nothing libelous *there,* so don't waste time and money on lawyers!"

It occurred to me that this little speech was a bit highhanded, but Mr. Gayelorde-Sutton did not resent the advice. He just stood blinking heavy-lidded eyes, his head looking more and more like a pink egg balanced on the extreme end of a collared cabbage stalk.

"My wife is naturally upset," he said very civilly. "She feels that this unfortunate incident has been magnified into something calculated to make her a laughingstock among her friends. I did point out before she called, however, that the local press could not be held responsible and I feel your explanation is a fair and an honest one, sir. I would, in passing, like to proffer my apologies to this young gentleman, who might have made a good deal more capital of the occasion than in fact he did, yet still acted within his rights as a er . . . gentleman of the press! Good day, sir, and thank you for your courtesy."

He left us then and Uncle Reuben looked after him sympathetically. I felt a little dizzy, partly with relief but also with elation, for up until then I had never taken Gayelorde-Sutton into consideration as a man or the father of Diana. He had been a mere symbol of wealth, and a caricature of one at that. I had never forgotten his pitiful appearance at the Heronslea meet on Boxing Day. Diana hardly ever mentioned him and I suppose I had already written him off in my mind as a henpecked nonentity. I saw now that he was more than that and I was now able to regard him if not as an ally, at least as neutral in the conquest of Diana. A man like that, I reasoned, would at least be fair-minded about his daughter's choice of a husband.

I could hardly wait to recount the scene to Diana and when I saw her at the Folly that same evening I was deflated by the discovery that she not only knew all the essentials of the interview but had, in a sense, engineered her father's attitude by taking him on one side and pointing out that Mrs. Gayelorde-Sutton's attack upon a local paper would only injure the cause of the Conservatives in the district. I was warmed, however, by her comment upon an aspect of the matter that had not even entered my head—my honoring of the promise I had given her to keep her part in the matter a close secret.

"I wouldn't have blamed you if you'd blurted out the truth, Jan," she said. "After all, I don't see why you should get a rap over the knuckles for something I did and I don't mind saying I had the wind up a bit when I heard that Mother intended storming into your place about it. You see, for all I knew, it was you who had sent the piece to London!"

It saddened me to reflect that she could even contemplate a betrayal of confidence on my part, to say nothing of presumed willingness on my part to see her family ridiculed. When I told her this she laughed and gave me one of her side-tilted looks.

"You're a real old-fashioned one, Jan! I believe you're a masochist and would enjoy dying for me. I believe it would give you no end of a kick. What is it, Jan? I'm not beautiful and sometimes I'm not very nice to you. I'm not going to pretend that I don't *like* having a true-and-gentle-knight, and I'll always come back to you in the end, you can be quite sure of *that*, but—"

She broke off, as though suddenly deciding she had said enough on the subject. I was far from satisfied, however, and pressed her to say whatever she had begun to say. This brought an obstinate expression to her face.

"It doesn't matter," she said, pettishly. "I'm not in the mood to say it right now and I won't!"

Earlier in our association I should have pressed for an explanation but I was learning very quickly about Diana, and took the hint. It was never the slightest good goading her into explaining anything. Her mother had followed that course throughout her childhood and all she had earned by it was resentment that came close to hatred. We let the subject drop there and then, and whenever we touched on it in the future we did so in a mood of hilarity.

3.

The next glimpse I had of a hidden facet in Diana's character was afforded by a trivial incident that took place at the Whinmouth Fancy Dress Parade.

[146

One of the annual events on my calendar was the Whinmouth Winter Carnival, a week of local entertainment sponsored by a veteran committee and aimed at popularizing the town and raising money for the Cottage Hospital and St. John Ambulance Association.

Few British annuals are as profitless as the seaside carnival, and our local affair was no better and no worse than the average small-town carnival. The Englishman is fundamentally devoid of carnival spirit and even if a sense of civic duty, and frequent draughts of alcohol, induce him to don a paper hat and prance about his familiar streets, the weather is usually at odds with the forlorn strings of bunting and determined good cheer.

Our event was organized by tradesmen who were prevented from staging a summer carnival by the demands of their businesses during the period, May to September. Thus the carnival was always held in the third week of October and had to compete with the autumn gales, as well as the national distaste for public enjoyment.

The torchlight procession of tableaux was usually a spectacular affair, providing the rain held off, but somehow the carnival, as a carnival, could never divest itself of its overcoat. The only weather-proof event of any size was the Baby Show and Children's Fancy Dress Parade, both held in the Church Hall, in Fish Street.

I was very busy throughout this event, collecting the names of countless Bo-Peeps and Jack Horners. I had, indeed, been busy throughout the week, so much so that I had overlooked the fact that Mrs. Gayelorde-Sutton, in her role of local patroness, had agreed to preside over the panel of judges for the children's parade. I did not remember this interesting fact until I arrived at the hall for the final selection of prize winners.

The children had been divided into various age groups and there were prizes for the first boy and first girl in each class. The organizers, however, had overlooked the dire need for consolation prizes, and as some of the mothers had gone to very considerable trouble to dress the competitors the stewards were faced with the problem of coping with a dozen or so bitterly disappointed finalists in each group.

We were accustomed to trouble with the Baby Show mothers, and the acrimony among the parents grouped at the far end of the hall after the judges had made their final selections was always regarded as something of a joke among Whinmouth tradesmen. Invariably there were threats that children who had failed to win a prize would not be called upon to face humiliation the following year, but nobody took these threats seriously. Each year the number of competitors increased and the two events were enormously popular, over a hundred children entering the parade in costumes that made judging a difficult task.

Not that its demands worried Mrs. Gayelorde-Sutton. She sat on the dais like an Ice Queen, flanked by a self-effacing Chairman of Council and his even more self-effacing wife. Neither of these worthies had the slightest say in the selections. Deftly and mercilessly Mrs. Gayelorde-Sutton sifted the grain from the chaff. When she had made up her mind she beckoned the winner and extended the palm of her hand to the rejects. The latter gesture was exactly like the Phoenicians' rejection of Celtic furs, in the famous picture dealing with early British trade.

It may have been her regal manner, or it may have been the fact that this year's competitors included a larger sprinkling of intractable children that caused this year's six-to-eight class for girls to develop into a scene of lamentation. Rejects were required to move away from the dais as soon as they had been judged and pass behind the stage and through to the dressing rooms. The hall was packed and spectators were sitting in the aisles, so that there was no way in which the spurned Maid Marians and Columbines could fly to their mothers for comfort. They had either to move around behind the stage or stand blubbering under the eyes of the judges.

There were, as I remember, nine rejects in this class, two others having been warned to stand by for the grand parade while the judges passed on to the nine-to-eleven class.

The trouble began when one little girl, dressed in sacking meant to represent the tatters of a scarecrow, burst into tears the moment she realized that she was not a prize winner and then made an unsuccessful dash for the phalanx of spectators.

She was headed off by a grinning steward and the event caused a titter, but the laughter died under the volume of howls touched off among the other rejects. In a few seconds eight children were screaming their heads off and Mrs. Gayelorde-Sutton, more than equal to the occasion, began to strike a compeer's gong and shout, "Cleah the areah! Ai can't continue while *thet's* going on!"

Mrs. Gayelorde-Sutton intimidated most people. Two of the stewards leaped forward to shoo the wailing children into the dressing room, but none would willingly be removed, so the most active steward tucked one child under each arm and tried to shepherd the others with his knees.

At this juncture several indignant mothers jumped up from the body of the hall and began to contribute to the outcry. Mrs. Gayelorde-Sutton sullenly continued to beat her gong, and the laden steward shouted for help.

It arrived from an unexpected quarter. At the height of the uproar Diana swept from the dressing-room arch, lifted the squealing scarecrow, placed a fairy doll almost as large as the child in her arms, pointed to the arch through which she had moved, and then held up seven fingers!

The action was so expertly timed and so deftly executed that all the children, including the two held by the perspiring steward, ceased their squalls and gazed ecstatically from Diana to the doll and then back to Diana again.

Mrs. Gayelorde-Sutton stopped beating the drum and stared bleakly down on her daughter but the audience cheered, as well they might. I remained staring at Diana as she gathered the children in a bunch and swept them into the rooms behind the stage.

It all happened with the speed of a dream sequence. When I had recovered from my surprise I sidled away from the stewards' table and went into the dressing rooms, but inside I stopped short near the door, looking in upon another extraordinary sight. There was Diana, surrounded by children, each of them squealing with delight as she placed a large package in each pair of upraised arms. Scarecrow was seated at her feet, crowing over the fairy doll.

Another child, wearing a ballerina's frock from which most of the tinsel was missing, was nursing a huge Dutch doll. A third child had just torn the wrappings from a cardboard box and found an exquisite doll's set, in blue and gold china. Each of the others had an expensive-looking gift of one sort or another and Diana was exercising complete control over the brood. There were no bickerings, no displays of greed, just a rhapsodic harmony that recalled the visit of Mrs. Do-As-You-Would-Be-Done-By to Kingsley's water babies. It was as though some other and infinitely mature being had taken possession of Diana and appeared miraculously to arbitrate among us lesser mortals, as though she had suddenly burst from the chrysalis of adolescence and become a patient, tender woman, with a vast experience in the art of handling small children. They looked up at her as though she were a goddess sent to extricate them from an intolerable situation and when I drifted into the room not one of them noticed me, or lifted their eyes from Diana.

I don't think I have ever been as moved, or as genuinely surprised, as I was at that moment, but when Diana greeted me she did not appear to regard her situation as anything other than commonplace. She said, very offhandedly, "Oh, hello, Jan! I rather hoped you'd pop in; go out to the car and help Redman to bring in the rest of the boxes. I think there will be enough to go around."

Mutely I did as she asked. Outside in the forecourt the Bentley was parked and Redman, the aloof chauffeur who had driven me home that first autumn evening, was unloading crates of toys from the back of the car. Together we carried the boxes through the stage door, and as we unpacked them I noticed that here and there was a toy from which paint had been chipped.

"Are these all yours?" I asked Diana. "I mean, you didn't buy them specially, did you? They aren't carnival consolation prizes, are they?"

"Good Lord, no," she said, impatiently, "as if those clots would ever dream up a consolation prize for the poor little toads! I came here with Mother and when she was judging the toddlers before the tea interval I saw what happened, so I nipped out and made Redman take me home for a good old rummage in the playroom. I was never very hard on my toys, Jan. To tell you the honest truth, I didn't go for them very much. I always preferred ponies!"

She began distributing gifts to the next lot of rejects, who came hurrying in from the main hall. Apparently word had got around among the losers that they were in for a far better deal than the prize winners; soon every dressing room was crammed with delighted children. I had a quick look at some of the gifts. The least of them must have cost someone a pound note and some were absurdly expensive-looking—tortoise-shell dressing-table sets, dancing shoes, party frocks, a mother-of-pearl Alice band, set in imitation pearls, books still in their cellophane wrappings, teddy bears, golliwogs, and every other kind of toy and trinket. The bounty represented the Christmas and birthday yield of Diana's entire childhood and it was just as she said, she had not been hard on her presents. Most of them appeared hardly to have been unwrapped.

I waited around until the judging was over. I ought to have gone back into the hall and collected the rest of the winners but I had lost interest in the contests. The music began to play and the children were rounded up by stewards for the grand parade. Only the little girl with the Dutch doll remained behind, tugging Diana's pleated skirt. She had an alien accent, placing her somewhere around Hoxton. Diana told me she was Keeper Croker's daughter.

"Please, miss, 'is eye's aht!" she stated, not unhappily but as one who states a simple fact.

Diana stooped and cocked her head at the one-eyed Dutchman.

"Ah, but it's *meant* to be out, Susan! You see, he lost it in the war, fighting the wicked Germans, didn't you, Hans?" And she lifted the doll close to her ear, paused and nodded thoughtfully, before restoring the doll to the child.

"He says he's glad you've got him, Susan, because nobody else wanted him with only one eye! You'll take care of him now that I'm grown up, won't you?"

The child looked very closely at Hans and nodded, emphatically. It crossed my mind, idiotically perhaps, whether she would still possess the doll when she was old enough to learn that Holland had passed the World War as a neutral. Then the thought was lost in wonder at the assurance and maturity of a girl whom I had always thought of as a high-spirited tomboy, with a penchant for getting in and out of scrapes.

"You're absolutely marvelous with them, Di," I said, as Susan Croker trotted after the others.

"Oh, I like kids," said Diana, yawning. "They don't pretend like all those jackasses in there. Do you have to go back? Couldn't we go and see your printing works? I've never seen them, you know, and you promised me years ago!"

"All right, Di," I said quietly. At that moment I would have taken her to Samarkand or Delhi if she had asked me.

We went along Fish Street and into our squalid little office, empty at this time, for Uncle Reuben was on the committee and the printing staff was working on the tableaux we had entered in the Trades Section. As we stood beside the old flatbed I suddenly put my arm around her shoulder, pulled her toward me and kissed her hair. It was only the second of our embraces in which I had taken the initiative and I think it startled her, so that she had to turn it aside with a little joke.

"Say it with printer's ink!" she said, but she found and squeezed my hand hard. I went out into the street feeling like a man who has stumbled upon the lost treasure of the Incas.

Up to this time—that is, until the summer preceding my eighteenth birthday—I was untroubled by active jealousy. Diana was at school for eight months of the year and during the holidays she was mine almost exclusively, for her parents spent a great deal of their time abroad or in London and only used Heronslea for holidays or special occasions, such as the Conservative May Fayre, when they came down for the weekend.

I was still vaguely suspicious of the French boy, Yves, but he and his family came to Heronslea only very occasionally and Diana had few contacts with local families. She wrote to me regularly when she was at school and the moment she came home we picked up the threads of our association without any trouble. I was always conscious of a threat to our friendship in the person of her mother and I never quite lost the dread of an open challenge from this quarter, but she had conditioned the staff at Heronslea to her erratic and unpredictable programs during the holidays and we were thus often able to spend whole days together in Sennacharib without anyone except dear old Drip being aware of our association.

It seemed to me then that this happy state of affairs might continue indefinitely. It never once occurred to me that sooner or later some other young man, with far greater social advantages than I possessed, would notice that, in addition to being the most eligible girl in the district, Diana was also one of the prettiest.

If I had thought about this at all I should have been alarmed at the prospect of some matchmaking mother entering the field on behalf of her son. At this time, when she was sixteen, she retained all the elfin prettiness of adolescence. Her blue eyes usually held in them a glint of mischief, her heavy chestnut hair was always untidy but its texture was smooth and fine and when the sunlight struck it, or she tossed it back to laugh or exclaim, a shower of stardust seemed to explode in your face. Her skin was smooth and pale, and no amount of sunshine would give her face an outdoor tan. Her ears were unusually small, white and flat, almost as if they had been overlooked and planted there as the afterthought of an affectionate creator. Her mouth was ripe and usually smiling, its broad curve matching the fun-sparkle in her eyes, and it was a mouth that always appeared to be on the point of uttering a gay observation, something of no consequence perhaps but expressing the simple pleasure of being alive.

If you looked only at her face she did not impress you as being more than a pretty and intelligent child, but it was otherwise with her figure, which excessive horseback exercise had prematurely developed. Her shoulders were braced and trim and her bust already that of a grown woman. Her narrow waist accentuated muscular hips and long, perfectly shaped legs, but she was vain only regarding her beautiful hands. They were certainly very shapely hands, with long, slender fingers and perfectly shaped nails. I never saw her ride or row without gloves.

"They're like Queen Elizabeth's," she once told me, with a laugh, and when I challenged this (after carefully studying a Holbein print, in one of Uncle Luke's illustrated *World Masterpieces* she added, "Oh, I mean the hands on Elizabeth's tomb, in Westminster Abbey! They're supposed to be the most perfect pair of hands ever carved in stone."

I was suddenly made aware of opposition in the field toward the end of the summer holidays about a month after the fiasco at the Heronslea fete. All the wealthy local families had attended the fete and among them were the Brett-Hawkins clan, a flock of gentlemen farmers, all interrelated, who held large farms and a communal shoot over in the Brackenhayes country, some five miles beyond Teasel Wood.

The acknowledged chieftain of this yeoman family was Colonel Brett-Hawkins, V.C., a hearty, professional soldier, with an active interest in dairy farming and cattle breeding. He owned a large herd of Guernseys and was always winning prizes at the county shows. He also had a trio of tall, broad-shouldered sons, all at Repton or University, and I first noticed the youngest of these, Gerald, when he had distinguished himself at a local gymkhana. As a matter of fact it was Diana who pointed him out to me and told me that he was leaving school to attend an agricultural college and train to take over his father's farms. I didn't pay much attention to him until I attended a Point-to-Point meeting in the area, and noticed that he was riding Diana's bay mare, Sioux. I had looked forward to the meeting and discussed it with Diana, so that it struck me as odd and disquieting that she had not mentioned to me that she was entering Sioux in the local hunter class. When I challenged her after the race

(I was delighted to witness Gerald Brett-Hawkins fall on his hat at the last fence but one!) she was irritatingly casual about it.

"Didn't I tell you? I'm sorry, I must have forgotten. It was a last-minute arrangement anyhow, as Lance Fayne was down to ride her but funked at the last moment."

Lance Fayne was the only son of Major Fayne, the M.P., and I knew him as a frequent visitor to Heronslea. He had squired Diana on the occasion of his sister's twenty-first birthday party but I had never regarded him as a serious competitor because his physical disadvantages canceled out his social qualifications. He was small, thin and undistinguished, a tough and determined rider to hounds, but so narrow-faced and foxy that it was ridiculous to imagine Diana would ever want to be kissed by him.

Gerald Brett-Hawkins, however, was a much more serious challenger. He was an inch or so taller than I and possessed florid good looks, of the type Diana would classify "dago." He had, in addition, an air of aggressive self-confidence, as I soon discovered when Diana introduced me to him in the car park, where she was drinking claret and nibbling chicken in aspic with her jockey's boisterous family. I had seen her go there and was hanging about impatiently, hoping that she would leave them and rejoin me, when she called me over.

"I say, Jan! This is Gerald . . . did you see him come a frightful cropper down there by the brook? Gerald, this is an old friend of mine, Jan Leigh. He's a journalist and he'll describe the lovely figure you cut, somersaulting over the bank!"

We shook hands and he gave me a single, bleak look. I could see that he deprecated Diana's readiness to introduce us, for his quick glance took in my cheap lounge suit and the fact that I was not wearing riding clothes or sporting tweeds. The word "journalist," however, made him pause.

"Really? What paper?"

"The *Whinmouth Observer*," I muttered, flushing.

He dropped my hand as though it had been a soiled dishcloth and resumed his talk with Diana about her mare's propensity to sweat as soon as she came in contact with other horses.

I stood about awkwardly for a moment or two and then left, mumbling something about having to collect the results of the last race for the paper.

Nobody heard my excuse and nobody looked after me when I moved away. I mooched down to the paddock sick with rage, for it seemed to me utterly unfair that I should have to compete with someone like Gerald Brett-Hawkins, a boy with the terrifying advantages of a public school education, good looks, a powerful physique, well-cut clothes, money and, what was more valuable than all these things put together, a background that gave him complete poise in the company of his equals and an ability to dismiss people like me with a limp handshake. I was glad that he had fallen so heavily and wished heartily that he had fractured his arrogant skull. The feelings of dismay he stirred in me that afternoon, however, were insignificant compared with the alarm I experienced when Diana told me that he was taking her to the Point-to-Point dance, at Swanley Lock Hotel on the following Tuesday.

"With him? With that lout?" I exclaimed. "Why, he can't even manage Sioux! What can you see in a chap like that?"

She looked at me levelly. She had a way of making you feel very small when you lost your temper. I never saw Diana lose her temper over a trivial issue; she reserved all her fire for targets that she could hardly miss.

"I don't 'see' anything in him, Jan," she replied, quietly. "He's a good dancer and he's good-looking but he's not my type. He's the kind of man who would always try to keep-the-little-woman-in-her-place, and you ought to know by this time that I'm not the kind of a girl who wants to be mastered."

This was a subtle dig at my challenge to her freedom of choice but it brought with it a crumb of comfort. I only had to think about it for a moment to realize that Diana and Gerald Brett-Hawkins would quarrel bitterly after an hour or so in one another's company, so long as they weren't distracted by noise and movement.

"All the same, that isn't true about his riding," Diana went on. "Sioux is too excitable for a Point-to-Pointer and neither you nor I would have got her as far around the course as Gerald did!"

This was true, of course, but I continued to sulk and Gerald's invitation to go dancing spoiled what might have been a pleasant evening's ride in Sennacharib. We were on the point of parting at the lane that led to Whinmouth Hill when I roused myself, for I always hated to part from Diana in a sour temper.

"Suppose I was able to get a motorbike?" I proposed. "Would you come to the regatta dance at Highchurch with me on Saturday?"

She was delighted with the prospect. The sheer lawlessness of a night out on a pillion made an instant appeal to her.

"Jan!" she said. "You don't mean you're buying a motorbike?"

"No," I admitted, "but old Coleman, our keyboard operator, owns a secondhand Douglas and he's taught me to ride it in our yard during the lunch breaks. He'll lend it to me, I know, and without some kind of transport we'd never get over and back, for it's a good thirty miles each way. The point is, could you get out of the house and back in again without anyone knowing?"

"Why of course!" she said. "I've done it before. Drip will be away for the weekend because Mother's coming down . . . no, don't look so hopeless, it makes it easier, because Drip always comes in and says good night but Mother never does, for she goes to bed much later. I'll tell you what"—she hopped about, her eyes shining with the prospect of an adventure—"come around to my window at dusk and whistle 'Dolly Gray' and I'll be dressed ready and come down over the conservatory roof. I'll leave a little ladder in the laurels and when you see my light you can get it and put it up for me. It'll be just like that Rowlandson print I've got—you know, 'The Road to Gretna'!"

We said good-by, our humor miraculously restored, and I at once set about making my preparations. First I had to buy a dinner jacket, for I had seen in the advertisement we printed that flannels and lounge suits would be frowned upon by the regatta committee. The town of Highchurch was a kind of rich relation to Whinmouth, a much larger and more popular resort, on the western side of the river. It had a nationally famous yacht club and the dance that concluded its annual regatta was a notable West Country event. Highchurch was too far away, and too awkward to reach by bus or train, for the dance to attract people from our part of the country, so I felt fairly sure we should not be recognized or, even if we were, that word of our presence would be unlikely to reach Heronslea.

I ordered a suit the following morning and it was promised for Saturday midday. It cost me six guineas and was made by a little tailor in Church Street. I wore it for years. Today it would probably cost about thirty pounds.

Coleman, the keyboard operator, was doubtful about encouraging me to risk my neck on his machine and insisted on my having several more lessons and taking out a license. It was before the days of driving tests and L plates, and I soon considered myself sufficiently expert to carry a pillion passenger.

I went in for my suit fitting on Thursday and afterwards met Diana in Shepherdshey in order to perfect final details. She said that everything was going according to plan. Drip was leaving that night and her mother and father were coming on Friday and dining at home on Saturday, which meant that there would be no danger of them coming in late when we arrived back at Heronslea about two A.M. She had earmarked the ladder but would not remove it from the tool shed until Friday afternoon. She had also surveyed the escape route from her bedroom window to the edge of the conservatory roof and located a strip of lead guttering that would serve as a path between the roof panes.

It was dusk about eight-thirty that night and I wobbled over to Heronslea at twilight, wearing leggings and an old mackintosh to protect my new suit. It wasn't the most suitable outfit for a long ride on a moterbike but I had been very pleased with my appearance when I had inspected it in the wardrobe mirror. The suit was a good fit and I now felt capable of doing battle with the Gerald Brett-Hawkinses and Lance Faynes of the world on more equal terms.

Diana had explained to me why she had chosen "Dolly Gray" as a signal. The Gayelorde-Suttons employed a man-of-all-work called Gaff, who sometimes pottered about the premises half the night, attending to horses, boilers and electrical plant. He was a persistent whistler but the only tunes he liked were Boer War music-hall melodies. Diana's devious mind reasoned that a snatch or two of "Dolly Gray" would not be commented upon if overheard by her parents or anyone else on the staff.

Luckily the dining room and main hall of Heronslea were on the side of the house farthest from her wing and as far removed from the glassed-in terrace where the Gayelorde-Suttons and their guests took their coffee. I hid the motorbike in some bushes halfway down Shepherdshey Hill and cut across the paddock from the west, using the cover of the oaks and beeches and remaining at a safe distance from the house until it was quite dark.

It was a warm, dry night, with the promise of a bright moon later on, and I thanked my lucky stars that we were not faced with the choice of abandoning the expedition or driving to Highchurch through West Country drizzle.

Shortly before nine I saw Diana's light flash off, on and off again. I moved into the open, crawled through the laurels outside the conservatory and found the ladder immediately. It was a light, ten-runged affair and I was able to drag it noiselessly out on to the gravel and set it up against the glass. Then I whistled "Dolly Gray" and it was answered from above. A moment later Diana's window squeaked and I stood back, waiting for her to appear on the guttering.

The minute or two that elapsed before I saw her seemed at least an hour. In the woods behind me owls hooted and once a rabbit screamed. The rest of the house seemed silent and deserted.

At last I heard Diana call softly from the edge of the roof and I steadied the ladder as she descended. She came down with a prolonged rustle of skirts and a whiff of heady perfume. When she reached the ground she turned and kissed me gently on the mouth.

"Thanks, Jan," she said, with a chuckle, "that was beautifully managed."

"You'll get terribly blown about in that outfit," I warned her, but I should have known better, for out of her beaded handbag she at once produced a compressed oilskin, complete with clipped-on hood.

"I'll put it on when we start," she said. "It will crackle too much if I unroll it out here."

We hid the ladder, stole across the paddock and climbed the low fence into the road. Diana donned her oilskin, and after a few terrifying failures on the part of the kick start we set off, her arms around my waist, her hair tickling the back of my neck. The journey was uneventful and we arrived about ten-thirty, when the dance had got into its stride.

I can recall every detail of that wonderful evening. I can remember what she said, what the band played, how the hall was decorated in club colors, with the stage a blaze of sweet peas, dahlias and early chrysanthemums, how many ices we had and the one dance that we sat out to eat them while Ted Bristow's Rhythm Eight wailed "Mean to Me" before beckoning us for the next fox trot, a peppery little tune called "The Wedding of the Painted Doll."

Diana said I looked "lovely and sveldt," whatever that meant, and I had no need to tell her how exciting she looked in her dance frock of yellow organdie, with a white rosebud pinned under her breast. We might have been dancing as partners since we were children and as the evening wore on, and we swung to and fro among the hilarious couples, reality faded altogether and we conversed with little pressures and glances.

When they had played "God Save the King" and we went out

into the harbor car park to find our Douglas, the moon was full and the moored sailing boats, anchored in little groups under the jetties, bobbed up and down on a silver plate so bright that it hurt your eyes to look at it.

"Jan, it's been wonderful, wonderful!" she said, as she slipped into her oilskin. "I wish tonight could go on for ever and ever, because I'm sure it's the happiest night we'll ever have together."

Happiness buzzed in my head. Gone were vague doubts about her mother, her background, her money, or haughty competitors, like Gerald Brett-Hawkins and Lance Fayne.

"We'll have thousands of nights like tonight!" I promised, with the blind faith of a seventeen-year-old. "Besides, it isn't over yet, we've still got to get home. Hold on, here she goes!" and I jabbed joyously at the kick start and started the engine first time.

I had thought that it might be cold on the way back, particularly as we had only missed a single dance and were both very warm when we came out, but the air was as soft and balmy as Mediterranean spring and we cooled down gradually and comfortably as we chugged along the deserted moonlit roads to the Whin swivel bridge that crosses the river four miles up the estuary.

I had no trouble with the bike and from time to time Diana shouted complimentary remarks about my driving.

When we were coasting down Shepherdshey Hill she thumped my back and shouted something that I failed to catch, so at the junction of the village approach road I stopped on the grass verge.

"We'd better park it here while I see you up the ladder again," I suggested.

"Oh, *no,* Jan," she said, pressing my ribs with both hands, "don't let's go in just yet—in for a penny in for a pound! Let's drive on down to Nun's Bay and have a dip. It's a glorious night for a moonlight bath and I've never had one, have you?"

This seemed to me to be tempting Providence. It was already after two o'clock and if we went down to the coast and bathed it would be getting on for dawn before she was back in her room.

"It's a good idea," I temporized, "except that you daren't risk going in for towels and suit and anyway, even if you get yours, I haven't got mine."

"Oh stuff and nonsense," she said, impatiently, "don't be so prudish, Jan! We'll bathe in the nude and if you're too shy you can keep

159]

your briefs on. Come on, this is a night to make history! If we don't go we'll be sorry when we're old and tottery—start her up!"

I drove on down to the sea with a flutter of nervousness in my stomach. I was not much afraid that we should be seen—you could wander about in Sennacharib any time of year after dark and rarely see a soul until you met an early plowman plodding up Teasel Lane —I think my uncertainties stemmed from the exciting prospect of sharing a moonlit bay with a nude Diana and the sense of doom that attended the possibility of her mother learning of such a profligate act.

When I saw the water, however, and the dark huddle of cottages that marked the eastern half of the bay, I could hardly wait to pull my clothes off. I had a good deal of trouble with dress studs and cuff links, but Diana had slipped out of her diaphanous dress in a matter of seconds and was running down the beach long before I was ready. The ripple of her laughter reached me together with her splash, as she dived from the edge of the fishermen's miniature jetty. A few moments later we were swimming out into deeper water, Diana using her unstylish but adequate breaststroke, me overhauling her rapidly with the crawl taught me by the Council School instructor in Brixton Baths, long before I ever dreamed of moonlight swims in Devon.

The water was colder than it looked and after fifty yards or so Diana, gasping, made for a moored dinghy and gripped the anchor chain. After a moment's rest, however, she let go and rolled over and over like a porpoise, her lovely white body shining like a lily petal, her thick chestnut hair trailing behind her like weed. I was too shy to swim close to her but I kept her in view and presently called from the other side of the dinghy:

"You look like a mermaid, Di!"

"I feel exactly like one!" she called back. Then: "Oh Jan, Jan, why do we ever bother with silly clothes? I feel more a part of the sea than I've ever felt in a tight bathing suit and one of those headachy caps."

Then she dived clumsily under the boat and bobbed up alongside me. "Cheat!" she laughed. "You've left your pants on. How deep is it here? Could we reach bottom?"

I threw up my heels and kicked my way under water. It was not more than twelve feet deep and I easily touched bottom. I was in the act of reaching for a pebble when she touched me, her arms encircling my neck, her lips brushing mine. Effortlessly we drifted, without the will to disengage.

It was the oddest sensation, an embrace down there on the floor of Nun's Bay, as though we were sailing gently through limitless space, our limbs freed of all substance and solidity. There was nothing shameless or even sportive about it; it was as though we were partners in some kind of ritual that belonged to a cult as removed from everyday life as a nymph's dance to the music of Pan. The kiss was symbolic, quite unlike any previous kiss she had given me, and when at last we rose together to the surface and struck out for the jetty, neither of us remarked on it, for to do so would have been to break the spell and convert symbolism into ridicule.

The spell held through the time we were drying ourselves on the lining of my old mackintosh and struggling into our clothes. The clothes themselves seemed incongruous, as though, by the mere act of donning them, we were deliberately removing ourselves from a world of enchantment and returning, glumly and resignedly, to an existence that was drab and futile.

I felt this so strongly that I remarked upon it. She didn't answer immediately but sat tugging at her hair with a comb taken from her bag. Presently she said:

"Come and sit beside me, Jan. Don't say anything, just sit here and put your head on my lap!"

"You must be cold," I argued, in spite of myself. "I'd better get you home now, Di."

"No, I'm not a bit cold," she replied, and then, with deliberation: "As a matter of fact I'm glowing. You see, Jan, I think I've discovered something, I think I'm in love with you, really and deeply in love! I don't think I could ever love anyone else after tonight and I don't think anything else will ever matter very much to me, not deep down I mean, except to know that you're in love with me and that we'll always be together. Do you think we've sort of hypnotized ourselves into believing this? You know, the music, the dancing, the moonlight and just being here, with everyone else in Sennacharib fast asleep? Or do you think it's simply that suddenly—just now—we both grew up?"

I thought about this a moment. It was like pondering a symphony of great, stirring chords. Then I said, "I've felt like that about you a long time now, Di. I don't think it's much to do with growing up. I felt it ever since that day you rode out of the larch wood and rescued me from Croker!"

Her admission, sweet as it was, did not electrify me, as I should have imagined only a few hours ago that it might. It seemed a natural and inevitable sequel to the embrace under the water, it only confirmed a subconscious conviction that I had had for almost two years now—that Diana Gayelorde-Sutton and I were predestined to grow up together and inherit, in the spiritual sense, all the slopes, coverts and copses of Sennacharib, and that our coming together then and now was simply a small swirl in the rhythm of the universe, like the unhurried patrol of the buzzards who sailed over Teasel Wood, like the flow of the brook under Shepherdshey Bridge, like the mating and flowering of everything that lived and grew in the few square miles we always thought of as our own.

I turned the damp mackintosh inside out and laid it across her shoulders. Then I crouched beside the little rock on which she was sitting and covered her hands with kisses while she lowered her head and laid her cheek against my head.

We sat there a long time, hardly moving, saying nothing, listening to the steady suck-lap of the wavelets on the shingle. And then, when I felt her shudder, I stood up and held her closely in my arms, kissing her damp hair, her eyes, her ears and mouth. I had never kissed her in this way before. Such kisses as we had exchanged in the past had nothing to do with the yearning we experienced for one another at this moment. We had forgotten where we were or how we came to be there. We had no shared past and no future, only this sweet, solemn hour that had coaxed us from childhood into anxious maturity, and changed us from a couple of children out on a moonlight spree, into a man and woman who wanted and needed one another so urgently that at this moment we could not imagine an existence apart.

A faint glow of headlights, moving rapidly along the distant London road seen through the cleft of the cliffs, restored to me but not to her a vague sense of time and place. I led her up to the quay where we had left the bike and slowly we rode back to Shepherdshey, stopping once again on the grass verge of the crossroads.

"Don't come across the paddock with me, Jan," she said, suddenly. "Let's say good night here. I'd much rather do that and I'll get back on my own, I promise you."

"What about the ladder? How will you be able to put it away again after using it? If anyone found it there—"

"Dear Jan," she said, slowly running a finger down my cheek, "do you imagine that I shall sleep when I get in? *Tonight?* After all the wonderful things that have happened? I'll change and wait until I hear the maids stirring. Then I'll slip out as though I'm going for Sioux, take the ladder away and put it back in the shed before old Gaff shows up. It's his day to gravel the drive and he won't come around to my side of the house until after breakfast."

I let myself be convinced by these arguments. It was almost dawn anyway. Already there was a faint glimmer in the sky over Shepherdshey Church and I reasoned that one pair of footsteps outside the conservatory would make less noise than two; besides, in the unlikely event of Diana's being caught, my presence would make matters ten times worse. Alone she might be able to talk herself out of being on the conservatory roof in a yellow dance frock at four A.M. on a September morning.

"What about tomorrow?" I demanded. "You'll be going back to school at the end of the week and I want to make the most of every minute. I won't see you again until just before Christmas!"

As I said this I could have wept but she bobbed forward, pecked my cheek and said, with a rueful laugh, "It isn't 'tomorrow,' it's 'to-day,' silly! I'll phone you between one and two and fix something for the evening. It depends so much on what Mummy and Daddy are doing. They might be going somewhere and expect me to go with them."

We had used this kind of arrangement in the past. When she was unsure of how and when we could meet I stayed behind at the office throughout the lunch hour, waiting for her to phone while I had the premises to myself. I agreed to leave it at that and kissed her once more while helping her over the fence into the copse bordering the paddock. I listened until I could no longer hear her footsteps cracking the twigs and then pushed the bike up the hill, starting it well out of hearing of the house.

When I got up to my room it was almost daylight and although I too intended to remain wide awake and recapitulate every moment of the past few hours, I confess that I failed to keep the tryst, falling asleep half-undressed and remaining so until I heard Aunt Thirza bustling about in the kitchen, with her usual accompaniment of rattling crockery as she assaulted the night's dust on the dresser. I pulled off my clothes, held my head under a running tap, threw on a pair of flannels and went down for a cup of tea, but Aunt Thirza was not fooled for an instant.

"Been out gallivanting half the night. I 'eard 'ee!" she grumbled, in her rich brogue.

I never had to apologize to Aunt Thirza. I was a grown man in her eyes and took shameless advantage of the knowledge that she had one set of rules for me and another for everyone else.

"Well, youm on'y young once, John!" she relented. "Yer, 'ave zum tay, boy, and dorn 'ee hurry to work, zeein' tiz Zat'day!"

I had forgotten what day it was. I had so much else to think of that it was fortunate for the readers of the *Observer* that Saturday was the day I collected no facts and typed no copy.

Uncle Reuben noticed my preoccupation but put it down to a late night. He didn't hold with dancing and motorcycling, and began to counsel a more serious approach to life, pointing out that I was now nearly eighteen and ought to be thinking of implementing my decision to widen my professional experience on a more important paper.

This gave me an opening and I think I rather surprised him with the sudden enthusiasm I showed for bettering myself. I did not tell him that my reason for wanting more money and greater responsibilities had to do with supporting a girl whose father was reputed to be the wealthiest man in the district. He was always so deeply immersed in his own affairs—the paper, his lay preaching, the treasurership of the local Liberal Party, and many other activities—that he had no knowledge whatever of my friendship with Diana. He had, however, carried out his promise about finding me a better job and had been awaiting a favorable opportunity to discuss it, together with another and more sensational proposal that had been maturing for some time.

"It will probably work out very well all around, John," he told me, "because after you've had a year or two on a bigger paper you can come back here on an entirely different basis. You see, since we're now embarked on the subject, I think I can tell you a good deal more than I was inclined to admit when we had our last discussion about your future. Mr. Priddis is leaving the *Observer* and works to me in his will, and who should I have to pass it on to but you?"

His information, so casually imparted, overwhelmed me. Coming so quickly upon Diana's declaration, it converted my entire future into something reasonably foreseeable. I had never thought of myself as the owner-editor of the paper but simply as a junior employee of the present proprietor, whose health was deteriorating very rapidly and giving all employed on the paper and printing works a certain amount of anxiety about our livelihood. Only the previous day Coleman, the motorbike owner, had drawn my attention to the possibilities.

"If Priddis kicks the bucket what's to happen to us?" he had speculated. "I'll lay you six-to-four the paper will be bought by one of the big chains and they'll put their own chaps in, you can bet your life on that!"

Unemployment was rife at the time and there was some justification for Coleman's gloom. Our local population in Whinmouth was about twelve thousand but our unemployment figure already stood at over four hundred and would go higher when the season ended.

If the business passed to Uncle Reuben we were likely to remain undisturbed and if, in the course of time, it then passed to me, I had an assured if limited future for as long as I cared to remain in the district.

"How does it appeal to you, taking on here after I've gone?" asked Uncle Reuben, eying me doubtfully.

"It couldn't be better!" I told him and smiled when I saw his face light up with pleasure. "I've been very happy here, Uncle Reuben, and things being what they are, where could I expect to do any better?"

He jumped up and thumped me on the shoulder. "God bless my soul, it does me good to hear you talk like that, John! You know, I expected you to be lukewarm about it and mumble a lot of nonsense about Whinmouth being a dead-and-alive hole and no place for a chap of your age! I still think you ought to have a bit of daily paper experience, mind you, but if you've got something established like this to come back to it makes all the difference in the world, it gives you roots, and a purpose in life. Now I'm off to see Mr. Priddis this weekend and perhaps we'll get something on paper. In the meantime I'll jog him for that introduction to a daily. It would mean leaving here, you understand, and I daresay you'd be away three or four years. How do you feel about that?"

"It depends where it is," I told him, with secret visions of frequent meetings with Diana in London and all the advantages of a press card with which to entertain her. "If it was London I think I should like it very much!"

He looked a little puzzled at this. "But I thought you were a converted countryman, John. Luke tells me you spend all your spare time up on the moor, or pottering about in the bay."

I was tempted to tell him then about Diana and ask his advice, which was always objective. In the light of what happened I rather wish I had, but something prompted me to continue to keep my unlikely courtship to myself and I replied, "I wouldn't care to leave the West Country for good, Uncle Reuben, but it's like you said, the more experience I get at my age the better journalist I'll make in the end."

It sounded rather pious but he was a pious man and took the explanation at face value. He beamed on me, paternally.

"By George, I wish you'd been my boy, John! I think I must have misjudged your father when he took young Miriam away from us all those years ago. He must have had some good stuff in him somewhere."

I felt guilty at deceiving him so outrageously but not nearly so abject as I was to feel a few days later, when his opinion of me was to dip to zero.

He went off to North Devon to see Priddis and I forgot him the moment I had the office to myself. I wasn't able to concentrate on anything but sat drumming my fingers beside the phone, waiting and waiting for Diana's call, and hoping with all my heart that she would be able to meet me at the tower that night. I had so much to say to her, so much to promise, and my yearning for her nearness, for the touch of her hand and the sound of her voice, was so intense that I ached.

One o'clock came, then two, but no call; I was ravenously hungry but afraid to leave the office. I phoned Uncle Luke, using the phone with demoniac speed lest it should block Diana's call, and asked him to tell Aunt Thirza that I was busy and couldn't get home. Then I tried to read, hanging about until late afternoon and pacing the deserted printing works like a man awaiting a reprieve. Over and over again I told myself that there was a perfectly simple explanation for her silence and that her parents had whisked her off on a social visit to a place where she was unable to use a telephone.

By five o'clock I was driven by hunger to call it a day and hurry home to my warmed-up dinner. I decided that I could not hope to get news if I stayed in the town, that my best plan was to go up to Heronslea and hang about on the fringe of the paddocks, hoping to catch a glimpse of her and perhaps get a signal.

By this time I was becoming alarmed, but not seriously so, for I reasoned that even if she had been missed during the night it was unlikely that I would be connected with her escapade. I was equally convinced that her mother knew her well enough by now to regard a descent from the bedroom as something entirely characteristic of Diana and punish it as a mere prank.

There was the dance frock, of course, and then, to complicate matters, her dripping hair, but Diana was a very accomplished liar where her mother was concerned and I had every confidence that she would be able to talk her way out of the situation and persuade her mother to accept it as just one more childish whim on the part of a tiresome daughter.

I went to the tower first but it was silent and deserted. I looked about for a note or message but there was nothing, so I crossed the patch of common and went on down through the larch wood into the paddock behind the house. Sioux was there and Nellie, but the rear of Heronslea was empty of humans. I skirted along the edge of the copse, taking good care to keep out of sight of the windows, and then sat down to wait for darkness, when I could approach the house in comparative safety.

It was a long time getting dark. The wood was full of scuttling life and as the sun went down behind the larches, blackbirds sang and once or twice a rabbit frisked across the lawn beneath the beeches. It was a lovely, pastoral scene, with the old, beautifully proportioned house in the near distance, bedded down in a wide circle of deep green timber and tussocky lawns, with the deeper green of the laurels and rhododendrons half-screening the pink walls of the kitchen quarters and stable yard. As I waited, the last rays of the sun struck the sloping panes of the conservatory and they flashed a dull ruby. The air was so still that the swift, rending sound of Sioux's rhythmic grass cropping carried right across the enclosure to where I sat, waist-high in bracken. I was not very receptive to the peace and beauty of Sennacharib that evening, however, for Diana's declaration had changed the direction of my thoughts and feelings about our relative status. I was no longer content to hang about awaiting the fall of Heronslea crumbs, keeping out of sight, and taking advantage of the Gayelorde-Suttons' absences in order to woo

their lovely daughter. All this time I had accepted the barrier between us as something in the natural order of things, like a desert
to be crossed, or a mountain range to be climbed, but now I wanted
to blast my way through the barrier and tell the whole world that
Emerald Diana Gayelorde-Sutton was in love with me, that we had
swum naked by moonlight in Nun's Bay, that we had pledged ourselves to one another and that, come what may, Gayelorde-Sutton
millions notwithstanding, I was going to marry her, care for her and
share my life with her, somewhere in this vast green silence with
which we, and no others, were in true accord.

It did not occur to me, then or later, that I might with some justice
be regarded as a youthful fortune hunter or that I was doing Diana
a wrong by encouraging her to imagine that she was in love, at seventeen, with a boy unlikely to earn more than one of her father's head
clerks. I never thought of Diana as an heiress, only as the daughter
of wealthy, snobbish people, and my daydreams did not embrace
Heronslea House but laid claim to Sennacharib as a whole, to its
woods, commons and beaches. Somewhere inside this realm I
dreamed of building a home of our own, a haven that would be in
sharp contrast to the elegant pile that dominated the estate.

This was admittedly illogical but I make no excuses. I was seventeen, and deeply in love with a pretty girl. There was pride and
wonder in the knowledge that Diana loved me but it was not the
kind of pride that Mrs. Mabel Gayelorde-Sutton would have understood.

When it was dark, and before the moon rose, I slipped out of the
wood and went around to the front of the house. Moving very cautiously I approached the glassed-in terrace. It was uncurtained and
I peeped into the dining room, the main room upon which the terrace opened.

There was a dim light inside and the door was half open. Presently
I saw the butler's figure cross the aperture and then, by crawling
crabwise along the outside wall of the terrace, I positioned myself
to look right into the dining room.

What I saw brought no relief to my anxiety. The Gayelorde-
Suttons, father, mother and daughter, were at their meal, waited
upon by Masters, the soft-footed butler. The radio was playing
"Sleeping Beauty Waltz" and the family did not appear to be con-
versing. Mr. Gayelorde-Sutton sat at the table end nearest to me,
his wife was at the other end, and Diana, wearing a dark evening

dress, was sitting midway in between, half facing me. They all looked rather solemn and helped themselves to dishes absent-mindedly, as though they were eating not because they were hungry but because someone had struck a gong and told them that it was time to eat.

They had reached the dessert stage before I had an idea. Then, catching my breath with nervousness, I whistled a line or two of "Dolly Gray" and was instantly rewarded by the sight of Diana's head coming up. Her father and mother took no notice of the start but continued to peel fruit. After a pause I tried another note or two, and this time Diana did not look up but Mrs. Gayelorde-Sutton said something to the butler, who crossed over and closed the door, cutting off my view.

Baffled and irritated, I crept back to the main drive and stood indecisively beside one of the largest beeches, ready to bob out of sight if anyone appeared in the front of the house. About a quarter of an hour passed and then I saw a chink of light and heard a dog bark. Almost at once there was a scamper of paws on gravel and a moment later Sheila, Diana's golden Labrador, lolloped up to me, snuffling a welcome and panting with pleasure at being released for a few minutes' probe among the rabbit runs of the paddock.

Sheila and I were old friends. She had accompanied us on dozens of rides and not a few dips in the bay. She was small for a Labrador but very active and almost stupidly affectionate.

"Here, Sheila, here!" I whispered, as she located me and jumped up for a pat. "Where's Diana? Is she with you? Is she coming out?"

Then I noticed that a fold of paper had been tucked into her collar and wound around two or three times to make it fast. I grabbed the dog and unwound the spill, resisting Sheila's attempts to snatch it back and take it in her soft mouth.

It was too dark to read any message that might be written on the paper and anyway at that moment Mr. Gayelorde-Sutton, his cigar end glowing, moved out onto the terrace. I slipped behind the beeches and made off back to the copse, Sheila following until a distant whistle recalled her to the house.

Deep in the wood I sat down and struck a match. The message was only a few words of scrawl and had obviously been written in a desperate hurry. It said: *Don't write or phone. Awful row. You not involved yet. Come to church. Sophia Grangerford's trick. All my love, Di.*

My feelings on reading this extraordinary note were very mixed. I was thoroughly alarmed about the row and apprehensive at the obvious reference to last night's affair implied in the word "yet," but at the same time I was comforted by Diana's ingenuity in warning me, by her alertness at responding to the "Dolly Gray" signal so quickly and, above all, by the invitation to attend church and learn more of what had taken place since we had parted. I had no difficulty at all in ciphering the "Sophia Grangerford" piece. Among the books that Diana and I were fond of discussing was *Huckleberry Finn,* and Diana's favorite chapter in that delightful story was the one in which Huck spends a period with the feuding Grangerfords on the river plantation. We had often talked about Sophia, the girl who caused massacre by running off with Harney Shepherdson, and Diana had remarked that Sophia's trick of exchanging plans with her lover through the medium of a note left in her prayer book was a "marvelous wheeze." It was now obvious that she intended to use the same medium and this, I decided, was very clever of her, because there was nothing to prevent me from attending morning service at Shepherdshey Church tomorrow morning and retrieving a letter from Diana's prayer book when the congregation had filed out. The Gayelorde-Suttons were conventional churchgoers when they were in the country and they occupied a pew near the front. Here they sat, surrounded by their estate employees, like a feudal family at church in Plantagenet times. It was a gesture that must have given Mrs. Gayelorde-Sutton a good deal of satisfaction. This was one occasion when I appreciated her game of squiress.

Sharp at ten-fifty the following morning I was in position a few pews away from Diana, in the pretty little church of Shepherdshey. Worshipers were sparse and I knew them nearly all. Nat Baker, the big sexton, was doling out hymnbooks, Half-a-Crown Sam, the cretin, sat moonfaced under the lectern, Ada Macey, flanked by her official and unofficial husbands, sat close to the door, and most of the other villagers I knew were in attendance, including about half a dozen keepers, gardeners and their families from the Heronslea estate.

I was very glad of their company, for I had entertained a horrible suspicion that, apart from the Heronslea contingent, I might prove to be the sole parishioner and this would make the inspection of Diana's prayer book a risky undertaking.

The rector droned through the service and the last hymn, I recall, was Whinmouth's most popular wedding hymn, "The Voice That

Breath'd O'er Eden," which I took to be a very good omen. Diana was taking no chances at all. If she saw me she didn't advertise the fact but kept her eyes straight before her as she stood, a small, trim figure in a blue two-piece and white straw hat, between her mother and father in the second pew from the front.

When the service was over I waited until the family had moved past my pew and down the center aisle, burying my head in my hands but keeping a wary eye on Diana as she went by, in order to note any signal she might want to give. She did give one, a slow, solemn nod, and as soon as the church was cleared I hurried to the Gayelorde-Sutton pew and rummaged frantically among the hymn-books in the rack.

I was unable to find a prayer book but then I noticed that one of the hymnals had an envelope in it. I quickly gathered it up and thrust it into my pocket, allowing a little time for the churchyard to clear, and hurried out into Teasel Lane. From here I made my way up toward the gorse slopes, to the spot where I had watched the hunt move in pursuit of the fox I lied about.

The envelope contained two pages covered with Diana's neat, stylish handwriting; it took my breath away.

John dear, it began (latterly Diana had not been so lavish with written endearments; when she used the word "darling" it meant something).

Thank goodness you had the sense to get in touch! As you will have gathered, I was collared on the way in last night and I'll tell you all about that when we meet. Right now there are much more important things to discuss, so here goes! To begin with Mummy doesn't know the truth, or any part of it. She *thinks* I was at a village hop, with Lance Fayne, the M.P.'s son, and I let her go on thinking so (without actually admitting it) because it spikes her guns. The one person she doesn't want to quarrel with right now is the M.P., not just because he is who he is but because of the coming election! She has, however, made an awful decision. I am not to go back to school at all but to go straight off to the Finishing School, the one in Switzerland that I was booked for next year. It is a country place, stuck away in a place called Thun, in the Bernese Oberland, and I haven't the faintest intention of going! At first I planned to do a bunk en route and get a job in London, where we could still see each other as you said we might later on, but I see now that my disappearance in that way would start a national hue and cry, and get into all the papers, whereas if it happened down here Mummy would sweat blood to keep it dark until I was located. So I'm going to run away *now*, and stay hidden for about a week, or until they find me. You might think that won't help much but it will, because Daddy will be in such a state by the time I'm found that he won't let me go to Switzerland and all that will happen is I'll leave school and stay on at Heronslea most of the year. Now my plan—hold your breath—is to go and hide on Nun's Island, where no one will ever think of looking for me. I have to get there, of course, and this is where you come in. Get the dinghy and bring it along to the place where we bathed after dark last night. Bring anything you think would be useful to a castaway. I'm bringing food but there is a limit to what I can carry. Can you find a waterproof sheet and perhaps some rugs or blankets? I am absolutely determined on this, Jan, because I think it is the only way to make her see sense and I'm dreadfully afraid that if she finds out about us I'll be sent even farther away, and probably never see you again, and that I just couldn't bear, Jan, because you are the only person in the world I really care about, darling, and I know now that I'm really in love with you, as I said.

Your own,
DIANA

My head began to spin. There were so many fantastic statements in the letter that I had to read it over and over again before I could absorb the gist of it. My first reaction to the island plan was that it could not possibly succeed, and was no more than the semihysterical ravings of a spoiled, sulky child. I began to think about Diana as the person I had known over the past two years, and then, somehow, it did not seem irresponsible but vaguely Machiavellian, particularly when one reviewed the balance of power at Heronslea. If I had not had an opportunity of studying the real Mr. Gayelorde-Sutton, during his visit to the *Observer* office about the pig, I might have rejected Diana's claim that her father would ultimately step in and take her part about going to Switzerland. After that glimpse of him it did not seem so unlikely. He was a man who would stand so much nonsense from his wife and then, when the limit was reached, quietly intervene and issue all the orders. Also, Diana obviously knew him much better than I did, and could better assess the likelihood of his championship. Then again, she was quite accurate in her estimate of the press reaction to a sudden disappearance. If she left a note, as I imagined she would, it was unlikely that local police would take her flight very seriously, whereas if she jumped the train or boat en route for Switzerland, there was sure to be no end of a fuss. Fleet Street would probably hint at White Slavers and invent other dramatic angles and the prominent social position of the family would lay them wide open to national coverage.

Her introduction of Lance Fayne into Friday night's escapade was a stroke of genius, although, incongruously, I found myself resenting his blameless role. I imagined this part of it could be cleared up by a phone call on the part of her mother but as long as Diana would not actually admit to having danced the night away with Lance, Mrs. Gayelorde-Sutton could hardly complain about it without risking a snub, which was something she would not care to receive from a Conservative M.P. Her object in sending Diana away almost immediately was obviously designed to safeguard her as well as prevent a quarrel between the families. What action she would take if she stumbled on the truth I hardly dared to contemplate.

As to the practical aspect, the plan to hole up on Nun's Island, that was not as silly as it seemed, either. Scarcely anybody went there now that the holiday season was ending, and if the recent good weather continued, the old cabin of Crusoe Jack, the recluse lobsterman, would prove adequate shelter once the roof was repaired. Getting there unseen might be difficult but it was by no means impossible, providing we chose our time and the sea remained calm.

I then moved on to examine my own role in the escape and was surprised to discover that, once the first shock of her letter had been absorbed, I began to feel pleasurably excited about it. It was an essay into the realm of pure romance, a flight of desperate lovers to a desert island, with the object of preventing prolonged separation. From the standpoint of maturity I suppose it all sounds harebrained and even cruel, for whatever happened, the Gayelorde-Suttons were certain to suffer a good deal, but from the standpoint of a lad of seventeen, fast in the web of first love, it was a great and glorious adventure, a chance to prove my devotion to the person I admired more than anyone else on earth.

Thinking along these lines, it was a short step from the role of accessory to that of a full partner in the enterprise. The more I thought about it the more certain I became that I could not possibly take her to the island and then return home, but would be obliged to share her period of voluntary exile.

The prospect uplifted me and I thought less and less of the rights and wrongs of the matter and more and more of the bliss of being marooned with Diana in a place remote from human contacts. After considering this for a spell I worked myself into a mood of reckless abandon and set about making plans with the dispatch and resolution of Willie Douglas, whose rescue of Mary Queen of Scots from Loch Leven castle had always occupied a cozy corner of my imagination. Having made up my mind, I deliberately turned my back on common sense. Diana and I were in love. Diana was about to be spirited away. If she had the courage to fight back then so had I, enough to challenge half a dozen Mrs. Gayelorde-Suttons.

I cycled back to town and gobbled my way through lunch in order to have the rest of the day clear. By two o'clock I was down at the quay, inspecting the dinghy and loading it with things we might need. I took a tarpaulin sheet from the Furniture Mart, and half a dozen tattered rugs used for conveying fragile goods to and from the auction rooms. They were very soiled and smelled strongly of linseed oil but castaways could hardly be bothered by a thing like that. I then raided Aunt Thirza's spotless pantry, filching some flour, sugar, biscuits, cans of fruit, a can opener, a whole Dutch cheese and a packet of salt. As an afterthought I took a bottle of Camp coffee, two cups, two plates, a saucepan, a mended kettle and a bull's-eye lantern.

By the time I had it all stowed away under the tarpaulin it was evening, and while Uncle Luke and Aunt Thirza were at chapel I wrote two letters, one to Uncle Reuben and another to Aunt Thirza. I told Uncle Reuben that I had had a sudden notion of a job and had gone after it, and that he would hear from me shortly. I told Aunt Thirza much the same, but added that I intended combining a job hunt with a week's camping holiday and that I had therefore helped myself to a few stores from her pantry. I knew that both Reuben and Thirza would be astonished by my precipitate departure but it was the best story I could think of at the moment, and if there was any publicity about Diana's flight I wanted to do all I could to avoid our absences being linked.

About dusk I pushed off along the edge of the bay, timing my arrival under Nun's Head with the fall of darkness.

It was not until I had tied up under the deserted jetty that I began to wonder how Diana would escape the house and, having managed this, walk the three miles from Shepherdshey to Nun's Steps carrying such kit as she had decided to bring. I was not overconcerned with these problems, for it was clear that a girl who was sufficiently determined to run away from home and isolate herself on a rock a mile out to sea would certainly contrive the preliminaries, notwithstanding the fact that a close watch was being kept upon her movements.

Fishermen were loafing about on the higher quay until after nine o'clock, so I did not dare to leave the boat for fear of being seen and recognized. I lay in the bottom, looking up at the stars and watching the moon play hide and seek with tatters of blue-black cloud. Out beyond Nun's Island I could hear the bell buoy toll and this meant a swell, but the water inshore was flat calm and the tiny wavelets poured over the shingle with barely a sound. I was anchored in two feet of water and soon the gentle rocking motion sent me to sleep, for I was very tired after two nights' broken rest. I was awakened by the sound of something clanking down beside me and I jumped up to see Diana, duffel-coated and hooded, climbing into the boat with an attaché case in one hand and a large canvas bag in the other.

"Lord, I was scared!" she said. "I was quite worn out when I got here and at first there didn't seem to be any sign of you. I kept wondering if you had got my letter—push off, that's everything!"

It was as casual as that! No explanations, no excited tale of her flight, or nervous speculations on the future; just "push off, that's everything!" and she was gathering up the anchor and fending the boat from the jetty.

The extraordinary thing about that long pull to the island was that I was almost speechless with embarrassment. I don't know why this should be so; I had never been embarrassed in her company before but I now found it almost impossible to begin a discussion on the situation. When we were three parts of the way across, and had entered the choppy water beyond the long finger of Nun's Head, I at last forced myself to say, "I'm staying with you, Di, I'm not going to let you stay there alone, no matter what you say about it! If you don't agree or think this will only make matters worse, then we'll turn around now and go home."

She looked surprised for a moment and then laughed. "I knew you would, Jan, but I wanted that part of it to come from you. Quite honestly, I'd be scared stiff out here on my own but I could have faced it, so long as you promised to row out every night, or very early each morning." Then: "Won't you be missed? And won't it mean they'll be hunting for two of us?"

I told her about the false trail I had left and she said I was clever and that she had left a note on her dressing table in true eloping style. In her letter she said that she was running away because she hated the idea of leaving England but had money and would be quite safe. She promised to write within a week. "That should give them time to have a jolly good bust-up about it all," she said, cheerfully, "and the bit about leaving England will get Daddy right under the ribs! I think he dislikes the idea of my going anyway, but Mummy says she won't be answerable for what happens if I don't, I'm so terribly out of hand."

I pondered this as we swung east and rowed inshore.

"What would be your father's attitude if he knew the real reason —about us?" I asked.

"I don't know and I don't care," she said, gaily. "He's so weak that I've lost all patience with him. I hate the way they've brought me up, all this snob stuff, and trying to keep me a child as long as they can. Something like this had to happen soon, Jan, and it was making up my mind about you that sparked it off. If I don't strike a blow for myself now I'll be chivvied along by Mother all my life, first this finishing-off nonsense, then being presented, then a 'suitable marriage,' and finally complete boredom with some awful droop like Lance, or a starched shirt, like Gerald Brett-Hawkins! I'll just be pitchforked into leading the kind of life *she* leads!"

"What kind of life does she lead, Di?" I asked, realizing that I had never really known, despite all the oblique references Diana had made to it in our talks.

"Oh, playing at Big Business with Daddy and falling over herself to be noticed by the right people in all the right places," said Diana, savagely. Then, very seriously: "It might seem to you that what I'm doing is a desperate thing, and I suppose it is, but then I *am* desperate, Jan, desperate of having my life mapped out the way she maps hers out, in a kind of fantastic calendar—Ascot, Wimbledon, Hurlingham, Henley, the 'Season'—you know, and not because she enjoys the actual events but simply because somebody's told her these are the right places to go and the right time to go there, d'you see?"

I saw a good deal more clearly than she realized. We had had these kinds of discussions before but she had not always been so explicit. I understood, for the first time I think, what caused Diana to go to such extraordinary lengths to resist her parents. It was as though she was being forced to serve an endless apprenticeship to a trade she loathed, and in which she could see no personal future beyond the ennui of aping the gentlewoman. It was her essential honesty that caused her to despise her mother's incessant charade but, in addition to this, her resistance had to do with the inherited outlook of the seedy old ferryman whom she claimed as a grand-father. Inside her, calling loud for release, was a peasant determined to do battle with the shams prescribed by her mother and buttressed by her father's wealth. I learned a great deal from that conversation in the boat. It became very clear to me (though I would not, at first, admit it to myself) that it was not on my account that she was making this gesture of independence. Her flight was instinctive be-cause, as she emerged from adolescence, she felt her resistance weak-ening with her threatened removal from the familiar, from Sennach-arib that had been a kind of sanctuary all these years, and possibly from me also, for I was the talisman of her freedom.

I do not mean that she did not sincerely believe that she was in love with me but simply that I was of secondary importance in a struggle to develop her own personality. I did not resent this knowl-edge, then or later. For the moment it was enough for me that she found solace in my company and was drawn to me physically and spiritually. I was confident, as are most males at seventeen, that I could soon convert this warmth into a blaze as bright as my own and here I was, with a wonderful chance to prove it! As the boat grounded and we jumped ashore I set about doing just that.

It was fortunate that I had brought the bull's-eye lantern. In its beam we made a careful examination of the shanty and I was soon able to patch the roof with the tarpaulin, weighting it down with heavy pebbles. We then recovered our kit and climbed the gulley to the copse, gathering armfuls of bracken for beds. We were too busy for the next two hours to appreciate the beauty of the night, but when the shanty had been made habitable we stood together on the little rock shelf outside the shattered door and looked out on the huge expanse of moonlit Channel.

The shanty faced south, which was a lucky chance, for it meant that our fire would be screened from any observer on the coast and we could also move about fairly freely without the chance of being observed by the pilot boat or trawlermen, who passed inside the island on their way to the open sea.

To the west we could see the necklace of tiny lights that marked Whinmouth quay and the steep streets of the town; to the east there was only the blurr of Nun's Head. The hamlet from which we had set out was obscured by the knoll and its copse. It was very quiet here, the only sound apart from the steady swish of the water being the irregular clang of the bell buoy three or more miles to the southeast.

"What are we going to do about drink?" she wanted to know.

I told her there was a spring somewhere, for Crusoe Jack had used it for years, but because I knew we should have some difficulty in locating it I had brought along a can of water and we could now make our first pot of tea.

"We can have some toast, too," she said, "because I brought a loaf and we'd better eat it before it gets stale. Oh Jan, this is quite heavenly! It's a kind of secret honeymoon! How long do you think it will last?"

"Don't let's worry about that," I said, grimly, for in spite of the *sang-froid* with which I had entered the adventure, I had a far more active conscience than Diana and could not quite banish thoughts of the hurrying and scurrying there would be when the hunt was up.

We had a hard task to find firewood by flashlight but we finally gathered a pile and I lit a small fire behind a carefully screened fireplace. The kettle took a long time to boil but when it did, and we had access to the red-hot ashes, Diana made some toast and I got out the plates and sliced the Dutch cheese. Rummaging about among the stuff we had brought with us, I discovered that the case she had carried wasn't an attaché case at all but a portable phonograph.

"Why on earth did you bring a phonograph?" I demanded, for it seemed to me a ridiculous thing to have on a desert island and must have proved a dragging weight to lug over to Nun's Head.

"Well, you see, I wasn't at all sure you'd stay, Jan," she said, laughing, "and I thought I might get very lonely. I only brought two records, a Gilbert and Sullivan medley and 'Student Songs.' They're both rather pets of mine."

We set it going and listened as we munched our toast and drank our smoked tea. The recordings were good and it added zest to the adventure to sit there listening to "The Lord High Executioner" and "The Duke of Plaza Toro." Somehow it made the shack more like home and banished the eerie loneliness of the rock we shared with sea gulls and the bones of long-dead seamen. I was thinking of these men when Diana, who was uncannily accurate at reading my thoughts, brought the subject into the open.

"I'm jolly glad now that we had that service and put up that cross," she said. "If their ghosts are still not laid then they're absolutely certain to be benevolent."

After supper we had the students' songs and then I was very glad that she had thought of the phonograph, for the strong choruses reintroduced a devil-may-care atmosphere into the cabin. We joined in the ones we knew, *Gaudeamus*," "The Eton Boating Song," and the Harrow school song, humming an accompaniment to the German songs on the other side of the record. When we had played them over twice I said it was time we went to bed and she lay down on her bracken couch fully dressed. I tucked her up with the least noisome of the rugs and she looked very like a child when she pronounced herself warm and cozy.

"Dear Jan," she said, sleepily. "Good husband! Kiss me good night!"

I did so very willingly, my love for her sweeping over me like a strong, warm flood.

"Everything is going to be all right about us in the end, Di!" I told her and believed it, deep in my heart.

Her arms wound around me and she kissed me a dozen times.

"Darling, darling Jan!" she whispered. "You're quite the nicest thing that's ever happened to me!"

I made up my own bed on the side farthest from the fireplace but although I was tired out with all the excitement and exertion it was a long time before I dropped off to sleep. I lay awake listening to the mournful notes of the bell buoy, and to Diana's slow, regular breathing, wondering what would be the end of it all and feeling humble and helpless, as well as immeasurably grateful for the opportunity to share the same world as Emerald Diana Gayelorde-Sutton, of Heronslea, Devon and Palmerston Crescent, W.2.

It was a bright day when I awoke and Diana's place was empty. I jumped up and looked wildly around, terrified that she had been spirited away during the night, but almost at once I noticed that the fire had been made up and the kettle was on. A moment later she came clattering into the cabin in slacks and sweater, carrying a large armful of driftwood.

"You were so efficient and come-come-little-womany last night that I thought it was my turn to show off," she said, kissing me lightly. "I've found the spring. It's over on the Whinmouth beach, so I think you had better refill the can before people are about. It's nearly seven already!"

We used the can for washing and I prowled cautiously around the spur of sand to refill at the spring. The distance from this side of the island to Whinmouth was too great for us to be spotted with the naked eye but there were always people on the quays and jetty with telescopes and binoculars, so I decided to take no chances.

We tried to make some salty little cakes with the flour I had brought but they were very unappetizing, so we agreed to ration ourselves with the bread. Diana opened a can of corned beef and we fried slices, exchanging many jokes about one another's cooking abilities. After breakfast we had a swim, then we made more tea and set the phonograph going.

"I wish you'd brought more records," I chaffed her. "We're going to get frightfully sick of 'Three Little Maids' and 'There Lived a King' by the time we're rescued. My favorite isn't here, anyway. It's *The Pirates of Penzance*, the one the amateurs did in the spring."

This led to an amiable discussion on Gilbert and Sullivan, and thence to musical comedies, films and books. During the time we were alone on the island we explored one another's literary and dramatic tastes very thoroughly, for we spent a great deal of our time inside the shanty, being nervous of daylight movement on the western or northern sides of the island.

I remember that first morning we talked a great deal about desert island books and I was rather surprised to discover that her acquaintance with them was slight. I told her the story of *Coral Island* and we discussed *Robinson Crusoe* at length, for she was vaguely familiar with this one. She knew nothing, however, about *Treasure Island* or *The Blue Lagoon*, and was very intrigued by Emmeline's production of a baby without the benefit of Marie Stopes, who was one of Diana's heroines.

I had not been all that impressed by *Blue Lagoon* but I know long passages of Stevenson's classic by heart and recited them with relish. We speculated a good deal on how the vast treasure came to be buried on the island and then moved on easily to poetry, in which field she was far more advanced than I. My acquaintance with verse at that time was limited to ballads like "The Armada" and Kipling's jingles, but she was very scornful about my taste.

"That isn't poetry at all!" she exclaimed. "Those are just rhymes, like longer Jack Horners and Little Miss Muffets! Real poetry is quite different. Miss Thorpe says it's 'emotion remembered in tranquillity' —you know, lovely, lovely groups of words, like in Tennyson's *Princess*.

My knowledge of Tennyson was confined to "The Brook," *Morte d'Arthur* and *The Lady of Shallott* so I asked her if she could quote me some of her favorite pieces.

"My favorite piece of Tennyson is the first and last verse of the song from *The Princess*," she said, and quoted:

> "Tears, idle tears, I know not what they mean,
> Tears from the depth of some divine despair
> Rise in the heart, and gather to the eyes,
> In looking on the happy autumn-fields,
> And thinking of the days that are no more.

> "Dear as remember'd kisses after death,
> And sweet as those by hopeless fancy feign'd
> On lips that are for others; deep as love,
> Deep as first love, and wild with all regret;
> O Death in Life, the days that are no more!"

Only a few days ago, after an interval of more than twenty years, I came across these verses and they still retained enough tired magic to restore to me a detailed memory of Diana, sitting with her long legs coiled under her, her small, earnest face frowning with the strain of recollection as she recited them against the background of the rough-hewn logs that formed the fireplace wall of Crusoe Jack's cabin. Then, without effort on my part, the sounds and scents and talks of our idyl came back to me as fresh and gay as growing daffodils, and I remembered how she had run on about poetry, and opened up a new field of cadences that have since brought joy and color into my heaviest hours.

"Miss Thorpe, our English Litt. teacher at school," she told me, "is the only mistress who really understands people our age. Some teachers have a calling, like parsons," she added, "and Thorpey is one of them. She's introduced us to a lot of modern poets, nearly all killed in the war, poor dears, and her favorite, and mine too, is Alan Seager, the American boy. I like everything he wrote because . . . well, because nothing that happened to him could take the sparkle away!"

"What did happen to him?" I asked, curiously.

She told me about Alan Seager, how he came to France a few years before the war, and how, when Paris was threatened by the Germans, decided that he was under an obligation to defend the city that had been his inspiration; how he served through three years of trench warfare and died, obscurely, at the barricade he had visualized in the best known of his verses. When she was discussing something that had captured her imagination she acted quite shamelessly, and as she quoted "Rendezvous with Death" I could see Alan Seager penning the lines among the debris of a shattered Champagne village.

"Do you know any more of that kind of stuff?" I demanded, eagerly. She was flattered by my enthusiasm and went on to quote her favorite verse from Seager, a little poem inspired by the memory of a prewar love. Later on, much later on, I found and learned the verses myself:

"Out of the past's remote, delirious abysses
Shine forth as once you shone—beloved head,
Laid back in ecstasy between our blinding kisses,
Transfigured with the bliss of being so coveted.

"And my sick arms will part, and though hot fever sear it,
My mouth will curve again with the old, tender flame,
And darkness will come down, still finding in my spirit
The dream of your brief love, and on my lips your name."

There was magic in the way she recited those lines, the kind of magic, I think, that Seager himself would have understood so readily, and as she said them it was not the ghosts of the Negro seamen who hovered over Crusoe Jack's shabby cabin, but the benign ghost of someone to whom the ecstasy of first love was still a strong, bright flame, strong enough and bright enough to light a candle in the hearts of two romantic young idiots and persuade them that it was enough to light them down the years.

Toward evening, when there was not much chance of being observed on the south side of the island, we roamed the beach and knoll and caught some flatfish in a pool left by the tide. We took them home and fried them, telling each other that they were delicious, and after our evening record recital we talked again until it was late, neither of us caring to admit that, as the hours passed, we were progressively conscious of the enormity of our situation and terrified of its outcome.

So passed three idyllic days, days spent in cautious sun-bathing, talking, preparing picnic meals, gathering driftwood for the fire and a good deal of innocent love-making of the kind that makes sweaty nonsense of the love-making to which film audiences have been conditioned since the advent of Metro-Goldwyn-Mayer and Paramount.

Such kisses as we exchanged, and they were not as many as we might have exchanged in that solitude, were spontaneously given and received, and all our caresses were gentle and playful. I don't know why this should be so; we were young, eager, and very well pleased with one another. There was nobody to surprise us or embarrass us, as young lovers are so tiresomely surprised, and so easily embarrassed. We had outgrown the shyness of displaying a mutual desire for affectionate exchanges; we acknowledged, with delight, that we belonged one to the other, and therefore had access to all but the innermost chamber of one another's thoughts and feelings. Yet we were not lovers in the real sense of the word, not then, not when we could have been and with such complete innocence.

I think we held back for different reasons. On her part she treasured the magic web we had spun, month by month and day by day, since our first meeting in the larch wood. She treasured it, yet was aware of its extreme delicacy. She wanted leisure to enjoy its beauty before moving on to explore its intricacies, for there was a kind of timelessness about this period in our lives and although both of us were acutely aware that the immediate future was perilously uncertain, we were yet able to look beyond into the years when we would have outgrown the prohibitions of the present and could contemplate them with laughter and nostalgia.

I, for my part, had another, darker reason for holding back when her lips touched mine and she murmured my name over and over again like an incantation. I wanted to emerge from this strange, sweet interlude free of guilt. I wanted to be ready to challenge her parents and her gilded background without having to explain my deepest feelings for Diana to people who could never measure them in terms of human emotion. I wanted to stand upright and meet their scorn, not to kneel and have it poured over me like scoldings leveled at a willful child. I wanted, even if I had to wait for years and years, to claim Diana as a right, not to beg for her, as one beseeching an impossible favor. This much her trust and declaration had done for me and they brought with them a current of steady triumph, as if the sap of manhood had been pumped into me by my unlooked-for responsibilities. I was no longer afraid of the Gayelorde-Suttons and their money. To a degree Diana's underwater kiss had banished that fear, come what may, threaten who would.

On the fourth night I was awakened by a frightful clamor through which I could hear my name being called, plaintively and urgently.

It was pitch dark and during the night a southwesterly gale had whipped up and was howling across the island like an army of dervishes, piling the sea on the beach in a long thunder of sound.

As I fought the tug of sleep there came a particularly vicious gust that ripped the tarpaulin from the rear end of the hut, exposing us to a downpour of slanting rain, cold and mercilessly direct, as though the storm-tossed clouds had singled out our particular corner of the coast for a thorough drenching.

I scrambled up and called back to Diana, torn between the desire to reassure her and the need to save the tarpaulin before it billowed across the island and was lost.

Diana won; we collided in the blustering darkness and instantly her arms went around me.

"Jan, oh Jan, you're there! What's happened? It's so dark and awful . . . !"

I made a great effort and pulled myself together.

"It's all right, Di," I soothed, stroking her streaming hair, "it's just a storm and the wind has ripped the tarpaulin off. Wait, I'll take the light and get it!"

"Don't leave me alone," she wailed. "I can't stay here alone, Jan!"

"All right, then you come too . . . where's the damned light . . . we've got to find the light!"

We groped around the hut, stumbling over items of kit and finally locating the bull's-eye near the fireplace. Its weak beam revealed a sorry state of affairs. When we had turned in, the cabin was a warm, cozy haven; now it was a half-flooded ruin, with seventy-mile-an-hour gusts sucking at what remained of its roof and torrents of rain streaming down the ramshackle timber walls.

I took her by the hand and together we staggered out and around behind the hut, flashing the beam from side to side in the hope of spotting the tarpaulin.

The wind was so strong out here that it hammered us like a rain of punches and we had difficulty in remaining on our feet. The loose sand of the hillocks came at us like a volley of darts and the roar of the breakers, fifty yards below us at high-water mark, was deafening. We groped our way, drenched and half-blinded, across the sandhills. On the far side of the island, where the rocks sloped away, the force of the wind abated somewhat, enabling us to reach the inshore tide mark, and here we at last stumbled upon the tarpaulin, soaked and tattered, held in a crevice between two rocks. Somehow we dragged it back to the rear of the shack, where we crouched under the lee of the chimney breast, doing what we could to shelter ourselves under the miserable remnant of tarpaulin. Soon Diana's teeth began to chatter and I thought about trying to light the fire and trying some-how to make a hot drink. Then I remembered that all the driftwood would be wet and anyway, in this kind of chaos how could I find kindling and strike matches?

There was nothing to do but wait for dawn, and it was a long time coming.

We lay there, pressed together, sharing what warmth remained in our bodies, until the wind began to drop, the gusts grew more widely spaced and, at last, a gray, reluctant light showed in the sky over Nun's Head.

Then, with infinite difficulty, we stood and spread the tarpaulin over one corner of the cabin, weighting it down with the largest stones we could find. It wasn't much of a shelter and the downpour had given place to a heavy, persistent drizzle, but it was a good deal better than remaining in the open. When it was quite light I scouted around for some paper and sticks. I found a small pile of driftwood that might be coaxed into a fire, but there was nothing to get it going with. By this time, however, Diana had rallied somewhat.

"Use the phonograph records," she suggested. "They're waxy and they've been under cover in the lid."

I found the records and broke them into jagged pieces. After one or two failures we soon had a frail fire going, Diana collecting likely pieces of damp wood, while I slopped along the desolate beach to refill the water can, upset in our groping during the night.

In the half hour the kettle took to boil we surveyed the ruins. Our rugs were soaked and there was no promise of sunshine to dry them. Our food stores, such as they were, were reduced to a soggy paste and the only things left to eat were Diana's two remaining cans of fruit. Neither of us much fancied a breakfast of cold peaches or pineapple, but the tea warmed us and gave us sufficient heart to discuss the situation.

"We'll have to pack it in, Di," I told her. "We can't stay here in this weather without food and shelter. I daresay we could dry out the rugs somehow and maybe patch up the cabin, but suppose we do? By tomorrow we'll be famished."

She said nothing for a moment or two, her small face pinched and strained with the ordeal of the night, her wet hair still plastered in glorious disorder across her cheeks. She sat quite still, hugging her knees and staring into the slow, smoky fire. At last she said:

"Right! Then I'll go back and give myself up, providing we do it separately and providing you aren't involved, Jan."

"How can we do that?" I asked. "It's broad daylight now and we're sure to be spotted going across, or landing."

"Then we shall have to put up with it until dark," she said, firmly. "Then we'll pack up and row across to Nun's Bay. You can drop me there and go on home yourself. I'll get in touch somehow. We'll think up a plan before we actually part."

I turned this over in my mind and it seemed about the best course open to us. We dried wood, built up the fire, and decided to take the risk of the smoke being seen, for we could not face the prospect of staying there, wet through and shivering, without the cheering glow and frequent draughts of hot tea.

The weather settled in drear and hopeless, so much so that at midday I was doubtful about making a dinghy trip across open water, but later on, although the rain persisted, the wind dropped altogether and the sea was no more than choppy.

Bad weather has a devastating effect on romance. All the sparkle had died from our island adventure and the rock itself had been changed by dripping skies and chilling southwesterly winds from a remote Eden to a dismal place of exile. We were depressed, too, by the inevitability of a prolonged separation. Perhaps, I thought, we had been away just long enough to persuade Diana's father to cancel her Swiss plans, but whether this was so or not, it was quite certain that the escapade would lead to a much stricter watch being kept upon her and from now on every meeting would necessitate complicated planning and considerable risks of discovery.

We worked out a kind of letter post, inspired, I seem to remember, by an old print Diana possessed, depicting a girl in frills and flounces making her way through a tangled wood to a letter box in a hollow tree. I agreed to call at the "box" every night and pick up any messages, leaving my replies. Even a night and a day under seeping skies could not extinguish Diana's enthusiasm for exploring the secret passages of romance.

Toward dusk the rain ceased, although the sky remained overcast and whitecaps flecked the surface of the bay. Diana said we ought to take the things down to the boat and bale it out before we pulled her down the beach.

"After that downpour last night she'll probably be half full!" she said, gloomily.

I had overlooked this, and we picked up our belongings and went out across the sand pit to the head of the gully, where we had landed and dragged the boat clear of the tide line. When we climbed the dune that looked down on the shallow cleft we stopped and gazed at one another with horror. The gully was empty and the dinghy was gone!

We ran shouting to one another along the entire beach as far as the old wreck. There was no sign of the boat until we reached the extreme southeastern corner of the island and there, left behind by the tide, was one of the floor boards. Apart from that there was nothing but driftwood, cork floats and ragged whiskers of ruined lobster pots. We made a complete tour of the coast in the deepening twilight but there was no sign of the boat. She must have been washed out of the gully by rain and carried away by the ebb tide.

I knew what I must do and I set to work at once. In the last glimmer of light we rooted among the overhang of the dunes for dry or semidry kindling and driftwood. When we had gathered several armfuls we dragged it to the westerly point of the island, directly facing Whinmouth. Then, with dismal solemnity, we carried out the remains of our fire in the saucepan and set the pile alight, heaping the brushwood up until we had a good, strong blaze. I knew that old Tom Yelland, the pilot, would want to know who was tending a fire on Nun's Island the evening following a heavy storm, and it was not long before we saw the light of the pilot boat swing out into the estuary and head out to sea to catch the easterly swell and bear down toward us.

About half an hour passed before the lights bobbed inshore and during that interval we said very little. Finally Diana stood up and tossed back her hair.

"Let me do the talking, Jan," she said. "I'm better at it than you."

"He'll take us back to Whinmouth first," I told her, "and he'll put two and two together at once, so it's no good pitching him an unlikely yarn."

"Listen, Jan," she said, "we've only got a few more minutes and after that it might be months—years even, before we even see one another again."

Her warning bored into me like a drill and involuntarily I began to protest.

"It's true," she went on, relentlessly, "so listen, Jan, and don't interrupt! Promise?"

"I promise, Di."

"Well, then," she said, speaking very levelly, "first I want to say thank you for everything, for coming here and for looking after me so wonderfully. Nobody could have done it so well, not even the real Jan, who was much heavier and stupider than you and really a bit of a bore when he wasn't in action!"

I managed a wry grin at this. It had crossed my mind more than once in the past that Diana would have found Jan Ridd infuriating, notwithstanding his masterful masculinity and heroic mold.

"Secondly, I want you to know that I'm more in love with you than ever and always will be, no matter what happens from now on. Anyone else would seem terribly feeble after you, Jan, and even if they had your kind of he-manship they wouldn't understand me nearly so well as you do, or be anything like so patient with *my* impatience, if you see what I mean. As soon as all this blows over I'll be packed off somewhere, if not Switzerland then somewhere else a long way away, but it can't be forever, because when I'm twenty-one I can do as I jolly well like and I will, don't you fret! I'll come back to you and find you wherever you are and we'll be together, for always. We'll find another Sennacharib maybe and we'll pick up where we left off, doing all the things we like doing and being the sort of people we want to be, d'you understand?"

"Yes, Di, I understand and I feel the same way about everything!"

"I'm glad," Diana went on, "because there's one other thing and that is, we've both got to stop struggling for a bit. Things are too strong for us at the moment and we've got to save our strength and drift with the tide like our poor old boat, waiting until we're in a position to go our own way in spite of all the opposition. That means that you mustn't make a scene when we get back, Jan, and you must just sit quiet and let them say anything, do anything, and treat the whole thing as if it was just a silly sort of a prank and hadn't any real meaning behind it. That's very important, because if they go on thinking that, they'll let up on us sooner or later, and forget about it and that'll be our chance, d'you see?"

It was very sound reasoning for a girl her age and temperament and I compared it, to its advantage, with the sour resentment and defiance that had been smoldering inside me for a long time now. Any kind of honest declaration on our part would be received with anger and contempt, not only on the part of her parents but on the part of people like Uncle Reuben and Aunt Thirza, who would be sure to share Mrs. Gayelorde-Sutton's scorn for a love affair between people as young and as socially remote as Diana and myself. Before I could comment on this, however, Tom Yelland hailed us from the shallows. I picked up our sopping bundles and turned toward the beach.

"Just a minute," said Diana. "I want to kiss you, Jan!"

I dropped my bundles and put my arms around her. My lips tasted the salt on her cheek and she shivered as I murmured her name.

Tom hailed again and Diana whispered, "Darling Jan, darling, darling Jan!" as I stood back and called to Tom. Then, without another word, we crossed the hillock to the mouth of the gully and waded out to the boat.

Chapter Seven

UNCLE REUBEN was the hero of that dismal week. I had always known that beneath his outward crust of holier-than-thou respectability was the core of a social rebel, but until now I had been inclined to share his brother Mark's opinion that, in many ways, Reuben was a hypocrite, that he thundered against others' shortcomings from pulpit and political platform because he had always lacked the courage to expose himself to a man's ordinary temptations. I was wrong and Mark was wrong. Uncle Reuben was a man who drew his inner strength of character from the Old Testament, who really did worship at the altar of self-denial and personal integrity, who believed not only in a fair day's work for a fair day's pay but in a handshake instead of the contract, and in the preservation, at almost any cost, of human dignity in terms of work, truth and resistance to the Devil. He was gruff, intolerant, and sometimes harsh in his judgments but he was no hypocrite; he had more moral courage than anyone I ever met.

In the days that followed our surrender I came to know and respect Reuben in a way that the lobster-helmeted troopers of Cromwell must have revered their Bible-thumping leader in the field. By some standards, I suppose, he was a narrow-minded old stick-in-the-mud but he was also a man, and a good deal more of one than anyone else involved in the repercussions of our flight.

There had been more fuss about our disappearance than I had anticipated. Diana's note about getting a job in a city had fooled nobody and the police were informed of her absence that same night.

Extensive inquiries were made and these soon resulted in a report that we had been seen together at the regatta dance on the previous Friday. This at once involved me, and when it was known that I too had left town at short notice, it did not need a trained detective to unravel the basic facts of our long association. Even Keeper Croker was called in to describe how we first met and poor old Drip, the governess, faced recriminations that came near to giving her a nervous breakdown.

There were one or two stormy interviews between Uncle Reuben and Aunt Thirza on the one hand, and Mrs. Gayelorde-Sutton and her solicitors on the other, but the upshot of these was that the hunt veered off on a false scent, for it was assumed that we had run away to try to get married at Gretna Green, in imitation of another teenage couple about whom the papers had had plenty to say a month or so before.

As Diana had prophesied, no one thought of looking nearer at hand, and by the third day, when some of the details had leaked out to the press, Heronslea was picketed by local linage men and so-called special correspondents. These were given a very cavalier reception by Mrs. Gayelorde-Sutton, who always considered that a free press was the principal drawback of democracy. The result was inevitable. The more she clamped down on news, the wilder and more improbable were the stories printed, and when Diana had been found and packed off home in a taxi by Tom Yelland and the local police, the Heronslea keepers had a full-time task keeping reporters at bay.

We had our share of the press siege but Uncle Reuben was an old hand at dealing with newspapermen and they did not bother us nearly as much; partly, I suppose, because the Heronslea background and Mr. Gayelorde-Sutton's notoriety in the City made Diana a more tempting target.

It all died down after a few days. The story was killed by an earthquake in Japan, then by Germany's abrupt exit from the League of Nations, and later by Diana's heavy cold, which kept her in bed and helped her mother to prevent the press from interviewing her until the story was stone cold.

I stayed indoors most of the time and Uncle Reuben did my work. I was glad of Aunt Thirza that week, for she reserved all her natural belligerence for callers but behaved toward me with extraordinary tenderness—far more, I felt, than I had deserved of her.

Talking to her over our meals (Uncle Luke was already insulated by silent contemplation of the migratory habits of martins and swifts), I realized how wise Diana had been to urge me to encourage the adult world to look upon the whole episode as a teen-age prank.

"Giddon, did 'ee ever zee such a fuss over a couple o' chits takin' it into their ades to go'n live on a desert island?" Thirza snorted, heaping my plate as though I had a dinosaur's capacity for vegetables. "They papermen want something to do, I reckon, writin' all that ole nonsense about something as happens yer every time kids go near the zea!"

The romantic or "sex" angle of the situation entirely escaped her. Diana and I might have been a pair of city toddlers who had succumbed to the magic of blue water and golden sands and sailed away from the harbor to play pirates.

"T'iz all on account o' they Zuttons"—Aunt Thirza would never concede Mrs. Gayelorde-Sutton her double-barreled name—"havin' too much money!" she declared. "If they 'ad to turn to, an' work vor it, zame as most of us, they'd smack her bottom an' think no more of it, so there! Yer, 'ave zum more tatties, boy," she added. "You couldn't have had much to feed 'ee up on that ole rock out there— bliddy silly plaace to go this sort of weather!"

Uncle Reuben, of course, took a much more serious view of the matter. The sheer extravagance of our gesture outraged his common sense and I think my willing participation in such a wild adventure permanently lowered his opinion of me as a future editor of the *Whinmouth & District Observer*. What worried him even more, however, was the vague implication, in one of the Sunday newspapers, that we had enjoyed a bizarre honeymoon on the island, and it was this aspect of it that led him to call around and demand to talk to me in private, closing the door on a muttering Thirza and a completely bewildered Brother Luke.

It was the first time we had been alone since I returned, and his brooding presence embarrassed me. When he tried to speak of what was in his mind, however, he became the more embarrassed of the two and finally I had to help him out, for he could never quite bring himself to admit that a child made its appearance via its mother's vagina, or still less that this rather shameful fact was preceded by an even more undignified one in which men played a degrading part.

"If you're wondering what really happened while we were alone out there, you can stop worrying, Uncle," I told him, and was glad to see that my words brought instant comfort to him. "It wasn't that kind of love at all, although I daresay lots of folk around here will always think it was. The whole thing would never have happened if Mrs. Gayelorde-Sutton hadn't decided to send Diana away to a finishing school in Switzerland."

This inclined him more to our side. Despite his ceaseless League of Nations work and Free Trade theories, he was a fanatical isolationist. Deep down he hated and distrusted all foreigners, even the blameless Swiss.

"Why on earth do people like her want to send their daughters to foreign schools?" he growled. "Aren't there good enough schools over here, where she can learn to behave herself properly?"

"It's all part of the setup," I told him, and explained a little of Mrs. Gayelorde-Sutton's plans for Diana's future. He shook his head, despairingly.

"Arrant snobbery! That's all it is!" he muttered. "Too many of those people about nowadays and it's where the Tories get their money from, I imagine. How can you want to go about with a girl like that, John? They aren't our sort at all!"

"Diana is," I said, stoutly. "She hates it as much as you do, and hated it enough to run away from it all."

"But why did you have to get involved? You aren't being sent to a finishing school in Switzerland."

I was tempted to try to explain to him how I felt about Diana, and how she felt about me. It occured to me that he might be able to understand a little of our love for Sennacharib and the glorious avenues of freedom it offered us, but in the end I thought better of it and simply mumbled:

"We get on, Uncle Reuben. We've grown very fond of one another after all this time and it seemed such a shame to spoil it all!"

He sighed and stood up, awkwardly patting my shoulder. There was a good deal more genuine affection in the gesture than he was able to convey.

"Very well, John," he said, "let's forget it all and start afresh. Come back to work tomorrow, and I daresay it'll all blow over in a day or so. Most of these things do, even in places like Whinmouth."

He was wrong in one sense. Whinmouth would have forgotten it almost at once, but the townsfolk were by no means as deeply involved as was Mrs. Gayelorde-Sutton. The day I went back to work we had a visit from her, and it was then that I had an opportunity of estimating Uncle Reuben's full stature.

2.

I thought I knew Mrs. Gayelorde-Sutton as well as anyone by this time, but I was nevertheless amazed by the viciousness of her attack. The moment she saw me she jabbed a trembling finger at me and squealed: "*Thet's* him! *Thet's* the boy! What's he doing here? He ought to be in a reformatory, thet's where *he* ought to be!"

I was badly shaken but stood my ground, reminding myself of Diana's final injunctions about this interview and how it should be handled.

Uncle Reuben, however, was disinclined to be hectored in his own office. He not only disliked Mrs. Gayelorde-Sutton personally but detested everything that she stood for, socially and politically.

"If you've come here for an apology for John's part in this silly business you'll get one, Mrs. Gayelorde-Sutton!" he said, stolidly removing the pipe from his mouth and laying it down on his cluttered desk. "On the other hand, if you've simply called to make trouble, and scream idiotic accusations at everybody, I'll have you removed, if necessary by the police!"

Mrs. Gayelorde-Sutton opened and closed her mouth twice. Her color mounted so rapidly, and her hands fluttered so violently, that I thought for a moment she was going to have a seizure. When at last she did manage to speak, her voice shot into a high, unnatural key and she had to try again, after a few rapid intakes of tobacco-laden air. This made her cough and we waited, with studied politeness, until she had quite recovered. Then Uncle Reuben nodded gravely at me and I took my cue.

"I'm very sorry Diana caused you so much worry," I mumbled, flushing. "I don't think she meant to and I'm sure I didn't!"

As an apology it left a good deal to be desired and Mrs. Gayelorde-Sutton gobbled it up like an insignificant crumb, glaring hard at me, her slightly poppy, green eyes almost starting from their sockets. I had always thought of her as a handsome woman but she did not look handsome now; she looked almost pathetic, like a badly spoiled child who has been goaded into a hysterical temper. Even she realized this, I think, for in the next few moments she made a great effort to calm herself.

"I could hev put you in prison for this," she said. "And I would, too, if Aim'ald hadn't been so . . . so utterly *wicked* about it!"

I wondered what this meant and made a guess at it; on Diana's return, no doubt, and after studying the newspapers, Mrs. Gayelorde-Sutton had probably told Diana that she intended prosecuting me on some obscure charge, possibly abduction, or something of that nature. Diana must have countered this by saying that if her mother did anything so stupid she herself would come into court on my behalf. Uncle Reuben, however, cut short my speculations by once more reducing the wretched woman to the point of self-strangulation.

"You couldn't do any such thing, Mrs. Sutton," he said—and I noted that he had taken a leaf from Aunt Thirza's book and dropped the "Gayelorde" in order to reduce his opponent to size. "John certainly did wrong in helping your daughter to run away, and also in not telling you about it when she did, but as the whole thing was your daughter's idea and not his, you could only charge him with being an accessory, and they'd laugh you out of court on that! Believe me, madam, I've a long experience in these matters. If you really want to bring a charge go right ahead and do it!"

Mrs. Gayelorde-Sutton then changed her tactics. Suddenly she began to snivel and her sniffs did nothing to restore her dignity. Uncle Reuben continued to contemplate her gravely until finally she blew her nose into a very expensive-looking handkerchief and wailed:

"It was a *terrible* thing to do! *Terrible!* No *nice* boy would do such a thing, I'm sure." When she said this her vowel-torturing accent disappeared. It was the first time I had ever heard her speak like anybody else and it somehow made her a little more human. Uncle Reuben, however, was unmoved by her tears.

"I'm not sure about that," he said heavily, "but if it is so, then no nice girl would do it either."

This rocketed Mrs. Gayelorde-Sutton out of the doldrums and she began to scream again.

"Ai'll tell you something, Mr. Waht-ever-your-name-is!" she began, her accent returning as all trace of tears disappeared. "The moment Ai hed Aim'ald back Ai called in mai doctor, in order to make a certain examination and set mai mind at rest, once and for all. If his report had been other than it was, then you can be quaite certain that this would be a matter for the police, notwithstanding what yew hev to say about it!"

Her statement so horrified me that I felt physically sick. I saw, as one might regard a series of pictures resulting from a thumb-flick of a book, the sequence of events implied by her admission—the solemn arrival of moonfaced Doctor Barnes, their family physician, his brief interview with Mrs. Gayelorde-Sutton, his heavy tread up the staircase and along the white passage to Diana's room, his routine pulse-feeling of the patient pending the real examination that was to follow, and so on, up to the moment when Diana was face to face with a humiliation that converted our love into an obscene joke. Yet, even while my imagination shied away from this scene, I was ashamed for Uncle Reuben and I think I might have flung myself at Mrs. Gayelorde-Sutton and bundled her out of the room had I failed to notice the curious expression on my uncle's face.

He was not miserably embarrassed, as I had fully expected him to be, and he did not seem to be as irritated as he had been earlier in the interview. He was looking straight at Mrs. Gayelorde-Sutton with a mixture of pity and disdain, as though he had just heard somebody say something that was certain to bring ridicule and disgust upon them, and had said it out of sheer ignorance and lack of ordinary consideration.

He stood up, reaching for the comfort of his pipe and hammering the bowl on his open palm at regularly spaced intervals. When he began to speak he continued this emphatic gesture, punctuating each phrase with a distinct rap, as though hammering nails into the coffin of Mrs. Gayelorde-Sutton's taste and breeding.

"Madam," he said, without raising his voice, yet somehow contriving to enlarge its volume enough to be heard above the clack of the presses in the works, "I feel bound to tell you that I find you a contemptible creature! Thoroughly contemptible, do you understand? If you were a man I should have the greatest pleasure, *the very greatest pleasure*, in picking you up by the scruff of the neck and dropping you into the nearest dustbin!"

I forgot to be horrified when I heard this. I just gaped at them, staring at one another as they stood barely a foot apart. Uncle Reuben was still rapping away with his pipe, and Mrs. Gayelorde-Sutton, colorless now, was staring at him like a rabbit facing a huge, hungry stoat.

"That you should find it necessary to take such steps with your hapless daughter is one thing," he went on, in the same level tone, "and although I most sincerely pity her it is really none of my business. That you should find it necessary to come here and scream such disgusting admissions to me, in my own office, *is* my business, and I find it insupportable, d'you hear me? *Insupportable*, madam! I am not myself a father but if I was, and it came to my knowledge that you had sought to betray your trust in a girl of mine in that . . . that . . . unspeakable fashion, then I should turn you upside down and deal with you as I fear you neglected to deal with your daughter when she might have benefited from that form of correction! And now, Mrs. Sutton, go back to your big house and endeavor to regulate your family without wasting my time and making me despair utterly of the entire human race!"

With that he strode across to the door and flung it open, waiting beside it while she remained motionless midway between me and the cluttered desk.

I looked away from her then. It hurt me to see a woman in the grip of such a frightful temper. I believe that if she had been within reach of a lethal weapon she would have killed him on the spot. She trembled violently from head to foot and her face, pink with temper a moment before, was now as white as her long, elegant gloves. At last she made an indeterminate sound that might have been a word, a cough, or an intake of breath. Then, before I could look at her again, she whipped around and walked jerkily through the open door and out of my life. It was years before I spoke to her again and when I did it was in vastly different circumstances.

I got up and drifted over to the smeared window, craning my neck around the intervening stack in order to see her climb into her car and shoot off up the incline in a flurry of blue exhaust. Uncle Reuben went back to his chair and slumped down in it, his Victorian eloquence spent and his heavy breathing betraying the fact that now the interview was over he was badly shaken by the turn it had taken. He sat for a moment pressing his hands on the desk and then muttered hoarsely, "Close the door, boy!"

I closed it and sat down near the window, exhausted, embarrassed and utterly wretched.

"I don't blame you doing what you did, John, and I certainly don't blame her daughter," he said, suddenly. "If she was my mother I wouldn't run away from her, I'd make her some toadstool soup, or push her under a bus when no one was looking!"

I said nothing; there seemed nothing adequate to say; and he mistook my silence and subjection for fear.

"You don't want to worry about any of her crazy threats, boy," he went on. "There isn't a thing she can do and her solicitor has already told her or she would have done it. I'll tell you something else, though. I think it would be a good idea all around if you cleared out of here for a bit. With her around and you going about your business, you never know what trouble she might go out of her way to begin! Go for a walk, boy, and let me think this out. Whatever we do ought to be done at once!"

I got up and stood beside him. "Thanks, Uncle Reuben," I said, and meant it, from the bottom of my heart.

I went out and through the town, turning my back on Sennacharib and taking the riverside road. For the first time since I had gone to Heronslea on the afternoon of my fifteenth birthday, Sennacharib was somewhere I did not want to be. At that particular moment it suggested scribblings on lavatory walls.

3.

It was mid-September when Diana and I surrendered. By the second week in October I had left Whinmouth and, apart from an occasional holiday, was to remain away for nearly three years. Uncle Reuben must have moved with uncharacteristic speed, for within a few days of Mrs. Gayelorde-Sutton's visit to the office, I was installed as glorified office boy on the staff of *The Illustrated Echo,* off Bouverie Street, E.C.4. Here I remained for my period of exile, my home a bed-sitting room, within a twopenny Underground ride of the City.

It was sound judgment on Uncle Reuben's part to spirit me away from Whinmouth. The roar and bustle of London and the excitement of a new job in new surroundings enabled me to get my preoccupation with Diana into some sort of perspective and to isolate it from my everyday life of work, snack lunches and interminable journeys on the Underground. Soon I was able to enclose it in a kind of glass case, like a man living a shabby, hand-to-mouth existence who owns a single object of great beauty, something that is a source of comfort and inspiration to him.

Every night during those first autumn weeks, when my feet were aching from pounding asphalt pavements, and when I was shut off from the endless murmur of London and crouching over a minute gas fire in my second-floor back room, in Guilford Street, my mind would return to Sennacharib as an exile's seeking home, and I would follow again the wide curves of Teasel Brook, or climb up through the larch wood to the oak paddock and watch for buzzards.

I cannot honestly say that I was unhappy. Sometimes the very consciousness of exile brought with it a curious satisfaction, as though I were doing an enforced penance for some unrepented sin, and when I remembered Diana it was not with a lover's yearning. Part of my mind was occupied in preparing for the future, our future, and pondering the economics of our problem. With the other part I ranged the museum of the past, examining and analyzing each hour we had spent together and recalling every significant remark we had exchanged during our expeditions on the common, to the tower, or during our stay on Nun's Island.

I made no effort to get in touch with her, knowing that a botched attempt would jeopardize the future and very probably make things unpleasant for both of us. I had no idea where she had been sent, or what she was doing, and for a long time I made no attempt to satisfy my curiosity in this field.

Once, during a week's holiday in Devon, I nerved myself to creep through the Heronslea copse on the Shepherdshey road, but the house looked deserted and Nat told me that the family never seemed to come now, although they continued to maintain a large outdoor staff. After that I went back to my job and my uninspiring lodgings, waiting for her to find a means of getting in touch with me, and as the months passed it became easier to put aside all thought of her, often for days at a time, and catch up on a youth that seemed, in some ways, to have been petrified since the day Keeper Croker applied his half nelson and she rode out of the woods like a princess in a fairy tale.

I made a few friends among the junior staff. I even took one or two of the girl clerks and packers to the cinema. I learned to drink. I explored London and parts of Kent, improved my French at a night school, and even attended an Italian class one night a week. *The Illustrated Echo* was a pleasant office in which to work and the job suited my inclinations very well at that time. The *Echo* was a weekly magazine that made two quite separate approaches to its subscribers. The main part of the publication was devoted to what might be called social and historical flashbacks; the remaining pages were crammed with a wide variety of literary competitions, quizzes, and crossword puzzles, all rather more original than was customary in this type of periodical during the thirties. The editor, Edwin Blackler, was a former *County Observer* reporter and an old friend of Uncle Reuben's. That was how the job had been secured for me, and I think I did my best during that first year or so to acknowledge this debt and convince Mr. Blackler that I was a very ambitious young man, anxious to advance in my profession and grateful for the opportunity to arrive in Fleet Street before I was twenty.

My work was at first limited to errand running and stamp-licking, but after a few weeks, when I had impressed myself upon the chief subeditor by giving him an idea, I was promoted to a very junior position on the editorial staff and given a raise that brought my salary up to five pounds a week. Out of this I had to pay out more than two pounds for fares and lodgings, but even so it was a great advance on what I had been getting in Whinmouth, and by economizing on lunches I was able to accumulate money in a post-office savings account. The first year I was there I was tipped the winner of the Grand National and made an extra twenty pounds. This might have tempted me to speculate further on racing, but luckily for me Mr. Blackler heard about it and being of the same nonconformist cast of mind as his friend Reuben, he called me in and read me a terrifying lecture on the evils of gambling. This would not have deterred me from joining in the office pastime of spotting winners but I was anxious at that time to make a good impression on him and left the bookies alone.

A week or two after that I went to Blackler with a sheaf of ideas and he welcomed them, for it was difficult to find something new and sensational in the flashback field every week of the year. He at once set me to work collecting material and old photographs for a ten-page feature on Jack the Ripper, and afterwards on the South Sea Bubble and, later still, material for a pictorial inquiry into the assassination of the Archduke that had touched off the First World War.

It was exacting but absorbing work. Most of the day I trotted about London, keeping a careful tally of my bus fares and visiting record offices, embassies, museums, picture galleries, and the like.

Sometimes I would have a slice of luck, as when I found someone whose aged father had been associated with the actor Booth who murdered President Lincoln, and I was able to hand in some unpublished photographs of the sixties and a wedge of secondhand theories about Booth's motives. Whatever its drawbacks, the job was never dull and left me free time in the evenings; I used this time to make myself thoroughly familiar with London and loiter in the Charing Cross Road bookshops.

This was not simply a means of passing the time. It was the result of some constructive thought about my future. I was determined, by now, to become a full-time writer, but the theatre interested me far less than it interested most young men and I greatly doubted my ability to write a novel. My strongest suit, I soon decided, was history, and I decided to put it to work in a way that was probably influenced by the *Echo*. It was an easy step from raking up material of a sensational aspect of the past to turning the same stories into full-length narratives.

My method of approach was naïve but nonetheless practical. I went through all the reference books relating to each subject that interested me and when satisfied that nothing had been published on it for the past half century, I noted it down and finally emerged with a curious list of characters who had never been presented to the reading public as anything other than two-dimensional people in the national biography.

My favorite among these was Margaret of Anjou, wife of Henry VII and leader of the Lancastrian cause throughout the Wars of the Roses. When I had amassed all the data I could find on her, I got a reader's ticket to the British Museum and from then on spent a good deal of my spare time under the famous dome. I bought a fat exercise book, a folding card table and a battered old typewriter, and with these tools joined the martyred army of literary geniuses living in the square mile around Euston Station. I think I was more in love with my role than I was with my material, but for all that the book began to grow under the title of *The Royal Tigress*.

It was cold and desperately lonely up there in a narrow bed-sitter, overlooking a car breaker's yard and acres of somber houses, but the room and the aspect were valuable stage properties, and as the story of the dynastic struggle took shape I congratulated myself on graduating from hack journalist to unrecognized genius. It was a kind of game I played and it helped to compensate me for the loss of the southwest wind off Whinmouth quay and the golden glare of the gorse thickets climbing Teasel Edge.

I suppose I had been working on *The Royal Tigress* for about three months when I came across an item in the gossip column of an evening paper. I had, as I said, made up my mind not to approach Diana, and because I saw no ready means of doing so I had been able to maintain this resolve. All the same, I kept half-hoping that she would contact me by writing to the *Observer*, in Whinmouth. When the months went by without her doing so, I began to wonder if Uncle Reuben, acting on the principle of doing something for someone else's good, might have received and held back a letter or letters. This doubt nagged at me so persistently that I was at length forced to write to him and ask if any letters had come for me. I knew I would get the truth. Uncle Reuben never committed a lie to paper.

He replied innocently that there had been no letters, and his reply bothered me. I began to lose some of my smugness about Diana's fidelity and, in the intervals between tracing the route the beaten Lancastrians had taken after Towton and in digging up photographs and material for the *Illustrated*, I wondered whether she had forgotten all about our pledges and had now regarded me as what she would have described as a "sixth-form pash." Every day I began to doubt her a little more, and every tug of doubt disturbed the comparative tranquillity of spirit I had painfully acquired since we had stood together beside the island bonfire awaiting the arrival of the pilot boat.

By midsummer I was in a ferment about her and my anxieties, added to a heat wave that made central London an insufferable place in which to work and sleep, combined to make me a very wretched and homesick young man.

I was in this self-pitying frame of mind when I got my first lead. It came at the cinema, during a brief newsreel dealing with Goodwood races. The winner of the cup that year was a Frenchman, and although I did not recognize the name when it was spoken by the commentator, I sat up when I saw Diana's French boy, Yves, mincing along beside his father as the winner was being led in after the race.

I searched the screen for Diana and would have been grateful to recognize Mrs. Gayelorde-Sutton among the spectators, but the item soon flashed by and although I sat through the desperately boring feature film twice in order to scan the newsreel again, I learned no more than the bare fact of Diana's friend's triumph.

That night, sleepless and half suffocating in my airless little room, I went over the social calendar of Mrs. Gayelorde-Sutton—Goodwood, Wimbledon, Hurlingham, Ascot, and so on—wondering if Diana was likely to return from wherever she was to accompany her mother to any of these functions, and if she did so, assessing my chances of seeing her at one or other of them and attracting her attention without risking a snub or worse from her parents.

I decided the chance was slim. Our paper did not cover social or sporting events, and the Gayelorde-Suttons always had the most expensive seats. Lacking a press card I was unlikely to get within hailing distance of them, even supposing they were present. Toward daybreak I thought up another half-baked plan, that of phoning the Gayelorde-Sutton's town house under an assumed name and accent, but this was a humiliating failure when I put it into operation the next day. A manservant at the other end of the phone at once asked my name and business and seemed entirely dissatisfied with my mumbled replies. Finally he rang off and I slunk away, telling myself that I was no good at this sort of thing and had no right to be within miles of Fleet Street. Any cub reporter, I knew, would have managed a good deal better than that.

I studied the glossies around Ascot time, hoping I might glean some information from the gossip column. Then I spent an evening or two picketing the house in Palmerston Crescent but gave it up when an elderly constable, after eying me distastefully from the opposite side of the road, crossed over with the obvious intention of moving me on or charging me with loitering.

All this led nowhere and only served to increase my anxiety and frustration. Gone was the resolute attitude of my first months of separation. I had to get information of some kind. The next time I was in Whinmouth I made another cautious tour of the Heronslea copses, and even went so far as to get into casual conversation with an estate gardener in the public bar of The Rifleman. From him I learned that Mr. and Mrs. Gayelorde-Sutton were in America and "the maid was abroad somewhere but not along of 'em." It was the first definite knowledge I had had in almost a year that Diana was still alive, and although it comforted me somewhat (for I reasoned that this went some way toward explaining her failure to write) it did nothing toward re-establishing contact.

Nobody at home referred to Diana. Uncle Reuben had had a satisfactory report about me from his friend, the editor, and I could see that he had now completely forgotten the part Diana had played in removing me to London in the first place. Although, in some ways, I liked going back to Whinmouth, I was always glad when it was time to return to the privacy of my bed-sitter and the demands of *The Illustrated Echo*. In London I was able to keep Diana in her glass case some of the time. Down here she popped out of it every few moments, and the closer I went to Sennacharib, the more painful and depressing became my thoughts.

It was after my return on that occasion that I made my first real effort to put her out of mind altogether. I had written barely a page of *The Royal Tigress* since the night I saw Yves on the newsreel and now I forced myself to contemplate the empty prospects that faced me if I failed to get over Diana and discovered, after years of waiting perhaps, that I was nothing more to her than the partner in an adolescent prank. Sometimes I imagined I could hear her discussing me with a sophisticated friend, over a coffee on some exotic terrace by the sea. "Jan? Oh, we had a lot of fun when Mummy wasn't looking! He was frightfully stuck on me I believe, but the weeniest bit dreary, darling, taken all round."

I was certainly becoming a dull young dog, and one day Twining, the friendly, pimply subeditor, who was several years my senior, told me as much. Twining had married the previous year, after getting his girl into trouble, and now lived out at Twickenham in a semidetached. At the office he frequently bewailed his premature loss of freedom and inveighed against the economic miseries of marriage and parenthood.

"By God, young Leigh," he told me when he overheard me saying that I had no plans for the evening, "you single blokes don't know when you're well off, I'm damned if you do! Look, son, you're free, you've got dough in your pocket, you can go where you like and you can stop there until morning, with no one to chew the fat over you when you turn up with a hang-over and a contented cow's look on your mug. What's eating a kid like you? Why the hell don't you see life while you've got the chance and before some calculating Judy puts tabs on you?"

Twining was no more than a chance acquaintance and never, during my stay in London, did he qualify as a friend, but by this time I felt a desperate need to confide in someone, so without reflecting much upon the matter I told him about Diana. I was surprised and slightly flattered by his interest. He asked me scores of questions about her and gave my answers a good deal of thought. Finally he blew out his cheeks and regarded me with amused contempt.

"Christ, kid," he said, "you've got it bad, haven't you? It's a good job you told me about this, though, because Uncle Twining is the very man to see you through it! I'll tell you what, let's knock off and go down to the pub for a jar. We can talk it over in comparative privacy down there."

I instantly regretted having told him. I was not much attracted to him and I was young enough and green enough to be shocked by his casual attitude to marriage. I had met his wife, a fluffy, talkative little blonde, and I pitied her. Their marriage seemed a very shallow and tawdry partnership when measured against my dreams of marriage to Diana. However, there was no help for it now, so we adjourned to the local pub and carried our beer to an alcove, where he became jocularly confidential.

"Listen here, son, I'm years older than you and maybe it's none of my biz but damn it, I don't like to see a chap hooked the way I was and that's what you're heading into—you'll get married on the rebound to the first bit of skirt you meet the day the lady of the manor gives you the brush-off! Yes, yes, I know, that can't happen, you'll say, but it will, Buddy, it will and I'll tell you how and why."

He then launched into a colorful description of Diana's set, and he knew them well, for he had worked for a time on the gossip page of a daily.

"They're as hard as nails, son, and just as mercenary as their mothers, so don't get any ideas to the contrary. Oh, they're okay for slap and tickle when they're on the point of 'being launched,' and you really can't blame 'em, because the men they eventually do marry never have any lead in their pencils and somehow they know it, even at that age. That's why they run off with chaps like you and make hay while the sun shines, but when it comes to marrying, brother, they keep their eye smack on the ball! Nothing less than three to five thou' a year and a title if they can hook one. You can't blame 'em for that either. If you'd been brought up with someone to wait on you hand, foot and finger, and if you'd kipped in the Carlton at Cannes from the time you could remember, would you trade it to change shoes with an unpaid char and a fortnight at Margate with the kids every August?"

"But Diana isn't like that," I protested, angrily. "She hates the way she's been brought up and there's not an atom of snobbery about her."

He laughed unpleasantly, and although he was genuinely trying to help me I could have struck him across the mouth.

"I didn't expect you to believe me," he said. "You're a bloody little romantic and you've got it coming to you, but you'll believe me in the end, son. You'll look back on this conversation and say to yourself, 'Old Twining was spot on! Old Twining knew his way around. Everything he said would happen *has* happened!' Damn it, man, forget the moonlight and roses for a minute and look on it from the practical viewpoint. How in God's name do you reckon you'll ever be able to keep a girl like that? Suppose you make the grade here? Suppose you land a good job with a national daily? Even then you won't take home more than thirty a week, and I daresay she spends that on clothes and make-up right now. Have another jar, on me this time—you look as if you need one!"

We had another drink and then two more. By the time I had seen Twining onto his train at Waterloo I was slightly drunk and very desperate. He leaned out of the compartment window and gave me a final piece of advice.

"What you need, Leigh, is a woman. Boy, oh boy, do you need a woman! *Any* woman! Take my advice, son, get yourself one tonight and start fresh."

I didn't take his advice at that time. I was far too timid to come to much harm in London and on the few occasions that a prostitute had accosted me I had always mumbled something unintelligible and hurried on my way, with my eyes at pavement level. I told myself, of course, that this was because of Diana but I don't think it was, not at that time. Uncle Reuben had forced himself to lecture me on this subject before he turned me loose in town, and when a closer familiarity with men like Twining encouraged me to take some of his dire warnings with a large pinch of salt, I was engrossed in my book and in grandiose dreams of the future. There was no room in my life for casual encounters.

The conversation, however, did have a sequel.

A week or two later Twining rang down from the subs' room and said that his wife had gone over to her sister's for the weekend and had taken the baby with her. He was on the loose for one Saturday afternoon and evening, and would I care to join him in a pub crawl?

I said I had nothing better to do, and when we left the office about 2 P.M. he piloted me toward a battered Austin Twelve tourer, parked in our truck ramp.

"It's my brother-in-law's," he told me, gleefully. "He said I could have it until tomorrow and it's given me a swell idea. What do you say to a run out into the country, just to see what's growing down there?"

I much preferred this to the cinema and an aimless drift around the suburban pubs, but it was soon clear that Twining's curiosity about the country had nothing to do with wild flowers. We headed straight for Tonbridge, where he had once worked as an estate agent's clerk, and from an inn on the outskirts of the town he made a phone call and rejoined me in high feather.

"I've fixed a date with Peggy," he said. "She's a nifty little piece, an old girl friend of mine, and she's promised to find a friend. There's a hop over at Penshurst, you see, nothing much, but good for a lark, and listen—she says we can go back to her place after for coffee and sandwiches. We're in luck, son! Her old man kicked the bucket years ago and her old woman is deaf as a post and goes to bed at nine anyway."

I felt a certain amount of pleasurable excitement at the prospect of such an evening. Looking back, it seems incredible to me that I had arrived at my eighteenth birthday without ever having been interested in a girl other than Diana, but I know that this was so. I think I was more curious than eager to hold another girl in my arms and try someone else's kisses. Suddenly I began to feel almost grateful to Twining for including me in this philandering expedition.

We had tea and picked up the girls at Peggy's home, a largish, cottage-type house in a quiet, tree-lined cul-de-sac. Peggy was a slim, boyish-looking blonde—Twining was only interested in blondes —and she seemed delighted to welcome him back. I learned afterwards that they had been engaged for a time and it was obvious that she had no idea that he was now a married man.

The girl she brought for me was called Madeleine. She seemed at first a vaguely disinterested young woman. Later I realized that this air was only assumed for my benefit, for when she forgot to pose she became friendly and talkative.

"I'm so glad you're tall," she told me, soon after we had been introduced and had settled ourselves in the back of the car. "I can't stand little men at any price!"

"A little goes a long way," chuckled Twining, who was small himself.

He had already started to paw Peggy in the front of the car and settled down to enjoy himself with desperate resolution.

"Well, girls and boys, off we go! First stop The Bull, Hildenborough, second stop The Cock, Leigh—pronounced 'Li,' Mr. Leigh! Bull and cock! Highly appropriate, what?" and he laughed uproariously at his own feeble quip.

I glanced at Peggy to see how she would take this, for secretly almost everything Twining said was inclined to shock me a little, but she was obviously accustomed to his type of humor and only said, "Now George, behave!" as we roared out of town, Twining showing off madly with a series of rapid gear changes, and Madeleine looking out of the window with studied unconcern, as though already raising a line of defense against tepidity on my part.

I stole a cautious look at her as we went along. She was dark and pale to the point of being pasty. She had a full face and slightly pendulous cheeks, but her eyes were large and brown, with curling lashes that reminded me of Diana's. She had a ripe, sulky mouth and now that I was able to look at her more closely, I saw that she was a good deal older than Peggy, twenty-two at least, and apparently experienced with men. On the way out I rather wished we could swop girls, for Peggy's freshness and vitality appealed to me far more than Madeleine's sultry charm, but there could be no question of that, so I made up my mind that the sooner we had a drink or two, the better would be the prospect of a pleasant evening. I might lose my embarrassment at being paired off with a complete stranger, and she might loosen up a little and come halfway to meet me.

We stopped at the two pubs Twining had named. The girls had gins and lime and we drank beer. Peggy soon became very giggly, but I was right about Madeleine. After the second stop she made the running, nestling close to me, lifting my hand and putting it on her lap.

Soon I began to enjoy myself in a mild sort of way and the evening passed pleasantly enough. The dance was a jolly uninhibited affair, with plenty of loud laughter, bursting balloons, streamers, and squeals of delight from the patrons. We stayed until midnight and then made our way back to Tonbridge, Twining driving with one hand and mounting the curb as we swung into the quiet cul-de-sac where Peggy lived.

Peggy told us to be very quiet, and we all filed in through the back door. The coffee and sandwiches were there but they were mere pretexts. After a sip and a nibble Twining and Peggy retired to the front room, Twining winking at me as he left and pinching the little blonde's bottom with an air of a customer sampling goods.

There was an awkward silence after they had gone. Then Madeleine said, "You haven't been out with many girls, have you, John?"

I was prepared to bluff but she smiled and gave me a peck on the forehead. She looked much more attractive when she smiled and my shame at being spotted as an amateur was reduced by her good-natured approach.

"Never mind," she said, "I'd much sooner have you than that nasty piece of work in there! He's an absolute stinker and for the life of me I can't understand what Peggy sees in him."

I said that nobody could ever see what anyone else saw in anyone. I also admitted that her guess about my lack of experience was accurate. Her interest in this confession surprised me.

"Why?" she wanted to know. "Did you once go steady with someone?"

"Yes," I said, "for a long time—ever since I was a kid."

"But you're only a kid now," she laughed, and then, quite gently: "What happened? Come unstuck?"

"More or less."

"Want to talk about it?"

"No."

"I'm glad," she said. "Most of the chaps I get landed with do. I'm a universal aunt and it isn't very flattering."

She said this so solemnly that I felt sorry for her. I put my arms around her and kissed her, lightly at first but more enthusiastically when she responded with a kind of desperate eagerness. She was a nice girl to kiss and I lost all my shyness after we had stood swaying for a moment or two.

"I like you, John, you're a decent boy, not at all the type I should expect George Twining to go around with," she said, rather breathlessly.

I told her that Twining wasn't a friend, just an office colleague, and she told me that she had recently been thrown over by a boy she expected to marry and that this was the second time, not counting friendships that hadn't amounted to much from the beginning.

"I can't understand that," I said. "You're jolly good company and I think you're pretty and exciting!"

I was alarmed by her reaction to this gallant speech on my part. I only said it with the intention of cheering her up but it had the effect of transforming her expression into something approaching radiancy. I had never had to say things like this to Diana. She didn't need to be flattered or courted, because it had been obvious to her from our first meeting that I regarded her as the most exciting person on earth. With Madeleine it was very different. She took my hands in hers and gazed at me with eyes as soft and wide as a heifer's.

"Do you think so? Do you *really* think so, John? Oh, I could hug Peggy for ringing me up tonight! Look—why are we standing like this? There's a sofa in the corner and we might as well make ourselves comfortable. Peggy and George will be necking in there until early morning."

My experience with girls might have been limited but it was wide enough to understand now why men had shied away from Madeleine. She wasn't content with rushing fences, she kicked her way through them. Before I knew what was happening, the lights were out, the back door key was turned and we were clinging to one another on the sofa. I don't remember taking an active part in these preliminaries.

It was an old and uncomfortable sofa and seemed to have been designed by someone who enjoyed making things difficult for lovers. It had a hard, shiny surface and any sudden movement was apt to deposit one or both of us onto the floor. After two such humiliations we settled for this and made ourselves comfortable as possible with cushions. Here, after a great deal of kissing and clumsy caressing, my enthusiasm overtook hers, but her protests seemed to me very halfhearted and I persisted, so that at length she whispered, "Wait a minute, John—please!" and removed herself from me in the darkness. A moment later I realized that her protests had been lodged in defense of her dance frock and not, as I had imagined, on behalf of her honor, for when she came back to me she had removed her dress and we had soon pressed the encounter to its logical conclusion.

I don't remember feeling as guilty or apprehensive in my life and she sensed it at once.

"It was what you wanted, wasn't it, John?" she asked anxiously.

I made a tremendous effort to convey a gratitude that I did not feel and kissed her, misjudging the distance in the dark and kissing her neck instead of her face.

"Yes, of course, Madeleine," I said, and while the answer seemed to satisfy her it sounded to me like the words of a man confessing to a crime that would hustle him to the gallows.

I don't know how long we sat there, tired, cold and crumpled, but at last she got up, humming a snatch of a tune we had heard earlier in the evening. I can remember the tune. It was "Little White Lies," and whenever I hear it now, it conjures up a small wavelet of that vast tide of guilt and fear that poured over me as we slouched about Peggy's kitchen, making fresh coffee and waiting for Twining to emerge from the front room.

We said very little but it was clear that Madeleine did not share my crushing load of dismay. As she tidied her hair, pausing in her pattings and combings to give me swift, sidelong smiles, there was an air of smugness and complacency about her. At that particular time I hated her for it.

4.

My feelings of apprehension about this incident persisted for some time but my sense of guilt disappeared almost at once. In fact, as time went on and no dire consequences resulted, I began to feel mildly defiant about it, as though, by making love to a stranger, I had scored off Diana and punished her for demonstrating that she had outgrown our pledges and had no intention of renewing them.

All that winter this resentment against her mounted, and alongside it there grew in me a deliberate intention to vindicate myself as a man ill-used by a woman in whom he had reposed trust. It was a painful, gradual process. The plant that Diana had nourished in me over a period of three impressionable years had grown very deep roots, and it was not easy to extract them. When I first came to London the most innocent friendship with an office girl would have constituted a shameless betrayal of our Sennacharib vows. I am not claiming that this was a sensible attitude for a boy of my age and experience, but am simply stating that it was so. Even my confidences to a man like Twining had seemed an act of disloyalty and the passage with Madeleine was a bonfire of all my hopes and ideals at the time. Later the sense of personal betrayal left me and I began to rationalize my behavior, and this became much easier as the months passed and I made more friends among the staff, and one or two fellow lodgers. Twining was one of the first to notice the change in me and having surmised, quite accurately, what had happened between Madeleine and me while he was closeted in the front room, he lost no time in taking the credit for it.

"What did I tell you, young Leigh?" he chaffed, when he overheard me making a date with the switchboard operator at work. "You're a changed man since that night out we had in Tonbridge. You ought to hand it to that pal of Peggy's, she's made a man out of you! Have you seen her again? Has she come down on you for seven-and-six yet?"

He meant this as a joke and I accepted it as such, but if he had known the hours of worry I had undergone regarding this very contingency he would have laughed his silly head off. As a matter of fact, I still had qualms about Madeleine and they were not wholly selfish. I could not forget her pathetic response to my lighthearted compliment and the eagerness she had shown to win my affection. If I had been as cynical as I am now, I should have wasted no sympathy on a girl who surrendered to a greenhorn like me after such a poor show of resistance, but in those days I was deeply ashamed of the fact that I had used her, not as a human being but as a means of defiance, a jeer at someone who had hurt me. It was because of these misgivings that I did not write to her, though she had pressed her address upon me when we parted. I don't suppose I should have seen her again, had she not passed a message to me via Twining, saying that she and Peggy were coming to town one Saturday and suggesting that we meet and go to a show. Twining, to his regret, was unable to accept, but he advised me to meet her, and we had tea in Fuller's, and then went to a film. I had regarded the expedition as an act of penance, but Madeleine looked so attractive in a little blue and white pinafore frock and matching beret, and proved so agreeable a companion up to the moment of parting at Victoria Station, that I recklessly made plans to meet her the following Saturday and even found myself looking forward to the occasion throughout the week.

We made no reference during our conversation to what had taken place at Tonbridge. Confronted with her again and lacking all hope of privacy in London, I was too shy, while she, sensing as much, was apparently learning the value of tact. I was determined that on the next occasion we met we should have some privacy and although it was against house rules to bring girls into our rooms, I determined to risk it and laid in a simple supper, planning the evening so that we should have a couple of hours alone before her last train at eleven o'clock.

It was not a cold-blooded maneuver on my part. I was fond of Madeleine, and the prospect of making love to her again filled me with the kind of excitement I had once felt in keeping an early morning appointment with Diana at the tower. Even so, I am not pretending that it was more than the normal anticipation any youth feels for the company of a girl who he knows will accommodate him. During that week, whenever I thought of Madeleine coming all the way up from Tonbridge to spend a few hours in my company, I did so with a male arrogance that was new to me. I no longer regarded her as a weapon against Diana's indifference, and that in itself was significant, for it meant that the embers of the Sennacharib fires were now almost extinct. Chance, or another miracle, was to demonstrate how hopelessly wrong I was in this respect.

Madeleine's train was due into Victoria at three-twenty, and I had a lunchtime call to make on behalf of the *Echo*, in Soho. After making the call and eating a quick lunch, I sauntered out into Piccadilly with an hour or so to spare, intending to walk slowly along toward the Ritz and cut across the park to the station.

I had reached Hatchard's and was idling beside the window absorbed in the new titles, when I heard a voice that made me spin around like a teetotem. There, paying off a taxi about five yards from where I was loitering, stood Mrs. Gayelorde-Sutton, and Diana waiting alongside her.

It was fortunate that they were not looking in my direction. I was so staggered by their appearance, and by the immense changes in Diana's appearance, that at least thirty seconds elapsed before I could collect myself sufficiently to turn my back on them and keep them in view in the plate-glass reflection. I stood there trembling as Mrs. Gayelorde-Sutton moved off past me toward the Circus and Diana crossed the pavement and disappeared into Fortnum and Mason's. Then, hardly able to believe my luck, I rushed in pursuit and watched her pass through the main part of the shop and turn into the dimly lit tobacco department. It was a convenient counter at which to observe her. I stood half-concealed behind a pillar and gazed and gazed at the elegant young woman who had replaced the tousled schoolgirl I had held in my arms under the tarpaulin on the night of the gale. I could never have believed that a person could change so much in so short a time.

She had developed a dress sense that rivaled her mother's. She wore a light, heather-blue coat with a wide fur collar and under the coat, which was open, a calf-length dress in a darker shade of blue, picked out with tiny white bows, like those on the dress of the celebrated Renoir girl. She had silk stockings, crocodile-skin shoes with three-inch heels, and a matching handbag as big as a satchel. Her hat was an outrageous piece of nonsense, a cross between a hussar's and a cossack's, flattened over the left eye and crowned with a blue tassel that matched her coat. Her thick chestnut hair had been severely disciplined, and although she was using plenty of make-up, the bloom and freshness of her complexion owed little to cosmetics but sprang from a radiantly healthy skin. Her cheeks had the soft glow of petals and her eyes, as huge and blue as I remembered, still held in their depths the laughter and mischief of Diana of Heronslea. It was all that was left, except perhaps the promise of her mouth.

Her figure had greatly improved. In her beautifully cut clothes she looked as trim as a model, her narrow waist emphasizing the firmness of her breasts and the long line of her shapely legs. My mind went back to the winter's day when she and her mother had come into Uncle Luke's quayside Mart to buy cottage furniture, and I recalled how gauche and insignificant I had felt when they inspected our seedy wares in the light of a single, naked bulb. Today the contrast was even more marked, for here she stood in one of the most exclusive shops in the world, once more giving the impression that she had paid the management a great compliment by entering it.

For a split second, as this memory crossed my mind, I was tempted to leave the place without speaking to her. Always unattainable, she now seemed to have removed herself to another planet, for how, I reasoned, could such an enchanting creature look at a down-at-heel wretch like me with anything but amused patronage? How could she be blamed for murmuring a few polite words and excusing herself gently but absolutely from a situation that could only bring us stuttering embarrassment? Then what remained of my pride came to my aid. It was an inadequate reinforcement but just enough to make me stand my ground. As she completed her purchase and moved away from the counter, I stepped out from behind the pillar and whipped off my ten-and-sixpenny trilby.

"Hello, Di!" I said, my voice not much above a whisper.

She stopped about a yard away, her lips parted, her eyes as serious as I had ever seen them. For several seconds we stood there facing one another, and then, with a rush of delight that made me want to shout at the top of my voice, I saw her cheeks flush with pleasure and she rushed forward to seize both my hands, hitching the shoulder bag to give free movement to her arms, and pulling me toward her so violently that the battered trilby I was holding slipped from my grasp and rolled on the carpet.

"Jan!" she exclaimed. "Oh Jan, *Jan!*"

I was so moved by the warmth of her greeting that I was unable to say another word. As I stared at her, feeling the strong pressure of her gloved hands on my fingers, all the doubts and dismays of the past two years fell away from me like Christian's sins and went tumbling down into limbo. I was left with a lightness of heart that I could not hope to express in conventional greetings, for inside me, buried under a debris of loneliness and drabness, the spring and glory of Sennacharib stirred, bursting through the sour crust of London and soaring like the buzzards above the paddock oaks.

I must have said something when she proposed tea in the adjoining lounge, and I must have followed her to the little whitewood table in the alcove where we spent the next hour, but I remember nothing of this and not much of what we spoke about after the first breathless exchanges.

"Jan, it's been so long, so long!" she said, studying me from head to foot, her eyes dancing and flashing with excitement. "You've grown so! Stand up! Let me look at you! Let me take you in!" And when I stood somewhat shamefacedly (for she was the same uninhibited Diana and made no effort to keep her voice low): "Mmmmm! *Mmmmmm!* You're bigger and broader and more masculine than ever! I knew you would be, of course, but you've filled out much more than I expected and you're still growing—you're over six foot now."

"Six-one-and-a-half," I said. "But now for heaven's sake let me sit down! I feel an absolute Charlie, standing up for inspection in Fortnum and Mason's tea lounge."

We both laughed aloud. That was what I found so remarkable about this meeting. Within minutes we were perfectly at ease with one another and the waiting months, which had wrought such changes in each of us, had been scattered like a drift of leaves.

"Well?" she said, as soon as the waitress had set down the tray and turned her back on us. "How about me? Do you think I've changed at all?"

"You look absolutely wonderful, Diana," I told her. "Grown up—frighteningly so—and so marvelously pretty that they must be absolute idiots not to sign you up as a film star!"

She was pleased and did not mind showing it. "As a matter of fact they've tried to," she admitted. "Not here, though—I'm not the Elstree type—but in France, you know, where they only make films about precociously sexy little misses, who keep running away from convents. Now tell me more about yourself. What are you doing in London? What kind of job have you got up here? How does a husky like you keep all the flappers away? Tell me everything—*everything*, Jan!"

I told her almost everything: how and why Uncle Reuben had whisked me away from Whinmouth, all about *The Illustrated Echo* and about the book I was writing on Margaret of Anjou, and how I hoped it would be published before I was twenty; also something of how I had hoped and schemed to get in touch with her over the last year.

She nodded gravely when I came to this and said, "We'll discuss that later, Jan. In the meantime, I want to hear exactly what you aim to do in the future. Do you want to be a real London journalist, you know, Fleet Street pubs, a stained raincoat, frenzied dashes to trouble spots and all that? Or would you much prefer to be an author who crams a special subject and then unloads it on an unsuspecting public?"

It sounded as though she was disinclined to take my writing very seriously and I was slightly piqued. She noticed this at once and added, hurriedly, "Oh I'm not pooh-poohing the idea, Jan. I always knew you'd turn into *some* kind of writer but right at the back of my mind I always had a different kind of hunch about you. I had it from the first day we met."

"What sort of hunch?" I asked curiously.

"Oh, I don't know . . . nothing really specific, just something to do with land—farming, dairy cattle, poultry breeding, market gardening—that's in your blood, Jan, whether you know it or not."

"Is it?" I asked, lamely.

"Yes, Jan, it certainly is. I always recognized that because you can't feel about a countryside the way you feel about Sennacharib unless it's a part of your nerves and blood and bone."

"Do you mean that you'd be disappointed if I stayed a journalist all my life, Di?" I asked, puzzled by the sudden turn the conversation had taken.

"Yes, I think I would," she said slowly, "and so, in the end, would you, Jan!"

We had our tea and she told me a little about what had happened to her—how she had been abroad practically the whole time, either at a school in Tours or, during vacations, with the French horsy family near Périgueux. I did not give her my full attention. I wanted to think about what she had said. It was odd, I reflected, that none of the conversations we had had while riding and wandering in Sennacharib had led us to this subject—the prospect of my returning to the occupation of all my West Country forebears, up to the time that Grandpa Leigh took to swilling rum and rode to his death on Nun's Bay rocks, but it was difficult to think objectively in her presence, I was far too elated and excited. All I wanted to talk about was us—how we could start again, where we could meet, how much personal freedom she had, how often she went to Heronslea, and dozens of other questions directed at a single target—how soon we could be as important to each other as we had been during those days of isolation on the island.

Before I could explore this vital subject she glanced at her watch and said that she had arranged to meet her mother at four o'clock, at Brown's Hotel, where they were staying while the decorators worked on their town house, in Palmerston Crescent.

"It's being renovated from top to bottom," she said, "and the party is being held there on the eleventh of next month."

She told me then that this was to be the first of her coming-out parties and that there were to be a whole series of them throughout her season. Later on, in mid-June, she thought, there was to be a country party at Heronslea and about the same time she was being presented, just the way it had been planned, years and years ago.

"Don't look so tragic, Jan!" she laughed, reaching across the table and patting my crestfallen face with her glove. "I expect I shall survive it. Everyone else seems to."

I knew very little more about young girls' seasons or presentations at court than I had known when she had first described the ritual, but what did depress me as she outlined her program was the conviction that I had no place in any part of it. The whole silly business would remove her from me more effectively than she had been removed during the past two years. What made it even worse was that she now seemed to be reconciled to all the fuss and glitter that attended a season. There was none of the pouting disparagement that she had shown in our Sennacharib days. Coming out, I brooded, would mean constant chaperonage and behind that the shadow of serious competitors.

I said nothing about all this, for she gave me no opening. Although, from the very outset of our meeting, her attitude toward me was very frank and friendly, she made no reference to our former relationship. When she looked at her watch again I called the waitress and asked for the bill, but I dared not let her go without some kind of reassurance.

"When can I see you again, Diana?" I demanded. "We can't just . . . just meet and part again like this!"

She began pulling on her gloves and frowned at her hands. For a second, as she did this, I saw a wraith of the old Diana, muttering terrible incantations against the thieves of her freedom. Then the frown disappeared and she gave me a brittle little smile.

"You must leave that to me, Jan dear! The fact is, we *can't* see one another just yet and for the moment it really is 'hail and farewell,' but if you'll be patient, very, *very* patient, Jan, then something will turn up, something exciting maybe, the way it always used to, remember?"

And with that I was obliged to be satisfied, for she walked briskly out of the restaurant, leaving me to pay the bill at the desk.

When I had collected my change I hurried down the steps to the floor level of the shop and saw her standing just inside the main door, looking in my direction. As our eyes met she put her hand to her lips and waved. It was a clear hint that she did not want me to follow her into the street, and because I was uncertain and bewildered I hesitated long enough for her to slip through the doors and enter a curbside taxi.

Then I thought of Madeleine, hanging about Victoria Station, and conscience drove me to hail another taxi and drive to the terminus, where I arrived an hour after the scheduled arrival of Madeleine's train. I made a halfhearted search of the buffet and along the bookstalls and platform exits, but there was no sign of her. An inspector told me that a train for Tonbridge had just left and I supposed she had boarded it and was already making the cheerless journey home.

I never saw Madeleine again and I can never pass Victoria Station without a sense of shame.

5.

The chance meeting with Diana did not solve very much, for I was now bedeviled by fresh uncertainties. I went over her cordial but indeterminate attitude toward me but I found it impossible to decide how she looked upon our former relationship and whether, now or at any time ahead, she would ever regard our association as a prelude to marriage. To me, throughout all the time we had been separated, there had been but two possible solutions—either she would defy her parents on the day she attained the age of twenty-one, or she had already dismissed me as a presumptuous hobblede-hoy with whom she had passed part of her girlhood. I had never demanded an "understanding" as to our plans when she was of age but I now felt that she owed it to me to clarify the situation. I had expected more from our reunion. I had hoped for a passionate re-avowal, but in the absence of it a frank and unsentimental "old-pals" approach would have told me all I wanted to know. As things were, I could form no strong impression of her attitude; regarding essentials she had remained mysteriously neutral. All the next day I studied my impressions. There was the hint that I ought to turn my back on journalism and learn farming; there was her refusal to commit herself about future meetings; there was her abrupt departure, without even a handshake or a good-by, and looking at it from these angles it appeared that she was putting me in my place almost as ruthlessly as her mother might have done. Looking at it another way, however, I believed that I had grounds for supposing that she had one or more of her aces in reserve, and was, in fact, on the point of bringing off a characteristic coup . . . "If you'll be patient, Jan, something will turn up, something exciting maybe, the way it used to, remember?" If she had persuaded herself that our love had been no more than a phase of adolescence, then why had she been so explicit about the future? Precisely *what* was likely to turn up? Another chance meeting? A day in Sennacharib together? Or a wedding, with a fairy-tale ending?

On the whole I inclined toward the more hopeful alternatives.

Diana had always been highly unpredictable, and I finally resolved to muster what patience I could command and settle down to await a summons. Fortunately for my employers it was not long in coming. All day my thoughts were full of Diana and there was no room left for research into the financial panic that followed the Young Pretender's march to Derby, or the Chartist agitation of 1832. In fact, I was becoming bored with the past and impatient with the present.

Less than a week after our meeting in Fortnum's, a Carter Paterson's man appeared in the office with a small crate, addressed to me personally. Inside was a magnificent Remington portable and a note from Diana on the label. All the note said was: *A little something to help poor Margaret over her labor pains! Love, Diana.*

I sat goggling at the wonderful gift for fully fifteen minutes, oblivious of everything save the astounding fact that she had made such a spectacular acknowledgment of my literary ambitions. Was it possible to read into her generosity a desperately serious intention to secure independence for both of us? All in all, I was elated with the turn of events and carried the typewriter home in triumph, taking up my manuscript and hammering away until the lodger underneath me knocked on his ceiling with a broom handle, something he had not had to do for months. I became so absorbed in the work, and found it so effortless after the maddening ribbon jams and type cloggings of the ancient machine, that I progressed at a very respectable rate and had the first draft finished by the last week in May. During those feverish weeks I stopped wondering about Diana. Perhaps her generous means of encouragement had reconciled me to leaving the initiative to her.

Then, halfway through June, I received a telegram. It read:

SEE LAST WEEK'S GLOSSY STOP HALFWAY HOME STOP PARTY HERONSLEA FRIDAY STOP GET WEEK OFF STOP TOWER EVERY MORNING 7 A.M. LOVE DIANA

I was not wildly elated by this communication, for journalism had been doing its best to convert me into a cynic and I began to suspect that Diana was now playing some kind of elaborate game. If she could send a telegram, I told myself, she could just as easily have written a coherent letter, and if she had to rely on a telegram, then why compose it like an agony column quote in a magazine serial?

I searched through the glossies in our morgue, thankful indeed that I did not have to go out and buy them all, and soon came across the feature to which she referred, a ten-page spread devoted to recent presentations, Diana's among them. There was the usual display of flashbulb photographs of debs at stately homes and night clubs, all the girls looking impossibly arch, and all the young men looking as though they would have preferred to be back in the Sixth, at Eton.

Diana's picture was no better or worse than the others. I found it impossible to identify the doll-like creature that blinked at the photographer over the hunched shoulder of an anonymous dancing partner, with the sveldt and elegant young woman who had greeted me in Fortnum's a month ago. The pictures and their captions made me even more impatient with the idiotic saraband that her mother was compelling her to dance, and I threw aside the papers and sat down to make what I could of the message.

The "halfway home" was easy. I supposed it to mean that the presentation part of the ritual was done with, and that the town parties, or the more important of them, had already been held. The date of the Heronslea party was plain enough but I might easily have read into the "get week off" a bold invitation to attend it, and clearly this was out of the question. I deduced, however, that she wanted me to be in the vicinity on the great occasion, and her last sentence, about a tower rendezvous, implied that no firm date could be arranged and that my best plan was to go there each morning in the hope that she could ride out on one or more occasions.

This was all very well and extremely promising in its way, but her theatrical secrecy and the obvious pleasure that she was deriving from it was instrumental in stoking up the resentment I had once felt while crouching like a thief in the Heronslea copse, waiting to escort her to the regatta dance.

Two years in London had done something to enable me to get Mrs. Gayelorde-Sutton into perspective. Although her spectacular snobbery and, more particularly, her tireless game of squiress-among-the-chawbacons had earned my disgust as a boy, it had nonetheless gone some way toward persuading me that she was a strong personality. Now I realized that there was nothing very special about her after all and that almost every district in Britain had a Mrs. Gayelorde-Sutton, most of them the product of rapidly acquired wealth in the period 1914–1918. I had discovered a little about the family, and how they came to acquire their money. Unlike his wife, Gayelorde-Sutton originated from a fairly prosperous industrial family, but they had never been reckoned as wealthy until Eric, the second son, secured large interests in a nitrate firm. His money now stemmed partly from this and partly from the timber business which had boomed so dramatically during the period of trench warfare in Flanders. Gayelorde-Sutton himself was reputed to have a first-class business brain and according to a city editor's clerk—the source of my information—would soon be knighted, even as Diana had once predicted.

I was on the point of trying to change my holiday week when something happened to make an office reshuffle unnecessary. Poor old Uncle Reuben was knocked down by a racing cyclist while acting as a judge at the annual grass-track meeting of the Whinmouth Wheelers, and his injuries included a broken thigh, something to be reckoned with at his time of life.

Somebody phoned my editor and I was given time off to go down and see him, my leave being extended indefinitely after Uncle Reuben had written and asked if he could borrow me to keep the *Observer* going until he was fit enough to return to the office.

He never did return and I never returned to London.

When I visited him at the Cottage Hospital I was shocked by his appearance. I had never thought of him as anything but an elderly man, although he was still a year short of sixty when I joined the *Observer* staff. Now he looked as though he was dying. His eyes were tired and his memory, once so accurate about Whinmouth affairs, was hazed by pain and shock. He was delighted to see me and gripped my hand with an eagerness that I found very touching.

"Ah, John," he muttered, "sorry you've got to see me trussed up like a Christmas fowl, and sorry to bring you back here before you've had your fill of smoke! The fact is, I don't know how we'll manage if you can't take over for a spell. That's the trouble with newspapers, boy, even little unimportant ones like ours. You can't put 'em in cold storage when you run into trouble. I remember old Joe Arscott, who ran the *Clarion* over at Ferndale—he had to put a carnival edition to bed on the day his wife and kids were killed in a road smash. How do you feel about staying down here until autumn?"

I said I should be glad to remain in Whinmouth until he was up and about, but said nothing about Diana or the party. In my heart I was glad of the opportunity. Diana's return had awakened in me a wild longing for Sennacharib and an equally strong distaste for my stuffy little bed-sitter and the fumes and roar of London. I comforted him as best I could. He was more worried about the *Observer* than he was about his injuries. This was the first time he had ever been laid up and the first going-to-press Friday he had missed since he was a printer's devil, in the eighteen-eighties.

"Come up here as often as you can and tell me what's going on," he commanded, as though he was a wounded general addressing a flustered aide-de-campe in the midst of a battle.

I promised and went home to Aunt Thirza, who was equally delighted with my unexpected return.

"Why bless 'ee, John!" she exclaimed, throwing her fat, freckled arms around my neck. "Us'll soon 'ave the color back in they cheeks, and a bit more spread to your belly. Praper pasty you look, and I don't wonder, breathing nothing but they ole vogs an' vumes all this time."

I went up to my old room, which seemed even smaller than the one I had abandoned in Guilford Street, but the moment I threw open the window I found myself blessing the chance that had brought me back.

It was a still summer evening and the estuary looked blood-red under the setting sun, its leisurely traffic of boats making hardly a ripple as they moved to and from the jetties. Far across the river, on a ketch moored beyond the tideway, a fisherman was hammering at something metallic and the sound of the blows reached me seconds after his arm was raised to strike. It made me think again of Huck Finn on the broad Mississippi, and I hoped that Diana was already at Heronslea and could see the bronze and heliotrope cloud formations over Nun's Head. Uncle Luke's favorite herring gulls, and lesser black-backed gulls, fished at their ease; Old Yelland, the pilot who had taken us off the island, stood on the quayside chatting to Ferris, the lobsterman, probably about football, for they were both vice-presidents of the Whinmouth Club. I stood there a long time, drinking the salt breeze and feeling older and more serene than I had ever felt in London.

I was up at the tower before seven. The Sennacharib bird chorus was deafening and the buzzards were there, looking as though they had been wheeling and mewing over the paddock oaks ever since I went away.

Foxhayes was aflame with gorse and heather and seemed to have put on its best clothes to welcome me home. From the tower summit I looked down on the long sloping larch wood and saw a wisp of smoke rise from the invisible chimneys of Heronslea, signifying perhaps that the family was in residence. Our room was much as we had left it but cobwebs had gathered and there was mold on the carpet strips, so I occupied the time tidying up and shaking the carpet from the window, keeping a sharp eye on the end of the ride from which Diana would emerge if she was coming.

She did not appear that morning or the next, but on the third day, the Monday of her birthday week, she came striding out of the wood and waved as soon as she had climbed the fence into the paddock. I was far too impatient to wait in the tower and ran down to meet her.

Even when we were hundreds of yards apart I saw that she was once more my Diana and not the girl I had met in London. She wore an old gray skirt and a sleeveless blouse, with a blue scarf tied countrywise over her hair. We both broke into a run and when we met rushed into an embrace, laughing breathlessly as a pheasant kuck-kucked from the bracken at our feet and then running hand-in-hand for the privacy of Folly Wood.

We exchanged no greetings. The place we were in, and the careless, girlish clothes she was wearing exorcised the awe she had created in me when we last met. I felt no awe for her now, only the wildest tenderness and delight in her presence. It was as though we had been parted for a day, or were still alone on Nun's Island before the storm, and I could not wait until we had climbed the tower steps but kissed her mouth a dozen times as we clung to one another on the brier-choked path to the porch.

One thing was changed, and that the nature of the kisses we exchanged. They were no longer the kisses of infatuated adolescents, owing more to the wonder of discovery than to physical desire. We kissed breathlessly and greedily, and all the time our lips were touching she strained her body to me so ardently that I had to brace myself against the masonry. Her scarf came off and I plunged my hands into her hair, speaking her name as I had spoken it during our island adventure and hearing my voice sound strange under the stress of emotion.

At last we climbed the tower and she looked ruefully at the signs of decay.

"I've never been here since, Jan," she said. "I often started out to go but I never got beyond the paddock. It seemed so depressing alone . . . look, there are our buzzards!"

"They were here yesterday and the day before," I said.

"But they shouldn't have been! They're only supposed to show up when we're together."

"They knew you were in the offing, Di, and anyway, we're together now. I'm home for several weeks. How long will you be here?"

"Not long, Jan. After the party we're all going to Nice and this week it isn't going to be easy to see you, not even in the early mornings. So many people are staying, and Yves likes to ride before breakfast. I had to tell half a dozen whoppers to get here today. Oh dear, I wish I could invite you to the party but that's quite hopeless, even if you come as a pressman. Mother will be certain to recognize you after that frightful to-do at your office!"

Her mention of the brush between her mother and my uncle reminded me of its cause—her examination by a doctor after our escapade.

"What happened that time?" I asked her. "How did it seem from your end of the business?"

She did not mind talking about it. She described how, on the day after surrender, she developed a frightful cold and was locked in her room for more than a week.

"I didn't care anyway," she said. "I wanted to think and think about it all. I've never forgotten how sweet you were that time, Jan, and that's what made Mother's suspicions so beastly and ungenerous. She believed we had been lovers, of course, and it was only for your sake that I stopped letting her go on thinking so. It was when she started talking about police court proceedings, and got our solicitor in to talk jargon about it, that I had to let them know I was still a virgin." She looked at me without a trace of embarrassment. "I *still* am! Are you?"

I found it impossible to meet her gaze but she only laughed, reached out and pushed up my chin with the tips of her fingers.

"Oh don't look so dreadfully hangdog, Jan, it's different for men, isn't it? Was it with one girl or several?"

"One," I muttered, but she didn't seem to notice my distaste for the subject.

"What was she like, Jan? Was she pretty? Were you in love with her?"

"No," I admitted, relieved by her attitude but still miserably embarrassed, "I wasn't a bit in love with her. I'll never be in love with anyone but you, Di, and I think you're quite sure of that and always have been!"

[226

"Yes, I think I am, Jan," she said lightly, "but I wouldn't have blamed you a bit if you'd found somebody else. After all, in most ways you've been a man for years. Sometimes I think you were born one."

"What are we going to do—about seeing one another?" I demanded, not only anxious to change the subject but worried about the difficulties that continued to beset us.

"Well, we can't do a thing yet," she said calmly. "If Mother gets so much as an inkling that you're back in circulation, she'll let Heronslea and we'll never see one another at all."

The morning clouded a little and suddenly the tower room seemed dank and sunless.

"How long have we got to go on like this, Di?"

"I suppose until I'm twenty-one, Jan."

"And what then? If I'm back in Whinmouth for good, and running the paper, would you have enough guts to tell her and your father to go to hell and get engaged—properly, openly—without all this hole-in-the-corner routine?"

She smiled and for some reason I was sure that the smile was slightly forced.

"That's the second proposal you've made to me in this old tower," she said, "and it puts you one ahead; the one on the beach in Nun's Cove was really mine, wasn't it?"

I was determined not to joke about it this time and pressed her hard for a direct answer. The maddening frustration of the situation was more than I could bear. I had held her in my arms again and believed I had learned from her response that she felt about me the same way as I felt for her, but for all that I did not get my answer, not then, not for a long time to come. She turned away and stood beside the window, looking down over Sennacharib.

"Well?" I demanded, after nearly a minute had passed.

"You mustn't stampede me, Jan. Women are a lot wiser than men about this kind of thing. You're entitled to an answer and you'll get one, I promise you that, but don't panic me, don't drag an answer from me that is only part of one and has to do with biology rather than all kinds of other things."

"Such as economics?" I asked, grumpily.

Her head came up and she looked straight at me.

"Yes! Why not? That's the basis of our trouble, isn't it?"

I was alarmed at this and tried to talk my way out of it. Looking back I can see that my attempt was ingenuous but it seemed logical at the time. Eagerly I told her about the owner of the paper and printing works having willed his property to Uncle Reuben and how Reuben had promised that it would pass to me.

"It isn't the kind of money you've been used to and never would be," I argued, "but it provides a good living and later on, when I've got another income from books, we shouldn't be at all badly off. We'd have plenty to live the kind of life we want to live, and I daresay we could even manage to hunt if you wanted to."

She heard me out and I think my case impressed her. She smiled again, genuinely this time, and kissed me lightly on the cheek.

"Dear Jan," she said, and then, in the old familiar way, "dear, darling, sober, solid, dependable Jan Ridd! Will you wait until Friday? Everything's gone haywire at home and there's been so many things to see to. I want time to think everything over. We'll talk more about it then, I promise, Jan!"

"But Friday is the day of the party," I protested. "We can't even see each other then."

"Oh yes we can," she said, with a touch of her schoolgirl cockiness. "In a funny way you might even be *at* the party . . . if you want to be, that is!"

"But Di, talk sense! If I . . ."

"Listen," she said, drawing her brows together in a way I remembered her doing when she was planning mischief in the past, "all you have to do is to be handy at a certain time and wait for my signal. Then you walk straight in and I'll keep you in cold storage until all the others have gone to bed. It'll be wonderful that way, a simply glorious score off everyone, and a way of eating my cake and having it too!"

"Wouldn't it be far less risky to meet in Nun's Cove at any old time? We don't want another scene to spoil your birthday!"

The mischief went out of her eyes and she took my hands in hers and said, with immense seriousness:

"It's simply *because* it's my birthday—don't you see—that you're going to be at the party, Jan. Everyone I don't care two straws about is there and I'm not going to dodge out and walk three miles to get a birthday kiss from the one person I really want to be kissed by! Does that sound unreasonable to you?"

I laughed, partly because she sounded so solemn but more, I think, because her words brought me great happiness.

"No, Di," I admitted very readily, "it sounds more reasonable than anything you've said so far."

"Well then," she continued, "you do just as I say. Now listen carefully—the party won't get going until the supper dance and . . ."

It was the usual hotchpotch of involved timing and theatrical nonsense. I was to come to Heronslea about ten P.M. and await her signal—the tune "Missouri City Waltz," played by the band, which would precede the buffet supper and provide my opportunity to enter by a little-used door that led through the flower room to the gun room. She undertook to meet me there and give me further instructions. We parted on this and I cycled back to Whinmouth with a sharp appetite and some misgivings, both outweighed in my mind by the memory of the eagerness with which she had run into my arms when I emerged from the tower to greet her.

It clouded over toward evening on Friday. I cycled as far as Shepherdshey Hill and left my bike in the gorse at the fringe of the big copse. There was no moon and I had a difficult time of it pushing through the wood to a spot where I could overlook the house. As I blundered along I wondered whether what remained of my boyhood was secretly enjoying this hocus-pocus, or whether I had consented to practice it because it was the only terms upon which Diana could or would continue our association. I never found a satisfactory answer to this query, the reason being, I suppose, that my reaction to the role of secret suitor was governed by the barometer of my faith in Diana. This went up and down almost hour by hour these days. Half the time I was convinced that she was only awaiting her moment of freedom in order to declare herself, at other times I was equally certain that she was using me as a kind of grappling iron to hang on to childhood. What she had said about my transition from boyhood to manhood was true. The lack of a father throughout infancy, and the death of my mother before I was fifteen, had bridged the gap between boy and man in a matter of months and the process of growing up was further accelerated by Uncle Luke's helplessness when I went to help him at the Furniture Mart.

It had been so different for Diana. Consciously or unconsciously, her parents had done everything in their power to arrest her development, not only by working to rule and charting a conventional future for her, but also by surrounding her with hordes of servants, a circumstance that prevented her from learning to do the simplest thing for herself. She had revolted against this, of course, and her

229]

rebellion showed itself in her furtive association with me and her readiness at all times to flout authority. At the time of which I write, when she was physically mature but in most other respects two years behind the average working-class adolescent, this defiance of her mother's pattern of behavior was little more than the deliberate act of a spoiled child; it was not until later that it developed into a deep-rooted characteristic and fed upon its own appetite for acts of calculated irresponsibility.

When I reached the edge of the copse bordering the fenced paddock in front of the house, I saw at once that Heronslea was very much *en fête*. From where I stood it looked more like a roadhouse than a beautiful country home. Greenery and balloons festooned the façade and over the pillared porch, which was extravagantly floodlit, was a vulgar set piece in colored bulbs, representing a giant birthday cake. It crossed my mind then that Mrs. Gayelorde-Sutton was redoubling her efforts to supply her only child with gigantic helpings of the wrong pudding.

Nobody knew better than I that Diana, viewed objectively, was basically an uncomplicated and extremely affectionate child, without false pride and without ostentation. All she needed at that time was someone who could understand her natural high spirits and pull firmly on the reins when she frisked over the rails of common sense. She wanted a just, tolerant rule, tempered by strong, demonstrative affection. She needed someone to canalize her abundant energy into something mildly creative. All she was getting was unlimited dishes of caviar and ice cream, to be eaten in the glare of spotlights. She only had to raise a finger to command the material wants of a sophisticated woman twice her age, but now that poor Drip had been banished she might look in vain for a shoulder to weep upon. Looking at the glitter of Heronslea in the dark bowl below, I began to understand what had prompted the childish eagerness of her kisses at the foot of the tower a few days ago, and it struck me as remarkable that she was as fresh and unspoiled as she was, for her mother by design, and her father by acquiescence, had done everything humanly possible to convert her into an impossible little brat.

I could hear the band playing a waltz, and by avoiding the circle of light thrown by the decorations and porch lamps I was able to approach the house quite closely and look in upon the celebrations.

Although the afternoon had been overcast and rain now threatened, the temperature of the night was unusually high, even for mid-June. There was not a breath of air in the open and inside the overcrowded house it must have been insufferably close, for all the French windows opening onto the terrace had been flung wide, and every now and again little groups of guests drifted out onto the raised flags and sat at tables or on the low windbreak to sip their drinks. I recognized several of the guests. Lance Fayne, the M.P.'s son, was there and Gerald Brett-Hawkins, the landowner's son. As I watched, Diana herself came out with Yves, the French boy, and a knot of six or eight young people surrounded them, saying something that made Diana throw back her head and laugh. Then the music recalled most of them to the dance floor but one couple remained in shadow at my end of the terrace and as soon as the others had gone moved into a passionate embrace. It was all very smart, streamlined and jolly, but I turned away quickly when I thought that I might have to watch Diana being kissed by someone like Lance or Yves, and retired sulkily to the rhododendron clump to await "Missouri City Waltz."

It was a long time coming, and before I heard it heavy drops of rain began to fall and drip through the leaves where I was sitting. The moment the tune struck up I scrambled out and went round to the flower-room door, which was shut but unlocked. I went in, pushing through the litter of ferns and flower stems left by the gardeners and into the paneled gun room, where it was pitch dark.

I remembered this part of the house from my tour of inspection and after waiting a moment, to make certain that my entry had passed undetected, I opened the door a chink and listened to the music and laughter coming from the central hall. A manservant clumped past, whistling in tune with the band, and I remembered that the passage outside connected the wine cellar and the housekeeper's flat, with a back staircase halfway along it. Then, soundlessly save for a swift rustle of her ball dress, Diana was beside me, whispering:

"Jan? Are you there, Jan?"

I found her hand in the dark and drew her to me. Her perfume banished the room's whiff of gun oil and resin and I kissed her bare shoulders.

"No, Jan, not now, there'll be plenty of time—I'll be missed, come quickly and don't say a word on the way!"

We stole out into the passage and crossed it to the stairs. The stairs led into the west corridor that branched off the central gallery, and a cacophony of music, laughter and plate rattling rose from the well of the big staircase. We turned our backs on it and slipped along the corridor to her side of the house.

"In here, *quickly!*"

She pushed me into her little suite and I saw that it was much changed from the last time I was there. It had been extended to include a little dressing room and a tiny bathroom, with a sunken bath. The simplicity of the room that had struck me as a boy was now buried under a vanload of hangings and antique furniture. It had the heavy, impersonal atmosphere of a modernized château. Although in good taste, the colors were too rich and the carpet was too thick. The rooms had Mrs. Gayelorde-Sutton's signature scrawled in every corner.

"I can't stay here, Di," I protested. "This is sheer madness!"

"No one comes in here and you can lock the door," she said, hurriedly. "Better still, *don't* lock it . . . leave it ajar, and if anyone comes along the corridor go into the bathroom and lock that. That's the last place anyone would expect to find a private boy friend!"

She giggled as she said this and I realized that she had been drinking. I think I might have resisted the idea of remaining hidden in her bedroom until the party finished in the small hours, but she gave me no opportunity. After drawing the heavy curtains she skipped out, blowing a kiss from the door.

It was about 10:30 by now and I knew that I could not expect her to return until after one A.M., at the earliest. Now that I was alone, however, I was exhilarated by the prospect of spending several hours isolated among her things. It brought a touch of intimacy to what had looked like being a damp and dismal evening, with my nose pressed against the pieshop window of Heronslea watching others enjoy themselves. There was triumph too, triumph over my dinner-jacketed competitors downstairs. Each was licensed to paw Diana in public, sharing her with a hundred others, but up here, cut off from the roar and clatter of the party, I was alone with the real Diana and secreted in a place where her dreams had flowered since she was a pony-mad schoolgirl.

I began to savor the privilege, stealing around and touching the things she handled every day, silver-backed hairbrushes, pots of make-up, the perfume spray, and even the pillow that held the scent of her hair.

I prowled across to the book alcove and found my own gift, the inscribed copy of *Lorna Doone*. Under the inscription was something written very indistinctly, in pencil, in Diana's handwriting. I took it over to the pink bedside light and deciphered it—*The tower, New Year's Day* and then a cross, signifying, I hoped, that this pencil mark was a record of our first kiss.

I examined her other books: Alan Seager's poems and several other books of verse, ancient and modern, Drip's classics that did not seem to have been read very much, and a row of Ethel M. Dell, Angela Brazil, Ruby M. Ayres that showed signs of constant use. I went back to *Lorna Doone* and sat down on a seat that looked like a pink, tilted plate resting on wicker legs. Outside heavy rain was drumming against the tall window and I read quietly until I heard someone cough in the corridor. Alarmed, I scrambled up and ran into the bathroom, locking the door and listening intently when I heard the bedroom door squeak, a faint clinking sound and then silence.

After listening for another five minutes I opened the door an inch and peeped out. No one was there but on the bedside table was a plate covered by a spotless napkin, and beside it an opened bottle of champagne. Diana had evidently remembered that I might want supper.

I was in fact extremely hungry and the sandwiches were very good. I had wolfed them all before I noticed two words scrawled in lipstick inside the fold of the napkin. She had written *Use toothbrush glass*. The message made me chuckle, for somehow it showed that the spiriting of someone like myself into a place of honor at her party was providing the hostess with more genuine pleasure than anything going on downstairs. I drank half the champagne and it gave me confidence and elation. I listened at the door to the sounds of revelry below—odd shrieks, bumps, *oohs*, *ahhs* and the constant undertone of saxophones. I tried to identify the tunes but failed, except in the case of "The Gay Gordons" which, judged by the uproar, seemed to be no end of a romp. My sense of private triumph mounted. I took off my shoes, tie and windbreaker and stretched myself on her bed, hazy with champagne, drunk with bliss. Suddenly I was quite sure that everything would work out perfectly, and lulled by reassurance I dropped off to sleep.

The prolonged rustle of her dress awakened me. I had turned off the bedside lamp and now only a chink of light entered the room from the corridor. I started up in alarm, cursing myself for being such a fool as to sleep with the door ajar. My mouth was dry from champagne and nervousness but Diana did not seem at all nervous. I heard her shut and lock the door. Then she called, softly, "Switch on the light, Jan, the small one."

I switched on and saw her smiling down at me. She was slightly tousled and her cheeks were flushed. There was the slightest suggestion of unsteadiness and this she exaggerated by clasping her hands behind her back. Her mascara had run a little and her lipstick was slightly smeared.

"I believe you're a bit tight, Di," I said, chuckling.

"Yes, I believe I am," she admitted deliberately. "Just the weeniest bit, that is, but not nearly so tight as most of them."

"Have they all gone?"

"All that *are* going. A baker's dozen are staying the night."

"I didn't hear any of the cars. I must have been sound asleep."

"Poor Jan! Have you been frightfully bored?"

"No, not a bit bored. I loved being up here, it was like being near you all the time."

She smiled vaguely, picked up the open copy of *Lorna Doone* and clicked her tongue in mock disapproval.

"Tch, tch! Jan Ridd wouldn't have gone to sleep uninvited in a maiden lady's bed!"

"Jan didn't get the chance," I told her.

She considered this, then dismissed it. There was something studiedly casual about her manner and I decided that it wasn't just the champagne.

"Do you want any more to drink?" she asked, suddenly.

"No," I said, "only water. My mouth is like a sandstone cave."

"I'll have a sip," she said, and poured a little into the toothbrush glass.

"Have you thought up how to get me out of here?" I asked.

"We'll think about that later. What time will it be light?"

"About five, I should say. What's the time now?"

"Two-thirty," she said, finishing her drink and glancing at her diamond-encrusted watch. "If we allow half an hour to get you clear that gives us two hours. Right!" She suddenly became brisk and businesslike. "Turn out the light!"

She said it as a command and when the room was in darkness she slipped around the bed, drew back the curtains and threw open the window. The current of air was like a kiss. Away in the wood a nightjar screeched but the only other sound was the faint plop of raindrops falling from the rhododendrons under the window.

She remained by the window long enough to make me impatient. Then I heard her dress rustle and realized that she was stepping out of it.

"I won't be a minute, Jan," she said, and there was a strong tremor in her voice. She went into the bathroom and I heard water running. I knew then that she meant to give herself to me, not only because she wanted to but because to do so, here at this moment, was part of a planned ritual. This was the ultimate defiance, a surrender that mocked everything in her past and present, and it was to be here, on this special occasion, in the tabernacle of the enemy's temple! She had planned it this way, down to the last detail. All the time her parents had been sending out their gilded invitations, all the time the staff had been furbishing and decorating Heronslea, all the hours that she had been drinking, chattering and dancing with people her parents had chosen as companions, her mind was racing toward a different kind of milestone, one that marked the very end of her childhood.

For a moment, a few seconds only, I resisted the invitation. I told myself, breathlessly, that she was not quite sober, that no good could come of a gesture as wild and reckless as this, and at the back of my mind there was another scruple, a miniscule of doubt that I was not being used as Jan Leigh, a human being whom she desired and who was hopelessly in love with her, but once again as the banner of the undefeated, advancing against the ramparts of convention. It all added up to the feeblest resistance on my part and was swept away by the first touch of her lips. For a moment, as she threw her arms around me, I was choked with a tenderness and gratitude so vast and intense that I played no immediate part in the embrace. Then I forgot to be grateful and all the tenderness I had for her was drowned under a sea of delight. I became rough and impatient to master what was so freely offered.

We lay without speaking for what seemed a long time. At first, so regular was her breathing that I thought she was asleep but she was not, for presently her hand moved gently across my face and began ruffling my hair, softly and rhythmically, as a mother strokes a sick child. Then I was bitterly ashamed of my roughness and almost wept to think of it. It was not the guilty feeling I had after my experience with Madeleine. As regards the act itself I felt only pride, but it seemed to me that my violence had given her cause to believe that she had been used impersonally and for that I wanted most desperately to apologize, only the words would not come. Like Madeleine she sensed my distress, using almost the same words.

"You're not sorry, Jan? You won't go away and hate yourself for it? You mustn't, you know, because it was how I meant it to happen and I'm glad it has! There's nothing furtive about us any more, you see, and nothing beastly either, as there would have been if it had been with anyone else. It's right that you should be the one and I'll never be sorry about it, *never*, do you understand?"

"I hurt you, Di!" I muttered. "And that's something I'll never be able to forget!"

"Oh nonsense!" she said, moving her arm and drawing my head onto her shoulder. "That wasn't your fault, stupid! It was inevitable. Anyway, don't remember that, just remember I'll always belong to you now, no matter what happens, or where I go, or what I do! Nothing can change that and it's what I always planned and wanted, right from the time I kissed you in the train that time, remember?"

Lying there, my head on her breast, I remembered so much, all of it sweet and uplifting. I remembered my first glimpse of her, riding out of the wood like a child-empress and banishing Keeper Croker with an arrogant glance; I remembered our short journey in the suburban train and her exultant claim as we pulled into the station. I remembered riding beside her into the wind on Foxhayes Common, under winter skies and in hot summer sunshine. I remembered even more vividly still our quiet days on Nun's Island, and her tremulous earnestness as we stood beside the signal fire awaiting the pilot boat. I remembered it all, every minute detail of it, and the memories filled me with a pride in my manhood that banished the shame of using her so fiercely and possessively. Her voice, and the nearness of her, healed the hurt and filled me with a sense of infinite peace.

I slept until she gently awakened me and I saw that the curtains were redrawn and the light was on. She was dressed in jodhpurs and yellow sweater and was beckoning, her hand on her lips.

"I've been on reconnaissance," she said, unsmilingly, "and it's all clear. We'll go out the same way as you came in, but don't say a word, not a single word, understand?"

We crept downstairs, through the gun room and out through the

[236]

flower-room door. The sky was gray over Shepherdshey, but still dark toward the copse.

"When will I see you again, Di? It has to be soon!"

She put her mouth to my ear, kissed it and whispered:

"I'll write the moment I find out what's happening, Jan. Go now, dearest! And thank you for loving me, Jan!" There was no opportunity to argue, and no real need. I knew now that she would make it possible and that these things were always best left to her.

"I haven't wished you many happy returns," I said.

"Wish me now, then."

"Many happy returns, Di, many, many of them, and all as wonderful as this!"

She nodded impatiently and gave me a little push. I slipped across the paddock into the last of the shadows. When I reached the edge of the copse I looked back and could make out the long, gray shape of the house, but the garden door was shut and she was gone.

I experienced the same small spurt of disappointment as on the occasion of my first visit to Heronslea, when I was whisked down the drive in her mother's big car and looked back at a closed door.

Part Two

Chapter Eight

IN SOME ways that period was the last of the old way of life, not only for me—I was hibernating and barely conscious of the events that led, step by step, to the Second World War—but for people like Uncle Reuben, Aunt Thirza, the journeymen in the works outside our office, for everyone who had seen the twenties and early thirties trying, and sometimes half-succeeding, to swim back into the easy water of the Edwardian decade.

Some people would have it that the old-world isolation of districts like Whinmouth disappeared in the slump of '31, but this was not really true of our part of the world. The slump never blighted Whinmouth. Down there wages were always low and, as I have said, most of us lived by taking in one another's washing. There are more people unemployed in Whinmouth today, after nearly two decades of the Welfare State, than there were in 1931, and Hitler was not even a concert-party joke with us until he massacred half his supporters in the summer of '34. It was only then, when the Nazis began to hit the world headlines, that we became aware that something shrill and hysterical was being shouted at us, something that made our annual British Legion rally and League of Nations Union meetings look genuinely parochial. Up to that time our interest in global politics was halfhearted, like our championship of Oxford or Cambridge in the Boat Race, or reaction to Amy Johnson flying to Australia. We heard about these things on the radio, and some of us read of them in the daily papers, but they were not as important to us as, say, the Chapel Hill tar-barrel race on Guy Fawkes night, and even when a

General Election came along only about 60 per cent of the local electorate turned out to vote. We were far more vocal over Councilor Rawlinson's proposal to remove the Boer War obelisk from Fish Square, and the only national event in which we took a genuine interest was the two-minute silence around the war memorial, and the sale of Flanders poppies.

We had slipped from the nineteen-twenties into the nineteen-thirties almost without noticing, and we were almost halfway through the new decade before Hitler's name began to crop up in the public bars of hostelries like The Rifleman at Shepherdshey. After that, however, the tide of events carried us along at a pretty round pace. Almost everyone had a radio set by then and when Germany invaded the Ruhr, Mussolini pounced on Abyssinia, Hitler grabbed Austria, and the papers began to headline the Spanish Civil War and the Sudetenland problem, we began to realize that a bad train and bus service was not an absolute guarantee against invasion by the outside world.

Even in Sennacharib one was made aware of this, for on the plain outside the market town they had built a small airfield and the mew of the two buzzards became even more plaintive when silver-glinting aircraft zoomed in from the sea and skimmed across Foxhayes to land.

As a newspaperman, even a small-town newspaperman, I should have been far more aware of all that was taking place than in fact I was, but my grasp of global events was not much better than Aunt Thirza's. During the first part of this Gadarene stampede I was content to get through my routine work and dream about Diana, and when Diana wasn't there to dream about, the soundproof wall of self-pity I built around me excluded objective contemplation of the antics of grotesques like Goebbels and Ciano, and even, to some extent, of Mr. Chamberlain and his umbrella. Coming from a professional reporter this is a very lame confession, but it is true for all that; I date this period of personal detachment from the night that Diana and I became lovers, and I pedaled dreamily into Whinmouth just as the sun came up over Nun's Head and the gulls went about their early morning shopping on the sandbanks.

I was blissfully content for about a fortnight. I did not expect to hear from her until the family had settled in Nice, where they were expected to remain for two months. Uncle Reuben's obstinate fracture kept him from taking any part in the weekly production of the

Observer, and as it was now high summer I had plenty to keep me occupied.

Then I had a postcard from her, just a wish-you-were-here gesture but enough to keep me happy for another month or so. Then Uncle Reuben was told by his surgeon that he would never walk again and my concern for him was strong enough to put even Diana out of mind for a time.

The business was reorganized. I was made official editor a week or so before my twentieth birthday and later presented with a thousand shares in the firm, now operating under the title of R. & J. Leigh & Co. (Observer Press) Ltd.

When things settled down a little, and we had moved Uncle Reuben into a new bungalow on Dune Terrace, overlooking the estuary, I longed to tell Diana everything that was happening, partly from reasons of pride in my new status but mostly, I think, because I believed that these changes would have a practical bearing on our future. I even sat down and wrote her a long letter, but I did not post it. I was unwilling to take any action that might prejudice our meeting when she returned to England, and I knew her mother well enough to realize that promotion from junior reporter to editor of the *Whinmouth & District Observer* was not enough to qualify for the role of son-in-law. I had an uncomfortable suspicion, moreover, that even my winning the Irish Sweepstakes, or my sudden elevation to the post of Foreign Secretary, would not induce Mrs. Gayelorde-Sutton to forgive my part in the island escapade. There was no other course open but to await Diana's twenty-first birthday and because, deep in my heart, I was now quite sure of her, I could await that date—June 18, 1937—with dignity if not with patience.

I was happy enough in my work and I was saving money at what seemed to me a prodigious rate. I took to ranging those scattered parts of Sennacharib where odd and isolated houses had been built, hoping to find one with a sale notice exhibited, or learn of someone living there who was old and infirm and not likely to need it much longer. Up to now it had been a vain quest. There were not more than a dozen homes in the area and two-thirds of them were large, detached houses, quite outside the range of my pocket.

Then, in November of that year, the bubble burst.

I came home from a Saturday afternoon tramp across Nun's Head and Foxhayes to find a fat letter lying on Aunt Thirza's hall stand. It was postmarked New York and the unmistakable handwriting set my heart racing like a dynamo. I tore off my dripping mackintosh and carried the letter up to my room, shouting to Aunt Thirza that I would have my tea upstairs and work there until bedtime.

Aunt Thirza came up with a tray and it was not until I had heard her descend, and had locked the door, that I slit the envelope and drew out four folded sheets and a wad of tissue paper about two or three inches square. I unfolded the tissue first. Inside was a small lock of Diana's hair.

It was softer and darker than I would have imagined but the sharp, neat twist reminded me of the broad lock that used to sweep down to her chin when I knew her first. Later on, when she began to attend West End hairdressers and the fashions changed year by year, this mutinous swath gave up its attempt to reach the corner of her mouth and fell in line with the long roll that touched her shoulders. I looked at the token a long time, almost forgetting the letter. Then I refolded the tissue, put it away in my wallet and settled down to read.

I have her letter still; this is what it said:

> Hotel Plaza,
> New York.
> October 21st.

MY OWN JAN,

This letter has been a long time coming, four months by my reckoning, and I suppose I could plead travel as an excuse. Since leaving the Riviera, in July, we have been two-thirds of the way around the world, and I could easily say that the reason I didn't write was because I was at sea, or packing, or sight-seeing, or anything else ordinary people say when they want to put themselves in the right. We aren't "ordinary people," Jan. We never have been and never will be. You've never pretended to me about anything, so I'm going to tell you the truth because I owe you that at least. The real reason I haven't written is that I hated telling you lies, and I was all this time finding the courage to say what I've got to say now, that we can't ever belong to one another as we thought we could all this time.

You've got to understand one thing straightaway. This isn't because of Mother—she doesn't even know we saw one another in London, or on my birthday, and I imagine she thinks I've completely forgotten you; maybe she has too, she's never mentioned you since that awful time she went to your office after the island business.

This is something I've thought about myself, day after day, since we became really each other's, and I knew it then, when I said good-by and perhaps it would have been more honest to call you back and say so, rather than sitting down and writing it cold-bloodedly, but I didn't and since then things have happened so quickly. We went away and have been on the move ever since. I've had to think about it at odd times when I was alone, which wasn't as often as I should have liked.

The thing is, Jan dear, I've learned so very much about myself in the last few months. I know now that it would be wrong to pretend I could be a good wife to you, and live in the country, even country as heavenly as our Sennacharib, because you would never have more than half of me. The other half would always be fretting for the kind of life you wouldn't even like, no matter how well-off you were, the sort of life your half of me has always sneered at when we've talked about it.

I said you had never pretended to me but I think I must have to you, although I do ask you to believe that I didn't do it consciously. The half of me that you've never met is the selfish half, that likes pretty clothes, smart hairdos, racing cars, meeting people, going places as I've been doing lately, and all the things that come naturally to people who don't actually earn money but just *have* it. Said like that, this seems dreadfully crude, even snobbish, but I've tried to write it other ways and it always comes out the same. If this is the truth then let it be the truth. I'm a thoroughly spoiled girl and I've got used to being spoiled. I can't cook, or sew, or make-do, and I don't think I'd ever learn. I could easily say that I would, for the man I loved, and I've heard heaps of girls say just that at school and even among the debs, but they don't mean it, not really, and all of them would rather be old maids than have to do it, or if they did they'd be hopeless at it and drive the man they married up the wall in the end.

I wouldn't do that to you, Jan, because you aren't just a schoolgirl pash but something much, much more. I've always known that and I'll always believe it, even if we never see one another again. The point is, going on and on like this isn't the least bit fair to you. It keeps you hoping and hoping when there isn't any reason to hope, but what is even worse, it stops you getting a proper kind of girl who would be a good wife, and that's the whole root of the matter—I'm living under false pretenses, and I've known that since about a year after we were separated and you went to work in London. It was very wrong of me to pretend when we met that time and even more wrong—something for which I'll never really forgive myself—to make you make love to me after the party. Any man, especially a man like you, would have a right to expect something different from this awful letter after that, and I can only plead that it happened because I do really love you in a terribly *private* kind of way, and when you put your arms around me and kiss me I just want you completely in a way I've never wanted anyone else who has kissed me or tried to make love to me. I suppose I wanted to *prove* this to myself! I had some sort of idea that if it happened the way I thought it might, then the "plushy" part of me that I've described to you would sort of wither away and leave just an ordinary woman in love with a man—the man being you, but you see, Jan, it didn't! Everything that's happened since—all the luxury cruising and travel and parties and what not—have only bolstered up this stranger to you and convinced her how impossible it would be to turn her back on it for good.

There is one way the half of me that you know will always survive and that's the physical way. Whenever I think of men *as men*, whenever I think of being made love to in the purely physical sense, I think of you and I suppose that will always be so and is just something that the person I marry (if I ever do) will have to put up with if he wants me. I can't alter this but I can be honest with you and say that this isn't nearly important enough to risk your happiness. People are quite right when they say sex is only part of marriage. If I've learned anything from the silly way I've been brought up, it's that. It would be a heavenly part of a marriage to you, Jan, but not enough to make me into the sort of wife you deserve and should have. When I was cut off from all the things I've been used to and (for all the jokes I've made about them) really *like* having, we should have dreadful rows. I'd get snappy and you'd get sullen, and in the end we wouldn't have anything left but bed, and all the wonderful memories we had of Sennacharib, and places like the island, would get blurred. I wouldn't want that to happen and I don't think you would either. For me you have always been a marvelous adventure and it's far better to keep it that way, something to think about when we're old, a kind of reason for having lived at all, if you understand.

I feel very wretched about all this and I've been weeping buckets all the time I've been writing, but all the same I'm glad I had the guts to write it and I hope I have some left to post it!

Good-by now, Jan darling, and thank you, thank you, thank you for everything, for getting into so much trouble for me, for being so faithful, for being so patient, for wanting me so much, but most of all for being just you—my Jan Ridd.

DIANA

I skimmed the letter at first, my hands shaking and a sound like crashing waves in my ears. Then I went through it line by line half a dozen times, pausing and thinking about every sentence and every thought behind the phrases of every sentence. In the end I knew it by heart, every word and every punctuation mark. I had forgotten to light the gas fire and the room was as cold as a tomb. I was shivering, not from cold but from sheer, physical shock, as though I had just avoided being knocked down by a runaway truck and was picking myself up in the gutter, not quite certain if I was still alive.

There was a finality about the letter that stunned me. It was like death, not simply my death but universal death, a sudden cessation of the processes of life, a kind of change in being that blotted out sun and moon, that stopped tides flowing and things growing.

I had had doubts before, serious ones some of them, but never a blow like this, never a denial of the most important thing in my life that came, not from external agencies, like her mother and background, but from Diana herself.

It was over; finished! No more secret meetings, no irregular correspondence, no kisses, no Sennacharib, no future! Over, and decreed so by her, in carefully reasoned terms that made argument futile.

All this time I had been waiting and planning to snatch her away from the places and people prescribed for her, and all this time she had never wanted to escape from them for more than a few moments, as someone might stick his head out of the window to take a few breaths of air, or a fish might surface for a second before returning to the underwater world where it belonged.

247]

That was what really hurt, the hideous, shattering sham of it all! For clearly it had been a sham, right from the night that she took me back to Heronslea on the pony, and we ate muffins and listened to Drip's musical boxes. Remembering this I recalled Drip's warning, and from this point it was fatally easy to gather together the clues that Diana had strewn along our path—her long silences between letters and meetings, her mysterious abstraction that time in Fortnum's, even the steady, almost calculating way that she had looked at me sometimes. It explained the odd remark she had made when we parted after the party night—"Thank you for loving me, Jan!" had not meant what I thought it had meant at all. In my male arrogance I had imagined it to refer to the act of physical possession, whereas it was now clear that she had begun composing this letter, or something like it, within an hour of our lying in one another's arms.

Blind rage ousted misery for a moment and I would have ripped the letter into shreds, had not Aunt Thirza called from the stairs at that moment.

"Supper, Jan! It's put out, so come and eat 'un while 'er's hot."

It is curious how compelling are the ordinary routines of life. I folded the letter, replaced it in its envelope, and went down into the kitchen, where Thirza mistook my glumness for overwork.

"Why bless 'ee, I dorn reckon you'd stop that there tap-tapping long enough to eat if I didn't drive 'ee to it," she grumbled, ladling out liver and onions and pushing a huge plateful in my direction.

I ate her supper in silence. It was like munching my way through a dish of sand.

2.

For a week or more I hugged my misery to myself but at last, whether I would or not, I was driven by sheer wretchedness to share it with someone. I had to find a confidant. I had scores of acquaintances in Whinmouth but no real friends apart from Aunt Thirza and Uncle Reuben, and I inclined toward the latter. After all, Reuben had already been introduced to the problem, and Reuben had met Mrs. Gayelorde-Sutton. Outwardly he was a narrow-minded old bachelor, but what drove me to confide in him was the certainty I had of his deep affection for me, and a belief that a man of his age and experience might be able to give me worth-while advice. I was not disappointed; to the day he died I never stopped discovering Uncle Reuben.

I went up to his bungalow and found him sitting like a stricken Cromwell in the big armchair, facing the superb river view. He had always been a very active man and he hated his inability to get out and about, and his dependence on the visits of cronies to bring him all the local news that did not appear in the *Observer*. He was always pleased to see me, however, and his face brightened up the moment I passed in front of his window. We exchanged a few banalities and then I went straight to the point, showing him Diana's letter.

He read it carefully, his hedgebank eyebrows drawing together in a puzzled frown. When he had digested it he said, very quietly: "All right, boy, you'd better tell me the whole of it now, right from the beginning."

I told him everything. I described how we had met and how I had once lied to him about going to London to put flowers on my mother's grave. I told him how he and others had been hoaxed by our cover story of the journalistic tour of Heronslea, and how for years Diana and I had used the local social and sporting events in order to meet without her parents knowing anything about me. I told him the full story of the island adventure, the dance that preceded it, and of our chance meeting in London. I finished with a truthful but shamefaced admission of what happened at the party, the previous June.

He didn't interrupt once but punctuated my story with a series of explosive little grunts. When I had finished he turned his big, gray eyes on me and I saw with relief that there was genuine concern in them, as well as pained bewilderment.

"Is that everything, boy?" he growled. "She wouldn't be in any sort of real trouble, would she?"

"That's everything I can remember, Uncle Reuben," I said, "and if she was in trouble you can be pretty sure we should have heard about it by now from the usual quarter."

"Ah," he muttered, "I daresay you're right at that."

He folded her letter and returned it to me. Like most printers he had been a snuff addict from boyhood and now he fortified himself with two enormous pinches and a volley of shattering sneezes. "Well now, tell me first what *you* make of it. Do you regard that letter as final?"

"There's not much doubt about that," I said.

He looked at me searchingly. "Isn't there? Then why did you come to me about it?"

Why had I come to him? Was it because I had been nursing this secret for years and had now allowed it to grow into an obsession, or was it because I wanted someone to blow on the ashes in the wild hope that a small spark had survived the cold douche of her decision? Had I come to him for sympathy or reassurance? To have my hand patted or to learn how to regroup my scattered wits for a counterattack?

He answered me himself, and the nature of his answer proved what I had long suspected—that underneath the harsh, radical shell of the Puritan there was an unrepentant romantic.

"See here, boy," he said, groping for his pipe and heaving his big frame half out of the groaning chair, "I'm a crabby bachelor, and have never had but one love affair in my life. It didn't amount to anything, not even as much as yours, you reckless young idiot, but it did teach me something about women. It taught me there's a right and wrong way to go about wenching."

I think I was more shocked by his admission than he had been by mine. Not only was it a great surprise to learn that he had once been in love, but his use of the word "wenching" was so uncharacteristic that it was almost as though he had started to tell me a dirty story.

"Who was she?" I asked wonderingly.

"She was the doctor's daughter, and in my young days a doctor was somebody in a place like this. Grace, she was called, Grace Dainton, tall and dark as a gypsy and as handsome a woman as you'd see anywhere, especially when she was up on her father's gig, driving a big gray up and down the town. We used to meet in the spinney, at the back of her father's place up on the Foxhayes road, and although I wasn't out of my apprenticeship at the time, and didn't have two pennies to rub together, she was mad to marry me and wanted us to run off when her father set about marrying her off to one of those Earnshaws, who owned the big brewery over at Whinford. Wealthy family and good-looking young chap, but she wouldn't have any part of him. You can't arrange these things, never could and never will! Here was me, several years younger than her and, as I say, without a penny in the bank, and there was this Earnshaw fellow, with all the money in the world and the first motorcar ever seen about here outside her door every night of the week. For all that, she'd get shot of him and come running down the spinney to me as soon as it was dark. Came in her nightdress once, aye, and bare feet at that!"

As he said this one of his rare smiles crossed his face. I was so astonished by his story that for a moment I forgot all about Diana.

"What happened, Uncle Reuben? Why didn't you marry her?"

He looked quite fierce for a moment and then, drawing on his pipe, relaxed and grinned again.

"Why? Well, for the same reason as you're disposed to take that drivel at face value," he said. "Mind you, this class nonsense was even worse in my young days! You were either born a gentleman or you were born to mind your p's and q's—none of this Jack's-as-good-as-his-master business you get nowadays. With Grace and me it wasn't only a question of money but a matter of birth and education. Now these Suttons aren't real quality, that's what makes the woman so insufferable! You're as good as they are and I daresay, if you went far enough back, you're the better bred of the two. When Grace Dainton begged me to run off with her I should have done it but I didn't, and not because I wasn't head over heels in love with her, because I was, but because I thought I'd be doing her an injury."

"You're sorry you didn't?"

He thought for a moment. "Yes, I am. I'm sorry for my sake but more sorry for hers. I was doing her the injury by letting her go, because in the end she didn't marry anyone and by the time she was thirty-five she was a leathery old maid, grumbling over a sick father and putting flowers on the altar of St. Luke's Church. She died before she was fifty and all the money that had kept me from running off with her went to the Whinmouth Animals' Dispensary. They built that red brick place at the top of Fish Street with it and I never pass the monstrosity without wanting to spit at it."

"But this is different, Uncle Reuben!" I protested, impressed by his story but far from appreciating the parallel. "This time the boot's on the other foot. It's *her* who has had second thoughts about it, not me."

"Ah boy," he said kindly, "don't you believe it! She's written the letter, but what brought her to the point of sitting down to write it? She's a girl of spirit, just like my Grace was before I turned her into a sour old maid by shuffling about and apologizing for being who I was and what I was. Now you're doing the same thing, standing aside and letting her make all the decisions. Don't do it, boy, make some yourself, and right or wrong she'll come to respect you for it.

If there's one thing a woman can't abide it's a man who lets her call the tune. Before you know where you are, it's unholy discord!"

I had expected censure and possibly kindly meant grow-up-sonny-advice, but certainly not an advocacy of aggression.

"I'll never have her kind of money, Uncle," I began, but he gave a loud snort of impatience and slapped his huge palm with the bowl of his pipe, the way I remembered him doing during the violent discussion with Diana's mother two years ago.

"*Money! Class! Keep your station! Keep in line!* What the devil has a generation of radical progress done for you, boy? There was some excuse for me when I was your age. You daren't let it be known you voted anything but Tory if you worked for a Tory or paid rent to a Tory landlord. But today—damn it, I don't often swear but you drive me to it—today there's more real equality than I ever dreamed possible. It's now, not 1884! You don't have to kowtow to people like the Suttons, just because they made a fortune out of nitrates and pit props in the war. If you want this girl as much as you say you do, then in God's name go in and get her! If she's been laughing at you behind your back all this time, then at least you'll soon know where you stand and be well shot of her! If she hasn't, if she's written you that mealymouthed letter because she thinks you've always accepted the situation and are therefore likely to go on doing so, then show her different. Thumb your nose at her background, tan her backside if you have to, and she'll want you the more for it! Maybe that isn't the kind of advice you thought you'd get from a dry old stick like me, but it's the kind I'm inclined to give you, seeing that you're no longer the moonstruck boy you were when you played truant on the island, but a man old enough to make love to a woman and then slink off with your tail between your legs, sniveling excuses about class and income!"

I was very much taken aback by this outburst but it did me a power of good, for it challenged my entire conception of the situation. He was entirely accurate in his assumption that I had never made more than a token attempt to kick over the barrier that separated us. I had accepted the limitations it imposed with a kind of masochistic fatalism, and although I had repeatedly told myself that I could do very little until she was legally of age, I now realized that this was only a cowardly way of evading the issue. The truth was, I had always stood in awe of Diana's background. Keeper Croker's agonizing half nelson still kept me in check. I raged at the necessity of coming and going to Heronslea by stealth, but I had never contemplated taking a stand in the middle of the big paddock and bawling defiance at the Gayelorde-Suttons. Uncle Reuben's comments, the first I had ever had on the subject apart from Twining's disparagement at the office and Old Drip's gentle dissuasion years ago, set me wondering whether Diana's behavior throughout our association had been conditioned by mine. I remembered now her curious, half-symbolic act in taking me over the Castle Ferry in order to show me her rough-tongued old grandfather; it seemed to me, looking back, that many times she had presented me with a tentative opening to challenge the opposition but had resorted to secrecy when she realized that I accepted stealth as a condition to our partnership.

All at once I began to feel a great deal more sure of myself. Uncle Reuben had greatly oversimplified the situation, but at least he was on the right lines, while I had been hopelessly off them for years. From confidant to whom I had been driven by unbearable loneliness he now emerged as a powerful and active ally.

"Look here, Uncle Reuben," I said, "Diana isn't twenty-one for more than two years yet. We couldn't marry without her parents' consent and, although I've got better prospects than most fellows my age, I haven't got enough to marry on. Just what is the best way of going about it?"

"Let me look at that letter again," he said, and when I gave it to him he sat hunched up for the better part of ten minutes, rubbing his nose with his forefinger and drawing his brows together so closely that they looked like a quickset hedge dividing his face neatly in two. Finally he looked up.

"I'd let her sow her wild oats for a spell, and then catch her on a rebound," he said.

"But she's been sowing wild oats ever since I've known her," I complained.

"Down here . . . rural oats! . . . Wait until she's sown a bag or two in Mayfair! I know her sort all right . . . they provide all the copy for the 'silly' seasons and they either end up with a loveless marriage, or an overdose of drugs. Point is, you'll have to watch your timing but that won't hurt, you're young enough in all conscience, and you can use the interval collecting ammunition—money in your instance. If you want the real key to all this it's *here*," he went on, rapping his pipe bowl on page four of the letter. "She won't get what she wants from those anemic guardsmen and younger sons, and the moment she realizes how badly she wants it, pounce, and good luck to you, boy! Now tell me what you've been up to this week and what you've laid by for the inside pages. I've had enough kiss-in-the-ring for one afternoon."

We talked on general matters, more easily and naturally than we had ever conversed in the past. When I left him there was a twinkle in his eye and he called as I reached the door:

"Feel any better for the heart-to-hearter, boy?"

"Better than I've felt for months," I admitted, gratefully, and hurried back to the office to give the Thursday proofs a good deal more attention than they had been getting since they became my responsibility.

3·

Uncle Reuben had lived his entire life in a rural backwater but his knowledge of the world was far wider than one might imagine it to be. His forecast in respect of Diana proved astonishingly accurate.

Over a year passed. It was December when I went to him for advice. The following spring, Diana was back in England and within two months of her return she was hard at work providing Fleet Street with silly-season material. She was doing it, moreover, in the company Uncle Reuben had predicted, that of guardees and younger sons, collectively known as Debs' Delights. Together with high-spirited companions of previous seasons they were recognized as the Bright Young Things. They were the very last legatees of the gay twenties.

Diana's recruitment into this set had its advantages. It made her movements easy to follow, even from as far away as Whinmouth. Regularly each month Diana and her boon companions made a bow to the newspaper-reading public, at first as participators in widely publicized charity efforts—balls, bazaars and dramatic entertainments—then as habitués of some of the more popular night clubs, later still as the organizers of bow-tie sprees and bizarre practical jokes, such as the digging up of a section of the Strand dressed as L.C.C. workmen, or the tarring and feathering of statues. It was all very gay and sophisticated, and I can imagine Mrs. Gayelorde-Sutton outwardly wagging a reproving finger but secretly being immensely proud of her daughter's antics, for they surely signified an acceptance of a way of life toward which the mother had been pushing her daughter since childhood.

Some of the left-wing newspapers were very scornful about these pranks and howled for less tolerance on the part of the police and a far tighter rein on the part of the parents, but the public as a whole gloried in the fun and I suppose most young people, living quiet dull lives in quiet dull towns like Whinmouth, secretly envied Diana and her set their uninhibited exploitation of youth.

Certainly the newspapers played up to them, often devoting more space to a Mayfair treasure hunt than they would allocate Mussolini's latest bluster over Abyssinia. It was on one of these crazy treasure hunts, then the peak of West End fashion, that Diana's escort, a young man known as the Hon. Newton Symes, overstepped the wide limits of public tolerance and gave the Socialist press a chance to compare the antics of these young British socialites with those of French aristocrats, immediately prior to the revolution of 1789. The comparison was somewhat strained. Diana and the young Honorable had not killed a peasant's child by driving a coach over it, they had merely driven head on into a coster's barrow and when the man's truculent attitude annoyed them, had refused to pay compensation without recourse to law.

The incident left a bad taste in the public mouth and from then on even the sensational dailies began to lead their columns against the Bright Young Things, and publish a steady spate of letters from Tunbridge Wells, and Budleigh Salterton, deploring their wild behavior in and around London.

I did not see Diana all this time, neither did I write or attempt to get in touch with her. I watched her pranks from a safe distance, and I kept an eye on the calendar. Then, one day after she had been in trouble over a motoring offense at Maidenhead, and had been threatened with suspension of her driving license, I decided that it was time for a reconnaissance and took a few days' holiday in London. Before setting out I wrote briefly to her town home, saying that I would be delighted to say hello and take her out to lunch. It was the letter of an old friend, resigned to his dismissal as a lover.

When I got to my hotel a phoned message awaited me. Diana suggested that we meet in the sherry bar of Martinez's in Swallow Street, so I went there, booked a table for lunch and sat down to await her in the bar facing the dim foyer, placing myself so as to see her before she saw me. I went about it coolly, without any of the bubbling excitement I had experienced immediately before our earlier meetings, but I was too smug by a mile. It was I, not Diana, who was caught off balance.

She appeared some ten minutes late and I almost failed to recognize her. There was a jerky brittleness about her walk and bearing, as if she was playing at being a marionette. She was exquisitely dressed and groomed, but somehow the general effect was unpleasing. When I had met her by chance, in Fortnum's, her smartness was a part of her, personality merging with clothes and accessories, but now it was as though a convention of talented couturiers and hair stylists had gathered together and drawn up a schedule decreeing "This is what the fashionable young woman of this season will look like; all else is drabness!" There was a cold uniformity about her appearance that banished the Diana of Sennacharib, replacing her with the kind of girl one saw leaning nonchalantly against an impossibly expensive coupé in magazine advertisements, and the transformation extended to her expression and features, from which the personality had been drained or neutralized. Her eyes had lost their glow, her mouth its mobility. Her chestnut hair still caught the light where it fell on the starched collar of her blouse, but it was no longer the kind of hair one wanted to stroke. It had a touch-me-not-it-cost-a-lot-to-arrange look about it, and this aura of prohibition invested her like an icy mist. It was as though the Diana I remembered and worshiped had died, giving birth to the Emerald that her training had conceived, so that for the first time since she had told me her name it suited her. She had a hard, greenish, gemlike quality that was fascinating at a distance, but repellent at close quarters.

She greeted me very cordially and I ordered two sherries. We chatted about one thing and another, much as two slightly acquainted cousins might have discussed members of their family. Then she ordered two more sherries and insisted on paying for them. It was during this second drink that I noticed that Diana was not yet dead but shut away in solitary confinement and trying, very feebly, to make her presence known. Twice Diana called to be let out, once in the bar, and again when we were lunching upstairs. The first time was when Emerald faltered for a moment and Diana reached out across the table, touching my shoulders with the tips of her fingers, saying, "They're so wide! I have to be sure they aren't padded, Jan!" The second occasion was when, halfway through the hors-d'oeuvres, she suddenly asked if I had been across Sennacharib lately. This time, however, Emerald was on guard and the word became *Senneckarib*, much as Mrs. Gayelorde-Sutton would have pronounced it.

It took me at least half an hour to absorb the transition and adjust myself to its almost macabre manifestations. When I had succeeded in doing so, our passages became a sort of game, each maneuvering to catch the other at a disadvantage, like a judge and a competitor in a statue dance, where all movement must cease with the accompaniment. I think that on the whole I had the best of the exchanges, for behind her façade of guarded frigidity I thought I could detect a tiny flicker of guilt. She was rather like a woman who had sat down opposite me to settle a claim for damages, determined to yield no more than she was obliged to, but held in check by a conviction that, if the matter went to court, the decision would surely go against her.

When we were sipping coffee the waiter came over to us with a bottle of cognac and Diana said she would like some. He poured a little into her glass but she laid her hand on his arm and kept it there, so that it became a treble. We had had a bottle of Beaune between us, as well as the sherry, and the effect of the alcohol now began to mellow her. She leaned back and smiled, no longer like a distant cousin, or a claim fighter, but like a rich aunt regaling a schoolboy nephew on a speech-day outing.

"Are you doing anything particular this afternoon, Jan?" she asked, and although the question was an idle one I knew that it was important to her that we should extend the reunion.

"Have you anything in mind?" I said.

"As a matter of fact I hev!" she replied.

There it was again; "hev" not "have," a formidable echo of her mother.

"Well, Diana?"

"I'd like you to take me to the Tower," she said.

"The Tower? The Tower of London?" It would have been an astonishing request from Diana; it was an absolutely outrageous one from Emerald.

"I've never been," she admitted, "and I don't know anyone else who would take me. I heard a broadcast about the ceremony of the keys the other evening and said to myself, I expect Jan knows all about that place. *Do you?*"

"I've been there several times," I told her, "mostly when I was

257]

writing the Margaret of Anjou book. We'll go if you really want to, we can get the Underground to the Minories."

She winced at the word "Underground" and I only just stopped myself laughing.

"I've got my flivver outside," she said, "providing you don't mind being driven by a woman!"

"No," I said, beginning to enjoy myself, "I'm sure you're a very good driver, Di."

She was too, as far as the mechanical processes were concerned, changing down soundlessly, judging distances with cool accuracy, and generally showing the same command over a car as she showed riding Sioux. I noticed, however, that she was impatient with less skillful drivers, and snarled at a man who slipped his clutch while trying to beat her over the traffic lights. In what seemed to me about five minutes we were on Tower Hill, where we parked and bought tickets at the gate. I showed her around. She did not seem specially interested in the block, the armory and the green, or even the crown jewels, which I thought might attract her, but she surprised me by dawdling beside the prisoners' inscriptions in the Beauchamp Tower, and asked me to tell her something about the people who had been imprisoned there. I was telling her about Lady Jane Grey, and how she had watched the headless body of her husband carried by shortly before her own execution, when I noticed that she was not listening. She had pretended to curiosity in order to allow time for other sight-seers to descend the spiral staircase, leaving us alone in the half-light of the winter's afternoon. As soon as their steps died away she said:

"Well, Jan, don't you want to kiss me?"

The odd thing was that I didn't, not in the least, but it would have sounded so unfriendly to say so that I replied:

"If you want me to, Di."

"I do," she said, flatly, and tilted up her face.

As our lips touched I wondered if contact would free the real Diana and reduce this unpleasant parody of Mrs. Gayelorde-Sutton to a wraith as insubstantial as Lady Jane Grey, but it did nothing of the sort. Her kissing habits had changed like everything else about her. This too had conformed, and now the conference of hair stylists and couturiers had bowed themselves out, to make way for Continental love experts, who had reduced the art of kissing to a graded scale of intimacy—so much pressure, so much time, a place for each hand, a specified angle for the body. She kissed me near the top of this scale, her lips parted and her eyes closed. There was sensuality in the kiss but no hint of bestowal. Its effect upon me was to harden my obstinacy.

I wondered, even while kissing her, whether her town escorts would regard this kind of embrace as something practiced by the lower orders in cinemas and parks. She must have sensed my detachment for she suddenly stepped back and stared at the floor. Doing this she looked so childish and pitiful that I felt a sudden and inexplicable sympathy for her, and at once tried to make amends. I kissed her again, softly and very respectably, but this time she did not attempt to respond, but tore herself free.

"For God's sake let's stop playing 'if-only,'" she snapped, and walked past me and down the stairs.

As we emerged on the green a Yeoman of the Guard began shepherding the last visitors toward the main gate. I drew level with Diana and looked at her sideways, expecting to find her flushed and irritated, but she wasn't; the hard, poised look was back again and as we walked past the Traitors' Gate she said:

"Those beefeaters—do they stay here or do they come out sometimes?"

"They come up for air every so often," I said. "There's usually two or three of them hanging about the ticket office."

She did not reply to this, and the significance of the question did not occur to me until, months later, I read that one of the trophies of a Mayfair treasure hunt had been a beefeater's hat.

Perhaps this was why she had wanted me to take her to the Tower. At the moment she was obviously anxious to be gone and asked me, with the air of addressing a hitchhiker, where I would care to be dropped.

"Nowhere," I said bleakly. "I've got to see a publisher and his office is near, I can walk."

It was a lie, but like her I had no wish to prolong the dismal occasion. She climbed into the car, started the engine, and revved up with unnecessary vigor.

"Well, so long, Jan! Thank you for taking me and thank you for a nice lunch."

We shook hands—that was the monstrously unreal part of it—we shook hands, and the gesture slammed the shutter on our adolescence. As she drove off, her engine making a series of sharp reports, a wave of sadness swept over me and the ache nagged at me all the way home to Whinmouth. Yet it was impersonal sadness. I was not mourning Diana so much as all things in life that promise so much and yield so little. I was sad for the sunny day clouded by rain, for the kitten that grows up to catch thrushes, for the juggler with the fixed smile who opens a glittering program and drops his clubs half-way through the first act, for anybody and everybody who grows up believing that the world is an oyster but never discovers the means of opening the shell. Behind this sadness, however, was a vague sense of relief. It was all over now! It was something that could be tied up like love letters and left to fade under a pile of holiday snap-shots and old phonograph records.

I was free, really free, for the first time since that autumn after-noon in the larch wood a century ago, and I believe I faced this fact with the same kind of resignation as a man faces the prospect of learning to walk with an artificial leg. It could have been far better, but it might have been much worse.

4.

I said nothing to Uncle Reuben about the visit to London, but I imagine that he noticed my application to work throughout that spring and summer and probably related it to Diana in some way. In July I read that, following another motoring offense, her driving license had been suspended for twelve months.

Week followed week, with its usual round of petty sessional courts, council meetings, funerals, weddings, sales-of-work and the odd mild sensation, a fire or a sea rescue. I slipped into a swift rhythm, sometimes covering as many as a dozen jobs a day, and spending what spare time I had in boating and bathing. I went to a few dances and made two or three tepid friendships with Whinmouth girls. I had a ten-day holiday in Brittany, partly with the object of improv-ing my French, which I had kept up by reading First Empire mem-oirs in the original, and occasional evening classes at the University. I went over to Uncle Mark's riding establishment now and again, and when the hunting season opened I even had a day or two out on one of his cobs.

It was a pleasant enough life. The riding and hunting, and some-times an occasional shooting expedition at the invitation of local farmers, kept me in touch with Sennacharib. I remember crossing it under a gray, lifeless sky soon after my twenty-first birthday and bagging a couple of rabbits on Foxhayes Common, but I no longer thought of its gorse and plantations as in any way associated with Diana. I absorbed its color patterns and contours subconsciously, much as Uncle Luke might have watched the flight of a heron over the estuary, but it was now a background, not an Eden.

Then the fun began again with the Bright Young Things. They got into trouble with the Customs and Excise, at Dover, and one of them, whose name had been linked with Diana in the past, received a short jail sentence for smuggling. Later, around about Christmas time, Diana herself figured in a more spectacular scandal. She was a passenger in a glider that crashed on a row of suburban houses in Kent. The pilot was injured, but she escaped with bruises and was photographed for the newspapers standing beside the wreckage. In common with most people I became rather bored with all this nonsense and sympathized with the comment of a vitriolic columnist in a "progressive" weekly, beginning: *If Hitler seeks proof that our expensively educated young people are decadent he should follow the careers of certain ornaments of Mayfair these days. . . .*

Ordinarily these pranks would have aroused little attention but they were given prominence because of the sharp contrast they provided with the main news of those times—endless death and destruction in places like Addis Ababa and Guernica, a constant overturn of threats from the dictators, and irritated gloom among everyone with enough intelligence to wonder what was due to happen next. What irritated people like the gossip writer I have quoted was the impression that people like Diana had turned their backs on the rest of us, and despised us for wondering about the future. They certainly did give that impression, as though they were not only determined to live for the day but intended making as much song and dance about it as possible. The majority, who had to work hard for a living, envied them their freedom and probably found compensation in regarding their childishly high spirits as evidence of degeneracy.

Then something happened that could not be written off as a Mayfair rag. Diana and a young man called Irving, who was the son of a wealthy cement king, were involved in a fatal accident on a country road south of London. Their car collided with a motorcycle combination, containing a young husband and his wife—an expectant mother. The woman was killed outright. Irving and the motorcyclist were critically injured. Diana escaped with two cracked ribs.

At first it looked like just another road accident, but at the initial inquest (later adjourned in the absence of the injured parties) it emerged that Irving had been far gone in drink and would face a criminal charge if he survived. He did not recover, dying a week or so after the accident.

The next day the injured motorcyclist died and the hunt was up. Relatives of the victims howled protests through the press, and feature writers jumped in with whoops of triumph. Diana, as the sole survivor of the crash, came in for some very sharp interrogation at the resumed inquest. As a mere passenger in Irving's car, however, there was no painful sequel for her, and the papers rounded off the story by publishing pictures of her leaving the court, one arm in a sling and the other shading her face from the cameramen.

Two days after these pictures had appeared, I came into the office to find a letter from Diana in my tray. It was a wild cry for help:

> My Jan,
>
> I don't deserve the slightest sympathy, least of all from you, but I've been in hell since the business, and no one else is the slightest use! If you could meet me, wherever you like, I'd never stop being grateful! If you won't, tear this up and forget it. I should understand. It wouldn't make me stop remembering you as the nicest person I've ever had the luck to meet!
>
> With love,
> Diana

I have said that I only remembered Diana impersonally, that when she disappeared in her cloud of blue exhaust on Tower Hill I had succeeded, at last, in turning my back on her. Since then I had adjusted myself to a routine in which she played no part at all. In essence this was true; I seldom thought about her these days, and when I did it was without bitterness. Her appeal showed me how grossly I had been fooling myself. The moment I read her cry for help I knew I must answer it, and I knew also that this would not be a matter of running to the aid of an old friend in trouble but the joyful stampede of a man hopelessly in love. Fortunately, I recognized this at once. It shocked me but I had the sense to go straight to Uncle Reuben and confide in him.

He was far more doubtful about her than he had been when I had sought his advice about her letter of dismissal.

"I don't know, Jan," he said, rubbing his chin, "she's gone from bad to worse, boy. Surely you can see that? There's a kind of devil in her, fed and watered by the kind of life she's been leading since you last saw her. I know that sort. Catch 'em young and you can do something with 'em, but now . . . how old do you say she is?"

I could answer that question with accuracy.

"She'll be twenty-one on the eighteenth of June," I told him.

"You want to go to her?"

"I've got to, Uncle!"

He looked at me sadly and nodded his big head. Inactivity had aged him. He looked more than his seventy years and tired to the breaking point of pain and half-life.

"I daresay you're right, boy. It never pays to defy instincts. Go and see how the land lies at all events, but don't commit yourself to any tomfool promises one way or the other."

I wrote saying that I would come to London that night, and meet her at the Swan and Edgar's corner at eleven A.M. Then I changed into my best suit and drove to the junction for the night train. It was like a parody of my first journey to meet her, the time she had played truant from school. The London pattern was similar, too; a hunched walk through the drizzle of the January small hours, a breakfast in the Covent Garden area, a whiling away of time beside the Embankment, and finally a bus ride to Piccadilly.

It was all there but somehow the parallel was not a pleasant one. It was as though I was the victim of a malign compulsion forced to re-enact a lost youth in order to prove to myself that the original journey had been a dream and that here, years later, was the reality. When I jumped off the bus and crossed over to the rendezvous, the first person I saw was Diana, anxiously scanning the faces of pedestrians as they hurried to and from Eros. It was the first time she had ever been the first to keep an appointment.

I approached her from behind and touched her shoulder. She swung around with a sharp exclamation and I saw at once that she was in a state of extreme nervous tension. When she saw who had touched her she almost cried out with relief.

"Jan! I was terrified you'd cry off! I got it into my head that your idea of arranging to meet me here again was . . . well, a sort of pay-you-out trick. Can we go somewhere and talk? Where shall it be? Martinez? Fortnum's?"

She spoke with extreme rapidity. Each statement was a question.

"It was Lyons the last time we met here, Di, but we've moved up a bit since then," I said, trying a joke in the hope of calming her nerves.

The joke fell flat. "Was it? I don't remember . . . everything's muddled . . . maybe it's the shock, or the bump I got on the windshield . . . you decide—somewhere quiet, somewhere *inside!*"

I took hold of her arm and noticed that she was trembling. She looked so pale, and seemed so helpless and distraught, that I wondered at her doctor allowing her out. Her state of mind was reflected in the clothes she wore. She, who had always been so trim and fashionable, now looked as if she had grabbed any garment that came to hand and had not even troubled to arrange her hair or tidy herself before leaving the house.

She was hatless and gloveless and her lovely hands showed traces of London grime. The varnish on her nails was chipped and her make-up was sketchy, too much lipstick having been applied to one side of her mouth and not enough to the other, so that the cupid's bow looked almost clownish.

I was so shocked by her manner and general appearance that I was obliged to take command of her in a way that would never have been possible in the past.

"We won't go anywhere where you'll have to make an effort, Di," I told her. "What about a snack bar I know, for coffee and a sandwich in strict seclusion?"

"Anywhere," she said, gratefully, "anywhere at all! It was marvelous of you to come so quickly, Jan."

She grabbed my arm and hugged it tightly, as though she had no confidence in her ability to negotiate the traffic. We crossed into Lower Regent Street and made our way to a tiny taximan's pull-up that I knew in a side street behind the Plaza.

There were no other customers at this time of the morning and the proprietor, a sallow young man with heavy sideburns, was out of earshot behind his zinc counter. I bought two coffees and two cheese sandwiches, carrying them across to an alcove at the far end of the shop. In the few moments it had taken me to get them she had made a brave effort to pull herself together and was now feverishly making up with the aid of a little hand mirror.

"I must look a terrible mess!" she said, sounding more like herself. "You've never seen me looking like this, have you, Jan?"

"Never mind that," I said, "just try to relax. We've got all day today and tomorrow as well, if you like. It's a lucky job your letter came on a Friday. I've put the paper to bed and I'm clear until the Petty Sessions, on Monday."

She sipped her coffee. It was very good coffee and she nodded, appreciatively.

"How much was this, Jan?" she asked, irrelevantly.

"Threepence a cup," I said, grinning. "I can run to that, Di!"

She smiled and it was exciting to see a trace of color return to her cheeks. She propped the hand mirror against the cup and, bending low, touched up her lips and tugged at her hair. Presently she replaced the things in her bag and straightened up, finishing the coffee in a series of quick gulps.

"I know places where they'd charge half a crown and it wouldn't be nearly as good coffee as this," she mused. "It was clever of you to know about a place like this but then, you lived and worked in London, didn't you? I keep forgetting that."

"On about thirty bob a week," I told her, "and it makes for careful housekeeping!"

I had been right to bring her somewhere like this. The traffic roar was very much subdued and there were no distractions, as there would have been in any of her usual haunts about the West End. She began to nibble the sandwich, gingerly at first but enthusiastically after the first bite or two.

"This is the first food I've had in forty-eight hours," she admitted. "I haven't swallowed a thing except pills since that awful inquest."

"What sort of pills?" I demanded.

"Oh, the usual . . . pheno and something else added," she said lightly, "but don't let's talk about pills, Jan. It's lovely being here with you; it's making me come alive again. I feel a lot better already, my Jan."

It was callous of me but I wasn't big enough to resist it.

"So I'm your Jan again, am I?"

For a moment she looked exactly as she had looked when we were skylarking up on the common.

"Yes," she said, "whether you like it or not!"

"Do you want to talk about the accident? I've read all the papers had to say about it. We do get London papers in Whinmouth," I added, noting her look of surprise.

"Yes," she said, firmly, "let's get it over and done with. I've got to have somebody's opinion about what to do or I'll end up in the bin! It's odd, Jan, you go on getting further and further away from life and then, suddenly, a single jolt pulls you up and you see where you've been heading and at what a fantastic speed. Do you see what I mean?"

"You'd better start from the beginning," I said, "but don't tell me anything you might regret telling me later on."

"All right, Jan," she said, meekly, "but order some more coffee and sandwiches first. Get ham and plaster it with mustard. I've suddenly realized that I'm famished!"

I went over and bought more coffee and ham sandwiches. Out of the corner of my eye, as I stood waiting at the counter, I saw her take out a cigarette, stick it between her lips, pluck it out again and return it to the case.

"The papers only got half the story," she began, when we were seated again. "We'd been down to a country-club dance, near Maidstone, and Irving was so tight that I made him let me drive, even though my ban doesn't expire until midsummer."

This really frightened me. "*You* were driving? You mean, when it happened?"

She nodded and did not take her eyes off me.

"But how . . . I mean, does anyone know?"

"No one but you, Jan!"

I began to understand the reason for her semihysterical condition. All the time she was giving evidence at the inquest she must have been stricken with guilt, as well as terrified of what might happen to her if the truth emerged.

"How the devil did you manage to persuade the police that Irving was driving?" I asked.

"That was easy . . ." She said it with a touch of the old Diana, planning mischief in Sennacharib. "There was no one about, not until later, and I was the only one conscious. I did it all instinctively —defense mechanism I suppose you'd call it. As soon as I sorted myself out, a minute or so after the impact, I climbed out and pushed Irving into the driving seat. After all, if he hadn't died he'd have still been for it, for letting me drive! I was with him when I was disqualified, so he couldn't have said he didn't know about the ban."

"But how about the others, the couple in the motorcycle combination?"

"I didn't even see them until the ambulance men arrived. I didn't even know what we'd hit! It was all such a frightful shambles. We were piled up under a bank and my side hurt so much that I must have passed out myself after somebody had stopped and carried me into a house for first aid."

It didn't need a vivid imagination to picture the scene—four badly injured people, three of them half dead, in the wreckage of vehicles on a dark, lonely road; a bewildered motorist concentrating on the one victim of the crash who was the least helpless; a sleeping householder dragged from bed by thunderous knocks on the front door; phone calls, ambulance men, solemn police poking about among the mess, taking measurements. As a reporter I was familiar enough with the scene.

"What happened afterwards? After you'd all been taken to hospital?"

"The police came in the afternoon and took a statement. They had already been ferreting around the club where we'd been, and when they hinted that Irving was tight when he left there, I saw at once it was no good lying about details. Then Daddy sent his solicitor in and I made a statement to him. I didn't say any more than I could help, I just said I was dozing and never even saw the motorbike and sidecar."

"*Did* you see it?"

"Just about . . . it's all a bit vague."

Suddenly she lost her grip again and her eyes filled with tears. "It was when they told me the woman was expecting a baby that I felt like a murderer," she said, her fingers drumming on the table. "Sometimes I don't think I'll ever sleep again . . . all three of them, and the baby inside her killed, just like that! I wish to God I'd been killed too! I've been wishing it ever since!"

There was no point in offering her the conventional consolations, telling her she'd feel better later on, that time was a healer, that what was done was done and couldn't be altered. She was in too deep to be helped by platitudes and shoulder pats. She was racked with a misery that stemmed directly from a deep sense of guilt, and would probably suffer even more when the physical and mental shock of the accident had been absorbed. I was not sure that I could help her but I was certain that no one else could, least of all her parents or any of her society friends. Yet the responsibility of helping her, of calming her down and trying to rationalize the circumstances, pressed down on me like a slab of concrete. Only one approach suggested itself. It seemed to me that the most promising line I could pursue was to try to steer her back to the high-water mark of our association, to the moment when we had parted outside the flower-room door on the morning after her party.

"If I hadn't answered your letter what did you intend doing, Di?" I asked her.

She blew her nose and avoided my glance.

"I think I would have gone to the police and told the whole truth," she said. "Come to that, I still might. I would if you said I should."

"How would that help?"

"It would help *me*," she said, biting her lip. "I'd go to prison, I suppose, and that would help to wipe it out somehow!"

"*Were* you tight, as tight as Irving?"

"No, I wasn't. I'd had a few, spread over the evening, but I've been much worse than that other times and got the car home without a scratch."

"Yet you can't remember anything about the moment before the collision?"

"No, just a glare of lights and then an awful crash!"

"Were you blinding along, just before that?"

"How could I have been? The crash was at the end of a steep hill and I'd only just changed from third to top."

I began to see a gleam of light. Her threat of a confession had scared me and my brain was now working at top speed. I wasn't looking for facts, not real, solid facts, such as they drag from witnesses in court. What I needed were a few threads that I could weave into something that she could hold on to during the next few weeks. With relief I remembered that I had kept two or three newspaper reports of the inquest and had put them in my wallet to re-read in the train. I took them out now and ran my eye down a column of print, stopping at the paragraph dealing with the evidence of the motorcyclist's brother, who had told how the dead man and his wife had left his home shortly before the crash. He admitted that the motorcyclist had "had a couple of beers." As one well versed in motoring cases I interpreted this to mean he had probably had five or six. Witnesses are generous to the dead, especially when big insurance claims are involved.

"Now listen, Di," I said, "and don't interrupt! First of all, forget that screwy idea of going to the police and confessing. It can't do anyone a ha'porth of good now and it will almost certainly land you in jail. Whatever claims there are will be fought out by insurance companies. I've seen a lot of this sort of thing and it's their job, and an absolutely impersonal one. If there were dependent kids it might be different, but there aren't and any admission on your part wouldn't amount to more than a bleat, and God knows how much it would complicate matters! That's point one—forget the confession angle, and don't even admit it to your solicitors, it would embarrass them no end. Point two is the accident itself. It's natural enough that you should feel to blame, but how do you know that you are? You only took a chance on driving because Irving was stinko, and if you'd let him drive you might have killed half a dozen people instead of two! As to the chap and his wife who were killed, they'd been drinking too—that's been admitted, and anyone who takes his pregnant wife out in a sidecar at night after sinking a few beers is sitting up and begging for it these days. It might even have been his fault, or at any rate, six of one and half a dozen of the other, so stop torturing yourself and write it all off as craziness on everyone's part. Look at it this way: if you had all four been injured and had come into court to give evidence on a motoring charge, what would have happened? I'll tell you. All four of you would have sworn on oath that you were doing about twenty miles an hour on your correct side of the white line, that you sounded your horn all the way up the road, that you dipped your lights like good little drivers and that you might have had one for the road but certainly no more before you set off! I've sat through dozens of these cases and they're all the same. No one is to blame. It's always the other fellow, and all it amounts to in the end is who is the better liar, or which of you has brought the slickest mouthpiece into court."

It was probably the longest speech I'd ever made and she heard it through, without taking her eyes off me. When I had said all I had to say she sat quite still, her head slightly to one side, her eyelids puckered at the corners, in a way that I remembered had heralded her short sudden laughs. The hunted look had disappeared. She had a natural color and her lovely hands, no longer fluttering, were clasped and pressed hard against her breast.

"You're marvelous, Jan!" she said at length. "You're an absolute tonic! You ought to have a room in Harley Street and get fifty guineas a time for sorting people out."

I wasn't at all sure whether she was trying to pay me a genuine compliment or half-laughing at me, the way she had often teased me when we had argued over something and I had seemed to her to champion stuffiness and caution.

"It's the way I see it, at any rate," I said, "and if you really want advice and not just a bit of 'there-there-now-now' I'll tell you something else while we're about it."

"Well?" She was smiling openly now, her teeth holding her lower lip, as though she was afraid a smile might offend.

"Cut loose from the Set and get to hell out of here, once and for all! Come back to Heronslea if you like but take it easy, at least for a spell. Stop chasing whatever your lot are chasing and grow up! We've all got to sooner or later."

She considered this a long moment, then she said, "When are you going back, Jan? Today?"

"I could," I told her, "but I shall have to travel down on Sunday night in any case."

"Would you take me with you—*now?*"

I had done my inadequate best to comfort her because it had distressed me very much to see her in such a pitiful state of depression. It had seemed important to me because, buried under the years of stress and disappointment that she represented, was the image of the person around whom my entire life had revolved, the girl who, somehow or other, had represented all the sweetness and joy of life. In the weeks that had followed our last meeting, on the afternoon we went to the Tower, I had persuaded myself that the Diana I had adored no longer had substance, that she had, in effect, been permanently superseded by the brittle, stilted upstart of Emerald, someone who, against all probability, had modeled herself upon Mrs. Gayelorde-Sutton and starved Diana of Sennacharib to death. Even the nervous creature that I had met an hour ago, outside Swan and Edgar's, was not really Diana but simply Emerald reduced to size, Emerald scared and threatened into something almost pitiful by worry and tragedy. Now, however, when this disheveled creature had sunned itself a little in my clumsy attempts at reassurance, it seemed to take on the flesh and spirit of a girl who had once galloped shouting through the larches into Big Oak paddock, and in as short a space of time I was back again at starting point, having my arm twisted by Keeper Croker, running to meet her from Folly Wood, holding her close as the raindrops splashed down on the laurels through a short summer night.

"You mean come home for good, Di?"

"I'll be twenty-one in June. I can go where I like, do what I like. For that matter, there's no real problem now. Daddy is up to his neck in mysterious deals—I hardly ever see him—and after the inquest Mummy buzzed off to the Riviera and left here in a towering rage because I flatly refused to go. I'm glad now that I had that much guts."

"Then who looks after you at home?" I asked, wondering again at the strange callousness of parents who could smother a child with material benefits and yet be so niggardly in accepting responsibilities one associates with parenthood. "You can't mean that they stood aside during this business and let you battle it out on your own?"

"More or less—they got the best lawyers, of course, and Daddy paid the barman at the country club to say I had been wallowing in tomato juice," she said lightly. It was clear that she did not resent this incredible disinterestedness on their part and was so accustomed to it that it did not even strike her as unusual.

"It's something I just can't understand," I said, remembering anxious and carefully dressed parents in Whinmouth Court who invariably put in appearances when their sons or daughters were in trouble with the law.

"That's reasonable," she said, "for you've never really understood anything about our sort. You see, Jan, once you get caught up in big business, and the kind of life that goes with having a lot of money, you step right outside life as most people live it and sooner or later it warps you altogether. You don't have the same set of values about anything at all. I noticed that with Mother. That motorcyclist was a bricklayer, and once she knew this, Mother's sole reaction to the smashup was irritation arising out of unsavory publicity! Apart from that she didn't turn a hair. Daddy was a bit more concerned but, as I said, he's been terribly preoccupied with business lately and what happened to me was a sideline."

"But it's absolutely bloody inhuman!" I protested.

She lifted her shoulders, another gesture I had forgotten but now recalled.

"It's just *us*," she said, calmly, and left it at that.

We went out of the café, down Lower Regent Street and across the Mall to St. James's Park. She walked freely now, swinging her arm and moving with long, even strides. There was no tension about her as we crossed the road, threading our way through slowly moving traffic, and her recovery left me free to think about the implications of her return.

Did her remark mean that she wished to cut loose from her parents forever and implement the pledge made on Nun's Island all that time ago? Was she agreeing to marry me after all, to turn her back on Heronslea and become a small-town wife who kept house and went shopping in Whinmouth? I suppose I should have asked her this at once, establishing our new position from the very beginning, but it did not seem to me a sensible thing to do at that time, it was too much like taking advantage of my temporary ascendancy and her highly emotional state. I knew that when I did get an answer to this vital question I wanted it to be an absolutely honest one. I was tired of finding her and losing her, and was sick to death of this interminable game of hide-and-seek. In addition, at this moment, Uncle Reuben's parting warning occurred to me—"Don't make any tomfool promises one way or the other."

I knew also, however, that I wanted her back. Diana had again banished the ludicrous Emerald and the only thing that really mattered was that Emerald should stay dead and buried, with Irving and the other victims of the crash.

"How about your things?" I demanded, suddenly. "There's a train at three P.M. from Waterloo. Could you make it?"

"If I don't then I never will!" she said.

I looked at my watch. It was ten minutes to one. We hurried out into Horse Guards Parade and hailed a taxi.

"It's platform ten," I said. "I'll get there early, buy your ticket, bag seats, and wait for you at the barrier."

She embraced me impulsively, and at the touch of her cheek I knew I was once more fully committed, in spite of Uncle Reuben's warning and in spite of my own secret misgivings. We were beginning again, right from the start, and I could have shouted as much from the top of Nelson's column.

I made my way over to Waterloo, claimed my hand luggage and had a wash and brush-up. Then I felt I needed a drink and I had two double brandies with barely a splash. At half-past two I bought her single, first-class fare, and ten minutes later I was back at the barrier, having tipped a porter to save us two corner seats in a smoker.

At four minutes to three there was a small swirl among the crowds beyond the bookstall and Diana emerged, driving two porters before her like mules. Each man carried two heavy suitcases and each had smaller luggage wedged under his arms. Diana was carrying, of all things, an unwrapped saddle to which long, trailing girths were attached.

The little procession swept past, gathering me in its stride. There was absolutely nothing about the laughing, breathless girl who seized my hand that one could associate in any way with the hesitant bundle of nerves I had greeted exactly four hours ago. I had no time to wonder whether this was a good or bad sign, whether it indicated that I alone was responsible for the transformation or whether it implied that her mind was so shallow that shame, misery and guilt could find no lodging there.

We bundled into our compartment and she gave the porters ten shillings each. Then the whistle blew and the train began to move.

"Made it!" she said, triumphantly. "Sennacharib! Here I come!"

It was as though someone had been juggling with time, whirling the clock back through the years to the summer evening when we set out for the regatta dance on the borrowed motorbike. It was as though everything that had happened since was the slow unfolding of a long, muddled dream, in which joy jostled misery and triumph defeat, a dimly remembered seesaw of delight, laughter and heartache. I looked from her to her mountain of luggage and back again. Suddenly the sheer idiotic improbability of it all set me laughing until my eyes filled with tears, and Diana bounced down beside me and curled up like a kitten, tucking her long, elegant legs beneath her and throwing her weight against me in a way that sent her hair tumbling across my face. Then, still chuckling, I listened to the rhythm of the wheels.

Five minutes after Clapham she was sound asleep.

Chapter Nine

THAT was the best time of all, early spring home-coming.

I must have misjudged Diana when she bustled up to the barrier at Waterloo with her hundredweight of luggage. She hadn't wriggled from under the accident as easily as all that and during the first weeks in the West Country there were times when I sometimes wondered if her apparent recovery had been the last flicker of the flame that had burned in her so strongly throughout her adolescence. Her ribs still pained her and she was not sleeping well. She would meet me on Foxhayes, or on the wooden bridge over the Teasel inland from Shepherdshey and for an hour or so would talk and laugh in the old, familiar way. Then her expression would cloud over and she would move out of reach and at these times her hands were the clue to her thoughts. They were never still but constantly moved up to her hair, or plucked halfheartedly at whatever she happened to be holding, a riding crop, a twig, or, if we were riding, Sioux's mane.

It was the springtime of Sennacharib that started her real convalescence. Toward the end of the cold snap, when the long slope from the larch wood across Big Oak paddock was silent under February snow, her moods became less erratic and she was less disposed to soar from gloom to the brittle elation that I associated with Emerald and then, perhaps, drop back again, setting me the job of finding something to level off her mercury. We spent a great deal of time together, walking and riding on the afternoons when I was free and sometimes taking a Sunday picnic farther afield. When I was unable to be with her she spent much of her time with old McCarthy, the Scots gardener, who had always been a pet of hers. They worked together at potting in the big greenhouses and I did what I could to encourage this activity, for McCarthy, a gruff, unsentimental old body, always treated her as though she were an irresponsible child of eight, growling at her when she handed him the wrong tool and even slapping her hand when she did something that outraged his surly professionalism. He was fond of her for all that and championed her aggressively when I mentioned the accident and asked if he thought she was on the mend.

"There's nae wrong with yon lass," he muttered, "as couldn't have been put right by a lick with a razor strop years since. It's her folk that want it now, for raising the bairn the way they did! She'll do, if she bides down here in the open."

This brief conspiracy began an unspoken conspiracy between us. McCarthy held Mr. and Mrs. Gayelorde-Sutton in contempt, and would have been sacked long ago had he not been the means of Mrs. Gayelorde-Sutton's winning prizes at fruit and flower shows for miles around. I like to think that, in his view, I compared very favorably with most of the young men who had been Diana's guests at Heronslea. He knew everything that went on and Diana had probably confided in him from time to time, so that in the absence of the Gayelorde-Suttons I was able to come and go quite freely about the estate. The supercilious chauffeur, who seemed never to have recovered from the indignity of having to take me home in the Bentley that first night, continued to regard me as a tradesman delivering goods at the back door, whereas the butler, on the few occasions I encountered him, always looked fixedly over my left shoulder, as though determined to pretend that I was an optical illusion. The remainder of the staff, all Shepherdshey folk, were friendly.

My easy access to Heronslea had a curious effect upon my new relationship with Diana. The very complications we had encountered in earlier stages of our courtship had, almost in self-defense, encouraged me to think of the future in terms of marriage. Now, with the clandestine element gone, the urgency of establishing right of access to Diana had disappeared. In those first weeks I concentrated solely on getting her well and later on, in the continued absence of her parents, there seemed to be no urgency in planning ahead.

I suppose, away at the back of my mind, I still thought of marriage as the ultimate outcome of it all, but I was not inclined to explore improbable ways and means of achieving it, as I had done so often and so fruitlessly in the past. It was enough, for the time being, to know that I was necessary to her and to watch her salvage more and more of the real Diana. It was enough for the time being, to hear her laughter ring through Sennacharib and watch her hair stream into the wind as she urged Sioux up the slope of the paddock. In some ways it was like reliving my happy boyhood but without the anxiety that had always attended our meetings here. There was Sennacharib, Diana and I, and with each day that passed, Sennacharib stirred more vigorously under its winter vest of sodden leaves and snowdrifts, and the southwest wind passed whispering through the marching woods as patters of rain coaxed dog violets, wild daffodils and crocuses from the banks of Teasel Brook.

One day in early March Uncle Reuben died, and much as I loved him I could feel no real sorrow at his death. He was tired of lying propped in a chair, watching the tides rise and fall over the estuary, and more than once had hinted that he was impatient to be gone.

We buried him beside his father and mother in the steeply sloping churchyard on the Foxhayes road, and went home to Aunt Thirza's to eat an immense funeral tea and hear what old Hawthorne, the Whinmouth Press executor, had to say about the future of the business.

The will was a very simple document. There was a modest cash legacy to Uncle Luke, another to the chapel, and a third to the Whinmouth Liberal Association. Reuben's shares in the paper and printing works were equally divided between the sister and nephew of the original proprietor, and myself. These shares, together with those already given me, made me a full partner in the concern, with a guaranteed salary of four hundred a year, so long as I continued to work on the paper.

Diana questioned me at what I considered unnecessary length about my future as editor of Whinmouth's little newspaper. She had never been able to take the *Observer* very seriously, even less so after I had invited her into the printing office one Friday night to watch the old flatbed trundling out the weekly edition.

"It's all so terribly 'Caxtony,' Jan," she protested, laughing. "You really ought to sell out to someone much older and then use your little bit of capital to do something important. How much do you suppose it's all worth—your part of it, I mean?"

I discussed this with Hawthorne, the solicitor, who estimated that my share in the Whinmouth Press would now fetch some two thousand pounds on the open market. It might have been double this amount but Uncle Reuben had laid no claim to the freehold of the premises.

Two thousand pounds seemed a far larger sum to me than it did to Diana.

"It's not a fortune," she said, "but I daresay you could make a start with it. Daddy started with very little more but somehow I don't think you're cut out for his kind of hanky-panky. I suppose you wouldn't know what to do with stocks and shares if you had any, would you, Jan?"

"No, I wouldn't," I told her, rather crossly, for although I had by no means resigned myself to spending my life as a small-town newspaperman, it still seemed to me infinitely preferable to the complicated occupation pursued so profitably by Mr. Gayelorde-Sutton. I was a bit of a snob about high finance and I suppose this distrust had been nurtured by my fear and hatred of Diana's mother.

"Since we're discussing the subject, what *am* I cut out for?" I demanded. "I'm a good enough journalist for Whinmouth, but what I saw of Fleet Street while working in town didn't whet my appetite for anything more ambitious in that particular line."

Diana screwed up her eyes and her voice grew persuasive.

"I always see you as a farmer of one sort or another, Jan," she said. "After all, it's in your blood and you're never really yourself unless you've got mud on your boots. What I mean is, you always look like a fish out of water in town, whereas down here you're sort of . . . well . . . sort of *real* and *belonging*, if you see what I mean?"

I understood well enough what she meant. The older I grew the more I regretted that I had not spent my youth acquiring some up-to-date agricultural knowledge. Some of my happiest days had been at the county shows, plowing matches and other competitions organized by the Young Farmers Clubs in the area. I was keenly interested in forestry and land conservation and by this time I was on friendly terms with most of the farmers in the district, even those as far afield as Castle Ferry. In fact, farming and its tributary occupations had always seemed to me so much more vital than industry or shopkeeping, and Diana's vague encouragement started a smolder of thought that blazed up like a heath fire when an opportunity came my way to change course a week or so after Uncle Reuben's funeral. Before that, however, Diana piloted me on what was to prove a sentimental journey.

We had been cantering west from the head of Teasel Brook, intending to drop down the steepest part of the common toward the Folly Wood and then ride home via Big Oak paddock. At the junction of heath tracks, a mile from the main road, Diana pulled Sioux's head to the right and before I could catch her we had dipped down into Foxhayes Hollow, the farm once occupied by my grandfather.

It was years since I had been that way and I was surprised to find the old farmhouse shuttered and unoccupied. We hallooed, thinking that there might be someone living in the cottage beyond the farm buildings, but nobody answered, so we made a circuit of the yard and soon realized that the farm was derelict. Docks grew in the sties, a heavy barn door swung loose in the wind, and closer inspection of the buildings showed that the place was well on the way to becoming a ruin. Winter gales and the weight of February snow had shifted pantiles from the roof and beyond the begrimed windows of the kitchen we could see pools on the stone floor. The barn door creaked dolorously and there was such an air of decay about the premises that I called to Diana to mount and race me back to the common. She stood, legs apart, looking up at me.

"What's the matter, Jan? Don't you like the old place any more?"

"Not the way it is," I said. "It gives me the creeps!"

"There's nothing here that couldn't be made shipshape by a jobbing builder in a matter of weeks," she said. "Did you know old Yeomans, the tenant, had left?"

I remembered then that Yeomans had died more than a year ago, and that Uncle Reuben had told me he understood Yeomans' son was selling a holding in East Anglia and coming home to take his father's place. I told Diana about this as we cantered back along the rutted track to the open common but all the way home she remained preoccupied, and it wasn't until we were on the point of parting that she called, "Wait, Jan, I'm coming into town with you!" and climbed into my fifth-hand Morris Cowley and asked me to drop her off at the Gilroy Estate office, in Chapel Street.

"I've just remembered," she said, carelessly, "I've got to see the agent about some timber. Daddy wrote about it yesterday and anyway, I've shopping to do."

It was Thursday and I had all the proofs to read, so we arranged to meet on Saturday morning when the paper was out.

The next day, however, I had a visit from Hawthorne, the solicitor. It seemed that the nephew of the original proprietor of the paper was showing an unexpected interest in the property and had offered to buy me out, while retaining my services as acting editor at the same salary. He offered me eighteen hundred for my shares and a ten-year contract, breakable on either side at five years.

Hawthorne advised me to decline, pointing out that if I wished to continue as editor it was obviously better that I should retain some part of the control, but recent discussions with Diana on this topic had unsettled me and when I met her on Saturday afternoon I suggested we should leave the horses at home and tramp over the moor to the source of the Teasel. It was never easy to talk to Diana when she was astride a horse. Each conversation was spaced by a mad gallop or a breathless scramble over banks and ditches.

"You look terribly solemn today," she chaffed, as we crossed the covert and made our way upstream.

"And you look as if you were hatching up one of your harebrained ideas," I countered.

She did indeed. There was a familiar "if-you-did-but-know" sparkle in her eyes, but I viewed it with tolerance, for it was clear evidence that she was now almost herself again. All the sun and wind we had shared during the last few weeks showed in her clear skin and lively bearing. I had never seen her look healthier or prettier. Emerald was banished and it was plainly Diana who skipped along in country brogues and a faded yellow sweater, moving like an eager girl discovering the country after a long spell in a city. Her thick chestnut curls looked as if they had never been within miles of a Bond Street stylist, and when the April sunlight fell on them they caught and held all the life and sparkle of the valley. The serenity of the countryside was reflected in her calm, untroubled gaze but its springing vitality was there also, as she bounded down the bank and hopped across the steppingstones at Teasel Curve and up again to the narrow footpath under the northern edge of Teasel Wood.

When we were a mile or so on our way, I told her of Hawthorne's visit and she showed the liveliest interest.

"Why, Jan, you must do it! It's the very thing! It couldn't have come at a better time, surely?"

I was by no means clear what the time factor had to do with it and said so, but she headed me off, strengthening my impression that she was deliberating some plan of her own that directly or indirectly involved me and perhaps both of us.

"It all adds up to what we were saying the other day, Jan," she chattered. "The local rag is all right in its way, but it's . . . well, it's stuffy and parochial. It can never give you the chance to develop the real *you*, if you see what I mean? Do you remember that talk we had years ago, up in the tower, when I told you the kind of man I admired?"

I remembered it far better than she imagined; I remembered every last word.

"I know you still prefer the Scotts of the Antarctics," I grumbled, reflecting that, in spite of all the bold resolutions I had made on that winter's afternoon, I had done little enough in the intervening period to model myself upon the heroic lines she demanded. True, I had learned to ride, learned to speak French and risen from furniture delivery boy to acting editor of a weekly paper with a circulation of about five thousand, but I was sure that all this fell far short of her exacting standards.

"I gather you're in favor of selling the shares," I said, "but how about the job itself? I shall have to make up my mind soon and it seems to me that one thing is dependent on the other."

"Not necessarily," she argued. "Sell out, keep the money in a deposit account and say you'll stay on and run the paper just as long as you've a mind to, with a month's notice on your side only!"

"They won't wear that," I protested. "It's far too one-sided."

She stopped and caught hold of my hand, laughing and holding her head on one side.

"Oh Jan, Jan," she chuckled, "you're the world's worst when it comes to business! Can't you see this nephew is just drooling to get full control of that potty little outfit and that he'll agree to anything, so long as you part with your holding?"

"Suppose that's true," I said, "doesn't it indicate that he'll get rid of me the moment he gets his hands on them?"

"Well it might, but I doubt it. You're a jolly good reporter and it wouldn't be at all easy to find anyone to do all you do for the pittance you get. And even if it does, what matters? What can you lose, apart from the few pounds a week they pay you? You might have started something else by then anyway, so do it—*do* it, Jan —sell out but don't be stupid enough to sign any contract about staying on as an employee, d'you hear me?"

She said this so aggressively that I was quite convinced that she was holding something sensational up her sleeve, something that had a direct bearing on the subject we were discussing. I knew her sufficiently well, however, to realize that no amount of probing on my part would persuade her to divulge until the suitably dramatic moment arrived.

"I know you're up to something, Di," I told her, "and I don't pretend to know what, but since we've gone this far we might as well go the whole damn way. I love you and I'm going to marry you—how or when I don't know, but somehow, someday, and not all the obstacles your people will put in the way are going to make a jot of difference in the end! I haven't harped on this subject before because I didn't think you were settled enough to talk about it, but you're more yourself again this afternoon than I ever hoped you'd be when I fetched you back here. Fine! I'll do what you suggest. I'll even explore the possibilities of getting a farming course at the Munhayes Agricultural College, over the river, but if I do, then I think you owe me two things, one following on the other."

"Well?" she said, looking a good deal surprised but not, I thought, in any way put out by plain speaking.

"First I've got to know if you really want to marry me, soon or a long way ahead, I don't give a damn which. Secondly, if the answer is what I hope it is, I'm jolly well going to speak to your father and tell him the truth about how things stand between us!"

Laughter still lurked about the corners of her mouth.

"Jan," she said, her eyes dancing, "that must be about the fourth or fifth proposal I've had from you. I'm beginning to lose count!"

"I'm not joking, Di," I told her, stubbornly. "I want to know exactly how you feel about it, for since you've grown up I've never honestly known whether you're serious, half-serious, or playing a long-winded game of bluff for both of us. Sometimes I thought I knew—that time after the dance, and again on the island, and again on your birthday, but every time something crazy happens. Now that I've got to make a decision about the paper I want something a bit more solid to decide me one way or the other."

She stopped walking then and stood looking at me, one leg crooked, with the sole of her shoe pressed against the last Scots fir in Teasel Wood.

We had now reached the point where the little river curved sharply westward, biting deep into the fringe of Foxhayes Common and forming a gully screened by young poplars, dwarf elms and flowering hawthorn. The water here was very shallow and the little shingle beach that sloped from the river bed to the sandstone overhang was as colorful as a fairy-tale bower. Primroses, periwinkles, windflowers, celandines and huge glowing dandelions grew there, against the whitish-green pattern of hedge buds. It was a favorite place for the blackbirds of which there were vast numbers in this part of Sennacharib. Their pipings rose shrilly above the steady wash of the stream and the whisper of Teasel firs. The inevitable buzzards were about: I had already seen them twice that afternoon, and now they were showing off over the distant larch wood, two wheeling, drifting specks, trying to pretend they were indifferent to admiration of their aerobatics.

After a long moment Diana took my hand and led the way down the cattle ford to the grassiest part of the beach under the hedge. There had been little or no rain for a month and the grass, facing sunwards, was as dry as straw.

"I've been a pig to you, Jan," she said, seriously, sitting and hugging her knees, "and you shall have something more solid, as you say, even though it does sound a little like another helping of treacle pudding. Sit down, take that Jan Riddish scowl off your face, and listen!"

She waited while I sat down beside her. "Nothing the Doones could do would stop me loving you more than I've ever loved anyone, so hang on to that for a minute and give me time to sort out my thoughts. First of all, I'm going to town again . . . no"—as I opened my mouth to protest—"not for good and not even for a week, but there's something I must do up there, something that has a bearing on us. It's not the slightest use pestering me to tell you what it is because it's still in the air and you'll have to trust me just once more, for three or four days, do you understand? As regards the sale of shares, don't do a thing until I get back, but keep it simmering. Tell them you want a day or so to think it over. If my idea amounts to anything, and I'm almost certain it will, then that little business will solve itself and we can settle the rest in five minutes."

"Is that all?" I demanded, as suddenly she shot out her legs and lay back, clasping her hands behind her head and looking as if she was done with talking and intended to luxuriate in the warmth of the sun.

"No, Jan, but it's all I'm going to say about business matters. I've got a lot more to add about loving you and needing you. I've been several kinds of a bitch to you over the last few years, and although I'm sorry for that, because you've been so wonderful to me particularly, when I was cracking up, I'm not promising that I'll ever be any different, because I know jolly well I won't be, not until I get the middle-aged spread, and by that time you won't care, because you'll be too busy reminding yourself that I wasn't always lined and stringy, or bulging and shapeless. There's something else—I wouldn't admit it to anyone but you—I'm like I am, not because of Mother and the way she's tried to push me since I was so-high, but simply because wildness and unpredictability are part of me. I've only got to be told that I must do something when a little imp pops up inside me and says 'I'll be damned if you do!' and that goes for settling down, and saying good-by to being young."

All this had the effect of relaxing me, and I chuckled.

"Don't talk as if you were getting in line for the Old Age Pension," I joked, but she was not disposed to share my mood and continued, very solemnly:

"I'm serious, Jan! I'm not the same as most people our age, not at all the same. Every person our age is frightened of growing old, I imagine, but with me it's not just the fear of growing old but the fear of growing *up*, and it's not simply worry either, it's a kind of blind panic that gives me nightmares. Sometimes, when I'm away from you, it gives me such a dreadful feeling of depression that I could run out and jump over Nun's Head!"

She said this so earnestly that it was impossible to tease her. In a way, indeed, I recognized it as the truth, a limited truth, for the fear she spoke of was all mixed up with the freedom of wealth as well as freedom to remain irresponsible, to go where she liked, say what she liked, and, if necessary, ride roughshod over all standards of behavior in her own world as well as mine.

"I daresay I'll grow out of this silliness sometime, and maybe it's as much a stage as every other stage a woman goes through from the pony craze onwards," she went on, "but in the meantime, and *because* I love you so much, Jan, I want to . . . well . . . to kind of insure against it in my own special way. What I've got in mind *is* a kind of insurance, as I hope you'll see after I've been up to London and back."

I chewed a grass stem, waiting for her to continue, but she fell silent and when I looked at her again I saw that her eyes were troubled and that her hands, freed from the clasp that had given her so relaxed a pose, were now nervously plucking at the leaves of some periwinkle stalks that clustered beside her. Suddenly, with a movement that was a kind of reflex, she twisted on her side and threw her arms around me.

"Jan, dear Jan! Don't ever leave me, not altogether! Not for good! Always come back, always *be* there! And love me now, Jan, love me in this heavenly place! Let it be a sort of marriage, our marriage, in Sennacharib! That would mean so much more to me than all the fiddle-faddle ordinary people have to go through . . . just love me, and make it certain, no matter what happens!"

I was to recall and ponder on that final qualification a great deal in the future, but I hardly heard it at that moment. My love for her and for the place we were in now mingled like two great streams, converging after independent courses down the steep hill. I gathered her up and covered her face with kisses, straining her to me as though we would merge ourselves with the very soil and fibers of the bank. It was much more than desire on my part, it was a consummation of all the years of longing and hoping and scheming to possess her. It was as she had demanded, a marriage before the altar of Sennacharib, a ceremony in which the setting assumed a personality, for as we clung together the hills and woods and valleys of Sennacharib seemed to reach out green and golden arms to enfold us in a vast, sensual embrace.

So vivid was this impression that to me the physical act was almost insignificant. It was immeasurably transcended by a spiritual accomplishment that gave me a sense of possessing her far more completely than anything stored in my memories.

We lay there in one another's arms until the sun passed beyond the big larch wood and its warmth left us for the estuary on the far side of the hill.

Then at last, we climbed back to the footpath and went along under the steep edge of Teasel Wood to the steppingstones, saying nothing and, for my part, conscious of nothing but a surfeit of tenderness and gratitude.

Chapter Ten

AFTER that events followed one another with the speed and improbability of a dream; indeed, in some ways the period that followed was more dreamlike than real in that I lost all sense of time. Even now days and weeks are jumbled together and events group themselves in what I know to be a perverse and inaccurate sequence.

Diana went to London on Monday, promising to return by the weekend at the latest but probably before. On Wednesday morning the phone rang in the office and when I answered it a soft, slightly sibilant voice asked to speak to Mr. John Leigh. When I told the caller that I was the person he sought there was a long pause; then the voice apologized rather gravely, and went on:

"This is Gayelorde-Sutton here, speaking from Heronslea."

I was so surprised that it took me a moment or so to recover but the caller had evidently anticipated this, for he allowed a period of grace. I could imagine him sitting there, erect in the study chair, his big head balanced on the long, thin neck, his mild eyes blinking at nothing.

"Are you sure I'm the person you want?" I asked at length, and when the voice assured me that this was so, I had to fight down a brief spasm of panic. It was no more than a spasm, for almost at once fear was succeeded by irritation and finally by a spurt of defiance. I felt that I had had more than enough of the Gayelorde-Suttons and their feudalistic notions. I was sure of Diana and that was all that mattered. If her father wanted a showdown then he could have one, and her mother too if she was standing behind her husband's chair, making the bullets that he was told to fire.

"Well?" I demanded, bluntly. "And what can I do for you, Mr. Sutton?"

His response disarmed me. If anything the voice was milder and more amiable than before.

"Ah, Mr. Leigh—I—er I—wonder if you would be good enough to call at Heronslea at your own convenience, and perhaps have a drink with me?"

"Well . . . yes," I managed to stutter, "I should like to, Mr. Sutton. I could come now if that suited you."

There was a flicker of enthusiasm or possibly relief.

"You could? Splendid! I'll expect you in half an hour, shall I?"

"Yes," I said and only just prevented myself adding "sir."

I backed out the old Morris and drove to Shepherdshey at about twenty miles an hour. I wanted time to think. I had known this family now for a number of years but this was the first occasion I had exchanged a word with Diana's father. I had no real quarrel with him, for as far as I was aware he had taken no active part in his wife's callous treatment of Diana after the island episode. From what I could piece together from Diana's conversations about her parents, he was the purely passive force in the ordering of her life. She had often spoken of him contemptuously, as of a man hopelessly under his wife's thumb, and I remembered now how helpless and pathetic he had looked when they hoisted him up on that big horse at the Heronslea meet. Quite apart from the summons, I was surprised to learn that he was in the West Country, having taken it for granted that Diana had gone to see him in London, and I could not imagine why he should suddenly take it into his head to invite me into his house for a drink, as though I were one of his daughter's friends whom Mrs. Gayelorde-Sutton approved and accepted. It occurred to me that this might be the result of Diana's "something concerning us," and that perhaps she had said something that caused him and his wife to hurry down to Devon in order to interview me, but I dismissed this at once; his manner on the phone had certainly not been that of an irate father, driven by a nagging wife to take the offensive.

I drove up the main approach and parked the car beside Gayelorde-Sutton's Bentley. Limousine and two-seater looked like a vehicular parody of the picture "Dignity and Impudence." I was hoping to demonstrate my determination by a fierce tug on the bell chain, but I was cheated of this by the sudden appearance of Mr. Gayelorde-Sutton on the doorstep. He had evidently been awaiting me and had come out as soon as he heard the car. We shook hands, casually on my part, limply on his, and crossed the hall to the study adjoining the pretty room that I remembered as being Mrs. Gayelorde-Sutton's morning room.

What struck me as unusual was that there seemed to be no servants about the place. Inside the study it was very quiet, so quiet indeed that I could hear a farm tractor bub-bubbing on the arable slope south of Teasel Wood almost a mile away. Mr. Gayelorde-Sutton's manner was so subdued that I thought at first that he was giving me the silence treatment and hoping thus to put me at a disadvantage. When I looked at him more closely, however, I soon realized that he was by far the more nervous. His hand shook as he poured a brandy from a Waterford decanter and his aim with the soda-water siphon was grossly inaccurate.

"You'll have brandy, Mr. Leigh?" he said, suddenly.

"Thank you," I said, sitting on a ribbon-backed chair near the tall window. I felt I could do with a brandy, and his was a very generous one.

He took his glass over to the desk, set it down and stood stiffly beside one of the bookcases. It was several years since I had seen him and the very first occasion that I had had an opportunity to study him at close quarters.

At this range the size of his head and thinness of his neck did not appear so ludicrously unlikely, but the over-all impression he gave was one of timid, secretive flabbiness. Face to face with him it was impossible to be awed by his presence, and I remember thinking how strange it was that a man with such a nervous disposition and possessing such an undistinguished physique had made his way so successfully in the city jungle. Yet when you thought about this perhaps it wasn't so strange. It was easy to imagine him sitting in board rooms listening to loquacious chairmen and accountants, saying nothing, blinking, drumming his long fingers, and then going away and sorting through the information he had acquired, filing it, weighing it up, discarding all irrelevancies before making a few telephone calls and going home the richer by several thousand pounds. He was the kind of man who would neither encourage nor discourage people but would let them talk and talk and writhe under his stolidity. Then he would use them, laughing dryly at their weaknesses, so less apparent than his own but infinitely more vulnerable.

Perhaps I have been unfair to him. These were my first impressions and they were to be modified greatly as the interview proceeded. The moment my stubbornness emerged he became more human, and I think I helped to thaw him by taking the offensive.

"I suppose you're wondering what this is all about?" he said, after we had both taken a sip or two.

"Not really," I said, shortly. "I imagine that you want to talk about Diana."

He smiled, a very fleeting smile, the kind of grimace that fond mothers sometimes claim as a smile when their babies burp.

"I know that you and Emerald have been close friends for a long time," he said.

"Since my fifteenth birthday," I told him, "and now I'm getting on for twenty-two."

"That's a long time to court a girl and an early age to begin!" he said, without taking his eyes off me, and without ceasing his rhythmic blink.

I was mildly surprised by his use of the word "court." It implied a certain regularity about an association that had always been clandestine, but before I could reply he suddenly stepped outside his board-room manner and became, if not affable, then at least heavily sincere in his approach. It was as though he had decided upon one approach but, after the preliminary exchanges, switched to another, suddenly making up his mind to project himself as a parent and not as a company director.

"Look here, Leigh," he said, lowering himself into his desk chair and placing his palms downwards on the red leather, so that his forearms formed a neat rectangle, "I don't think I'm being quite fair to you. The onus of this discussion is on me, since I invited you here, and the fact is, I know a great deal more about you than you imagine. I knew a little about you a long time ago and when I heard you had whisked Emerald down here after that unpleasant business in town, I made it my business to find out a great deal more. Now I daresay that appears somewhat presumptuous to you, but my daughter ha—*has* money coming to her, and certain inquiries on my part were obligatory. Do you follow?"

One thing puzzled me more than anything he had said. He was going to say "had money" and changed it, at the very last moment, to "has money." It was the kind of slip that a man like him ought not to have made and because my wits were razor-sharp that morning it told me more than it need have done.

"I've always known your daughter as Diana," I said, with the air of a man clearing the ground, "so can't we call her that for today? I can never think of her as Emerald."

"Very well," he said, gravely, "let it be Diana if you wish. I had a talk with her the night she came up to town and your name came into that talk. You won't mind my being frank?"

"Not in the least," I told him, folding my arms and looking, I hope, a good deal more self-assured than I felt.

"Right!" he said. "I take it you are genuinely attached to my daughter?"

This was something I could bite upon and I did, without the slightest hesitation.

"I'm a good deal more than that, Mr. Sutton. I'm in love with her and it's only fair to tell you that I'm going to do my damnedest to marry her. I don't know how or when, but nothing you or her mother can do or say will make any difference to my trying!"

It was a deliberately provocative statement on my part and I made it in the hope that it would galvanize him into terminating the interview. The situation was beginning to irritate me, partly because his board-room cat-and-mouse act was an affront to my pride but more, I think, because it somehow cheapened my estimate of Diana. All the years I had known her we had never found it necessary to spar as this flabby, blinking man and I were sparring now. If we had anything to say we had said it and if we hadn't, then we respected one another's privacy in a way that this man could never begin to understand.

My words, however, had an extraordinary effect upon him. He neither recoiled, nor flushed, nor displayed any reaction at all but sat perfectly still, blinking at an accelerated rate, so that I soon began to feel like a man who has pressed the trigger of a large blunderbuss and produced nothing noisier than a half-audible pop. Then, as I floundered about in this anticlimax, I was slowly conscious of his curious change of manner and expression. Quietly and smoothly his whole body relaxed, as though the frame of ice that had kept him so rigid had suddenly melted, leaving him free to stretch himself, uncurl his long fingers and flex his knees; but the strangest thing about this almost physical thaw was that it somehow reduced his stature and made him look as helpless and as pitiful as when he was astride the big gray at the Boxing Day hunt. His face crumpled and his pursy little mouth twitched, as though he was on the point of tears. He realized this and it shamed him. He got up and turned first one way and then another, like a man suddenly awakened in a railway compartment and told he has slept past his station. Then he saw the glass of brandy on his desk and he snatched it up and drained it, slamming it down with such violence that I was surprised the vessel survived the shock. The brandy helped him to collect himself but he said nothing during the moment that it took him to come out from behind the desk and cross to the tall window, where he remained standing with his back to me.

"I'm glad you told me that," he said, quietly, "it helps a great deal. You see, my boy"—he suddenly swung around and faced me—"I'm going away . . . quite soon . . . a long way off, I'm afraid, and I shall be gone some time, some considerable time, do you understand? I asked you here because . . . well, because I wished to satisfy myself on certain things regarding my daughter."

He broke off but continued to look down at me. I sat twiddling the stem of my empty glass.

"Here—have another drink!"

I handed him the glass and he almost filled it. This time his aim with the siphon was totally inaccurate and I suddenly realized that he was a dreadful bundle of nerves. The board-room techniques that had sustained him throughout our opening gambits had now disappeared and he was quite lost without them, so much so that I began to feel slightly sorry for him. For the first time he looked as though he might be Diana's father, but the kinship was limited. He was as remote as ever from the Diana of Sennacharib but within hailing distance of the frightened girl I had watched scanning the crowds outside Swan and Edgar's a few months ago.

"I believe your name is John, isn't it?" he asked, after another brief silence, but before I could reply added: "Do you mind if I call you John . . . or Jan, is it?"

"John!" I said, hating the idea of his using Diana's pet name, and longing for him to return to his board-room seat and drop his clumsy skittishness.

"Well, John," he said, "as I told you, I made certain inquiries, and I discovered two things—two things that led up to this talk we're having. One was the fact that you actually work for a living and the other is that you must think a great deal of Diana, or you would have sold out long ago."

"Just where does that get us, Mr. Sutton?" I asked him, but he had a much thicker skin than I supposed and clung desperately to his embarrassing affability.

"I'll tell you my boy, I'll tell you!" he squeaked. "You came up here on the defensive, didn't you? You imagined that I was going to make the same kind of scene about your association with my daughter as my wife once made in your newspaper office some years ago? Well, I'm not. Not at all! . . . As a matter of fact, I . . . I'm in favor of it. I've no objections at all and as far as I'm concerned you can marry my Emerald tomorrow, if she's agreeable. Now what do you say to that, eh?"

I had nothing at all to say to it. Once I would have been immensely flattered by this astonishing declaration but in those days I was far less certain of Diana and was also young enough to be taken in by an animated adding machine like Gayelorde-Sutton. Today, as a man full-grown, I was so incredulous and suspicious that I sat grasping his enormous brandy and glowered at him. There was something grotesque about his eagerness to put himself on the right side of me, and I found it impossible to accept anything he said at face value. His tongue seemed to be working independently of his brain, as though his head and mouth were master and apprentice, with the latter having been sent out by the former to try his luck at bamboozling the public. All the time he babbled on I could see the instructor squatting like Fagin behind the furiously blinking eyes and watching his bungling little Oliver make a fool of himself. Taken all around, it was a very unsavory experience, rather like a prolonged interview with an excited idiot.

"I was very glad when you persuaded her to come down here for a spell," he went on. "Those people up there are no good to her, you know, and she's such a madcap that she'll probably get into worse trouble if she goes back among them. Now a nice, steady, pleasant young fellow like you . . . I daresay that's what she really needs, *all* she needs maybe, and if I was in your shoes, do you know what I'd do?"

"What?" I said, flatly.

"Why, I'd marry her and *keep* her down here! I'd give her some work to do, a family to look after . . . nothing really wrong with her that a decent home and roots wouldn't cure. . . ."

He said a great deal more in the same vein, but I recall very little of it, because I was no longer listening. What appalled me, I think, was not so much his arch line of patter—that might well have been borrowed from a second-feature film on the father-daughter relationship—but his complete and utter ignorance of Diana as a human being. He was as dismally miscast in this role of encouraging parent as it was possible to be, but with every word he uttered he convinced me that if indeed he and Diana had discussed our prospects, then neither of them had said anything worth saying. In other words, he was lying outrageously, but why? Uncle Reuben had discovered more about Diana after a glance at the single letter I had shown him than this man had discovered during a period of more than twenty years under the same roof. Where had he been all the time she had been growing up? What did he know about her that he could not have learned from reading newspaper reports on the antics of the Set, or a glance at one of her school reports?

Then, as I climbed slowly out of my disgust, and tried to peer at his hidden purpose objectively, I saw that there was something quite terrifying behind his blather, something so strange and unnatural that it almost stank. What this something was, and what made it so frighteningly evident to me, I had not the least idea, but it was there all right and it made me shiver, not only for myself but for Diana and everything surrounding her. I felt I wanted to take him by the shoulders and shake it out of him, like money from his trouser pockets. I wanted to thrust my face within an inch of his and shout: "*Stop it, you old fool! Stop it, for Christ's sake! What's happened to you? Why are you suddenly handing me Diana as though you couldn't wait to get rid of her?*"

Then he was handing me a blank sheet of notepaper, with an embossed heading printed on it.

"I said I was going away," he ended at last, "and that's the address of my solicitors . . . good firm . . . sound people . . . go to them if you want to, but not until Emerald is of age, understand? We don't want her mother making more difficulties, do we, eh?"

"Where is her mother now?" I managed to ask, folding the paper mechanically, and stowing it away in my pocket.

"France," he said, offhandedly. "South of France. Spends most of her time there nowadays."

"You said you had a talk with Diana the night before last," I asked him, in a final attempt to extract a grain of realism from this senseless interview. "Did she give you to understand that we were eng—"

I never finished the question, for at that moment his desk phone rang and he snatched up the receiver like a greedy child grabbing a lollipop.

"Yes?" he snapped, and instantly his features took on the board-room mask of impassivity that they had worn when he ushered me into the room. All the eagerness and excitement ebbed from him, like air from a balloon. He even began to hold himself stiffly again, nodding and blinking an accompaniment to the insistent rasp of his caller's voice.

"Right!" he said at last, and then, still into the phone, "Excuse me a moment, I have someone here."

He put down the receiver and turned to me.

"I'm afraid that's all for the present," he said, distantly. "This is one of those timed, transatlantic calls and it happens to be rather important. Thank you for coming. I'll see you to your car."

I think this bland dismissal surprised me more than anything else that had taken place, but I was so grateful for the interruption that I made no protest and let him lead me into the hall and out onto the porch.

"Are you down for any length of time, Mr. Sutton?" I asked, for even then I found it impossible to believe that he could leave matters between us to remain as they were and would be obliged to ask me to call again after I had discussed this extraordinary interview with Diana.

"I can't really say," he said, vaguely, "but you'll be seeing my daughter again very shortly, I imagine."

"Before the weekend," I told him, "but . . ."

"Please excuse me now," he said, "that call . . . I've so much to do, so much to see to!" and he was gone, leaving the door ajar and myself standing openmouthed on the top step.

I did not return to the office but drove up over Foxhayes, to the highest part of the moor. Here I parked and tried to empty my mind of everything but four distinct puzzles that presented themselves as a direct result of the interview. There was a great deal I failed to understand, but to explore the subject as a whole would, I knew, result in lunatic confusion, so I deliberately separated the particular from the mass, and examined the most obvious puzzles one by one.

First, what had prompted Diana's father to send for me at all?

Second, having sent for me, why had his initial reception been so formal and distant? Third, why had my frankness regarding the relationship between Diana and myself produced such a startling change in his manner? Finally, after having almost begged me to elope with his daughter, why did his interest evaporate at the sound of a telephone bell?

I looked at it carefully, point by point. He had sent for me, no doubt, in obedience to a demand on the part of Diana expressed during their talk the night she arrived in town, and this talk had a strong bearing on puzzle number three—his almost indecent eagerness to accept me as a son-in-law. It now seemed fairly clear that Diana had not only nagged him but threatened him, with what I could not even guess, for I knew absolutely nothing of the relationship of father and daughter. His stiffness on my arrival at Heronslea might have a simple explanation. He was obviously a very shy man, constitutionally ill-equipped to make headway with any conversation outside the realm of business, but his abrupt switch from embarrassing amiability to downright rudeness was not so easy to explain. It was possible, of course, that the call represented the gaining or losing of thousands of pounds, and that the caller had jolted him back to the principal interest of his life, but this hardly explained the way in which he had rushed me out of the house and skipped back to the study without even pausing to shut the door. If the call had been of an excessively private nature he would surely have made certain that I was clear of the premises before he returned to the phone.

I teased myself with these speculations until late afternoon and I gave some thought to other aspects of the conversation, notably his slip of the tongue when he mentioned Diana's monetary prospects. This, in some ways, was the biggest mystery of all, for while I found it difficult to doubt the sincerity of his wishes regarding our marriage, it seemed odd that he had already made up his mind to disinherit Diana if she did what he appeared to want her to do. Had man and wife disagreed on this matter? Was the phone call an unexpected call from Mrs. Gayelorde-Sutton, thus presenting him with the opportunity to win her over or justify his sponsorship? Did Mrs. Gayelorde-Sutton know anything at all of what was going on? Was the slip about the money not a slip at all but an assumed one, intended to let me know that if I did marry Diana after her twenty-first birthday we could expect nothing in the way of a settlement? Did he still think of me as a person on the lookout for a substantial dowry?

Was he such a poor judge of character that he failed to understand that I hated the very idea of marrying Diana without separating her, once and for all, from her family background? God knows, I had endeavored to make this much clear to him, but had he lived and worked among moneyed folk for so long that he could imagine no other spur toward marriage?

Finally I gave it all up and drove slowly back to town. There was plenty of work to be done, an inquest and two weddings to be written up, proofs to be read, the layout to be sketched in, and I was hard at it, trying to make up for lost time, when the phone rang and I was relieved to hear Diana's voice on the line.

She was calling from London to warn me that it was unlikely that she could return until Monday. In the meantime, she wanted me to do something on her behalf, something rather urgent. I was so eager to tell her about the interview that I interrupted her before she had said more than a few words. The telephone was not the best medium for such an involved story, but I was so certain that she would want to hear every word that I began to gabble into the receiver at top speed. I was halfway through before I sensed that she was not nearly as surprised or as interested as I had anticipated. I broke off and said:

"Are you listening? Don't you want to hear all about it?"

"Of course I do, and of course I'm listening. Go on!"

I was by no means reassured. She still sounded bored and impatient, but I finished the story and breathlessly awaited her comments.

All she said was: "I see! Poor Jan! It must have been dreadful for you!" Then, completely dismissing her father, she began: "Now listen carefully to what I want you to do. . . ."

I was so dismayed by her lack of response that I did listen, but with growing bewilderment.

"First thing tomorrow I want you to drive up to Foxhayes Hollow, and give a verbal message to Harrington," she said, as if she had been a schoolmistress issuing orders for homework. "I want you to tell him to go down to the Gilroy Estate office, ask for the agent and get the papers from the Heronslea file. Tell him it's all satisfactory this end but Harrington is to take the papers home and read them, and have them ready for me when I come. Did you get that?"

"I'm a journalist," I said, grimly. "I'm accustomed to taking phone messages."

She chuckled at that. "Dear Jan, I can't wait to be hugged!" she said.

"If this is a Heronslea chore," I grumbled, "why the blazes don't you ring Harrington direct? He's your foreman, not mine!"

"Don't be so churlish, darling! Harrington is hardly ever at Heronslea and he's a frightfully difficult man to lay by the heels. Don't worry about Daddy, he'll be gone long before I get back and the weather up here is hot enough for swimming, how is it down there?"

"I'm damned if I'm going to talk weather with you, Di," I said, "and I'm getting bored with all these mysteries. Come on home and let's go riding."

"Monday," she said. "'Bye now, darling."

She had only been away a few days but the sound of her voice made me ache for her. I sat on in the stuffy little office, copy and proofs forgotten, pondering her message and the strange, schoolmarmy manner in which it had been delivered, wondering at her lack of interest in what seemed to me a momentous development in our lives. Then, suddenly, I was tired of mysteries and complications. All the years I had loved her we seemed to have been enmeshed in an intricate web of conditions, provisos and prohibitions. I wanted to cut every strand, throw her over my shoulder and walk out into the open to a place where we could behave like a normal man and woman in love, like a normal couple who planned their own destiny and led normal, unrestricted lives. I pitched the proofs and the reports into the copy tray and locked up, slamming the door on the musty little office that had enclosed so many dreams since my wild need of her had driven me to seek my living there. Illogically my sense of frustration extended to the *Observer* and to the silent array of machinery that nursed it. The whole premises became mean, squalid and inadequate. Maybe she was right, maybe a man could never develop in a field as small and restricted as this business and this town.

I went home to have supper with Aunt Thirza and she found me very grumpy company.

2.

Early the next morning I drove up to the main road and down the cart track to Foxhayes Hollow. Long before I reached the dip in which the ramshackle farm was situated I noticed that something was astir in the area. When we were last here the track had been grass-grown and straggling bushes almost met at several points; now deep tractor ruts showed in the lane and the undergrowth had been cut back to allow the passage of carts or trucks. One or two new bricks and traces of cement lay about and I wondered whether a new tenant had been found, perhaps some fancy friend of Diana's, who had enlisted her considerable influence with the Gilroy Estate.

Notwithstanding this, I was quite unprepared for the sight that greeted me when I bumped into the clearing. The farm and buildings had been transformed. A new slate roof had been laid in place of the weather-beaten pantiles, the ground had been cleared of rubbish, the barn door had been rehung and the greater part of the premises repainted in white and horizon blue. The farm now had a raffish, gaudy look, as though the person responsible for this work had borrowed some chintzy ideas from a magazine article on amateur farming. Builders' materials lay everywhere, and two early risers were already at work on the sties, operating a cement mixer. I recognized one of them as Davey, a member of the Heronslea permanent maintenance staff.

"What the devil is going on here?" I demanded, when he greeted me.

"Us is doin' the ole plaace up!" he said, phlegmatically. "Do 'ee know who's taaken the ruin?"

"Not a clue," I told him. "I'm looking for Harrington, the foreman. Is he around anywhere?"

"Aye, he'll be yer any minute, maister," said Davey. "Praper slave driver he be! Us be workin' overtime on this yer job, dawn till dusk. Praper bliddy hurry they be in!"

"Who?" I wanted to know.

"New tenants, pals o' the family I yeard, London townees, zo they zay. Bought into the big house lease, 'er is," he added, nodding toward the farmhouse. "Always a freehold plaace in Ole Maister's time, but 'er's bought in now, zo they zay."

I knew by Old Maister he meant my grandfather, for Davey was a Shepherdshey man and was just old enough to remember him. I don't think he recognized me as a Leigh or he would have remarked upon it. At that moment Harrington the foreman drove up in his old Ford and came over to us. He was a stocky, efficient man, who seldom wasted a word on anybody. He gave me a curt nod and told the concrete mixers to "put a jerk in it." Harrington knew that I was friendly with Diana. He had seen me riding with her and standing about in the stables. I gave him her somewhat cryptic message and he nodded, briefly.

"I'll see to it during lunch break," he said, and then scratched his chin and gave me a shrewd glance.

"You're a Leigh, aren't you?" he asked, suddenly. "Your people farmed here back along, didn't they?"

I told him that this was so and mentioned Uncle Mark, at the riding school, and Uncle Reuben, both of whom he had known as young men.

"That's funny," he said, "that's funny and no mistake!"

He shot another sidelong look at me. "You behind all this?" he asked, flatly.

"Me? This renovation lark? No, I'm not, and what on earth makes you think I am?"

"I dunno, maybe the fact that your name is Leigh," he said. "It all adds up."

"What adds up?" I demanded.

He told me then that his instructions regarding the extensive renovations on the farm had originated from Diana, who had told him that she was acting on behalf of her father because he was exceptionally busy. "He was down here yesterday, I heard, but he had left when I rang up this morning," he went on. "I've committed them for a real packet on this place. I didn't realize it was so far gone. It needed reroofing and pointing and some of the outbuildings will have to be pulled down and rebuilt. I suppose it's all right, but I would have liked an okay from Mr. Gayelorde-Sutton before I went ahead with it. No sense in doing half a job. If they've had the place included in the Heronslea lease, they might as well make it habitable and workable but they'll be a damned long time getting their money back, if I'm any judge! The work that needs doing here will stand them in about three thousand."

"Do you mean to say that you haven't had direct instructions from Mr. Gayelorde-Sutton about the job?" I asked him, my stomach contracting.

"Not a word of 'em," he said, and his voice now sounded slightly anxious. "It all came through Miss Emerald. We rode out here together and saw what needed to be done."

I thought furiously for a moment, then I said:

"Look, Mr. Harrington, it's none of my business, but if you'll take a tip from me, go straight down to the Estate office, get those papers she talked about, see the agent and find out who talked to him about including this place in the Heronslea lease. Then, no matter what the Gilroy agent says, get on the wire to Mr. Gayelorde-Sutton as soon as ever you can."

He looked pained and indecisive. "It must be authorized," he argued. "Miss Emerald wouldn't do a crazy thing like that without consulting her father."

"Wouldn't she?" I said. "You don't know Diana Gayelorde-Sutton as I do! Take my advice and check up right away."

I left him standing there, hands deep in his breeches pockets, a puzzled frown on his brown countryman's face. Suddenly my brain fog had cleared. I was no closer to a solution of Gayelorde-Sutton's strange behavior, but I had rumbled Diana's plot. The penny had dropped when Harrington referred to my family link with the farm, and it had gone home the moment he told me that she had been acting independently in this matter. It was so simple that I was amazed I had not seen through her clumsy scheme long before, and I raced along the main road and down Foxhayes Hill to Whinmouth at a speed the old Morris had not traveled since she was new, in the early nineteen-twenties.

This was her idea of a bumper surprise! This was her plan to force me out of a profession that she despised into one that she considered far more befitting a gentleman-husband. This—a tarted-up Foxhayes Farm—was my advance wedding present likely to cost her father three thousand pounds, plus whatever advance rent had been promised for the inclusion of the farm into the Heronslea lease. Whether I liked it or not, I was to become a yeoman, operating a newly renovated 250-acre farm, as a Heronslea tenant, and all this before I had had so much as a day's training for the job.

I wasted no time wondering how this plan of hers tied in with Gayelorde-Sutton's sales talk of the previous day. Obviously he knew something about the farm, and was probably under the impression that I had far more capital than was the case. I could almost hear Diana lying to him: "He's only a journalist now, Daddy, but he's come into money and wants to farm!" I began to sweat at the thought of all the blarney she must have talked about me in order to bring a busy man like her father hotfoot to Devon, to have a look at his yeoman son-in-law.

The fact that here was proof that Diana really did intend to marry me, that she had abundant faith in my ability to become a farmer, and that she was willing to commit her father to heavy expenditure on my behalf made no impression at all upon me. The fantastic recklessness of her gesture made me shudder, and so did her estimate of my pride. All this time I had been her slave. Nothing she had proposed was too risky or improbable for me to condone it and act upon it. Twice she had claimed me as a lover and over and over again she had assured me that no other man meant two straws to her, yet she was still able to go calmly about the business of buying me with her father's money and enlisting me as tenant dependent upon her family's grace and favor as landlord and patron.

Before I clattered down Fish Street into Whinmouth I had a plan of my own. Gayelorde-Sutton had schemed, Diana had schemed, but neither had showed the least willingness to take me into their confidence. It was high time, I felt, that I started scheming, and I marched straight into Lawyer Hawthorne's office and ordered him to sell my *Observer* shares for whatever he could get, providing the sale went through in twenty-four hours. He was startled and counseled delay, but I would not even listen to him. I had other things to do and shot off out of town again to my Uncle Mark's stables, behind Teasel Wood.

Mark had aged in the last few years and I knew that he was finding his muddled little business irksome and unprofitable. He was giving some promise of settling down at last and marrying one of his old flames, a hearty little widow who kept a boardinghouse in Jetty Road. He had been a frequent visitor there during her husband's lifetime and the last time I had seen him he had joked about her wanting to look after him. "Though 'er's a bit past it now, John," he added, with one of his lewd grins.

I found him standing in the little yard bullying Ned, his dull-witted stableman. When I said I had a proposition to put to him he led the way into his tumble-down cottage, which stood about a stone's throw from the loose boxes in the shadow of the beech copse. It could have been a very attractive little dwelling if Uncle Mark had kept it clean, but now its big living room was cluttered with harness and dirty cooking utensils and the great open fireplace was blocked with a rusty old stove and litter of every description.

"Do 'ee want that there cob after all?" he asked, for we had previously discussed the purchase of a neighbor's skewbald.

"No," I told him, "I want the whole shooting match if you're disposed to sell it!"

He gaped at me. "You mean it?" he gasped, unable to believe his good fortune. "You really want to take over yer? Horses and all?"

"Stables, horses, cottage, grazing, the lot!" I said. "What's it worth, Uncle?"

His eyes narrowed and he began to mumble something about me being Miriam's boy and therefore entitled to a special price, but I knew him very well and cut him short.

"It's no good asking a silly price," I said, "for I haven't got much and I shall have to spend several hundred doing the place up. What about twelve-fifty, lock, stock and barrel?"

"Damme, the horseflesh is worth five hundred," he growled.

"Don't be silly," I told him, "you couldn't get three hundred for all six of them at the horse bazaar. I'm not daft, Uncle Mark, but I am in a hurry, and I've finished with newspaper work!"

"Well that's a relief, at all events," he grunted, for his contempt for Uncle Reuben, and all Reuben's works, had not been buried in his brother's grave. "I'll practically give 'ee the place, John—fifteen hundred."

"Thirteen-fifty," I said. "It's all I can afford!"

He was far more eager to sell than I had anticipated. "Youm a bliddy old Jew!" he shouted, but we shook hands and I hustled him back to old Hawthorne to draw up a provisional agreement. In my absence Hawthorne had closed for nineteen hundred, so that I had a surplus of five hundred and fifty, less legal fees. As I intended to do the repairs by direct labor and to assist in the work myself, I considered this was more than sufficient. I had no clear idea what I would do with the place, but I knew that there was a good living in the livery stable, providing it was conducted on up-to-date lines, and I was sure that I could earn something more with the land, which comprised nearly fifty acres.

By five o'clock that day the two deals were complete. I agreed to remain at the newspaper office until a substitute could be found and later on I drove out to Shepherdshey to enlist Nat Baker's help in getting cottage and stables in order.

The old sexton agreed to work by the hour and we went up there before dark. I made a list of the furnishings I thought we should need and Nat explored the structure, pronouncing it to be sound, despite its great age.

Now that I had a place of my own, and a plan of campaign, however incomplete, I was as happy as a boy on holiday. It was Thursday when I bought the stables and by Sunday night Nat and I had transformed it. We made a vast bonfire of Uncle Mark's rubbish and persuaded Ned, the stableman, to scrub the loose boxes and give the horses their first real grooming in months. Aunt Thirza and Uncle Luke rolled up with a truckload of their best secondhand pieces and Thirza stayed on to help with the spring cleaning, leaving the cottage reeking of strong carbolic soap that mingled with the stink of creosote Nat was plastering on the fence rails.

When they had all gone I toured the premises with a feeling of pride and achievement. I had a home, a small but promising home, and I had a means of livelihood, and both were inside the borders of Sennacharib!

I decided to move in the following day, and after giving instructions to Ned, whom I decided to retain, I left the car in the yard and walked home across Teasel Wood, down the escarpment and along the elm bank of Heronslea to Shepherdshey. For the first time in my life I looked at the big house with a feeling of equality. I awaited Diana's return with confidence.

3.

There was a letter on Monday morning, asking me to meet the eleven o'clock from Waterloo, due in Whinford about three-thirty. During the morning I had another idea. I went along to Awkright's Garage and traded in my old Morris for fifty pounds. He had some good secondhand cars in his shed, so I looked them over. There was a resprayed Alvis sports that had been involved in a crash. Awkright wanted two-fifty for it, but I beat him down to two-twenty-five. It had a long, wicked-looking bonnet fastened down by straps, and a deep-throated exhaust that sounded like an airplane warming up. I took it out on a trial run, paid him his hundred and seventy-five and drove home to the quay to change into my best suit. On the way to Whinford I stopped at Kennard's Nurseries and bought a huge armful of daffodils, narcissi, and purple iris. Then, feeling very artful and extremely pleased with myself, I drove to Whinford and awaited her train.

She came down the platform followed by the inevitable porter and luggage. I never knew Diana to travel light. Wherever she went, be it only for the weekend, she took about a hundredweight of baggage. She looked extraordinarily chic and carefree, in her neat little two-piece and a close-fitting, Juliet-style straw hat that compressed her curls just so far, then spilt them over her shoulders. The moment she saw me she waved, broke into a run and kissed me half a dozen times. I told the porter to bring the luggage to the Alvis.

"Why Jan!" she exclaimed. "What on earth have you got there?"

"One of several things," I said smugly and stowed the luggage in the capacious trunk.

"Flowers too! Why, Jan, you're becoming almost gallant! Oh, I do love you so!" she added, ignoring the fact that the porter was still bustling around hoping to earn a bigger tip.

He almost groveled when I gave him half a crown but it wasn't the money, it was the Alvis and Diana. She climbed in and snuggled down in the red leather, shooting out her long legs and giving one of her luxurious, catlike stretches.

"Mmmmm-*mmmmm!*" she cooed. "Whatever's happened? Have you cashed in on your newspaper money?"

"You'll see," I told her. "We'll be making a call en route for Heronslea."

"You did give my message to Harrington, didn't you?"

"Yes," I said, "but forget Foxhayes Hollow for the moment, we'll go into all that later on!"

She looked at me half-smiling as I let in the clutch and we roared off up the Station Hill.

"Something sensational has happened to you while I've been away, Jan," she said. "You've grown about two inches!" Then, probing me: "What did you think about the renovations at Foxhayes Hollow? Don't you think Harrington is making a good job of it?"

"Fine," I said, "if someone has the idea of converting it into a roadhouse!"

She did not know what to make of that, and it struck me then that we were beginning to learn the art of sparring after the manner of her father, a method of conversation we had never found it necessary to use before, not even when she was Emerald being conducted around the Tower of London.

"There's something funny about you this afternoon," she complained. "Is it the car that's making you sound so now-now-little-womanish?"

I made no reply to this so after a moment she said:

"What's wrong with what we're doing to Foxhayes Hollow?"

"It's chi-chi," I said, offhandedly, "the sort of place a man would build if his idea of a farmer was of a chunky man in tweeds, buckskin leggings and a pork-pie hat."

"A farm doesn't have to be a stinking midden, does it?" she said, rather snappishly.

"No," I said, "but it doesn't have to be quaint and hey-down-derryish either!"

We weren't getting along so well and I'm afraid it was mostly my fault. The car, the sudden break from the tyranny of a weekly paper, the business I had bought, and my still-smoldering resentment of her plan to convert me into a yeoman tenant without first consulting me combined to make me sound arrogant and patronizing. I stole a glance at her as we whipped along the road and noticed that she now looked unhappy. All the gaiety she had shown as soon as she stepped off the train was gone and she seemed to be groping for words that would resolve the curiously tense atmosphere of the cramped space under the hood. I wanted very much to stop, kiss her and tell her that everything was going to be all right, providing she granted me my little triumph, but pride, or more cockiness, still held me on a tight rein.

"What is it, Jan dear?" she said at last. "What's the matter?"

"You'll see in a moment, Di," I said, relenting a little. "Just have a little patience, five minutes' patience."

She fell silent after that and made no comment when I took the left-hand fork toward Teasel Wood instead of dropping down to Shepherdshey. I was beginning to be a little anxious now and my heart was thumping. I sensed her surprise as we turned off the road and dropped into low gear to negotiate the unsurfaced lane leading down to Uncle Mark's place. Then we were there and I was handing her out of the car and into the cottage. She looked around with a mixture of surprise and dismay.

"Why have we come here?" she said.

The expression of distaste on her face frightened me.

"It's mine—*ours*, Di," I said. "That Foxhayes Hollow idea of yours is crazy. I don't want your family to stake me and I don't even fancy the idea of being their tenant. You ought to have discussed it with me before you did a slaphappy thing like that, and anyway, it can't even be legal until your father approves of it!"

Her face fell and for a moment she looked as if she were going to burst into tears; then her mouth hardened and her eyes blazed.

"Have you sold out and spent your money on this dump?" she demanded. "Have you been idiot enough to buy those old screws from your crooked uncle and set up as a riding instructor?"

"I've bought the stables, the stock and the cottage," I said, "and even if it doesn't look much now it will when it's had a bit spent on it. There's fifty acres and I won't need more than half of it for the horses. There's free grazing around here and I'm going to use the rest of the land for chickens. The cottage can be made very pretty and there's a good living here, Di."

"A living!" she almost screamed. "An existence, you mean! Five pounds a week profit on horses and two more on eggs, *if* you're lucky. You must be out of your head, Jan! Why, once Foxhayes Hollow is back in production—"

"I don't want Foxhayes as a bloody dowry!" I shouted, for suddenly I was hysterical with rage and disappointment. "Can't you get it into your thick skull that I don't want anything from your family but *you?*"

She calmed down somewhat but the superior expression that replaced her angry look was not an improvement.

"Do you really expect me to live here, like . . . like a Devon version of a poor white in the Deep South?" she said, calmly.

"Yes, I did and I do!" I roared. "If what's happened between us all these years means anything to you at all, you'd be happy to do it and help make a go of it. Damn it, you've always loved horses, and together we could build this place up until it was known all over the county. We could get more fields and better horses. We could do something together for once, free of all interference, and we should be doing what I always imagined you wanted to do—living together, in Sennacharib."

The look of disdain left her and she now stared at me with solemn troubled eyes.

"Jan," she said, quietly, "this is real life. . . . Sennacharib was only a game!"

It was the most savage thrust that I had ever received from her and it hurt like hell, far more than any of the old wounds that her abrupt changes of mood, her eternal unpredictability, her erratic comings and goings in my life had inflicted. For a moment I was incoherent with rage and grabbed her wrist, pulling her toward me.

"You listen to me!" I thundered. "It might have been a game to you but it was never one as far as I was concerned! You say living here wouldn't be practical and you make it all sound childish and stupid, but I'm not going to let you walk out on me just like that, not after all I've been through on account of you! You can turn me and this place down with your mother's brand of arrogance but you won't forget me that easily. You'll remember me for at least a month every time you sit down, damn you!"

I had her fast with my left hand and with my right I reached out and snatched up a short switch from the window seat. It was a light, improvised crop that had been overlooked in the general turnout. I pushed her away and flourished the crop like a dancing dervish, cutting the air with it and cursing her at the top of my voice. I was beside myself with rage and, for a brief moment, there was real fear in her eyes.

"Jan!" she said, and her voice seemed to come from the far side of Teasel Wood. "Jan, don't, *don't!*"

I struck her then, a single blow across her shoulders, and she shivered, pressing her hands flat against the wall and staring at me, her eyes wide with incredulity. The action did more to sober me than anything she could have said or done. I threw down the switch and for several seconds we stared at one another without moving. Then the fear left her eyes and her mouth began to pucker. She put up one hand and slowly rubbed her shoulder, without taking her eyes off me.

"You hit me!" she whispered, so quietly that I lip-read rather than heard what she said. "*You hit me, Jan* . . . nobody, ever . . . nobody . . ."

Her voice trailed away to nothing but her lips continued to move and her hand went on massaging the smart. Then, still without taking her eyes from me, her expression changed again, passing from utter bewilderment to a kind of savage intensity that I had never seen in the face of anyone, man or woman. The tears that had brimmed the moment before remained static in her eyes, giving them a kind of glaze and somehow magnifying them, as if I were looking at her through a powerful glass. Her mouth, which had crumpled like a child's, twitched into a firm line and two bright spots of color glowed on her cheeks, pulsing through the make-up. Her breast was heaving and she stood so tensely that, for a moment, I thought she was going to project herself forward and fly at me, clawing and biting, but suddenly her body relaxed and her head went back, her chin shooting up like the chin of a person suddenly and immoderately amused.

All my rage was spent. I ran to her and threw my arms around her, kissing her cheek and neck, burying my hands in her hair.

"Oh, God, why did you make me . . . *why*, Diana . . . ? What's happened to us? What *is* it?"

"Don't talk, don't say anything, Jan!" she said, and her voice sounded harsh, almost guttural. "Don't worry—fuss—we belong—always, so take me, for God's sake take me!"

She began kissing me then, not as she had in the dell beside the Teasel, and not even as she had kissed me when she was Emerald in the Tower, but like a predatory savage, starved and desperate. Her straw hat slipped off and was trampled underfoot and we clung together in a frenzy for how long I do not know, perhaps for a few minutes, perhaps an hour.

At last I lifted her and set her down in the deep window seat, lowering my head to kiss her hands and wrists, fearful of breaking contact and conscious, as my lips touched her fingers, of their steady pressure on my face. Then I laid my head on her lap and she stroked my hair, gently and regularly, each sweep beginning at my temples and ending on the nape of my neck.

"I was mad, Di," I said, at length. "I felt like killing you and it scared me more than it scared you. I've never felt like that about anyone before."

"Forget it, Jan, I asked for it and I've always asked for it from you, right from the very beginning."

I looked up at her and saw that she was crying now. She looked about fourteen, no more, and I felt closer to her than at any time since we had stood together beside the island bonfire awaiting the arrival of the pilot boat.

"I'd really set my heart on the farm," she said, presently. "I'd got it all worked out and I felt terribly Machiavellian. It was because of that I was so beastly about this place, but I suppose my disappointment wasn't nearly as keen as yours." She looked around the half-furnished room. "It was a wonderful thing for you to do, quite wonderful, but then, why should I be surprised? You've always done things like this and I've always repaid you by being me."

She spoke very quietly and presently extricated one of her hands, opening the bag beside her and dabbing her eyes. While she applied lipstick I sat down beside her. Inside the cottage it was very quiet but outside the thrushes in Teasel Wood were singing their early evening chorus. I noticed Uncle Mark's switch on the floor and turned my eyes away.

"Did it hurt very much, Di?"

"Just enough, Jan!"

She smiled and then looked quickly away and I saw that she was blushing. "It's funny," she said, as though in explanation, "I've always heard that it's true, though I can't honestly say I really believed it when I read about it. Women like brutes but just in short, sharp bursts, I imagine. I've never wanted you so much in my life. If you'd run out of the cottage, as I thought for one awful moment you were going to, I should have run after you, shouting that you'd forgotten your stick! I wonder just how much of our trouble in the past has been due to that? I wonder if the primitive part of me is terrified of your inclination to overplay your strong suit, Jan, and it's that that makes me want to run away every now and again?"

"What exactly is my strong suit, Di?"

She laughed and ran a hand down my cheek. "I told you years ago! Male gentleness—'Jan Ridd' gentleness—and only the really hefty men have it."

She got up and retrieved her hat, studying it ruefully.

"This is a write-off, like the farm idea. Wait here a minute."

She went out into the kitchen and a moment later appeared beside the car. Through the window I saw her gather up the armful of flowers that I had bought and carry them into the kitchen. Then she brought a large bowlful into the living room and put them down on the table. The gesture blew on the small spark of hope that remained in my heart.

"Why did you do that, Di?"

She gave one of her sly, mischievous grins and began combing her hair, glancing into her handbag mirror propped against the flower bowl. As she stood there, tugging at the knots, I was reminded very vividly of how she had looked during our island adventure, when she had combed out her hair in front of a handbag mirror propped on stones.

"I hate seeing flowers out of water," she said, "and anyway, this place needs color."

"Does that mean you'll give it a go?" I asked, trying to keep the tremor from my voice.

She went on combing. "This is how I see it, Jan," she said. "The thing I said that made you so angry—about Sennacharib being a game—well, that's a fact, you know, whether you like it or not. But there are other facts, and now seems to be the time to face them. What have you and I got in common, apart from our physical appetites and kind of spiritual hunger for the few square miles in which we grew up?"

"I believe we're in love with each other, Di," I told her. "That isn't a game, or is it?"

"You're in love with me, Jan, I'm sure of that, and whenever we're together in this place I'm very much in love with you. When I'm away from you I'm not, but for all that, I lust after you, the way I did just now. What qualifications have I got to marry a decent person like you? I can't cook, I haven't the faintest interest in housekeeping, I'd make a hopeless mother to children, and there's nothing I can do with my hands apart from spend money like water, the kind of money you'll never have! Mind you, I think it's damned sporting of you to want to take me on, and you do, don't you? You do, in spite of everything?"

"More than anything in the world," I said, "but not at the price of being financed by your family."

"Then your personal independence is more important than just marrying me?"

I considered this. I wanted to give her an absolutely honest answer. There was no point, at this stage, in bluffing her or myself.

"Independence wins by a short head, Di."

"You wouldn't have our maintenance staff up here to renovate the place and you wouldn't let me borrow from Daddy to restock the stable and lay out the rest of the place as a poultry farm?"

"No," I said, more definitely, "I wouldn't! I'd sooner risk waiting another five years and then make another pounce, by which time, I think, you might have found out what's worth having and what isn't."

"But you'd still be willing to risk it now? You'd still risk starting us off on the wrong foot and maybe making a terrible hash of it?"

"Yes, I would, Di! Taken all around, I believe that to be the lesser risk."

She was silent for a moment. Finally she tossed back her hair and carefully replaced the comb in her handbag.

"All right, Jan dear, we'll do it! All I'm promising is that I'll try, I'll try damned hard, but you'd better keep this handy. You may need it oftener than you think!"

She picked up the crop and laid it on the table, regarding it seriously before turning and smiling down at me.

"Failing that there's always bed," she added.

I had imagined, over the years during which I had dreamed of this moment, that it would have the glow and excitement of an elopement, but now I discovered that it was far more like taking the first step of a journey into a remote corner of the world. Nothing was certain about it save that Diana was coming with me and nothing was certain about her beyond the fact that she only had to enter a room or pass within yards of me, to paint my world with the rainbow colors of joy and adventure. I did not ponder with these uncertainties but let go, happy to drift and careless of the quicksands and rapids that almost surely lay ahead. I got up and kissed her on the tip of the nose.

"Come on, Di," I said, "let's go down to Shepherdshey and put up banns before you change your mind!"

4.

We saw the vicar, an eager, gnomish little Welshman, and put up banns for a wedding in Shepherdshey Church on the Saturday following her twenty-first birthday. She did not regard the date as being of much importance, commenting on the certainty of her mother's continued absence in France, but I was taking no chances. If the vicar was taken aback by our frank discussion in front of him he had the good manners not to show it. He was a comparatively new man in the parish and his knowledge of the Gayelorde-Suttons was based almost exclusively on hearsay. We should have had a great deal more difficulty with the old vicar, who had been a regular diner at Heronslea.

We had high tea at a farm over on Nun's Head and when I took Diana back to Heronslea at dusk she suggested that we should wet the banns with a bottle of champagne.

"Hardly anyone's there," she said. "Most of the staff have been given a holiday, or shuttled up to the town house for some do or other. Anyway, I bought a record for you in London, and I'd like to play it. It's part of what you might call the Sennacharib overture, so I'm quite sure you'll approve."

The big house was oddly quiet. There seemed to be no one about but two or three living-in maids. The butler and chauffeur were missing, and for this I was grateful, but it seemed to me that, tonight of all nights, our healths should have been drunk by dear old Drip. When I asked Diana what had happened to her, she told me that soon after the island business Miss Rodgers had been pensioned off and now shared a bungalow with her sister in a remote part of North Wales.

"I write to her sometimes," she said, "but not as often as I ought. Before I found you, Jan, she was the only real friend I had. I tell you what. We'll honeymoon up that way and look her up. I've been everywhere on the Continent and never even seen Wales, or the Lake District. How about that?"

I said I should like that very much. Just to hear her use the word "honeymoon" was bliss.

She found some champagne, of the same year as that brought up to the bedroom the night of her party, and we opened it with a good deal of difficulty and laughter. Then she put the record on and sat watching me as music dripped from their impressive-looking radio phonograph. It was a more modern recording of the record we had burned on the island to start the signal fire, and I loved her for remembering. The nostalgic effect of the harmonies was so powerful that I could have wept, and seeing that her little surprise had succeeded, she came and sat on the arm of my chair, so that her nearness, her perfume, and the wildly improbable end to a very difficult day made me almost drunk with delight.

"I always thought those Student Corps' bellowings were a funny kind of theme song for two crazy kids marooned on an island," she said, "but I could never hear them afterwards without picturing you on your hands and knees in that leaky old cabin, puffing away at damp driftwood and trying to boil the kettle. Why, Jan, about a year after I was sent abroad, Yves' family, the French people I stayed with, took me to Heidelberg and I disgraced myself at a concert by bursting into tears and refusing to explain why."

As the record began to run down the phone rang and she got up to answer it. I was so deep in my trance of delight that I missed the first part of her conversation and only began to pay attention when I heard her say, "Is he in the hospital, then?" in a crisp, anxious voice.

"Who is it, Di?" I asked and, as though I had known that this phone call was going to shatter my dream as casually as a gale strips the petals from a rose, I scrambled up and hurried across to her. She made an impatient gesture, devoting her full attention to the phone.

"All right, Masters," she said, sharply, "I'll come at once. I can be there by soon after five. I'll catch the night train from the junction. Have the chauffeur meet me and we'll drive straight there, do you understand?"

She put down the phone and looked at me without seeing me.

"Daddy's had an accident; he's in the hospital, seriously hurt!"

"What kind of accident?"

"I don't know, Masters was very evasive, so I've got a strong suspicion Daddy's already dead and he was trying to break it gently. I shall have to go up right away, Jan!"

"Of course," I told her, slipping my arm around her shoulder, "but why catch the train? I'll run you up in the Alvis. We could be there about the same time." And I made to hurry into the hall for my raincoat.

"No, Jan!"

She stood quite still in the center of the big room, one finger plucking the corner of her mouth. "It's your press day tomorrow and you've got so many things to see to down here. You can't leave the paper just like that, the people you're selling out to might think you're letting them down and cry off the deal. If they did that I'd never forgive myself and it might spoil everything. You said you were under contract to keep it going until they got a substitute, and besides, I think I'd much sooner go by train. I'm tired and I can try to sleep. I shall have plenty to do tomorrow, God knows. Masters says everyone is in a terrible flap!"

"How about your mother?" I asked.

"He says she's flying home but she won't get into Croydon until midday and anyway, she's not much good in a crisis."

"I'd gladly run you up, Di," I told her, "but in the circumstances maybe you're right about going by train. I'll stay here providing you'll promise to ring me breakfast time tomorrow and fetch me if I can be of the slightest use to anyone. Will you promise that?"

"Yes, of course," she said, and tried to smile. "Poor Jan! This was your big night and now . . ." Her smile faded, "Do you suppose there's some sort of curse on us?"

"If there is, it's not going to make a ha'porth of difference, you can rely on that!" I said grimly. Not even the thought that her father might be dying at this moment tempered my rage against him for snatching Diana away when we seemed at last to have emerged from the tunnel. "I'll run you to the junction. You'd better get some things, just a few things!"

"I'm not unpacked," she said. "I'll change and be down in ten minutes."

I occupied the time by phoning the junction and checking on the train. I had no real need to do this, for the train was the one that I had caught on my various dashes to town, after the *Observer* had been put to bed on Thursday nights, but I wanted to stop myself wondering how this thunderbolt would affect our plans and whether it would in some way postpone our wedding. There was a kind of desperation about my feeling for that coming-of-age date. For years now it had stood in the distant future, like a mountain peak that was clearly visible but unattainable. Only an hour ago it had seemed, at last, to be within walking distance, but now it had receded again and I was wretchedly uncertain of my ability to keep it in view. I told myself that this accident was a mere coincidence, that Diana had no real affection for her father and that we had agreed on the way down to the vicar's that neither he nor Mrs. Gayelorde-Sutton had any place in our immediate future, but these arguments did very little to reassure me and we drove to the junction in silence.

The train was in and I found her an empty compartment and bought two cups of thick railway tea. We sat sipping them and trying to make conversation until the guard walked along and slammed the door. I jumped out and caught her hands through the window.

"Di," I said, piteously, for I was now in a turmoil of doubt and depression, "you'll come back! You'll come back the moment you can!"

She pulled me to her as the whistle blew and kissed me very softly on the mouth.

"Dear Jan," she said, "don't look so tragic. I love you and I'll always love you. And even if I couldn't come back, I'd need you and holler for you, the way I did last time!"

I was a little comforted by this and stood back as the train began to move. She remained rigid, framed in the window, not waving but just regarding me with the fixed gravity of a portrait staring down from a gallery wall.

Then a cloud of steam hissed up and she was gone, the last of the carriages snick-snacking past and beating out a metallic dirge. It thumped in my head all the way home and throughout the greater part of the night.

Chapter Eleven

T H E next morning every London paper carried the story in headlines. There had been no accident but there had been a resounding stock-market crash, involving a group of large trusts and a string of other firms, some of which had names that were household words. It was a Hatry scandal on a smaller scale, but a scale big enough to prompt Gayelorde-Sutton, as one of the most prominent figures in the group, to attempt suicide. He had swallowed two dozen sleeping tablets and had been found unconscious by his secretary. Two of the papers carried a stop-press announcement that he had died soon after midnight.

I bought all the London papers and went into the office, locking the door and telling the foreman printer that I was not to be disturbed. The old fellow looked at me anxiously.

"You feeling all right, John?" he asked and his eye took in the bundle of papers I was clutching. One flaring headline was visible— CITY FINANCIER'S DEATH FOLLOWS MARKET CRASH—and the name Gayelorde-Sutton in the subsidiary headline. It was common knowledge in the printing shop that I had been mooning after Gayelorde-Sutton's daughter for years. You could never keep a secret of that kind in a town like Whinmouth.

"Yes, I'm all right, Fred," I told him, "but I've had a bit of a shock over this and I've got some important phoning to do. Keep everyone away for a bit!"

"'Ee b'ain't caught you for aught, 'as 'ee?" demanded Fred, whose knowledge of stocks and shares were as vague as mine.

"Good God, no!" I snorted, and slammed the door on him.

I read the reports but they did not make very much sense to me. As far as I could understand, Gayelorde-Sutton's firm, or the one in which he figured most prominently, had gone bankrupt for over half a million pounds, and their ruin involved other groups in which he and his partners were concerned. One of the partners had fled to the Argentine and it was on his account that the Fraud Squad had been called in. The story was written in the consciously dramatic style that Fleet Street bestows upon this kind of news. There were pictures of Gayelorde-Sutton and his wife at Ascot the previous year, and another at Heronslea, labeled: *A financier's place in the country*. The caption implied a sneer and it was obvious that the journalists knew a good deal more about the scandal than they could safely print at this stage.

When I had read all I could find on the subject, I asked for directory inquiries and tried to get through to Diana's town house but, as I suspected, the line was blocked and no calls could be put through, although I tried several times.

Afternoon came but no call from Diana. I raced through the most urgent of my work and then rang Hawthorne and told him that I had no alternative but to abandon the *Observer* to the printing staff and hurry to London. I just told him it was on account of an urgent personal matter, involving a relative's sudden death, and I left instructions with Fred the foreman to answer Diana if she did ring and tell her that I was on my way. There was no through train until four P.M., so I filled up with petrol and drove across country to pick up the main London road, west of Yeovil. I kept my foot down and traffic wasn't heavy. I was nosing my way into Hammersmith about eight o'clock in the evening and I made straight for Palmerston Crescent.

I had no need to look for the house. There were parked cars all around the entrance and a little knot of reporters and photographers picketing the short flight of steps to the front door.

"I'm a relative, not a pressman," I told a photographer who warned me that no one would answer the door.

"You could be King-Kong, chum, but you won't make it!" he said, flippantly, and then, calling a thickset young man, told him that I was a relation and might have a new line on the story. Other reporters drifted over and I soon had cause to regret my feeble bluff.

"Where's his wife?" they wanted to know. "Is she down in the country?"

[318

"I've just come from there," I said, "and the place is unoccupied. Mrs. Gayelorde-Sutton was supposed to be flying in from France today."

"She didn't turn up," said one of the reporters. "We've checked every airport."

I tried the bell again but the door remained shut. Bewildered and uncertain, I left the group and drove to the office of the *Illustrated*. I had a vague idea that the editor might be disposed to help me, for now I was beginning to regret my precipitate dash to town. I had no means of finding out where Diana was likely to be and, as always, I could only hang about waiting for her to get in touch with me. The editor of the *Illustrated* was sympathetic and made half a dozen phone calls, without the slightest result. Nobody knew where the Gayelorde-Suttons, mother and daughter, were hiding, but Fleet Street was anxious to find out before the story went cold.

It was a long time cooling off. There was even more about it in the papers on the following day, so I rang Fred at the *Observer* office and satisfied myself that Diana had not tried to get in touch with me. Then, in growing desperation, I made an exhaustive tour of her haunts—Fortnum's, Martinez's, various hotels, and even the homes of some of the Set with whom she had associated during her wild period.

It was all useless. Both Diana and her mother had vanished, and I came to the dismal conclusion that if the professionals in Fleet Street could not trace them my own chances were negligible.

On the third day I trailed back to the West, where I took old Hawthorne into my confidence, but he wasn't much help. All he could suggest was that I should ask the telephone people to put through all the evening calls to the cottage where I was now sleeping. I did this as a precaution, and then hung about, racking my brains for a lead, any sort of a lead that would offer the slightest hope of tracing Diana.

Suddenly I found one, a folded slip of paper that had been in my pocket all the time, overlooked in my mad rush to and from London and forgotten under the merciless cudgeling I had given my brains during the last few days. It was the letterhead that Gayelorde-Sutton had handed to me during our interview and it gave the phone number of his solicitors. As I read it I heard his voice saying, "Good firm . . . sound people . . . go to them if you want to."

I could hardly wait to get in touch with them and put through a call one minute after nine the following morning.

A dry, impersonal voice answered, saying that he was the managing clerk. I tried to speak quietly and reasonably, telling the clerk that I was an agent of the family, resident in Devon. Certain complications had arisen, I said, in respect of a farm Gayelorde-Sutton was purchasing, and as I was reluctant to worry the family at a time like this I had thought it best to contact the London solicitors. I gave the impression that I was in almost direct contact with mother and daughter.

The clerk went away and was gone for a few minutes. Then he told me that he was putting me through to Mr. Fellowes, one of the partners, and I repeated my story to him.

"I see," said a fruity voice. "Well then, I think perhaps you had better come to town and discuss the matter with us. None of our client's property can be sold or disposed of in any way, you understand, Mr. Leigh?"

I said that I realized this and made an appointment for the following day. Then I went up to the cottage and had the first real sleep I had had in more than a week.

2.

Mr. Fellowes, the owner of the fruity voice, was a heavily built man, about forty-five. He was so courteous, and made such a pleasant impression on me, that I decided to take him into my confidence. After presenting the letterhead as a kind of *bona fides* I told him how things stood between Diana and myself. I had to exaggerate the cordiality shown me by Gayelorde-Sutton, and I hinted that the family had intended to set up Diana and me in a farm newly acquired by the estate. I would have told any story to get to Diana and this was only half a lie.

Fellowes seemed keenly interested and when I had finished, and admitted frankly that Diana had vanished after I had put her on the night train at Whinford, his attitude became genuinely sympathetic.

"Why do you suppose she hasn't got in touch with you?" he asked. "Could it be she's ashamed of what's happened?"

This had not occurred to me and privately I thought it very unlikely.

"Young women are very unpredictable about that kind of thing," he went on, "and her father has come out of this business rather badly. I'm afraid a lot of people have lost a great deal of money. I've lost a few hundreds myself, come to that! How about you?"

I said that I had never owned a stock or a share in my life and he smiled.

"Wise young man," he said lightly, but I could see he was summing me up and was by no means certain what to make of me.

"Excuse me for a couple of moments," he said, at length, and rang through to the outer office for Gayelorde-Sutton's file. A typist brought it in and he sorted through it, drumming his fingers and humming tunelessly. Presently he plucked out a large, sealed envelope.

"I thought the name rang a bell," he said. "This is addressed to you. It came in ten days ago, actually on the morning of the crash. Perhaps you'd like to open it in my presence?"

I was dumfounded. Not only did my name appear on the envelope, but Aunt Thirza's address was there and beneath it, in brackets, the alternative address of the *Observer*. Then I recalled Gayelorde-Sutton's admission—"I know a great deal more about you than you imagine." Well, here was proof of it. Inside the envelope was a single sheet of notepaper and another sealed envelope, with bulky enclosures. On the notepaper, in Gayelorde-Sutton's spidery handwriting, was a brief note:

DEAR LEIGH:

I was impressed by our talk. When you get this I shall be in no position either to oppose or assist your somewhat prolonged courtship. In the event of your taking my advice, however, I am making you a personal bequest of one thousand pounds.

You will find Emerald a handful and I wish you joy. I believe you are interested in horseback riding and my advice, for what it is worth, is to keep her on a far tighter rein than I did!

Sincerely,

ERIC GAYELORDE-SUTTON

Inside the second envelope were ten hundred-pound notes.

I was so astonished that I sat staring at the letter until Fellowes reminded me of his presence by a discreet legal cough. I passed the letter to him and he read it, his eyebrows shooting up.

"Did you have any inkling about this?" he asked.

"Not the faintest notion," I told him.

"Then stuff that damned envelope in your pocket," he said, gruffly. "I've mislaid my damned glasses again—can you see them anywhere?"

I pocketed the money and handed him his horned-rimmed glasses that lay on the desk before him. He blew out his cheeks, like a motorist who has just avoided running over a dog.

"Will everything Gayelorde-Sutton owned have to be sold up?" I asked.

"Even his clothes," said Fellowes. "The creditors might get five shillings in the pound and then again they might not! He didn't own Heronslea but there's a fortune in antiques down there and he did own the London house and a place in Nice."

"What about Mrs. Gayelorde-Sutton?" I asked. "Surely she had money of her own?"

"She had until a few months ago," he told me, "but when things got sticky she transferred all of it to one of the companies. I heard from her yesterday. She's penniless!"

I digested this for a moment, then I said:

"Look here, Mr. Fellowes, I don't need this money and I . . ."

"What money?" he demanded, looking straight at me.

I thought for a moment. "Right, have it your way! Put me in touch with her and I think I might be able to help her," I said.

He looked hard at the ceiling. "I'm not authorized to give her address to anyone," he said, slowly. "If the press got on to it the story would take another week or so to die a natural death! You've been a journalist, I don't have to tell you about that, do I?"

"No," I said, "but it seems to me that if I find her I might trace Diana, and I'm going to trace her if it costs me a thousand pounds! Talking of figures, is that very much, measured against the sums involved in these deficiencies?"

He smiled, then swiftly composed his features. "Like giving a donkey one oat," he said.

As we talked I noticed that he was fidgeting with the open file in front of him. A small sheet of notepaper, similar to the one I had given him as a *bona fides,* was now detached from the main pile. It edged across the desk, until it was about halfway between us. It was the top sheet of a letter written in a strong, feminine hand. At the top of the page was an address:

21 *Drayford Gardens, Holland Park, W.9.* Having noted the address I stood up.

"Well, I don't seem to have got much further, do I?"

"No," he said, blandly, "but I'm sure I wish you luck, Mr. Leigh! Don't forget this, will you?" And he returned Gayelorde-Sutton's note.

We shook hands and he showed me as far as the outer office, where we parted. He was the most human solicitor I have ever met.

I took an 88 bus along the Bayswater Road and on the way I thought about Gayelorde-Sutton's gift in relation to our interview of a fortnight ago. Some of the things that had puzzled me so much were now becoming clear—his talk of going away, which I recognized as a conventional smoke screen for suicide; his anxiety to get Diana settled and cushioned, to some extent, against the disaster that was then only forty-eight hours away; his frantic desire to be rid of me in order to concentrate on the phone call, probably the final nail in his coffin. For all that, his last-minute efforts on behalf of Diana failed to impress me. Looking back on his grotesque heartiness, and knowing what was in his mind at the time, his clumsy bluff was like the action of a drunk urging a slightly less tipsy companion to do something calculated to make him look foolish in the eyes of the sober. His letter was not the kind of letter a man should have written a few hours before taking his life. There was a sneer behind every word and the sneers suggested that, to some extent, he blamed his wife and daughter for the position in which he found himself at that moment. Pondering this I realized that nothing would induce me to use his money, that I had to get rid of it as soon as possible. If it was able to buy information regarding Diana's whereabouts then I was prepared to use it for that purpose, but in any case I had to get rid of it, soon!

I left the bus at the stop beyond Notting Hill Station and made inquiries in a shop. Then I found Drayford Gardens, a long and depressing row of four-story Victorian houses, stucco-fronted, Ionic-pillared and as grim as a city cemetery. Number twenty-one was divided into flats and on the plate beside the bell push there was no card bearing the name of Mrs. Gayelorde-Sutton. I took potluck and pressed the bell of Apartment Number Three.

A middle-aged woman with peroxided hair opened the door and I told her that I was a clerk with an urgent message from a firm of solicitors for a lady living in one of the flats but that I had unfortunately forgotten which number.

"What's she like?" the woman asked, affably enough.

I described Mrs. Gayelorde-Sutton as accurately as I could.

"Oh, that'll be the smart one who doesn't go out," she said. "Top floor, and a bloody long climb!"

I thanked the woman and followed her up six flights of stairs. On the third landing she pointed and I climbed two more flights, arriving on the floor that had been occupied by the maids when the house was occupied by prosperous Victorians. The landing was uncarpeted and there were two doors, divided by a strip of peeling plaster. I chose the door that had an empty milk bottle outside. Beyond it I could hear a faint whirring sound, like the pleasant drone of a sewing machine. The sound ceased the moment I knocked.

"Who is it?" called a voice, after a lengthy pause.

"A clerk, with a message from Messrs. Lammett & Fellowes, the solicitors, ma'am," I called back.

"Wait a minute!"

I waited, my heart pounding like a steam hammer, not only from the exertion of climbing all those stairs but from the prospect of seeing Diana again.

The door opened and there stood Mrs. Gayelorde-Sutton, as trim and elegant as she had been when I had last seen her in the West End. Apart from that, however, she had changed a good deal. Her drawn expression reminded me of somebody listening from the dock to evidence on the second day of a tedious trial.

For a long moment we stared at one another. Then, as I detected a movement to slam the door shut, I said:

"I really have got something for you from the solicitors, Mrs. Gayelorde-Sutton! I've just come from them, how else would I have the address?"

She considered this, her greenish eyes regarding me curiously but with none of their customary arrogance.

"You had better come in," she said, quietly, and stood aside.

The apartment was small, dark and low-ceilinged. What furniture there was reminded me of the pieces she had once bought at Uncle Luke's Mart. A one-bar electric fire was burning and under a single-shaded bulb stood a Singer sewing machine; around it were crumpled folds of material. It seemed almost obscene to discover Mrs. Gayelorde-Sutton in a setting like this, and I had a curious feeling that I was dreaming and had interrupted a game of Heronslea charades. It was as though at any moment all the lights would come on, and people would laugh, clap and call out the word that she was acting out on her sewing machine. Then, against all probability, I felt a rush of warmth for her, such as I had not experienced for her husband when he had patted my shoulder and used my Christian name. There was something about her in this shoddy setting that suggested enormous dignity, a dignity that had always escaped her when she was high-heeling across the parquet floors of Heronslea, or climbing in and out of her vast, black Bentley during shopping expeditions in Whinmouth. Behind the dignity there was something else, humility, and a kind of dogged courage in the way she moved around the room, clearing materials from the one easy chair and lifting her hand toward it indicating that I should be seated. The simple gesture humbled me as I had never been humbled by her in her lady-of-the-manor days.

"You're looking for Emerald, I imagine?"

Something else struck me as hopelessly irrational. The monstrous affectation had gone from her voice. She spoke like a normal person, tired perhaps but politely patient. There was no hint of tightly corseted vowels and tortured consonants. It was "Emerald," not "*Air*-m'lde"; it was plain, simple "I," not "*Aies.*"

"Yes," I said, struggling madly to adjust myself to this complete stranger, "I got your address by a trick but please don't let that worry you. I'll give you my word of honor now that I'll forget it the moment I walk out of here!"

She pushed materials from the sewing-machine chair and sat down, resting her hands on her lap. I noticed that the fingers were long and tapering like Diana's and also that they were ringless. Even her wedding ring was missing.

"She isn't here, I'm afraid. Did you think she would be?"

"I hoped that she would be. Do you know where she is?"

She thought a moment and her eyes avoided mine. "How long is it since you saw her?"

I spoke briefly of what had taken place between us on the day before the crash and how we had put up banns to marry a few days after Diana's coming-of-age. I mentioned the circumstances in which we had heard of the disaster, and of our parting at Whinford Station. She listened carefully to every word I uttered.

"Emerald's abroad now," she said, when I had finished.

"In Nice?"

"No, not in Nice."

"Then where? Or do you still think I've no right to know?"

"Yes," she said, quietly, "of course you have that right, Mr. Leigh, and I intend to tell you if you'll tell me something first. Exactly what did the solicitor say about Emerald?"

"He didn't say anything about her," I said, with a good deal of surprise, for her approach was so unlike all I recalled of Mrs. Gayelorde-Sutton that I had to keep reminding myself that I was addressing the right person. "I told you, I got this address by a trick, a quick bit of snooping over the desk."

More in the hope of convincing her that I was on her side than with any ulterior motive, I handed her Gayelorde-Sutton's letter. "I was given this by Mr. Fellowes," I said and waited while she read the note.

Her expression did not change but I noticed that her hands trembled slightly.

"What did Mr. Fellowes say about this?" she asked, in the same gentle voice.

"He pretended he had lost his glasses," I told her, and her lips twitched. It was not a smile but it was the nearest approach to one she had ever given in my presence.

"Well, that's very nice for you, Mr. Leigh," she said, returning the note, "but you don't have to marry her in order to keep the money, do you?"

"I haven't the slightest intention of keeping it!" I said, gruffly. "Diana tried to bully me into taking over a Heronslea farm but I turned that down, and this money either belongs to you or the creditors, it certainly doesn't belong to me!"

"That's rather silly," she said. "I should hang on to it now that you have been clever enough to get it out of the lawyers' clutches."

"Well, I'm not keeping it," I said, slightly nettled. "I'm leaving it here, and if you don't want it, put it back in the kitty and ensure that the creditors get 5/1d in the pound. Now are you going to tell me where Diana is?"

"Diana—Emerald is married," she said. "She was married last Monday, to Yves de Royden, a French boy she had known for a very long time."

"*Married*—you said?"

What meager light there was in that cheerless little flat seemed to fade, so that the erect figure of Mrs. Gayelorde-Sutton, seen sideways at the sewing machine, became blurred. The shock was very great. It was as though someone had stolen up unseen and struck me a savage blow across the chest, and the illusion was so vivid that I put out my hands to avoid a second attack. The indistinct shadow in front of me rose from her chair and as she passed in front of me my vision cleared and there was Mrs. Gayelorde-Sutton, standing close beside me, her hand on my shoulder.

"Just sit still a moment," she said, "I'm making some coffee."

Even in the extreme stress of the moment I noticed that her voice was excessively gentle. It had never occurred to me that she might have a pleasing voice, for her natural speech had always been smothered under that stupid accent. Now the recollection of her accent was like remembering the voice of a silver-toned contralto whose talent is being rendered grotesque by a botched accompaniment. I fixed my mind on this curious inconsistency while she bustled about in the adjoining room, turning on the gas and rattling cups and saucers.

In what seemed to be a moment she returned carrying a tray on which were cups, a coffeepot and a plate of chocolate biscuits. She cleared the table, swinging the heavy sewing machine to the ground as though it had weighed a couple of pounds instead of at least thirty.

Gradually the shock of her information about Diana became absorbed in a kind of competition that was engaging part of my brain, a crazy game of trying to relate the two Mrs. Gayelorde-Suttons, the one I remembered and had loathed and the one now moving about in front of me, doing things that I associated with Aunt Thirza and the housewives in the steep streets behind Whinmouth quay. It was like trying to place ball bearings in little holes under the glass of one of those tiresome tricks found in Christmas crackers. Every time I resolved the two personalities into a unit they slipped away, dodging one another and shooting off at a tangent. Presently I could bear it no longer.

"Why are you here? What are you doing in a place like this?" I asked her. "How is it that you aren't with Diana and what in God's name made her go off like that?"

"Which question would you like answered first?" she said—and this time she really did smile. Her smile reminded me of Diana's when she was making a special effort to appear patient.

"How do you come to be in this kind of house and living by yourself?"

"It was the best I could find at short notice," she said. "I shall be moving on very shortly, at least I will if I'm any good!"

"Any good at what, Mrs. Gayelorde-Sutton?"

"Dressmaking and dress designing," she said. "I'm even enjoying it in a way. Wasn't there once an emperor who became tired of ruling and retired to a monastery to make clocks?"

She had no more power to surprise me now and the weight of misery began to press down again. Diana married! Diana gone forever! Diana the wife of that narrow-faced youth who had once greeted us in a cinema foyer at Marble Arch, and afterwards whisked us to Victoria Station in his glittering sports car! She had hardly ever mentioned Yves since that far-off day. She had seemed absolutely resolved to share the cottage under Teasel Wood and ride out beside me over Foxhayes on eternal summer mornings.

Suddenly Mrs. Gayelorde-Sutton spoke again:

"How well did you know Emerald, Mr. Leigh?"

"I thought I knew her better than anyone on earth," I muttered.

She nodded. "I wouldn't go as far as that but I thought I knew her reasonably well. I knew that she was wild, willful, reckless, utterly unreliable, selfish, greedy, disloyal . . . I knew all that! What I didn't know was that she was such a pitiful little coward, even a worse coward than her father!"

"Are you trying to say that she married because she was afraid to stay in England after what happened?"

"No, that had nothing whatever to do with it. She was afraid of being poor, of having no money for all the things she's had lavished on her since she was a child, and it's hard for me to understand that. You see, I enjoyed having money, nobody more so, but I'm not in the least frightened of being without it. It was a challenge to be well off but is an even more exciting challenge to sell clothes and jewelry in order to provide a float to keep one's head above water while making a fresh start. You've always had to struggle, so perhaps you can understand, Mr. Leigh?"

I understood it well enough, but what I failed to understand was why the sale of her personal effects had not brought in sufficient money to give her a far more promising start than the one she appeared to be making. Her jewelry alone must have realized thousands of pounds. I was so curious that I mentioned this.

"No money or shares," she said, almost gaily, "but I only kept two hundred pounds from my sale of furs and jewelry. The main sum went in last-minute efforts to stave off the crash—I had several weeks' warning of it, you see—and what didn't was handed over. I've been all kinds of a fool in my time, Mr. Leigh, but I'm not a thief. These wretched people are entitled to every penny they can get, surely you see that?"

What do we know about anyone? I had always thought of Diana as a strong, inflexible person, someone who would ride out any storm and shout defiance into the wind. I had always thought of Mrs. Gayelorde-Sutton as a vapid, futile creature, with no more honesty in her soul than there was in her accent. The sheer impact of her character now helped me to hold Diana at bay for a few moments and I said, "You say you'll be moving on. What kind of plans have you got, and where do you hope this dressmaking will lead?"

"To a nice little one-woman business, I hope," she said, brightly. "I've an idea that I might open eventually in the Market Square, in Whinford. They need a place down there, and I daresay I should attract the curious and afterwards keep them as satisfied customers."

"Tell me," I went on, "did Diana know about the crash in advance?"

"I think she had her suspicions after her father turned down an increase in allowance and said no to a settlement."

"What settlement was that?"

"She wrote asking for a lump sum settlement in event of her marrying. My husband was hard pressed at the time and told her he could promise nothing definite at the moment."

Other certainties were creeping out of the mental fog of the last few weeks. I realized now what had been in Diana's mind when she had tried so hard to bulldoze me into taking the farm. Obviously she had banked on cadging a sizable lump sum from her father and using it to stock the place, at the same time getting all the renovations done free by the Heronslea maintenance staff. An unpleasant picture of our marriage, as she had seen it, began to emerge—Diana continuing to lead the life of a county belle, with myself as man-about-the-place and a proven bedfellow. She had never intended that I should become a real farmer, just a stallion, partly for use and partly for local window dressing. It was not a very flattering picture and it made me grind my teeth with rage and humiliation.

"Does she love this French boy?" I burst out, slamming down my half-empty coffee cup so hard that the liquid splashed the table.

"Love him? God bless my soul, does she have to? His family owns a tire factory! They're three times as wealthy as we were in our palmiest days."

She stood up, took a duster from the mantel shelf and carefully wiped away the coffee splash. Suddenly she stopped wiping and stood leaning on her hands, her back to me.

"One other thing, John"—she used my Christian name far less self-consciously than her husband had used it—"and you don't have to tell me this if you'd rather not—were you and Emerald lovers?"

"Yes," I admitted, "on three improbable occasions and each a long time after the occasion you believed us to be, Mrs. Sutton!"

She straightened up and turned to me. "That makes it worse," she said, "because now that we've met you don't have to tell me that the initiative came from her. Frankly I always suspected her of being a sensual little baggage!"

My own thoughts about Diana were bitter enough but I did not want to listen to her mother's observations on the subject. I stood up to leave.

"Thank you for being so frank, Mrs. Sutton," I said, and held out my hand. "If you do open a shop in our part of the world, then I hope you'll let me know. I've got friends down there and I daresay I could pull a few strings with the local press. That usually helps with a new business."

"Yes," she said, pleasantly, "I might even take you up on that, John. I should like to see you again anyway, so perhaps you'll leave your address?"

I scribbled the name and phone number of the cottage on the back of one of her husband's envelopes and passed it to her.

"Teasel Wood Cottage. It's a pretty name," she mused.

"It's a pig in a poke," I said and started down the first of the eight flights of stairs.

I suppose I should have learned something important from that interview, something of lasting value and not simply the bare fact of Diana's betrayal and a few of the reasons behind her scheming of the last few weeks. I could have learned, for instance, the right way to take a beating and to face life, bleak as it was, with dignity and courage, but Mrs. Gayelorde-Sutton had more guts in her great toe than I had in my hulking body and I was soon launched on a spring tide of self-pity and alcohol, much as Grandfather Leigh had launched himself two generations ago. It was no fault of mine that I did not end like Grandfather, dead and drunk over Nun's Head.

I suppose it was putting an unnecessary strain on myself to go back to Sennacharib and live a Crusoe life in the cottage all that summer. My sole companion during the days was Old Fred, Uncle Mark's lugubrious stableman, and apart from him I had few human contacts. Uncle Luke and Aunt Thirza came up there at first but I behaved very churlishly toward them and soon they stopped coming, as did the odd visitor from Whinmouth and Shepherdshey.

I hired out horses to people who wanted a ride but I never accompanied customers on their hacks, or gave lessons to beginners. I disliked my own company but I hated everyone else's. I spent most of the days exercising the horses alone, or digging in the extensive vegetable patch behind the loose boxes. The nights I passed in drinking, sometimes in the private bar of The Rifleman but more often alone in the cottage. Gin and French was my tipple and I accounted for a prodigious amount of it during that summer and autumn. The weather was generally depressing, with whole weeks of rain, leaden skies and brief, gusty intervals when the sun tried to warm the sodden woods and waterlogged meadows.

Sometimes I made a halfhearted attempt to put Diana out of my mind and tire myself with heavy spells of work about the tumbled-down premises, but these bouts seldom lasted more than a day or so. Soon I was back to brooding over the bottle or, what was worse, brooding along the vales and gorse plateaux of Sennacharib where every bush, every pattern of copse and hedgerow reminded me of Diana, of something she had once said or the ring of her laughter as I had heard it when we had cantered over this ground during the past few years.

I recall very little of that period, only an odd day or two here and there when I was so defeated and depressed that I set Margot, the best mare in the stable, at hedges and ditches that were beyond her power to jump. I won't say that I behaved suicidally but I was certainly indifferent as to whether or not we parted company at a hazard, and sometimes I came home bruised and battered by heavy falls.

I deliberately cut myself from all contact with the town and village. My stores, such as they were, were brought up by Fred, and I seldom saw a newspaper. Had I possessed a radio, and kept in touch with the news, I might have derived savage satisfaction from the steady deterioration of affairs in Europe during those months. It was the period when Spain was bleeding to death, Mussolini was blasting and gassing his way into Abyssinia, and Hitler was screeching threats into loudspeakers at Nuremburg, Munich and elsewhere. As it was I had no interest in the victims of Guernica and slaughtered Abyssinians. I had plenty of troubles of my own and I was almost insanely jealous of them.

Sometimes, I think, I was a little mad, as on my twenty-second birthday, the cheerless anniversary of the day that I met Diana in the larch wood behind Heronslea. On that day, hell-bent on turning the knife in my wounds, I went out with the gun, eager to vent my spleen on any rabbit or pheasant that presented itself. I walked up to Teasel Bend, crossed the steppingstones and went along the edge of the wood as far as the Big Oak paddock. Here, just as I was climbing the rail, I spotted the two buzzards circling above their favorite hunting ground.

The sight of them convulsed me with rage. I jumped off the rail and ran shouting across the turf until I was about twenty yards short of the oak. It was at this very spot where I had first watched them, an hour or so before Keeper Croker pounced on me in the wood. I put the gun to my shoulder and fired both barrels.

They were too high to hit but on the report they mewed defiance and dropped swiftly down the slope to the trees. Then I felt a little ashamed of myself and abandoned the idea of shooting, humping myself back to the river and following it down as far as the track under the wood.

One of the few impressions I recall of that dismal interlude was the curious effect that one's mood has upon the aspect of a familiar landscape. Sennacharib had always held for me a holy significance. It was my private Arcady, my Isle of Avalon, my Never-Never Land, and my greatest joy had been to watch the seasons change on the two-mile slope between the common and the first cottages of Shepherdshey. I had looked across the woods for the cloud formations driven by the south wind and my greatest compensation for the passing of summer had been the slow march of copper and rust red across the tops of the Heronslea beeches. It was always exciting to find a late foxglove on Teasel Bank, or early wild daffodils in the marshy part of the larch wood. I had always felt better for a walk or a ride up here, but now Sennacharib's power to heal must have crossed the Channel with Diana. The autumn colors seemed jaded and nondescript, it seemed always to be drizzling and the wind was forever in the southwest, driving sleet and shredded cloud across the estuary. Even when the sun shone, the undergrowth had the poisonous brightness of Stevenson's *Treasure Island,* and where the water had failed to drain away, acres of alien swamp had spread to the riverbanks. I suppose much of this was my fancy but it was how I saw it that year. Where there once had been magic there was dullness that pressed on me like a rain-soaked cap.

Autumn passed, then winter, with no snow but still more rain. I rode, walked, dug, chopped wood, groomed the horses, and withdrew more and more into myself until I was little better than a morose recluse, inhabiting an isolated pigsty. It was ten months now since I had said good-by to Diana on the station platform and I had almost stopped thinking of her as a person. She now merged into the general tedium of my life, at one with the driving wind, the gray, empty sky and the eternal drizzle. Then, one February afternoon, my life changed course again, but this time Diana's contribution to the switch was remote and indirect.

I had been over to Castle Ferry to find a sweep and try and get him to do something with the smoking chimney of the cottage. It was dusk when I returned and as I trudged up the muddy track I noticed to my surprise that the oil lamp was glowing in the window. I quickened my step, irritated at the prospect of an uninvited guest and determined to send him packing as quickly as possible. When I threw open the door I was amazed to see Drip, the friendly ex-governess, tending the fire.

She seemed to be very much at home. The room had been sub-

333]

jected to an intensive spring cleaning. Freshly washed curtains were drying on a line over the fireplace, a week's accumulation of dirty crockery had been cleared, the table laid for supper, the slated floor had been scrubbed, and all the rugs brushed and beaten. It astonished me that one person could have achieved so much during my brief absence.

Miss Rodgers did not look a day older than when I had last seen her, now getting on for five years ago. She was one of those plump, breathless little women who display far more energy than the lean, stringy ones, and her round, good-natured face was shining with health and the heat of the huge fire. In the soft glow of the lamp the room looked cozier and far more inviting than it had ever looked in my brief tenancy, or during the lengthy occupation of Uncle Mark.

"Come in and take your filthy boots off, Jan!" she said, as though we had been sharing the cottage for months. "I couldn't find slippers, so I warmed a pair of outdoor shoes. The fish is nearly ready and the kettle's boiling. You make the tea, while I cut bread and butter."

"Where on earth have you sprung from, Miss Rodgers," I asked, "and how the devil did you get in? I locked up when I went out at midday."

"You don't hide the key in a very original place," she said, smiling. "After I'd drawn blank under the bricks outside the door, I tried underneath the water butt. This place was a disgrace to a Christian! It positively stank when I came in and until the wind changed I was half suffocated by smoke. You'll have to get that chimney seen to at once."

Not knowing how to reply to this I said nothing, changing my boots and warming myself at the fire, where some fillets of hake were hissing in the long-handled pan beneath the spit. I noticed that the pan had been scoured. The smell of cooking put a sharp edge to my appetite.

"I came down from Wales last night," she said, "and called at your uncle's on the quay. As a matter of fact I stayed the night there, and your aunt is very worried about you. She has need to be, in all conscience. What kind of a man are you to turn your back on everybody like this, apart from living like a savage, and a very dirty savage at that?"

"It suits me well enough," I grumbled, but my mouth was watering for those fillets and hunger coaxed the sourness from my voice.

"It doesn't suit you at all," she snapped, "because you're really a very sociable person. You ought to be ashamed of yourself, a great hulking lout like you, mooning over a bit of a girl all these months! Haven't you got any pride? I'd be a charwoman before I let a man do that to me! Not that one ever has," she added, and winked so saucily that I laughed for the first time in months.

"And don't call me 'Miss Rodgers' any more," she pattered. "I've always known that you and Emerald referred to me as 'Drip' and I don't mind a bit because, as things have turned out, I'm not nearly such a drip as either one of you has turned out to be! Here"—she lifted the pan from the fire and tipped the fillets into a dish—"get that into you and when you've finished you and I are going to have a very frank discussion, young man!"

We ate a silent but enjoyable supper, finishing the new loaf Drip had brought and making inroads into a pound of the best Cheddar that came up in the same basket. Afterwards I helped her to wash up, and when all the crockery was back on the dresser we built up the fire and I sat opposite her, smoking. It was by far the most peaceful hour I had ever passed in that room.

"Well," she said, breaking the long, satisfying silence, "where do we begin, Jan?"

I asked her to tell me about herself and she said that her sister had died, and that she had suddenly been homesick for the West Country and had come down with the intention of buying a small property and ending her days in the district where she had spent the happiest part of her life.

"I *was* very happy at Heronslea," she said, "although you may not have thought so. It almost broke my heart to leave and I kept in touch with the family right up to the time of the crash. I had a pension, of course, and it didn't stop when poor Mr. Gayelorde-Sutton killed himself. It wasn't very much but my sister and I ran a candy store and we managed very comfortably. Now I've got sufficient to last me out, providing I'm careful of course—but that's enough about me. Tell me everything about you and Diana—*everything*, mind you, no skipping the important pieces! Start from the time you two silly children were fetched home from that dreadful island."

I told her everything, how I had fared in London, how I had run into Diana outside Fortnum's, and all that happened afterwards, up to the day that I called on Mrs. Gayelorde-Sutton in Holland Park and began my nonstop sulk.

335]

She listened carefully and made no comment. Then, without looking up, she said, "I had a letter from Diana last week. She's got a little girl called Yvonne and she's living outside a town called Saumur. Do you know it?"

"Not that part of France," I said, "but I've heard of it. It's somewhere on the Loire, isn't it?"

"That's right, but I'm surprised you've never been to Anjou. You speak French very well, don't you?"

"Yes," I said, glumly. "I learned to please Diana!"

She flushed a little at that and her head came up, her eyes regarding me seriously over the rims of steel-framed spectacles.

"Is that *all* you did on that account?" she demanded, crisply.

"No," I said, "not by a long chalk!"

"What else, Jan?" The voice was much kinder now.

"I gave up secondhand furnishings for small-town journalism and then small-town journalism for this. I left home for London and then left London for home. I nearly broke my neck learning to ride horses in order to be with her. I learned how to ride a motorcycle in order to take her to a single dance. I was always in and out of hot water on her account, but I'm not grousing at that, for I judged it was worth it and I got my payoff at the time. What I do begrudge her is *time*, Drip—the whole of my blasted youth!"

She nodded as though she understood and sympathized and I fell into her trap. "All those years I never made a single friend," I said. "Do you know anyone else rising twenty-three who had grown up in a town like Whinmouth and not made a single real friend, male or female?"

"There was never another girl, Jan?"

"One, before Diana came back, but I only saw her twice. I dropped her like a hot coal after one fresh look at Diana."

Drip carefully removed her glasses and set them down. She did this as though she was playing for time before answering.

"Jan," she said, at length, "have you ever wondered what you might have done with your life if you hadn't met Diana?"

In all my moonings about Sennacharib during the past ten months I had never considered this. It was the sort of question that did not present itself, like a man wondering what it might have been like to have been born a woman.

"No," I answered, "I don't think I have, Drip. Can you tell me?"

"I can tell you precisely," she said. "If you hadn't met Diana that day in the woods you would still have been humping furniture around Whinmouth on your Uncle Luke's barrow!"

I considered this and accepted it as true but it did not seem to prove very much.

"I was happy enough pushing that barrow, Drip."

She made a gesture of impatience, a violent one for her.

"Don't you *see*, Jan? Everything you are as a person you owe to Diana! Diana performed a kind of miracle on you and in spite of what's happened I don't think you have any right to quarrel with it."

"Is it much of a miracle? I was Uncle Luke's errand boy at fifteen and at twenty-two I'm a bad-tempered hermit, living just as you said, like a grubby savage in a kraal."

"That isn't Diana's fault, it's yours! There isn't the slightest reason for indulging in this spectacular sulk, apart from the fact that I believe, deep down, you're enjoying it in a gloomy, perverse kind of way. Because of Diana you got yourself a better job! Because of Diana you learned to ride and manage horses! Because of Diana you learned a foreign language! Diana taught you to dance, taught you to look for adventure, taught you how to buy clothes, cured your accent, taught you your table manners if the truth's known, and goodness knows how many other things that you've forgotten or are in the process of forgetting, or have even come to believe you acquired by your own will power. *You make me sick, Jan Leigh!* Look at yourself in the mirror! Think about yourself! Talk to yourself if you like, but if there's a spark of honesty left in you, you'll end up admitting that Diana enlarged your life and gave it a shape and purpose that it could never have had if you'd married one of those bovine girls I used to see pushing their prams up and down Whinmouth quay on Sunday afternoons. Now you can get that car out and run me back to your uncle's, but don't imagine I'm going to leave you alone! I'm moving in here; for the time being I've found my little place in the country. You don't have to pay me but you do have to pull yourself together, and you won't see the last of me until you have, so there!"

It was a long and vehement speech for Drip and it left her rather breathless, so much so that I laughed outright and she laughed to hear me laugh. I drove her back to Uncle Luke's and we all had a pot of tea in the kitchen before I returned home. The next day she kept her word, moving in bag and baggage, and we lived there, like aunt and nephew, until our world went mad.

It was a happy time, those last two and a half years under Teasel Wood. The stable prospered. I started a poultry farm, and Drip kept the premises as bright and cozy as a tea cozy in an illustrated fairy-tale book. She stayed on when I took a middle-aged Whinmouth gardener-groom into partnership and joined the army, in the autumn of 1939, and on that birthday, my twenty-fifth, she sent a cake to the battery in which I was serving outside Lille.

She took a big chance on that cake. It was made in the cottage bread oven and she had piped it with a large, pink heart. In the center of the heart was my name, transfixed by an arrow, and the point of the arrow passed through her own initials, piped near the rim.

I was cutting into it during an air-raid alarm that had sent us to ground when Ginger Beavis, the bombardier, exclaimed, "Those marzipan dots around the edge! In this half-light they look just like emeralds!"

Chapter Twelve

THE fact that I had learned French all those years ago, and had been sufficiently interested to improve it during my London period and subsequently, stood me in good stead when the war came. Or did it? I was soon winkled out of the friendly antiaircraft battery and attached to Intelligence H.Q. in Paris. When the big breakthrough began, in May 1940, I was hustled down to Bordeaux to make arrangements for the evacuation of civilian personnel.

The great exodus had hardly begun, so that the journey southwest was tolerable, but by the time I arrived in Bordeaux it was a city of bewilderment and seething rumor, with nobody from politician to refugee knowing what was happening, or likely to happen, hour by hour.

When the panzers smashed through the Allied line and the British army began its retreat upon Dunkirk, I had urgent instructions to get my people aboard. My immediate superior, a major, was badly wounded in an air raid on the harbor, and from then on I had to use my initiative, sorting out the claims of the various groups, civilian and military, French, British, Dutch, Polish and even Spanish, who besieged me for a passage to Britain.

It was a thankless, harassing job. For a period of four days I went without sleep and on the fifth, when I had dispatched two crowded coal boats and had seen another sink under a Stuka attack, I was too dazed and dispirited to take much interest in the war. Then a Dutch skipper came to me and put his thousand-ton tramp at my disposal. I sent my sergeant to collect any stray units in the area and get them aboard as soon as possible, for the Dutchman was as impatient to be gone as everyone else in that fear-crazed city and told me that, empty or laden, he intended to clear the Gironde on the early morning tide.

The weather was insufferably hot. At that stage of the evacuation I was operating from a slipway and ferryboat landing at Blaye, just across the river from Bordeaux, and I had commandeered the ferryboat office, a squat, one-story building near the water's edge. The would-be immigrants formed a long, untidy queue down to the waterside and a line of battered trucks, military vans, and hideously overloaded Citroëns and Renaults stretched from the ferryboat office to the main road, more than two miles inland.

I have never witnessed such a scene of chaos. The French, ordinarily a brave, philosophical people, had completely succumbed to the virus of panic and defeatism. They fought one another for places in the vehicle queue that led down to the berth of my Dutch steamer. Some of them wanted to go to Britain and picketed my office, shouting and gesticulating, each urging his or her claim to be saved from the Boche. Others were not interested in being evacuated but were trying to reach Bordeaux and join up with relatives from whom they had been separated on the trek west. It was useless to try to organize the fugitives and their vehicles. Car and truck drivers persisted in edging out of line and creating vast jams, and every now and again a fight started with other drivers and gendarmes who tried to stop them. Pedestrians clambered over the line of interlocked transport in the hope of bypassing my office and reaching the ship's gangplanks. The scene reminded me of Ségur's description of the passage of the Beresina during the retreat from Moscow.

Toward sundown, I locked myself in and did business through the window and I was here, praying for darkness to descend on the lunatic confusion, when my sergeant found me, fighting his way through the crowd and approaching near enough to shout a message to me.

"There's a Judy back up the road who says she knows you," he bawled. "She's stuck there, with a tribe of kids, about a dozen of them. She sent a note . . . catch! Did you ever see such a bloody shambles?" Then, having thrown his note, he disappeared, clawed down by two men who held him and screamed into his ears.

The message, a crumpled ball of paper, sailed through the window and fell beside my desk. I retrieved it without much interest, smoothing it out among the litter of papers. Then I nearly hit the ceiling. The note, scribbled in pencil, was in Diana's handwriting.

It said:

> Heard you were here, Jan—come and get me again! Be gallant, like Mr. Ridd!
>
> Love,
> DIANA

Just that; just as if we had lost one another in a Cup Final crowd!

I sat on, facing the hideous turmoil immediately under the window, indifferent to the grinding crashes of colliding vehicles and the shrill fury and despair of their drivers.

So much had happened during the last few weeks that no thought of Diana had entered my head. I had not even remembered that she was resident in France and had a French husband, for at last, at long last, the affairs of Europe had lapped over Sennacharib and were submerging it like a drowned civilization. Now Diana's note acted like an underwater beam, probing through the deluge and revealing a well-remembered contour. Looking down at her scrawl, as the last rays of the sun slanted across the road, I saw another stream, the tiny Teasel, chattering over its stones to Shepherdshey Bridge and its outfall at Nun's Bay. I saw the looming shape of Teasel Wood high above the left bank and the two vain buzzards, soaring and drifting above the larches of the plantation. It was all as vivid as a film flashed on a cinema screen. I had not set eyes on Diana or her handwriting for four years, yet a few words, scrawled on a crumpled piece of paper, had that much power to move me.

The moment it was dark I escaped from the ferry office via a rear window and crossed the fields, joining the stationary queue about half a mile inland. I went slowly down the line, shining my flashlight into the interiors of trucks and cars. Forlorn voices called to me but I ignored them. I was interested in only one refugee and at last I found her, on the grass verge beside a road junction where the road ran between high, sloping vineyards.

She greeted me gaily. We might have met after parting at the foot of Shepherdshey Hill the previous evening. Her car, a large Renault, seemed to be packed with sleeping children and there was a mountain of baggage tied to the roof with fencing wire. She saw me just before I spotted her and called out, so that I flashed my powerful flashlight in her face. She was much thinner than I remembered, and a long, gray dust cloak gave her unexpected height. Her hair was clamped under a colored handkerchief, tied tightly beneath her chin. Her voice had an unfamiliar timbre, acquired through speaking so little English during the past few years.

"Well, Jan!" she laughed. "Lady-in-distress, as usual! You really ought to have ridden up on a big gray and then we might have done an Uncle Tom Cobleigh into Blaye. The numbers would have been right—I've got five more in there for Widdicombe Fair!"

Her gay courage impressed me so much that I forgot to be amazed by the wild improbability of our encounter. In any case, she answered my question before I could frame it:

"It isn't exactly coincidence, Jan," she said. "I put a call through to British H.Q. and then the Bordeaux consul. The Bordeaux Johnny said a certain Lieutenant Leigh was the Big Cheese at the quayside, so I said 'J. Leigh?' and he said 'Yes' and I said 'A husky great chap, with shoulders so wide?' and he said 'How did you know?' and I said 'We're buddies!' and that was that!"

She had me laughing again, just as if there had never been a market crash, a suicide, an atrocious personal betrayal and, to end it all, a bloody great war. She was irrepressible, unique, the final, final word in cool cheek and inspired selfishness! No one but Emerald Diana Gayelorde-Sutton would push blithely through the swirl of foundering nations in order to put through two long-distance telephone calls about shipping space for herself and five children, and no one but Emerald Diana Gayelorde-Sutton would have received anything but a howl of indignation from the other end of the wire! Even my own presence in that place and at that time did not strike her as incredibly providential but merely a kind of jolly surprise, like the acquisition of an unclaimed seat at a popular first night.

"Diana," I said, at length, "you're not only priceless, you're also the slightest bit tiddly!"

"Yes I am," she admitted, "but I wasn't greedy, I saved a noggin for you—and you look as if you could do with one, poor dear!"

She rummaged in the glove compartment of the car and handed me a half-empty bottle of cognac. I took a long, grateful swig. It was excellent brandy and helped me to match her mood.

"How did you really trace me? There must have been more to it than a couple of phone calls."

[342

I sat down on the broad running board of the car and she seated herself beside me.

"Yes, there was," she said. "I saw this coming months ago so I wrote to Drip to make . . . well . . . certain arrangements. She gave me your Paris address and I called there, soon after you'd gone. The conversation I had with the Bordeaux consul was true. I gave you a build-up there!"

"In the meantime what the devil has happened to your husband?" I asked. "Is he boxed up in the Maginot Line, or somewhere?"

"Yves?" She laughed, unpleasantly I thought. "No, dear, he and his papa have gone over to the Opposition."

"Joined Jerry? *The Nazis?*"

It was the first I had heard of active French collaborators and I was shocked.

"Great possessions, Jan!" she said, shrugging. "They usually incline you to the winning side. After all, I ought to know, shouldn't I?"

It was neither the time nor the place to hold an inquest on her madcap marriage, so I ignored the opening and said, "Do they really think Jerry is going to win?"

"Don't you?" she said, quietly.

Did I? It seemed to me that I had never had a chance to study the possibility. Up until April it had not been a real war at all and ever since I had been acting as a kind of whipper-in to a traveling lunatic asylum.

"He won't beat us, not in the long run!" I growled, and she laughed, more pleasantly this time, and squeezed my arm.

"That's the stuff!" she said. "Death to the Doones!"

"By the way," I went on, "why five children? You haven't been that enterprising, have you?"

"Only the youngest, Yvonne, is mine," she said. "All the others belong to our Spanish gardener. His wife was killed in an air raid and as a militant anti-Fascist he's already on the run. Shall I wake up the kids now?"

"Yes, and you'll have to ditch car and baggage," I said. "We can make it over the fields, but for God's sake keep them quiet or we shall have half the French nation behind us! Give the kids the old Whinmouth Carnival treatment."

She laughed again. "You remember that, Jan?"

"I remember everything! Every damn thing that happened to you and me!" I said grimly.

She opened a rear door and prodded the children. They emerged yawning onto the road. Her own girl, Yvonne, was a pretty little thing, with jet-black hair cut in a straight fringe and huge brown eyes that stared up at me with solemn intensity.

"This is my Jan, Yvonne," said Diana briskly. "You've heard all about Jan, haven't you?"

"*Qui!*" said the child, stifling a yawn and then, after subjecting me to another solemn stare: "*Il est très gros, Mamma!*"

Diana chuckled. "Yes, I told you he was," she said, lightly. Then, "Come on, you others—Philip, Manuel, girls—this English soldier is going to put you on a big boat and take you all across the sea!"

The Spanish children formed a ragged line, Yvonne standing a little to one side, like a tiny N.C.O. on parade. Diana said something in Spanish to a child a year or so older than Yvonne and when the girl asked a question she replied rapidly in the same language.

"She wants to know if she's being taken to her father," said Diana, "but I told her that her father has to stay and beat Franco first."

"Good God!" I exclaimed, for nothing would have surprised me overmuch that night. "Is he coming in against us?"

"It's the same war to her," said Diana, simply.

"Poor little devils," I said, and the sight of the children, standing in pathetic, quasi-military formation as they knuckled the sleep from their eyes, reminded me sharply of all the misery and bewilderment I had witnessed during the last few days. Rage against the Germans rose in my throat like bile. I stooped and lifted the smallest of the Spaniards to my shoulder and Diana lifted Yvonne.

"You others hold hands and Manuel is to keep hold of the back of the soldier's coat," she said. "Don't chatter, any of you, and from now on do exactly as you're told!"

Reflecting that I would sooner have Diana than anyone else in the world to share this sort of adventure, I led the way off the road and over the shoulder of the vineyard. I walked slowly and carefully, keeping my torch to the ground. The little procession straggled along behind, Diana and Yvonne bringing up the rear, and in this way, without exchanging a word we reached the rear of the ferry headquarters.

I left them all outside and climbed through the rear window, to find Sergeant Bowles sound asleep on the floor. He had shuttered the window that opened onto the slipway and everyone outside seemed to be asleep.

"Christl! I was pretty sick when I got back and you weren't here," Bowles said, when I awakened him. "That bloody Dutchman is casting off first light and had the gangplanks removed. Orders came through on the phone an hour ago—we've got to go with them. He's flying the Yank flag, so we stand an even chance against Stukas, but it looks as though we'll ride home on the anchor chains!"

"There are six more outside," I told him, "and we have to get them aboard right now."

"It's dicey," he said. "They're already five deep on deck and the crew have got rifles and orders to shoot last-minute gate-crashers."

"We've got to try," I said. "They'll have to come aboard with us."

"Wait a minute," he said, "I've got an idea!"

He was a useful sergeant, a thirty-year-old Terrier who had been a chemist's assistant in Hereford less than a year ago. "We'd better use the dinghy and pretend we're only crossing over. I put two of the gendarmes to guard it—it's moored under the jetty."

"Okay—take four of the kids and then come back for me," I said. "I've got stuff to burn and I'll need half an hour or so."

We rejoined Diana and I explained what was going to happen. She passed on the instructions in Spanish and the children remained passive. They were adults in everything but size. Without a whimper they followed Sergeant Bowles down the slipway and I climbed back into the office.

"Hand Yvonne through to me and then come in yourself," I told Diana.

She passed the child through and I noted that Yvonne was sound asleep. I laid her down very gently on an old leather sofa and covered her with my greatcoat. Then I helped Diana to climb through, shuttered the window and switched on the flashlight.

"If we show much light we'll have everybody clamoring at the window," I explained. "Did you bring that brandy along?"

She passed the bottle and I swallowed half the amount that remained.

"Keep it," she said. "I can get plenty more, Jan."

"You won't find every mod. con. on that Dutch tramp steamer," I said, gruffly. "They're standing on one another now!"

"I'm not taking passage on your smelly old steamer," she said.

Overwork, lack of sleep and probably the emotional shock of meeting Diana again had combined to make me extremely irritable.

"Now look here, Dil" I shouted. "Let's not have any bloody heroics!

This is everybody's last chance and if you don't believe me, take a peep outside."

"I never intended going, Jan," she said, "so please don't try to hector me! All I wanted from you was a chance to get the children away. I know what I'm going to do and my being here is part of the plan."

"You and your slaphappy plans!" I began, but she checked me by raising her hand.

"Listen, Jan, it's as I said, I've known this was coming all winter and that's more than Winston Churchill can say. The minute you've sailed I start back to the Loire to meet Ramond."

"Who the blazes is Ramond?"

"The father of those children, our gardener at Saumur."

"And what do you and Ramond intend doing? Fighting a civil war as a Lewis-gun team?"

"Not yet," she said, seriously, "but we probably shall as soon as the nights draw in, as they used to say back in Devon." She leaned back in the chair and clasped her hands behind her head, regarding me with that judicious mixture of amusement and affection that I had once found beguiling but now made me feel like a frustrated father coping with a willful child.

"Dear Jan," she said, "you haven't changed the tiniest bit! Still glum, truculent, explosive, but still utterly dependable! Just think," she went on, "in less than a week you and Yvonne will be in Heronslea. Will you promise something? Will you sit her up on old Nellie, and take her on the leading rein up the main ride and across Big Oak paddock to Folly Wood? I should like to think of her doing that for the very first time, with you."

I suddenly felt desperate about her. No trace of rancor remained and the hard shell of indifference that I had grown, scale by scale, since the damp afternoon that Drip had forced her way into my life and talked some sense into me, now cracked and fell away, leaving all the scars she had caused, sensitive to her glance, her touch, and the sound of her voice.

"Diana, you just aren't equipped to play cloak-and-dagger games with those bastards, and you've got to come!" I pleaded. "There'll be checkups, rationing, identity cards, God knows what kind of restrictions . . ."

She cut in, quietly but very decisively. "Don't be so insular, Jan. I'm French and I've lived over here a long time now. I know what's

[346

going to happen far better than you British amateurs. It's going to be tough but we've had plenty of time to arrange all this. We started getting an organization together months ago. That was why I took a duration lease on Heronslea."

She planned to surprise me and she certainly succeeded.

"*You what?*" I shouted.

"I did it through our old solicitors and it's all organized and paid for, with my funds transferred to London last January. Drip will explain everything when you see her. She's going to be in charge, you see."

"In charge of what? Damn it, when I was on leave last December they were making Heronslea into a Polish hospital!"

"That's all canceled," she said blandly. "It's going to be a refugee children's home and those Spanish kids and Yvonne will be among the first batch. As time goes on, I expect there'll be lots of others, all kinds of kids, who'll begin to turn up the minute they start bombing London."

"Are you operating through a government department?"

"Oh no," she said, "this is my own idea. It's a kind of dream I had when the war started, but now it isn't a dream any longer because meeting you has given it a kind of shape and solidity. You see, you've got a real stake in it now, because Yvonne is your child, Jan!"

She took advantage of my stupefaction to lift the flashlight and direct the beam on the sofa, where Yvonne was still asleep under my greatcoat.

"That child . . . you mean . . . ?"

She put down the flashlight and reached across the table for my hand. She was smiling but her expression was as gentle and serene as I ever recalled.

"Didn't it ever creep into that great wooden head of yours? Didn't it ever occur to you as a remote possibility? No, of course it didn't! I can see that now. Well, it's true, for all that, and if you take a good look at her you'll see it is. She's got your jawline, your hair, your coloring, and a quite unmistakably Leigh gait. She'll have your obstinacy too, so watch out, or you'll have a problem on your hands!"

"Are you sure—absolutely sure?"

"Good Heavens, of course I am! I can count, can't I?"

"Does . . . does Yves know?" I managed to ask, after a long pause.

She looked just as she used to look when she was on the point of revolting against one of her mother's edicts. "He didn't but he does

347]

now," she said, grimly. "I wanted him to have something to think about when his Nazi friends began lecturing him on racial purity, selective breeding and all that claptrap!"

We were silent for a moment while she gave me time to absorb the information.

"When was it, Di?" I asked. "Was it that last time, that time when we quarreled and I hit you in the cottage?"

"No, Jan, before that. It was the day we walked up the Teasel and suddenly got tired of arguing about what we were going to do with your newspaper shares, remember?"

"Are you sure about that?"

"Absolutely, but does it matter that much?"

Somehow it mattered tremendously. It seemed to be of enormous significance that the attractive child asleep under my greatcoat was a living manifestation of Diana, of me, and of Sennacharib. Sitting there, in that shabby, airless little room, with the human wreckage of Armageddon lapping up to the very door, it mattered more than anything that our love, and our need for one another, had combined with the sun and wind and springtime of Sennacharib to create something tangible, something capable of inheriting the yearning we shared for those few square miles between the estuary of the Whin and the firs of Teasel Wood. For the cottage, where we had healed our quarrel by an act of love, was not Sennacharib. It lay beyond the wood and had never, in my mind's eye, been included in the domain, but the hollow under Teasel Bank, the quiet place where we had lain in each other's arms that sunny April afternoon, that was the very heart of Sennacharib! The conception of a child—our child —in such a place, gave a kind of symmetry to all that had happened between us since she had come riding down the larch wood to vanquish Keeper Croker with a glance. It made sense of her hiring Heronslea as a refuge for children. It made sense of so much that had seemed to me, in the years since she had gone, so empty, wasted and sterile.

"Was taking over Heronslea to do with us?" I asked her. "Is that what you meant when you said that running into me like this gave shape to that dream?"

"That's exactly it," she said, joyously, "and I don't even have to explain it, do I? It's as if everything that happened to you and me in Sennacharib was . . . well . . . a kind of prelude, but a prelude so complete in itself that what's happened since doesn't amount to a row of pins! This idea of mine means that the prelude hasn't been wasted, that maybe we were meant to live it not for ourselves but for a whole tribe of children, a representative bunch, a kind of juvenile League of Nations if you like. You and I managed to squeeze every drop of delight out of growing up in Sennacharib and this way we're passing it on as a sort of answer to all the horror that's piling up everywhere right now. Ordinarily it might be years before kids get a chance to romp and ride and laugh in places like Folly Wood, and on heathery places like Foxhayes, but this idea of mine makes it possible for at least a few kids to have that chance before they grow up and things get out of control, the way they finally did with us."

She paused, breathlessly, and I waited. "I suppose this all sounds a bit precious and fanciful, Jan, and I'll agree that it's madly uncharacteristic of me, but I'm not fooling about this! It's the only really imaginative thing I've ever done and I *want* it to happen, I want terribly for it to happen!"

I was going to beg her to abandon her crazy notion of staying behind. I understood, suddenly, why she was making this additional gesture. All her life she had resisted regimentation, and to Diana the very word "Fascism" must have been like a whiff from a sewer. She had been devastated by her husband's cynical espousal of the creed and in her own unpredictable way she was trying to atone for his degradation. In the years ahead many French people were to react in an identical way to their country's collapse, and I could see now that Diana had absorbed a great deal that was Gallic in essence. I don't say that I fully understood all this at the time, but I understand it now as clearly as though she had written it down and asked me to learn it by heart.

She looked at me anxiously. "You're not going to try to force me to go, Jan?"

"No," I said, gloomily, "nobody ever succeeded in forcing you to do anything that you didn't care to do, Di!"

"Then we can say good-by in here," she said.

I crossed to the rear window, where Sergeant Bowles' round, anxious face peered up from the yard.

"They're aboard," he whispered, "and I've seen the mate—high tide is at two and the skipper has given us fifteen minutes dead! Can you make it?"

"Yes," I told him, "I can make it! Take this other child down to the dinghy."

Diana had already lifted Yvonne, still wrapped in my greatcoat, and was now standing at my elbow. I passed the child down to Bowles and told him to give me five minutes to burn papers.

"For God's sake don't hang about," he said. "Never mind all that bloody office bumph, let Jerry have fun with it!"

He disappeared and I closed the shutter.

"Turn on the light, Jan, just for a moment, I must see you properly," she whispered.

I switched on a low-powered bulb and Diana stood quite still, facing me, her eyes roving from dusty flying boots to the crown of my head.

"Darling Jan," she said, softly, and then, with a smile and a swift toss of her head: "You see, there were plenty of Doones left over after all! The whole of Europe is crawling with them."

It would have pleased me to have matched her panache but that would have been like playing horse holder to D'Artagnan. I could only take a long, long look at her, noting the strange and independent life of her chestnut curls under the kerchief, the luster of her skin and the wide, generous curves of her mouth. I held her in my gaze like that for about a minute. I memorized—as if I had need to memorize—everything about her, the strong grace of her neck, the swell of her breasts, the line of her thighs and the eternal promise of her eyes. Then I kissed her, not as a lover, but as a boy might kiss a mature woman who has been teasing him.

"Go now, Jan," she whispered, pushing me from her.

I remember de Maupassant saying somewhere that a deep and lasting love strikes the heart like a thunderbolt and leaves it a source of aching ruin, but my love for Diana was never like that. It was a slow-burning fuse that spluttered on and on throughout every phase of my life, sometimes sparking and sometimes smoldering but always inextinguishable.

I turned quickly and climbed through that wretched little window for the third time that night, and as I went I made an Orpheus-like resolution not to tempt fate by looking back. I broke that resolution and my final glimpse of her was standing framed in the window, her back to the light. It was a somber, theatrical picture, something to carry away, like the glowing memory of a Goya portrait.

I went down the slipway to the waiting dinghy. The broad Gironde, silent under the stars, looked uncannily like the Whin tideway from the summit of Foxhayes.

"Where's that damned woman?" demanded Bowles. "We can't wait . . . we . . ."

"She's not coming," I told him, "so for God's sake push off, *push off!*"

He gave me a quick, anxious glance. How was he to know that my life had been enriched by two loves, Sennacharib and Diana, or that one was the complement of the other?

I kept my promise and took Yvonne on the leading rein through the larch wood and across Big Oak paddock to Folly Wood. It was exciting to watch her big, solemn eyes study the parched country-side, comparing it, no doubt, to the green, flat country in which she had grown up. Later that same day, about an hour before sunset, I returned to the tower on foot and climbed the crumbling staircase to our room. Diana had once called it a "thought rendezvous" and I wondered now if its spell would work. It did, but not in the way I had hoped and expected. Standing against the window through which I had seen Diana come trotting out of the wood and across the paddock on Sioux, with Nellie on the leading rein as my first mount, I thought not so much of Diana but of the meaning of the struggle we were engaged upon. By this time even Shepherdshey had joined in, and at this very moment Nat the sexton was leading his patrol of L.D.V.'s over Nun's Head. They were armed with rook rifles and two small-bore shotguns with which they were ready, if necessary, to do battle with tanks. I had only been on leave forty-eight hours but it was long enough to discover that Whinmouth and Shepherdshey were enjoying the war. No one could blame them for that. This was the first time anything like this had happened around here since Napoleon lay encamped at Boulogne, a hundred and thirty-five years ago. There were blackouts, London evacuees, bustling A.R.P. wardens and all the outward trappings of total war, but to any who had been involved in the rout of France it was all rather like a group of children playing cowboys and Indians. Up there in the tower I wondered how long this mood would last, how long Hitler would suffer it to last, and then I remembered my boast to Diana as we sat side by side on the running board of her crowded Renault outside Bordeaux.

Was it really possible that one day arrogant young Teutons would come jackbooting through the ferns and gorse of Sennacharib?

Would high-explosives crash down on huddles of cottages like Shepherdshey? Would the road to Castle Ferry ever boil with panic-stricken women pushing handcarts piled with bedding? Somehow I couldn't imagine such things, and as I rejected the prospect I was able, at last, to think objectively of Diana, lurking about the woods and fields of Anjou in the company of homeless desperadoes like her Spanish gardener, risking her life—for what? Because she believed in democracy so passionately that she was ready to die for it? Or because she would find in this kind of adventure yet another excuse for hanging on to her youth and fending off the maturity that she hated to contemplate? I asked myself the question and told myself the answer. Diana never had and never would care two straws for democracy, but here was the best chance anyone had ever had of thumbing one's nose at strident autocracy. How long would the war last? How long would Diana last? How long would any of us last when Goering's air fleets had finished pounding the ports and airfields and switched to the cities?

It was very still up there in the tower. The Foxhayes blackbirds had gone to bed and the light was fading over Nun's Bay. There was no evening twinkle of lights from Shepherdshey or Whinmouth. People had had a long winter to perfect their blackouts.

Then the silence was broken by a pleasant sound that rose up from the central aisle of the larch plantation and carried right across Big Oak paddock to the edge of Folly Wood. It was the sound of the Spanish children laughing as they romped down the broad ride toward Heronslea, laughing perhaps at having evaded Drip's curfew, for it was past nine o'clock and they should have been in bed.

I listened carefully but the sound was not repeated. That did not seem to matter, for it had been unmistakable. Children were laughing in Sennacharib, so maybe there was something in Diana's crazy dream after all.

I went down the staircase to the wood. It was quite dark among the trees but I walked without stumbling. I did not need a light to find my way across Sennacharib.